Under

Al-Fariz refused to be [...]
his first tactical mission [...]
to be fired upon by the enemy. [...]

"Help!" he squawked on the radio. [...]
A missile—"

"Break right!" came the voice of Colonel Jabbar. "Turn right now! Immediately!"

The urgent command penetrated like a laser into Al-Fariz's paralyzed brain. *Turn!* He jammed the stick hard to the right, then pulled. The MiG wheeled hard into a right turn. . . . Nearly at the end of its envelope, the air-to-air missile swished past the tail of the hard-turning MiG-29, then sputtered out and lost guidance.

Al-Fariz was alive.

But the second missile, a quarter mile behind the first, stayed locked on. . . .

PRAISE FOR THE WRITING OF ROBERT GANDT

"Gandt . . . understands not only airplanes but the people who fly them."   —*Air & Space*

"Gandt has a way with words that will send the reader soaring."   —*News Chief*

"Gandt transports readers into the cockpit . . . about as close as one gets without arming the ejection seat."
—*San Diego Union-Tribune*

"[Gandt's] writing is for fans of air racing and warships and lovers of extreme sports."   —*Publishers Weekly*

"Gandt may be the best unknown aviation writer around."
—Stephen Wilkinson, *Air & Space*

"Robert Gandt is a former Pan Am pilot who also happens to have the pen of a poet."
—*The Christian Science Monitor*

"For anyone who is, was, or wants to be a part of the glorious adventure that is naval aviation. Gandt makes me wish I were doing it all over again."
—Stephen Coonts, author of *Flight of the Intruder*

WITH HOSTILE INTENT

ROBERT GANDT

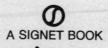

A SIGNET BOOK

SIGNET
Published by New American Library, a division of
Penguin Putnam Inc., 375 Hudson Street,
New York, New York 10014, U.S.A.
Penguin Books Ltd, 27 Wrights Lane,
London W8 5TZ, England
Penguin Books Australia Ltd,
Ringwood, Victoria, Australia
Penguin Books Canada Ltd, 10 Alcorn Avenue,
Toronto, Ontario, Canada M4V 3B2
Penguin Books (N.Z.) Ltd, 182–190 Wairau Road,
Auckland 10, New Zealand

Penguin Books Ltd, Registered Offices:
Harmondsworth, Middlesex, England

First published by Signet, an imprint of New American Library,
a division of Penguin Putnam Inc.

First Printing, October 2001
10 9 8 7 6 5 4 3 2 1

For Annie,
partner, best friend, sweetheart

ACKNOWLEDGMENTS

Special thanks to Lieutenant Commander Allen "Zoomie" Baker, USN (ret.), good friend, intrepid fighter pilot, and emerging writer. His literary talent and expertise in the nuances of air combat helped make this story as accurate as possible. May his own works light up the sky.

For this first sortie into fiction I was blessed with the masterful editing of Doug Grad, of New American Library, whose skills made this a better book. Huge thanks, as always, go to my literary agent, Alice Martell, of the Martell Agency, for her stalwart support.

Finally, a salute to all the gallant men and women who fling themselves from the decks of America's warships and fly into harm's way. They're awesome.

May God have mercy on our enemies;
they will need it.
General George S. Patton

In waking a tiger, use a long stick.
Mao Tse-tung

It is always the one you don't see that gets you.
*World War II Ace Major Tommy McGuire,
KIA January 1945*

0 Miles   100   200
0 Kilometers   200

ARMENIA   AZERBAIJAN
AZER.
TURKEY   CASPIAN
                                            SEA
SYRIA   IRAQ
                                            IRAN
AL TAQQADUM AIR BASE   AL TAJI AIR BASE
F/A-18 interception of Iraqi
MiG-29s, 1443 GMT, 18 April   ★ Baghdad
                           ✈ SHAYKA MAZHAR AIR BASE
⊗
LATIFIYAH WEAPONS COMPLEX

SOUTHERN NO FLY ZONE

                              Al Basra ●

                    KUWAIT   PERSIAN
                                GULF
                    USS Ronald Reagan, 0645 GMT, 30 May
                                          ⊗
                    SAUDI
                    ARABIA
                              Al Manamah (Manama) ●
                              BAHRAIN

EUROPE
              IRAQ
              area of detail
AFRICA   ASIA

© 2001 Jeffrey L. Ward

ONE

The Kill

"Fulcrum!"

The effect was always the same. Just calling out the radar contact never failed to spike First Lieutenant Tracey Barnett's pulse rate upward by twenty beats. She knew it was having the same effect on the other two controllers. In the spectral glow of the E-3C *Sentry*'s red-lighted command-and-control compartment, she could see them both hunched over their own consoles.

"Make that two Fulcrums!"

She had them tagged now. They were out of the Al-Taqqadum air base, just west of Baghdad. They were headed south, toward the thirty-third parallel, the boundary of the No-Fly-Zone. And she could label them as bona fide, no-shit bandits, meaning they were hostile. She had a good electronic I.D. on them and these guys were definitely MiG-29s—twin-engine, Russian-built fighters with the NATO code name "Fulcrum."

They were coming her way.

Tracey studied the two blips on her scope. It was not like the Iraqi Air Force to come out and challenge the allied air patrols. If they took off at all, they would make a fainthearted thrust at the NFZ, then cut and run back to the interior of Iraq.

At least, that's what they usually did. But not today. These guys weren't running. They were supersonic, about Mach 1.2 and accelerating.

Still coming this way. Headed south toward the NFZ.

Just to be sure, she called up *Rivet Joint,* the intelligence-gathering RC-135, in its own orbit over the Gulf. Like the AWACS, *Rivet Joint* was a version of the ancient Boeing 707, but without the saucerlike radome atop the fuselage.

"We confirm that, Sea Lord," said the controller in *Rivet Joint.* "Two Fulcrums in the air. Looks like the game's on. Hope you got shooters available."

Tracey went back to her console, giving the display a quick scan, checking her assets. She needed shooters—armed and ready fighters. Now, where were they . . . ?

There. Perfect! A flight of four Navy F/A-18s, just launched from the *Reagan,* still refueling on the tanker.

She called the fighter division lead. "Stinger One-one, this is Sea Lord. You with me?"

A mini-second's pause. "Stinger One-one is up, Sea Lord," the F/A-18 flight leader answered.

"Show time, Stinger. Got a hot vector for you."

"You called the right number, Sea Lord. You point, we shoot."

One hundred ten kilometers to go.

The desert was sweeping beneath them in a brown-hued blur. Colonel Tariq Jabbar knew that at this velocity—one and a half times the speed of sound—they would reach the thirty-third parallel in less than five minutes.

Ninety kilometers.

Of course, the trick at this speed was to time your turn to avoid penetrating the forbidden airspace. In fact, Colonel Jabbar did not intend even to get close to the so-called boundary, just rush at it in a threatening way. Taunt the Americans. Make them scramble fighters and go through yet another useless exercise.

An idiotic game, thought Jabbar. A senseless waste. It was all an extension of the Gulf War, which had been the mother of all idiotic games. He felt a wave of anger rise in him, just as it always did when he recalled the slaughter of thousands of young Iraqi men. For nothing.

Colonel Jabbar pushed the thought from his mind. He had a mission today, senseless that it was. If he wanted to survive another encounter with the enemy he had to remain focused. He already knew from experience that he was on his own out here. He could not obtain help from any quarter. What information he received from his own GCI—Ground Controlled Intercept—was not only sparse, it was often woefully wrong. Iraq's air defense network had been so pummeled by allied antiradiation weapons, they had only a single functioning intercept radar. It was co-located with the approach control radar at the Baghdad airport, which had saved it from being demolished like the others.

Without an adequate air defense radar, even sophisticated warplanes like Jabbar's MiG-29 were easy prey for the American fighters, who had the backing of their AWACS ships and a fleet of shipborne control systems. The Iraqi fighters were flying blind.

But Colonel Jabbar, commander of the Twenty-first Air Intercept Squadron of the Iraqi Air Force, was, if nothing else, a pragmatist. His task today was not to win wars or even to do battle. He and his wingman would merely feint at the allied-imposed No-Fly-Zone, cause some sphincters in the American warplanes to tighten. Then they could return in triumph to Al-Taqqadum. Their glorious humiliation of the cowardly Americans would be duly reported to the President. Both Colonel Jabbar and his wingman, Captain Hakim Al-Fariz, would be summoned to the presidential palace to have medals pinned on them by Saddam himself.

This would come to pass, Jabbar knew, because of one simple truth. Captain Al-Fariz, incompetent ass that he was, was the son of Saddam Hussein's second youngest sister. It was no secret that the young officer had been designated for rapid advancement in the Iraqi military. Even though he had just completed his initial training in the MiG-29, he was already assigned as Jabbar's assistant squadron commander.

Today was Al-Fariz's first tactical mission in the MiG-29. And he was useless.

Jabbar glanced over his left shoulder, checking on his neophyte wingman. At first, he couldn't find him. Then he spotted the MiG, down low, nearly a mile in trail.

"Close it up, Blue Wing," Jabbar barked on the radio. "Bring it abeam, and closer."

"Yes, Colonel."

Jabbar watched Al-Fariz's MiG slide forward. It was not enough. The oaf knew nothing about tactical formation. He was still too far out, still in trail. Jabbar felt like keying his microphone and telling the imbecile, as he would any other pilot in his squadron, what a worthless specimen of fly-encrusted shit he was, that he had no business driving a goat cart, never mind a supersonic killing machine like the MiG-29.

Colonel Jabbar kept his silence. The idiot nephew of the country's idiot President held the key to Jabbar's own destiny. If Jabbar returned from this mission with Al-Fariz safely on his wing, he would be covered in glory. Of course, if the unthinkable happened and something happened to the nephew, Jabbar would be peering down the muzzles of a Republican Guard firing squad. Such was life in the Iraqi Air Force.

Forty kilometers. Two minutes. Jabbar rolled into a bank, searching the pocked desert for landmarks. There were few good visual cues for the invisible thirty-third parallel. Again he cursed the worthless Iraqi air defense radar. They had no reliable way to guide him to the precise boundary of the NFZ. He would have to depend on the MiG's quirky navigational display and on his own knowledge of the Iraqi landscape.

There! A wavelike series of wadis, a twisting road in the desert leading to a rocky promontory. Jabbar recognized the landmarks that identified the boundary—the invisible line drawn in the sand after the Gulf War, beyond which the Iraqi Air Force was forbidden to fly. Jabbar figured that his headlong charge at the boundary would already have lit up the allies' radar screens and alerted their interceptors. Now he and his wingman would execute a hard turn, parallel the boundary, tease them like a cat taunting a leashed dog.

The trick was knowing how long the leash was.

*   *   *

Commander Killer DeLancey, leader of the four-plane flight of F/A-18E Super Hornets, watched his second section refueling from the KS-3 Viking tanker. DeLancey and his wingman, Lieutenant Hozer Miller, were finished with their own refueling. Now they were in a high perch position off the tanker's left wing.

DeLancey glanced at the MDIs—Multipurpose Display Indicators—on his instrument panel. With the afternoon sun streaming over his shoulder, he could see his reflected image in the glass screen—camo-drab helmet, oxgyen mask pressed against his face, sun visor pulled down over his eyes. He looked like a creature from science fiction.

While he waited, DeLancey assessed the tools of his trade. The Super Hornet was armed with an arsenal of air-to-air weaponry. With the touch of a button he could select three different ways to destroy an airborne adversary. On each wingtip he carried an AIM-9 heat-seeking Sidewinder missile. On inboard stations were mounted the AIM-120 radar-guided missiles. In the long pointed snout of his Hornet fighter nestled the twenty-millimeter Vulcan cannon with its horrific six-thousand-round-per-minute rate of fire.

With his right hand DeLancey kept a light hold on the control stick. The stick grip bristled with knobs and switches—cannon and missile firing trigger, the pickle button that launched air-to-ground munitions, the three-position air-to-air weapon select button.

DeLancey's flight had been scheduled for a routine CAP—Combat Air Patrol—of the NFZ. It was supposed to be a four-ship CAP. But that was before the call from AWACS.

Now he wanted to move out. He rolled his Hornet

into a turn and shoved the throttles up. Hozer Miller stayed glued to his left wing.

"Stinger One and Two will take the hot vector," DeLancey said. "Three and Four, rejoin after you've tanked."

"Stand by, Killer," came the voice of Commander Brick Maxwell, leading the second section of Hornets. Maxwell's wingman was still plugged into the tanker's refueling drogue. "We haven't finished tanking. This oughta be a four-ship."

DeLancey assessed the situation. That damned Maxwell was lecturing him again. Maxwell was De-Lancey's operations officer. He had been in the squadron three months and he was a royal pain in the ass.

DeLancey gave it a moment's thought, then reached a decision. Screw Maxwell. Screw the four-ship. This was war.

He swung the nose of his Hornet to the north. He was not going to wait while those two old ladies took their sweetass time refueling. Not with MiGs headed into the NFZ.

"Stinger One-one is taking the vector," DeLancey said. "Hozer, stay joined. We'll engage as a two-ship."

"Roger that, Skipper," Miller replied without hesitation. Hozer might be a suck-up, thought DeLancey, but he was a team player.

DeLancey knew the radio exchange was being monitored and recorded both aboard the AWACS and back in the Combat Information Center on the *Reagan*. He also knew he would catch hell from CAG Boyce, the Air Wing Commander. So be it. It wouldn't be the first time he had to explain his actions in front of some thumb-up-his-ass captain or admiral. This was combat, or at least the closest thing to it. In combat you had to seize opportunity.

DeLancey knew about seizing opportunity. On the side of his Hornet, just beneath his name, were the painted silhouettes of three fighters. One was a MiG-25. The other two were Super Galebs. The MiG was from the first night of Desert Storm, over Iraq. The Galebs were a flight of two in Yugoslavia. De-Lancey had caught them from behind and shot them both with AIM-9 Sidewinders. With three kill symbols on his fuselage, Killer DeLancey was America's top-scoring fighter· pilot.

Here was another opportunity. *Two bandits.*

The significance of the two Iraqi jets now aimed southward was fixed like an implant in DeLancey's brain. Another kill symbol on his jet would ensure his status as the world's top fighter pilot. Two more . . . The thought made him almost giddy. Killer DeLancey would be the only active-duty ace in the world.

He would be a legend.

Tracey Barnett could see the whole picture. It was a classic intercept. On her tac display, the shooters and the bandits were converging like glowworms in a meadow. "Stinger One-one, Sea Lord," she said in her microphone. "Bandits bearing zero-one-zero, range sixty-two miles, at thirty-one thousand. Looks like they're turning to parallel."

Tracey was beginning to relax now. This was going to be another of those cruise-the-boundary capers the Iraqis liked to pull. She wondered why they bothered. Why did they want to expose themselves? Maybe it made them feel good.

Sometimes Tracey marveled at how progress and

antiquity were melded together in this business. The lumbering four-engined E-3C, for example, with its saucer-shaped radome and array of advanced electronic warfare equipment. This big truck was the same basic Boeing 707 that first flew nearly fifty years ago. Yet it was the most sophisticated—and deadly—command and surveillance tool on the planet.

She heard the Hornet leader. "Stinger One-one has a lock."

Tracey stared at the screen. A lock? That meant the Hornet leader was targeting the bandits. What the hell was going on?

"Your weapons status is tight, Stinger One-one. Copy that?" "Tight" meant that the Hornets did not have clearance to arm their air-to-air missiles. They had to wait for an indication of hostile intent.

She waited for Stinger One-one's acknowledgment.

And waited.

Nothing.

"Stinger One-one, confirm weapons status tight."

Still nothing. Damn! He was stonewalling her. She could see the fighters—Hornets and MiGs—converging on the tac display.

Fifty miles. *Okay, guys, this is going too far.*

She jabbed her intercom button. "Butch, you better check this out."

"Coming," answered Butch Kissick, a graying, crew-cut Navy lieutenant commander. Kissick was the ACE—Airborne Command Element—who reported directly to a three-star general headquartered in Riyadh.

Kissick walked to Tracey's console and plugged in his own headset. He looked at the tac display, and a frown passed over his face. The Hornets were flying a pursuit curve that would put them in firing range in the next two minutes.

"Stinger One-one, this is Hammer," Kissick said. "Answer up, cowboy, or I'm gonna yank your ass out of there."

Three seconds passed.

Finally, "Stinger One-one copies, Hammer. We show the bandits turning nose hot." "Nose hot" meant that the opposing fighter's nose was pointed toward them. It was an indication of hostile intent.

"Negative, negative," Kissick replied, his voice rising. "They're gonna turn and stay north of the border."

Another two seconds. "Copy."

Kissick stood there, watching the glow worms on the screen come closer. If this peckerhead in Stinger One-one pushed any harder, Kissick was going to call the game off. But as long as they followed the rules of engagement, he'd let them play. At least they might scare the crap out of a couple of Iraqi fighter jocks.

Maxwell glanced to his right. A quarter mile away, in combat spread formation, was his wingman, Leroi Jones. Both jets were in full afterburner, hauling ass to catch their commanding officer, who had just charged off to engage the Iraqi Air Force.

Maxwell studied his situational display. The bandits were heading west along the border. They were obviously playing their game of feint and tease. The other two blips in the display—Killer and Hozer—were nose hot on them, in a ninety-degree intercept angle.

Maxwell was getting a bad feeling in his gut. He called on the tactical frequency: "Stinger One-one, confirm the rules of engagement. We gotta see hostile intent, right?"

"We already covered that in the briefing."

"I show the bandits nose cold."

"Get off the frequency," DeLancey snapped, "unless you've got something I need to hear."

In the cockpit of his Hornet, Maxwell smoldered. Everyone on the channel—AWACS, *Rivet Joint,* the rest of Stinger One-one flight—had heard the rebuff.

Okay, asshole, go for it. Maybe we can bail you out. Maybe not.

Chirp! Chirp! Chirp! Chirp!

Colonel Jabbar heard the aural alert from his *Sirena* RWR—radar warning receiver—and he felt every nerve fiber in his body tingle.

He had heard it before, of course. He expected it. It meant that the Americans—probably F/A-18 Hornets—were rushing toward the NFZ at high speed. Even his enfeebled GCI up in Baghdad had been able to pick them out and send the warning. So it was all very normal that Jabbar and his wingman would be getting an RWR warning from the inbound fighters. It was part of the game.

Still, that slow chirping of the *Sirena* made his blood run cold. Jabbar toyed for a second with the notion of turning hard *into* the Yankee bastards and engaging them. Stuff a couple of AA-10 missiles up their intakes. It would be glorious. It would correct a hundred past humiliations the Iraqi Air Force had suffered.

But not today. He did not have an expendable wingman to lose in such an engagement. Instead he had Saddam's idiot nephew to protect.

"Blue Wing, stay with me," Jabbar radioed Al-

Fariz. "We have fighters approaching from the south."

Jabbar started a gentle turn to the north. He would play it safe, show everyone that he was giving the border a wide berth. As he turned, Jabbar glanced over his left shoulder. Make sure Al-Fariz was following.

He saw nothing.

No wingman. Just empty sky.

"Blue Wing, where are you? Join up! *Now!*"

Captain Hakim Al-Fariz heard the warning. Enemy fighters inbound from the south! Even though Colonel Jabbar had briefed him that the Americans would probably send up fighters, the news that they were out there—*coming toward them!*—sent a surge of adrenaline through Al-Fariz's body strong enough to jolt a camel.

His immediate reaction was to go to his own radar. *Fighters! Where were they? From what angle?*

Fixated on the display, he twirled the acquisition knob. He was a novice with the complicated Russian-built tactical radar display. Why wasn't he picking up the targets? Where in God's name were they?

While Al-Fariz toiled with his radar, his MiG-29 rolled into a gentle left turn.

Southward. Into the NFZ.

They all saw it.

Tracey Barnett, in the E-3C AWACS, picked it up on her display. The trailer MiG was . . . Oh, shit! . . . The guy was turning *nose hot!*

Butch Kissick was peering at the same display. "Goddammit!" he roared. "Look at that. The sonofabitch is flying right into the NFZ."

Brick Maxwell, leading the second section of Hornets at Mach 1.2 toward the NFZ border, observed the MiG drifting across the border. He also saw the lead Fulcrum in a shallow turn—*to the right.* What the hell? Were these guys playing a game? Some kind of set up? The trailer Fulcrum was either playing chicken or he was totally out to lunch.

Maxwell felt a sense of dread. This was going to be ugly. The other pair of blips—Stinger One-one and his wingman—were closing fast from the left. DeLancey and Hozer were almost within the envelope for a missile shot. And so was the Fulcrum. He was still coming left.

Nose hot.

DeLancey wasn't worried about the Fulcrum pilot taking a shot. If the guy really wanted to fight, DeLancey figured, he wouldn't be so stupid as to make a shallow turn like that into two opposing fighters. Even if he managed to get a missile into the air, DeLancey was sure that at this range he and Hozer would have the time and tools to defeat it.

Only one worrisome thought now troubled him— this MiG jockey might get homesick and bug out for Baghdad.

He might get away.

Sure as hell, that's what the guy was doing. DeLancey could see it happening on his radar. He could see the bandit's nose cranking around back to the right. The sonofabitch was going to cut and run!

Well, maybe he'd get away, maybe not. If the stupid bastard was in the NFZ, he was fair game.

On his stores display, DeLancey selected an AIM-120 radar-guided missile. It would be at the far edge of his firing envelope, but it was the only shot he would have.

He rolled his Hornet into a right turn, leading the Iraqi jet's turn to the north. He superimposed the target acquisition box in his heads-up display over the radar symbol of the retreating Fulcrum.

Looking good . . . almost . . . hold it . . . *There!*

Fighter pilots called the AIM-120 a "wild dog in a meat locker." This was because the missile contained its own autonomous guidance system that when locked on to a target—any target—guided the weapon without further control from the pilot. Once launched, the AIM-120 pursued its prey like an unleashed hunting animal.

DeLancey squeezed the trigger on his stick.

Whoom!

He squeezed again.

Whoom!

Two AIM-120 missiles, one after the other, were racing out ahead of the Hornet. Behind each missile trailed a wisp of smoke and vapor.

"Fox Three!" yelled DeLancey, signaling that he had just fired radar-guided missiles.

Hunched inside the cockpit of his MiG-29, Captain Hakim Al-Fariz heard the slow chirping of the *Sirena* radar warning receiver. Then he heard it sharpen to a high-pitched warble.

Al-Fariz felt a stab of fear that nearly made his heart explode. Even though he had never been in combat, he recognized that shrill warbling sound: The *Sirena,* which had been receiving the American fighters' APG-73 radar emissions, was now hearing something else.

A missile! An air-to-air missile was inbound. From where? Was it targeting him?

Al-Fariz refused to believe what was happening. How could this be? This was his first tactical mission in the MiG-29. He wasn't supposed to be fired upon by the enemy.

"Help!" he squawked on the radio. "Colonel! The *Sirena*. A missile—"

"Break right!" came the voice of Colonel Jabbar. "Turn right now! Immediately!"

The urgent command penetrated like a laser into Al-Fariz's paralyzed brain. *Turn!* He jammed the stick hard to the right, then pulled. The MiG wheeled hard into a right turn. Al-Fariz hauled the stick back, grunting under the heavy acceleration. Five Gs, six, seven Gs. Seven times his normal body weight, the blood being forced from his brain. Turn! Make the missile overshoot.

The AIM-120 bored through the sky toward the MiG. The sudden angle-off and the seven Gs were more than the missile could manage. Nearly at the end of its envelope, the air-to-air missile swished past the tail of the hard-turning MiG-29, then sputtered and lost its guidance.

Al-Fariz was alive.

But the second missile, a quarter mile behind the first, stayed locked-on. As Al-Fariz's MiG-29 pulled hard in its seven-G vertical bank, the AIM-120 continued in a relentless arcing pursuit curve.

Tracking. Closer, closer, still tracking.

Kablooom! The missile impacted the MiG squarely in the cockpit.

The forward half of the MiG-29 disintegrated from the blast of the AIM-120's warhead. Captain Hakim

Al-Fariz, who had been an athletic, handsome specimen of young Iraqi manhood, was transformed into a
molten blob of protoplasm.

The aft portion of the jet, containing the engines
and the fuselage fuel tank, exploded in an orange
fireball. The flaming debris descended like a comet to
the floor of the desert.

"Stinger One-one, splash one!"

The radio call from the Hornet crackled like an
electric shock through the command cabin of the
AWACS. Butch Kissick stared at the tactical display
console. "What the fuck . . . ?"

Tracey Barnett was shaking her head. "He did it.
He shot him."

"I don't believe this shit," said Kissick.

"What do you want me to do, Butch?"

"Remember everything that happened. I guarantee
you we're gonna be standing in the general's office."

From thirty miles away, Maxwell saw the fireball. It
looked like a tiny Roman candle, arcing downward to
the earth.

On his radar display he could see the aftermath of
the engagement. The lead bandit was still in a turn to
the north. The blips from DeLancey's and Hozer's
Hornets were still pointed northward, into Iraqi
airspace.

"Stinger One-one," said Maxwell. "Heads up.
You're past the NFZ boundary."

"Roger that," said Killer. Maxwell could hear the
exhilaration in DeLancey's voice. "We're bugging out.
Stay nose on the bandit and cover us while we egress."

"Three copies. You're covered."

Maxwell saw the two radar symbols—Killer and Hozer—executing a turn-in-place to the left. In unison, their noses swung toward the south, back to the NFZ, egressing from Iraqi airspace. As they turned southward, Maxwell and his wingman swept past them with their noses—and missiles—trained on the surviving MiG. Just in case the MiG leader decided to come back and take a shot at the retreating Hornets' exposed tailpipes.

And that, Maxwell realized with a start, was exactly what the bastard was doing.

There it was on his display—the symbol of the lead Iraqi MiG-29. He wasn't turning north any longer. The MiG's nose was in a hard turn southward. Toward Maxwell and his wingman.

"Sea Lord, Stinger Three," Maxwell called. "Do you show the lead bandit coming nose hot?"

"That's affirmative," answered Tracey Barnett from the AWACS. "Looks like he's reengaging."

Maxwell cursed inside his oxygen mask. It was just what he was afraid would happen. The fight that De-Lancey started wasn't over. DeLancey had hosed this guy's wingman. Now the Iraqi wanted to take his own shot at someone.

Maxwell was the someone. It was going to be a face-to-face shoot-out.

Colonel Jabbar scanned the empty sky where Al-Fariz's MiG had been. No sign of a parachute. He was not surprised. He knew from the pitch of the *Sirena* warning that it was a radar-guided weapon, not a heat-seeker. It had been a direct hit. At least Al-Fariz did not suffer a painful death.

Jabbar felt himself filled with a white-hot fury. The

smoking trail of his wingman's destroyed jet was still falling to the desert. The arrogant bastards had executed Al-Fariz like he was a stray dog in a garbage heap.

He could see in his radar the two fighters—the ones who had killed Al-Fariz—egressing from the area. If he accelerated, pursued them into the NFZ, Jabbar could lock them up, take them both out.

But then he saw something else. Two extra blips that weren't there before.

He should have known. Two more enemy fighters coming at him. They were twenty miles, nose on.

Just as Jabbar reached to slew the target designator in his radar display to lock up the lead fighter, he heard the aural warning in his headset. The warning was in Russian. "Low fuel! Low fuel!"

For a second Jabbar considered. If he stayed in the fight, he would probably run out of fuel before he made it back to Al-Taqqadum. If he turned tail, he would be exposed to a shot from the enemy fighters. Either way, his chances were nil.

Jabbar's finger went to the missile launch button on the control stick.

He was about to depress the button when he heard another aural alert. *Chirp! Chirp! Chirrrrrrrp!*

The *Sirena*. It was going crazy. They had fired *another* missile! This time Jabbar was the target. The enemy had preempted him. Now he was defensive.

Colonel Jabbar made an instantaneous tactical decision. *Try to save yourself. Maybe, if you survive the missile, you might even escape a firing squad.*

Jabbar snapped the MiG into a seven-G right break. He shoved the throttles into full afterburner and dove for the deck. With its nose down, under full thrust from the two mighty Tumansky afterburners, the MiG-29 accelerated—Mach 1.5. Mach 2. The brown vastness of the Iraqi desert filled his windscreen.

Jabbar was in a deadly tail chase. Behind him the Mach 3 air-to-air missile was trying to overtake his Mach 2 MiG-29 fighter. It was a game of hound-and-hare, except that the hound possessed an eight-hundred-mile-per-hour advantage.

He could hear the angry shrill squeal of the *Sirena*. Sweat poured from inside Jabbar's helmet, stinging his eyes. *Chiiirrrrrrrrrrp!*

The chirping intensified. More shrill, more relentless. The missile was closing on him. Jabbar hunched down in his cockpit seat, holding his breath, waiting for the inevitable.

The chirping stopped.

Jabbar waited. The chirping did not resume.

He took his first breath in nearly a minute. He had outrun the killer missile and its fuel was exhausted. But the Americans were still behind him. Was another missile on its way?

Maxwell prepared to fire his second missile. His finger curled around the trigger.

His first shot had been launched at the extreme end of the AIM-120's range. The MiG pilot had made a smart move. He had dived and managed to outrun the missile. It had saved his life, at least for the moment. It had also persuaded him to haul ass for home.

But now, because the MiG had gone nearly vertical, Maxwell had closed the distance. He could take a second shot and still bag the MiG. Maxwell hesitated, finger on his trigger. *Should I kill this guy . . . ?*

The window was closing. He had perhaps three seconds. He could shoot now—and the MiG would be dead. Another anonymous Iraqi fighter pilot would be history.

Maxwell's finger touched the trigger.

Squeeze the damn thing. Shoot and get it over.

Another second.

"Position check, Brick," said Leroi, high off Maxwell's right wing. Jones's job was to radar-search for "spitters"—unobserved newcomers to the fight. Jones sounded worried. "We're thirty miles past the boundary."

So they were. The two Hornets were deep into Iraqi airspace, and going deeper. On his display Maxwell could see the blip of the Iraqi jet retreating northward at twice the speed of sound.

The MiG was still in range. Maxwell still had a shot.

He slid his finger off the trigger. *Okay, pal. You owe me one. Have a nice life.*

"Copy that. We're bugging out."

Screech. Screech.

The landing gear of the big Russian fighter squawked onto the asphalt surface of Highway U45, the main thoroughfare from Baghdad to the Al-Taqqadum military complex.

Jabbar saw an Army truck coming at him head-on. Jabbar's MiG was still rolling at over a hundred kilometers per hour. From the cockpit, Jabbar could see the truck driver's eyes. They looked like huge white lamps. At the last instant, the driver swerved toward the ditch, rolling the truck up on its side. Jabbar swept past, giving the driver a friendly wave.

Well, he'd almost made it back to Al-Taqqadum.

The full-afterburner race with the air-to-air missile had consumed the last of his reserve fuel. Knowing that he would not make it to the Al-Taqqadum runway, Jabbar had decided to plunk the MiG-29 down on the highway while his engines were still running.

That turned out to be a fortuitous decision. Ten seconds after touchdown, he saw the RPM indicator for the left engine begin spooling down from fuel exhaustion. And then the right engine. Now he was coasting down the highway in total silence.

Still rolling, Jabbar passed a sign declaring that visitors were ordered to halt. They were entering a restricted military area. Ahead he saw the main gate of Al-Taqqadum air base. Jabbar let the jet roll until the long, drooping snout of the MiG-29 was pointed directly at the door of the sentry house.

A startled guard, holding his Kalishnikov across his chest, came charging out of the sentry house. Suddenly aware of the immense object rolling toward him, the guard dug in his heels. Losing traction, he fell in a heap, still clutching the Kalishnikov.

Jabbar brought the MiG to a smooth stop. He opened the canopy and removed his brilliantly painted red helmet. The red helmet was the single indulgence by which he distinguished himself from his other squadron pilots.

Despite the searing afternoon temperature, the outside air felt cool. He gazed around him at the shimmering desert, the dumbstruck guard, the air base he hadn't quite reached. Overhead, the sky was a dull, hazy blue. Jabbar realized that he was soaking wet from perspiration.

Several hundred yards inside the gate, he saw a per-

sonnel vehicle coming. It would be the base commander and, surely, several Republican Guardsmen.

All in all, he thought, this had been a very bad day.
The worst was yet to come.

TWO

The Hero

The news traveled, literally, at the speed of light. It flashed simultaneously from the AWACS and *Rivet Joint* to the Commander of the Joint Task Force in Riyadh.

The reaction was predictable.

"Jesus fucking Christ!" roared Joe Penwell, the Air Force three-star who was responsible for all the United States forces in the Middle East. Penwell was a barrel-shaped ex-SAC pilot. He was famous for his volcanic eruptions of temper. "Just what we need. The Saudis are already having shit fits over the sanctions on Iraq, starving the poor Iraqi schoolchildren. Now a goddamn shoot-down!"

Penwell's Vice Commander was a bespectacled Navy commodore named Ashby. "Maybe it really was hostile intent," he said in his monotone voice. "We don't have the intel debrief yet."

"Maybe it was some Navy jock full of testosterone who wanted a notch in his belt." Penwell was on his feet, storming around his desk. "Tell the Hornet flight leader to divert his flight to Riyadh. I'm gonna debrief those clowns personally."

Ashby compressed his lips and waited a full five seconds, which was what he always did when Penwell went ballistic. "Let's give it a second, Joe. That would implicate the Saudis, bringing the Hornets directly to Riyadh after the engagement. You know where that could go."

Penwell fumed for a moment. He knew goddamned well where it could go. Ashby, the bureaucratic pissant, was right. That's why Ashby was Vice Commander—to keep him from making such mistakes, or, in this case, exacerbating a mistake some trigger-happy fighter pilot had already made.

Penwell had another problem. He knew with an absolute certainty that within the next hour he would receive a call from the Chairman of the Joint Chiefs. Or the Secretary of Defense. Or even the President. When the call came, Penwell wanted to say, *Yes, sir, I have the facts. A court-martial is already in session.*

But the Saudis were his first worry. To draw them into a belligerent action against fellow Arabs could unhinge the already fragile allied coalition. No telling where that could go.

"Okay," said Penwell. "Send the Hornets back to the *Reagan*. But shoot off a personal-for to the Battle Group Commander. I want all his debriefing intel— and a damn good action report—ASAP."

Penwell thought again about the Navy fighter pilots. They were crazy bastards. But what did you expect from people who landed airplanes on boats?

"Hornet ball, nine-point-three."

"Roger, ball," answered the Landing Signal Officer.

That was the ritual—rolling into the groove, approaching the carrier deck, you announced your aircraft type, that you had the "ball"—the optical glide path reference, then your fuel quantity. The LSO replied with a "roger, ball." It was the verbal contract that acknowledged the LSO's control of the pilot's approach to the ship.

Maxwell recognized the LSO's voice. It was Pearly Gates, a young lieutenant in Maxwell's squadron, VFA-36.

Maxwell concentrated on the Fresnel Lens at the left edge of the landing area. The illuminated amber "ball" was in the center of the lens, indicating that he was on the correct glide path to the deck. If the ball went high on the lens, it signaled that the jet was high. Unless the pilot corrected, he would overshoot the arresting wires. A low ball was worse. It meant that the jet was settling dangerously close to the blunt aft ramp of the flight deck.

The ball was drifting upward. With his left hand, Maxwell nudged the throttles back an increment. *A tiny bit . . . now put a little back on . . .*

Maxwell's hands were making infinitesimal corrections with the stick and throttle, nudging, adjusting, keeping his F/A-18 on a precise path to the deck. In his windshield the gray mass of the aircraft carrier swelled like an expanding apparition.

Landing a jet aboard a ship at sea was the most demanding feat in aviation. Since he'd been back to the fleet, Maxwell had added another forty-three traps—arrested landings—giving him a total of 522. Not a lot these days, at least for someone with the rank of commander. But pretty good, he thought, for a guy who'd spent half his career on the beach.

Until six months ago, Maxwell expected that he would never see another aircraft carrier. He had de-

parted the normal fighter pilot's career path back
when he was a lieutenant, still in his first squadron
tour. Maxwell was selected for the Navy's test pilot
school at Patuxent River, Maryland. He then spent a
tour of duty testing the new F/A-18 Super Hornet,
which was just rolling off the Boeing assembly lines.

Then Maxwell was selected for what he considered
the ultimate flying job in the universe—the space shuttle. He checked in to NASA's Johnson Space Center
and commenced training as an astronaut. It took two
years. Finally, on a splendid autumn afternoon, he
lifted off from the Cape's Pad 39-B aboard the orbital
vehicle *Atlantis* on his first space shuttle mission.

He didn't know that it would be his last.

Whitney Babcock hung up the secure phone that
linked him by satellite to the Pentagon. A broad grin
spread across his face. Just as he expected, the Secretary was delighted.

An air battle over Iraq. It was glorious! Like a gift
from Allah. And he, of course, would now ensure the
media reported that Whitney T. Babcock III was not
only on the scene, but he had been directly involved
with the control and execution of the mission.

It was what the Secretary of the Navy had sent him
out to the *Reagan* to do—look for an "opportunity."

At first Babcock hadn't understood.

"It used to be called 'gunboat diplomacy,' " the Secretary explained before Babcock departed Washington. "When Reagan needed some credit, what did he
do? He blasted the shit out of Gadhafi. Over what?
A little terrorist bombing. A pinprick, really. But Bush
Senior got the big prize. He got to send half a million
troops after Saddam. Why? Because America wanted

to keep cheap gas. Hell, this President deserves as much."

"You mean, sir, we—the President, that is—needs, ah . . ."

"A distraction, Whit. That's all. Just a little side show. The public loves it, and it makes everybody look good, especially the President."

Babcock understood. Like every staffer in this administration, Whitney Babcock understood the primary commandment of political life: *Thou shalt make the boss look good.*

For three weeks Babcock had been stuck out here aboard this great steel barge. He knew that the senior officers, especially the Battle Group Commander, Admiral Mellon, held a barely disguised contempt for him. The old mossback had made it clear when Babcock arrived that he regarded him as a guest aboard his ship. Look but don't touch. Ask questions, but don't expect detailed answers. As though he, a presidentially appointed senior official of the Department of the Navy, was some kind of outsider aboard the Navy's newest carrier. Well, the admiral didn't know it yet, but he was at the end of his run. Babcock had already tagged him for an early retirement.

During his rise through the labyrinthine agencies and secretariats of Washington, one shining truth had guided Whitney Babcock. He was of the governing class. With his rarified lineage and education and breeding—Exeter, Yale, Georgetown Law, a succession of State and Defense Department positions—he, more than any of these military-trained blockheads, was destined to command the affairs of the United States military establishment. Unlike these career officers, he understood the subtle nuances of geopolitics.

He possessed the innate ability to see beyond the simple deployment of weaponry and assets. By background and birthright, he could think *strategically*.

And now, into his lap, had fallen this—a matter of strategic importance. What would the Iraqis do next? What would the other Arab states say? What should the response be from the United States forces gathered here in the Gulf? Point, counterpoint. Babcock now had a chance to show his own true brilliance.

From his padded chair on the flag bridge, he gazed down on the aft flight deck. The four Hornets that had engaged the MiGs were landing back aboard the *Reagan*. Soon the pilots would be down below, debriefing in CVIC. The admiral and his intelligence staff would be there. And so would Whitney Babcock III.

Commander Devo Davis, executive officer of the VFA-36 Roadrunners, watched Maxwell's jet slam onto the deck. Over the bulkhead speaker he heard the voice of Pearly Gates, the LSO—"Ooooohh-kay!"—as the jet's tailhook engaged the number three wire. Of the four arresting wires stretched across the deck, number three was the target.

The LSO normally didn't hand out compliments on the radio, but Pearly Gates was the type who liked to reward a perfect pass when he saw it. "Okay," with no qualifying comment, was as good as it got.

As the jet lurched to a stop on the landing deck, Davis donned his gear—the float coat survival vest and the hard-shelled cranial protector that everyone had to wear on the flight deck—and headed down the ladder.

Maxwell was still in the cockpit when Davis arrived.

The plane captain, a nineteen-year-old sailor named Ruiz, was helping him with his straps and navigation bag. Maxwell saw Davis and waved down to him.

Of the few men in the Navy whom Davis could count as genuine friends, Brick Maxwell was the closest. Maxwell and Davis went all the way back to Kingsville, Texas, when Davis was a freshly minted flight instructor and Lieutenant Junior Grade Sam Maxwell was his first student. And, as it turned out, his best. It was Davis, at least indirectly, who tagged Maxwell with his call sign—the moniker that sooner or later is attached to the name of every Navy fighter pilot.

It happened the day the training squadron skipper stopped Davis on the ramp. "How's your student doing?" asked the commander. "Is he worth a damn?"

"Maxwell? Solid as a brick, sir."

A smile flickered over the skipper's face. He scribbled something in his notepad, and that was it. Old Solid-as-a-brick Maxwell had a call sign.

Over fifteen years had passed since that day. Now, watching Brick Maxwell descend from the cockpit, Davis felt a flash of envy. Here he was, fighting the same old battle against his thickening waistline and vanishing hair, while Maxwell seemed to be exempt from such problems. He had the same lanky build—six feet tall, his weight unchanged since his light heavyweight boxing days as an ROTC midshipman at Rensselaer. He even wore the same old Tom Selleck-style mustache, without any sign of graying in his dark brown hair. Life was goddamned unfair, thought Davis.

Maxwell stepped onto the deck. Davis shook his hand and pointed to the empty missile rail on the wing tip. "Shit hot, pal. Looks like you got yourself a MiG."

"Not me," said Maxwell. He nodded across the flight deck to DeLancey's jet. "The skipper."

A crowd was gathering around DeLancey's Hornet. He was shaking hands with the deck crewmen and officers, signing autographs, posing for the photographers who had come from the ship's public affairs office. He had removed his helmet, flaunting the rule against unprotected heads on the flight deck. DeLancey's curly black hair was ruffling in the wind over the deck. He flashed his white-toothed grin for the photographers, giving them a good shot of his handsome profile.

"Look at that sonofabitch," said Davis. "Strutting around like some kind of movie star."

"You know Killer. He's on stage now."

"He's gonna be on another stage in a minute. The admiral sent me down here with a message for all four of you. He says to get your asses to CVIC immediately. Don't go to the ready room, don't stop to pee."

"That bad, huh?"

Davis nodded. "Never saw the old man so worked up. I hope you guys have a hell of a good story for what happened out there."

"Sit down," said Admiral Mellon. It was an order, not an invitation.

Maxwell, DeLancey, and their two wingmen, Leroi Jones and Hozer Miller, all took seats at a long conference table. Each was still wearing his torso harness, carrying his helmet and navigation bag. Their flight suits were damp, stained with sweat.

CVIC—Carrier Intelligence Center—was a spacious

room on the second deck. It had a projection screen on one bulkhead, charts of the Persian Gulf and Iraq on another, and the conference long table in the middle.

Admiral Mellon was already seated at the table. Beside him sat Red Boyce, the Air Wing Commander, gnawing on an unlit cigar. Sitting in a corner chair was a civilian, a sandy-haired man in his thirties. He was wearing Navy khakis without insignia.

The admiral didn't waste time. "What the hell went on out there, Killer?"

"The MiG we were vectored to intercept turned nose hot on us, Admiral," said DeLancey. "The guy made an aggressive turn into me and my wingman. He was entering the NFZ. I didn't have any choice except to shoot."

Mellon's eyes narrowed. He turned to Hozer Miller, DeLancey's wingman. "Let's hear it from you, Lieutenant."

Miller pulled on his earlobe and glanced at DeLancey. DeLancey nodded. "Uh, just like the skipper said, sir. It was definitely hostile intent. The MiG went nose hot on us."

"Anybody get a radar tape of the engagement?"

"My tape was set on the HUD," said DeLancey. "No radar tape."

"Me neither," said Miller.

Admiral Mellon had been a strike fighter pilot. He knew that the Hornet's tape recorder could be switched from the HUD—Heads-Up Display in the windscreen—to any of several other cockpit monitors, including the radar.

"Sorry, I didn't get it," said Leroi Jones.

DeLancey crossed his arms over his chest and tilted back in his chair. A pleased grin spread over his face.

"Damn it," said the admiral. "Everybody from the Pentagon to the Joint Task Force command is screaming for the video of the engagement. Somebody should have taped the fight on his radar."

"Somebody did."

Every pair of eyes in the room swung to Brick Maxwell.

Maxwell reached into the pocket of his G-suit and produced a tape cassette. He set it on the table in front of him.

The grin melted from DeLancey's face. His voice took on a hard edge. "What the hell did you do that for? You weren't even part of the engagement."

"Leroi and I were assigned to cover you. I switched the tape to radar when you called a lock."

DeLancey put his hands on the table and leaned forward. "If you were supposed to be covering me, why didn't you take out the lead MiG?" His face was reddening. "The sonofabitch turned nose hot and you had a shot at him."

"Because there wasn't any need to shoot. The MiG was bugging out. There was no hostile intent."

"The hell there wasn't! He was hostile and you lost your guts."

Maxwell and DeLancey locked gazes. Maxwell slid the tape cassette across the table. "There's the tape. Let it show whether the MiG was hostile or not."

DeLancey stood and aimed his finger at Maxwell. "Listen, mister. I don't give a shit what's on that tape. I've shot down more enemy aircraft than all the pilots in this air wing combined. All the pilots in this whole goddamn fleet, for that matter. Don't you tell me about—"

Boyce cut it off. "Sit down, Killer," he ordered. "Everybody chill out for a minute. I know you're still tensed up from the engagement. You heard Admiral Mellon. He wants to see that tape."

DeLancey was still on his feet. "Listen, CAG, I was the first on the scene. I know what I saw."

"That's why we have the tape. So we can all know what you saw."

"Sir, I can tell you that—"

"Never mind what's on the tape." The voice came from across the room.

Every head swung to the man in the corner.

Whitney Babcock walked over to the table. "Commander DeLancey did exactly the right thing."

"Mister Secretary," said the admiral, "with all due respect, this is an intelligence matter."

"It's a lot more than that, Admiral. It's a national security matter."

The admiral looked exasperated. He sighed and said, "Gentlemen, in case you haven't met our guest, this is the Undersecretary of the Navy, Mr. Whitney Babcock."

"Just call me Whit," said Babcock. He went directly to Killer DeLancey and extended his hand. "Commander, let me be the first to congratulate you."

"Sir?" A quizzical grin spread over DeLancey's face.

"For your brilliant victory today." Babcock turned to the admiral. "I think our country owes a tremendous debt to a warrior like Commander DeLancey. He deserves a decoration for this accomplishment. At least a Silver Star. Don't you agree, Admiral?"

*   *   *

Jones and Maxwell walked along the passageway that led back to the squadron ready room.

"Whooee!" said Jones. "I've never seen the skipper so pissed. Did you see his face when you pulled that tape out? He looked like he wanted to kill us."

"Not us, just me," said Maxwell. "In case you haven't noticed, the skipper and I aren't exactly soul mates."

Jones nodded. It would be damned hard *not* to notice, he thought. DeLancey had already told everyone that he considered Maxwell a carpetbagger who didn't belong in his squadron.

Lieutenant Leroi Jones was the only black pilot in the squadron and one of only four in the *Reagan*'s air wing. He had not joined the clique of DeLancey devotees, like Hozer Miller and Undra Cheever and half a dozen others. He thought their behind-the-back contempt for Brick Maxwell was bullshit. Jones liked Maxwell and enjoyed flying with him.

Jones said, "I take it you and the skipper know each other from somewhere?"

"Another squadron, another war."

"It must have been real bad. Killer acts like he hates your guts."

Maxwell kept his eyes straight ahead. "What makes you think it's an act?"

It was already dark out on the catwalk. Maxwell made his way, one foot in front of the other, hanging on to the steel rail. The catwalk was suspended beneath the port edge of the flight deck. A ten-knot breeze blew over the deck, and eighty feet below he could hear the carrier's bow slicing through the choppy sea. Off in the distance, lights were twinkling on the western shore. Bahrain? Qatar? Some Saudi coastal port with a name he couldn't pronounce?

The lights reminded Maxwell again what a tiny stretch of water the Persian Gulf was. Here they were, bounded on either side by renegade countries that wanted nothing so much as to see them sent to hell. It really wouldn't be too difficult, he thought. He knew that against a serious enemy—one with sophisticated naval and aerial weapons—the *Reagan* battle group and its escorts would be as vulnerable as ducks in a pond.

Coming up here to the catwalk at night had become a ritual for him. It was one of the few places aboard the great iron barge where he could be alone and think. Up here at night, exposed to the wind and surrounded by the summer sky and the black sea, he could imagine himself cut away from all earthly ties. He could be adrift in the vastness of the universe.

Like a space traveler. He could look at the stars and imagine the way things might have been. He could fling his voice out into the black void, and nobody could hear him.

Nobody except, maybe, one person.

"Are you out there, Deb?" he said into the darkness.

The words were swept away in the steady wind. He heard only the wind and the waves. The lights twinkled back at him.

THREE

Baghdad

No blindfold.

That's the way he wanted it, and they had granted him that much. The Guardsmen would have to look him in the eye. Observe him watching them over the sights of their carbines. Colonel Jabbar would not cringe or beg or weep. He would not grant them the privilege of seeing a professional officer disgrace himself.

At least he had the pleasure of knowing the President was enraged. According to his interrogator and former colleague, Major General Zirun, the President had had such a tantrum when he was informed about the death of his nephew, he ordered the executions not only of Colonel Jabbar but of the base commander, the wing commander, and each of the lowly GCI controllers who had failed to save Saddam's nephew from the American murderers. Saddam wanted everyone associated with the death of Al-Fariz consigned to Allah.

Jabbar wished he could have witnessed the tantrum. Saddam's fits, it was reported, could reach such intensity that he would be transformed to a seething, spittle-dripping maniac. His fury was so towering that he sometimes dispensed with formal death sentences and immediately executed offenders with his own automatic pistol.

Of course, it had all been very predictable. Even before he entered the interrogation room, Jabbar knew he was a dead man. The irony was, he might have saved himself. Somewhere over the desert he could have ejected from the MiG instead of delivering it safely back to Al-Taqqadum. He might have been able to escape, shed his identity, blend into the peasant population of Iraq. He could have fled to Turkey.

But that was not Colonel Jabbar's style. He was not a peasant, not an unwashed goat herder like these ignorant Guardsmen who were gazing at him over their Simonov carbines. Despite his country's misguided leadership, Jabbar had always considered himself a loyal warrior. For his country's cause, right or wrong, he had killed many men and had risked being killed. Death did not frighten him.

The six riflemen of the firing squad faced him from ten meters away. A Republican Guard captain, wearing his dress blue tunic with a holstered pistol on his belt, barked an order. Jabbar saw the riflemen work the slide actions of the carbines, heard the metallic *clack!* as the 7.62mm rounds rammed into the chambers.

Another order from the captain. All six open muzzles were trained on Jabbar.

Where? he wondered. His chest? His heart? His face? Would he see muzzle flashes? Would he experience a nanosecond of terror—or exhilaration—before the lead projectiles shattered his body?

I must not blink, Jabbar told himself. He would

leave with his dignity intact. He would die like a
soldier.

Another barked order. Jabbar tensed his body . . .
Do not blink! . . . The bullets would arrive before the
sound . . . look for the muzzle flashes . . .

More barked orders. Jabbar tensed even more, his
breath held tightly in his chest.

Something was happening. Another Republican
Guard officer—a major, perhaps a colonel—was
shouting at the captain. The captain was arguing
with him.

Jabbar kept his eyes fixed on the firing squad. The
rifles carbines were lowering. The soldiers glanced at
each other, at the captain, at Jabbar. They looked
confused.

The officer—Jabbar could see now that he was a
colonel of the Republican Guard—was walking
toward him. The captain was shouting something to
the firing squad.

Jabbar heard a succession of metallic *clacks*! The
Guardsmen were unloading their weapons.

Colonel Jabbar resumed breathing.

Chris Tyrwhitt tossed down his scotch and gazed
around the bar. The big walnut-paneled lounge was
empty. No Lufthansa or Swiss Air or Sabena flight
attendants. No European secretaries finished with
work and out for a drink. Not even the semiprofes-
sional pickups that used to hang out here at the
Rasheed Hotel bar.

It should have been cocktail hour, but the place
was deserted except for a couple of safari-suited Iraqi
bureaucrats and a cluster of Eastern European types

who were drunk and arguing in a language Tyrwhitt couldn't understand.

"This is a fucking bore," he declared.

"A sign of the times, mate," said Baxter, the BBC correspondent. Baxter was Tyrwhitt's only drinking companion these days. "They lost a war, they can't sell their oil, and nobody with half a brain wants to come to Baghdad. The only reason you and I are here is to cover the next war."

"What war? This country is so poor it couldn't attack Ethiopia."

"Don't believe it," said Baxter. "Uncle Whiskers is always good for a few surprises." Uncle Whiskers was Baxter's name for the President of Iraq.

Tyrwhitt, being an Australian, made a habit of disregarding Brits like Baxter, especially when they rambled on like this. Baxter liked to pose as an expert on Saddam's hidden weapons. Tyrwhitt and Baxter were among the few reporters left in Baghdad, and the subject of Saddam's invisible weapons was about the only item of bar conversation they had left. Did Saddam have them or not? If he did, what would he do with them? If he didn't, why didn't he just comply with the U.N. resolutions and get the sanctions lifted?

In any case, Tyrwhitt was bored with the whole subject. He yawned and stared blearily at his image in the mirror over the bar. "You know something, Baxter? You're full of shit. The only surprise Saddam has is which poor bugger on his staff he will execute next."

Baxter waited until the bartender walked down the bar to where the Eastern European contingent was still arguing. "What I'm hearing is that he's cranking up the big weapons. He's gone berserk about that MiG he lost last week."

"One worn-out Russian MiG? Why would he care? You're getting desperate, Baxter. When you don't have a story, you invent one."

"Not the MiG. The pilot. He was Saddam's nephew."

"Which means one less family member he has to provide with a palace," said Tyrwhitt. "Two more scotches, Efraim," he yelled down the bar. "Your problem, Baxter, is you're not drunk enough. You have to be drunk to understand that nothing in Baghdad makes any difference. Nothing matters and nobody gives a stuff."

"How can you call yourself a reporter, Tyrwhitt? You don't care about anything except drinking."

"That's an absolute lie," said Tyrwhitt. "I also care about fornicating. Trouble is, here in Baghdad both activities are exorbitantly expensive and inferior in quality."

They had another round. And then several more rounds. Tyrwhitt observed that he was right about the scotch. It wasn't good, nor was it cheap, even in nearly worthless Iraqi dinars. But the Rasheed Hotel was one of the few establishments in Baghdad where you could still obtain whiskey. In the old pre-war days, it was a place where you could pick up European women. No more. A grimness seemed to have settled over the Rasheed, just as it had over all of Baghdad. No airline flight attendants were showing up, no secretaries, no women of any ilk.

Tyrwhitt felt depressed. Perhaps, he thought, he should go back up to his room and try calling Claire. She was on assignment in Dubai, probably checked into the Hilton. At times like this he missed her caustic wit, her laugh, even the flashing-eyed fury when he drank too much or flirted too much or came home a day too late. In his mind he could see her long, trim legs, the little freckles on her breasts, the way her chestnut-colored hair splayed on the pillow when they made love.

Forget it, mate, he told himself. She'd hang up, just like last time when he rang her in—where?—Tel Aviv? He couldn't blame her, really. But still, maybe he would try—

"Look," said Baxter, nodding toward the lobby. "Our escorts."

Tyrwhitt looked up. In the lobby, wearing their ubiquitous brown safari suits, sat a couple of unsmiling hotel guests. Tyrwhitt knew who they were. Agents of the Bazrum—the Iraqi secret service—were easy to spot. They didn't even bother trying to conceal themselves anymore. These days the agents were as common as the street vendors who sold fake watches and jewelry. They were there to observe the activities of each foreign correspondent stationed in Baghdad.

Darkness settled over the city. No one was left in the bar when the two reporters paid their bill. They wobbled unsteadily through the lobby and out to the street. Baxter spotted a lone taxi, a decrepit Trabant that looked like it had been through a sandstorm. "Let's go to dinner over at the Jinnah."

"I'm not riding in that thing," said Tyrwhitt. "You're on your own, Baxter."

Baxter climbed into the Trabant. "I know what you're up to, mate. Be careful. Don't catch a disease."

As the taxi clattered off with Baxter inside, Tyrwhitt saw a black Fiat pull out of a street-side parking area and fall in trail. That was another standard fixture in Baghdad—a shadow. Wherever you went, either in a vehicle or afoot, you could expect to be followed. You got used to it.

Tyrwhitt started off down the street, then stopped and glanced over his shoulder. One of the safari suits from the lobby was peering at him through the glass door of the hotel. Tyrwhitt gave him a wave, then continued down the sidewalk.

"Were you followed?"

"Of course," said Tyrwhitt. "He was an idiot. He's still looking for me in the Al-Faisah district, back at the whorehouse."

"Are you certain?"

"Don't worry. I've done this before."

Tyrwhitt didn't know the man's name. He only knew that he was an officer assigned to a senior position somewhere in the Iraqi military. This was their second meeting.

"You stink of whiskey. Can you remember what I tell you?"

"I'm okay. I remember everything."

Tyrwhitt hadn't seen the man's face, at least not close up and in the light. By his voice and his manner he seemed to be in his late thirties, maybe early forties. With Iraqis, it was hard to tell. He had the demeanor of a man accustomed to command. Tyrwhitt guessed that he was a colonel, perhaps a brigadier.

The souk—the open-air market—was the perfect meeting place. It was easy to lose yourself after dark in the teeming throng that swarmed through the yellow-lighted stalls. Baghdad's economy was in tatters, and almost all the essential commerce of daily life now took place here. There were money changers and black marketers and merchants hawking used appliances and dried fruits and live chickens. A hubbub swelled over the marketplace like the rumble of a distant storm.

Inside the Al-Faisah brothel, Tyrwhitt had replaced his blue denim shirt with the standard Iraqi beige safari shirt. Wearing a kaffiyeh, he was able to slip out the back of the brothel, then wind his way through the ancient streets to the souk. In his costume, even with his ruddy, red-haired features, Tyrwhitt could blend into the throng. After a fair amount of meandering among the vendors, he stopped at a stall near the exit of the souk where a toothless old merchant was peddling cheap carpets.

Stooped over, inspecting one of the carpets, was a nondescript man in a long kaffiyeh that shielded most of his face. Tyrwhitt glimpsed a hawklike nose, a black mustache tinged with gray. He stood with his back to the man. They alternated speaking in broken English, then Arabic.

"Your Arabic has improved."

"I've been studying," said Tyrwhitt.

"In the whorehouse?"

Tyrwhitt couldn't tell if the man was joking. He didn't know, for that matter, if he even possessed a sense of humor. It would be difficult, he thought, for anyone to make jokes in a situation so filled with danger. Tyrwhitt wondered again what motivated the man to take such a risk. Did he despise the country's leadership so much he was willing to betray them? Did he expect some reward? Did he have a personal vendetta against Saddam? Was he a patriot, or a scoundrel?

The officer spoke in short staccato sentences. Tyrwhitt listened, startled at what he was hearing. The information was so explosive, so unbelievable, that at first he thought that he had misunderstood.

He asked the officer to repeat the information. He hadn't misunderstood.

Tyrwhitt felt compelled to ask, "You know this to be absolutely true?"

"Do you think me a liar?"

"I mean, is it verifiable?"

"I have seen it myself."

It had to be true, Tyrwhitt thought. The man couldn't be making it up. Not if he wanted to maintain any credibility.

They made an arrangement for their next meeting, this one at another souk, the one near the B'aath building downtown. The officer lingered a few more minutes, examining another carpet. Then he laid it aside and wandered away from the stall.

Tyrwhitt took his usual route back through the souk, out the southerly exit onto a narrow, winding street. After several blocks he entered a darkened alley. He waited several minutes, making sure he wasn't followed. Then he shed the safari shirt, replacing it again with the denim. He removed the kaffiyeh and stuffed it into his tote bag.

The agent—the same one who had followed him to the brothel—fell into trail when Tyrwhitt was within a block of the Rasheed. Tyrwhitt nodded cordially to him. *No hard feelings, mate. I'm just better at my job than you are at yours.*

Once he'd let himself into his room on the sixth floor, Tyrwhitt wasted no time. What he had to do now was too important to wait. Too urgent to worry about consequences. In any case, he was sure that the

Iraqis did not yet feel the need to prevent or intercept or even understand what he was doing.

The Cyfonika was still in its satchel in the closet. Tyrwhitt knew that Bazrum agents had already searched his room, several times probably. They had seen the Cyfonika and figured out what it was—a handheld satellite communications device. It was a commercially marketed tool, manufactured in the United States, that anyone, including the Iraqis, could purchase. With the Cyfonika phone you could speak real-time with anyone anywhere on the planet. Using a constellation of dedicated satellites, devices like the Cyfonika were becoming the chosen communications medium for global businesses, news services, shipping companies, government bureaus.

And spies.

Already Tyrwhitt had been hauled in for violating the strict Iraqi censorship laws. He had managed to convince the Bazrum interrogators that what he transmitted via his satellite phone was already being monitored by them and consisted, in fact, of dispatches that had been cleared by their own censors. Because Tyrwhitt and his news agency were not affiliated with the devil-allied Americans, and because his dispatches usually portrayed the Iraqis in a sympathetic light, they allowed him to keep the Cyfonika. So long as he transmitted only pre-cleared dispatches, he could continue what he was doing.

What the Iraqis did not yet understand was the rest of the technology. Tyrwhitt himself had only a vague notion of how the thing worked. As it had been explained to him, the SatComm device contained a micro-router that bundled compressed packets of encrypted data. The data, when delivered by voice to

the mouthpiece of the Cyfonika, could be encrypted
and transmitted simultaneously within a parent stream
of uncoded data—and it was virtually undetectable.
On electronic surveillance screens and passive monitoring devices, the appearance of the Cyfonika transmissions had an almost normal wave-length pattern,
with just a few odd-shaped squiggles that suggested
poor antenna stabilization. Or perhaps, imprecise
wave propagation. Or just some peculiar atmospheric
anomaly.

The Bazrum, of course, already suspected him. But
in Tyrwhitt's opinion, that was not bad. In a way it
was good, because it meant that they were giving him
no special attention. The paranoia of the Iraqis had
reached such a level that they suspected every for-
eigner in Baghdad was a spy. Even Baxter, who loved
to pose as some sort of undercover agent, had been
dragged into an interrogation room and held overnight. He was released the next morning, thoroughly
terrified by the Bazrum.

Tyrwhitt extended the antenna of the Cyfonika and
positioned it in the open window. He knew that ob-
servers in the building across the street from the hotel,
or in the street below, would detect the antenna. That
was okay. They would also intercept and translate the
censored dispatch that Tyrwhitt had been authorized
to send to his editor in Sydney. The dispatch consisted
of a press release from the office of Deputy Premier
Tariq Aziz declaring, once again, that due to last
week's aggression by American warplanes inside sov-
ereign Iraqi airspace, Iraq would henceforth shoot
down any and all intruding foreign aircraft.

Ho-hum, thought Tyrwhitt. More of Aziz's standard
chest-thumping response to every encounter in the dis-

puted No-Fly-Zone. He could count on sympathetic foreign correspondents like Chris Tyrwhitt to accommodate the beleaguered Iraqis by passing their message of defiance to the rest of the world.

But there was more. What the Bazrum would not intercept—or at least Tyrwhitt fervently hoped they wouldn't—was the encrypted message within the news dispatch. Unlike the news about Aziz's press release, which would be passed by satellite to Sydney, the encrypted message was intended for a different audience. It would be received by an umbrella-shaped antenna atop a gray, slab-sided building in Riyadh, Saudi Arabia. Within the bowels of the nondescript building specialists of the United States Central Intelligence Agency would decrypt this latest and most urgent report from their agent in Baghdad.

FOUR

Aliens

Like a piece of meat, delivered fresh to the fleet.

All in all, thought Lieutenant B.J. Johnson, it was a lousy way to arrive on an aircraft carrier—sitting backward, strapped down like a hunk of produce in the nearly windowless cargo compartment of a C-2A turboprop.

The C-2A was called a COD—Carrier Onboard Delivery. The COD hauled everything out to a carrier at sea that would fit into its cargo compartment—mail, food, tools, toilet paper, tires. And replacement pilots.

B.J. Johnson was a replacement F/A-18 strike fighter pilot, and coming aboard a carrier in the back of a freight hauler like the C-2A was damned undignified. And scary. It was a feeling of complete powerlessness. B.J. could hear the engines of the C-2A advancing and retarding, the throttle movements getting more abrupt, more urgent. It meant that they were approaching the ramp of the deck. The COD pilot was flying the ball. And this guy sure as hell was no smoothie. He was snatching the throttles and yanking the controls like a bear with a beach ball.

Whump! The C-2A slammed down on the deck—at

least B.J. hoped it was the deck—and lurched to a halt. B.J. was thrown hard against the seat back, and appreciated for the first time why they seated passengers in the COD facing backward. It felt like they had hit a wall. A couple of seconds later, the engines were revving up again and the COD was taxiing out of the arresting wires to the forward deck.

B.J. looked over at the other replacement fighter pilot, Lieutenant Spam Parker, two seats away. The ride out to the ship had been just as hard on Spam as it was on B.J. Spam had turned a ghastly shade of white.

The aft loading door of the COD dropped open. A flood of daylight and wind and the howl of turbine engines swept into the cabin. A man wearing a flight deck cranial headset appeared in the door. He wore a yellow jersey with "VFA-36 XO" stenciled on it.

"Lieutenant Johnson? Lieutenant Parker?" He had to yell above the din of the flight deck.

"That's us."

"I'm Commander Davis, executive officer of Strike Fighter Squadron Thirty-six. Welcome aboard, ladies."

Brick Maxwell poured a coffee and settled back to watch the fracas.

"Goddammit, no!" DeLancey yelled. "Not in my squadron."

"Nobody asked if we wanted them, Skipper," said Devo Davis. "They're here. They've got orders."

DeLancey had assembled all his senior squadron officers in the ready room—Devo Davis, the executive officer; Brick Maxwell, the operations officer; Craze Manson, the maintenance officer; Spoon Withers, the admin officer; Bat Masters, the safety officer.

DeLancey was not in a mood to listen. "How the hell am I supposed to run a fighter squadron with *women* in the cockpits? You were supposed to get those orders canceled."

"Wing staff wouldn't hear of it," said Davis. "The detailers wouldn't talk about it. Women in combat squadrons are a fact of life."

Watching the exchange, Maxwell knew that it was an argument without end. For over two centuries, ships-of-the-line had been crewed exclusively by men. But in the early 1990s, the ban on women in combat was lifted. Warships—and fighter squadrons—were deploying with complements of women, officers and enlisted. Men no longer had an exclusive franchise in the cockpits of Navy fighters.

Killer DeLancey wasn't buying it. He gave Davis a withering look. "Fact of life, huh? Well, thanks, Commander Davis. That's really helpful. We appreciate that little homily about the facts of life."

Davis's face reddened. An awkward silence fell over the ready room. Davis took the rebuke like he always did. He stared at the far bulkhead, wearing the expression of a beaten dog.

Maxwell felt the anger rise up in him. DeLancey was violating one of the oldest tenets of command— you didn't humiliate a subordinate in front of his peers. DeLancey was famous for violating rules, and everyone in the squadron had seen him heap scorn on the executive officer. Devo Davis was DeLancey's favorite target.

DeLancey had gone too far. Maxwell thumped his coffee cup on the desk, causing everyone's eyes to swing to his end of the table. "Devo is right," he said. "Hear him out, Skipper. You don't have any choice."

DeLancey swung his attention to Maxwell, peering at him like he'd just discovered a new specimen of insect. "You—are telling me—that I have no choice?"

Maxwell locked gazes with DeLancey. "They're part of the squadron. Just like Devo said. Like it or not, we have to live with it."

"How do you propose we live with it, Commander Maxwell?"

"Treat them just like any other new pilot. No favoritism, no bias. No double standard."

DeLancey gave him the same withering look he used on Davis. "Oh, by all means," he said in a mocking voice. "Let's make sure our women warriors get treated properly." He gazed around at all the senior officers. "Listen up, all of you. You're gonna give those two split tails the toughest assignments on the flight schedule—weather, night, whatever comes up. Give them every chance to prove that they have no business in a combat squadron. After they've screwed up bad enough, I can ship their asses back to the beach. Everybody copy that?"

The other officers all nodded, glancing from Maxwell to DeLancey. They all copied.

Lieutenant Leroi Jones couldn't believe it. His equipment—helmet, torso harness, G-suit, navigation bag, all his goddamn flight gear!—was in a pile in the corner of the ready room. In his locker at the back of the ready room was another set of flight gear. The name card on the locker bore another pilot's name—
LT. P. R. PARKER.

"Who the hell is P. R. Parker?"

"An officer senior to you," said a voice behind him. Jones spun around, startled by the voice. It be-

longed to a woman. She was tall, with ash-blond hair
that flowed down to the collar of her flight suit. Another woman, shorter, with bobbed brown hair, looked
up from one of the ready room chairs. "I'm Parker,"
the tall woman said. "Call sign 'Spam.' I take it
you're Jones."

"Why'd you dump my gear on the deck?"

"Nothing personal. I'm senior, so I took over the
locker."

"New pilots in the squadron usually take one of the
empty lockers in the back room."

"Haven't you heard? We don't have to use the
back room."

Jones stood there for a moment, the anger boiling
up inside him. He was a wide-shouldered, muscular
young man who had played linebacker at Nebraska
before his Navy commissioning. If this new pilot were
a man, he would give the guy ten seconds to get his
gear out of the locker before he got it shoved up
his ass.

But in a tiny fleaspeck of Jones's brain, a danger
signal was going off. This was the post-Tailhook Navy.
He already knew too many male officers who'd been
hauled up on sexism or harassment charges.

Jones shook his head and began gathering his flight
gear from the corner. He headed for the door. "Welcome aboard, Lieutenant. This squadron's gonna love
you."

"That was really dumb. Why'd you do that?"

"Because," said Spam Parker, "we have to establish
our territory. We can't let them treat us like inferiors."

The two women were alone in the passageway outside the squadron ready room.

"You pissed that guy off," said B.J. "He's not gonna forget it."

"That's his problem. They'll know how to deal with us from now on."

B.J. hated confrontations. It was a bad way to meet your new squadron mates, she thought. "Maybe we oughta just keep a low profile for a while. You know, like new kids on the block."

Spam gave B.J. a withering look. "You're such a wimp. You always let someone else do the fighting for you. Then you come along and act like Miss Primble at a tea party." Spam was nearly six feet tall and towered by a head over B.J. In her gray-green flight suit, wearing her clunky steel-toed flying boots, Spam looked like an Amazon warrior. "You want all these Neanderthals to like us. Well, guess what? I don't care whether they like us or not."

B.J. had to admit that Spam was right about one thing. She wasn't a fighter. As far back as B.J. could remember, it was Spam Parker who waged war with the male military establishment.

B.J. remembered their Naval Academy days. In their third year at Annapolis, Spam brought a sexual harassment suit against an officer on the faculty. Though the matter was quietly settled outside the military judicial system, it put an effective end to the officer's career.

She pulled the same thing after flight training, when B.J. and Spam found themselves in the same class in F/A-18 replacement pilot training at Oceana. Spam's problems in the fighter weapons phase reached a point that an evaluation board was convened. Spam blamed her troubles on what she claimed was her instructor's bias against women. After an investigation by the

Judge Advocate General, the charge was dismissed,
but it carried sufficient weight to get Spam past the
evaluation board. She managed to complete strike
fighter training and graduate to the fleet.

Whenever Spam went to war with the male establishment, B.J. tried to be invisible. It never worked.
She always found herself guilty by association with
Spam Parker, and thus ostracized. She knew that male
pilots in fighter squadrons had a name for them.
Aliens.

In a closely knit community like naval aviation, it
was a lonely existence. Nobody trusted aliens.

Despite B.J. Johnson's pleadings to be assigned to
a squadron on the opposite end of the planet from
Spam Parker, the Navy had other plans. B.J. and
Spam received orders to the same squadron—the
VFA-36 Roadrunners, deployed aboard the USS *Ronald Reagan.*

Spam Parker hadn't changed.

"We have to kick 'em in the balls," Spam said over
her shoulder as she marched away. "It's the only way
those jerks are gonna learn."

The heels of her flight boots hammered like drum
beats on the steel deck. Watching her, B.J. had a sinking feeling in her stomach. She hated being an alien.

As Maxwell walked aft, along the port passageway
on the second deck, it struck him again. *The smell.* He
had served aboard half a dozen aircraft carriers. Each
of the ships had possessed its own unique belowdecks
smell—an evocative scent of jet fuel, sweat, paint, oil,
and steel.

But the scent of the USS *Ronald Reagan* had something else—newness. Maxwell could sense the freshly painted bulkheads, the clean metallic shininess of the ship's recently installed fixtures. The *Reagan* smelled like a freshly assembled weapon. At one hundred five thousand tons, the *Reagan* was the mightiest warship the world had ever seen.

He turned down a passageway toward the hangar deck ladder. Rounding the corner, he nearly collided with a young woman wearing a gray-green flight suit. She was exiting a door that bore large stenciled lettering: WOMEN OFFICERS HEAD.

"Excuse me, Commander," said the woman. Her face reddened. On each shoulder were two silver bars.

Maxwell glanced at her leather name tag. "You're Johnson. One of our new pilots. Welcome to the Roadrunners, Lieutenant. I'm Brick Maxwell, the ops officer."

B.J. Johnson looked petrified. She shook Maxwell's hand as if it were a pump handle. "Yes, sir. Sorry, sir, I'm still running into things. I'm, uh . . . it's my first time aboard . . . you know." Her face reddened further.

"Everyone does that. I've still got the scars from bashing into overheads and knee knockers on my first cruise."

B.J. looked around the passageway. "Uh, truth is, Commander, I'm lost. I was trying to find the ladder up to the hangar deck. Isn't there a ceremony we're supposed to attend?"

"Follow me. I was headed there myself. By the way, we go by call signs in the squadron. You can call me Brick."

"Yes, sir. I mean, Brick. And you can call me . . . B.J." She caught his surprised look. "It, uh, comes from my name—Beth Johnson." Maxwell said nothing, nodded, turned, and began walking. Red-faced, B.J. followed Maxwell to the ladder that led to the hangar deck. She was amazed Maxwell hadn't made the usual crude remark about her call sign.

White-uniformed officers were clustered around the podium. The ship's band, also wearing dress whites, was limbering up their instruments. In the background was a parked F/A-18, angled so that the four victory symbols were clearly visible.

The ceremony was supposed to begin at 1600 hours. Maxwell saw Admiral Mellon standing with his aide and a couple of staff officers behind the podium. The admiral wore a sour look. He looked, Maxwell thought, like a man waiting for a root canal.

Killer DeLancey and Babcock, the civilian Maxwell remembered from the mission debriefing yesterday, were huddled together. DeLancey was listening to Babcock, grinning as if he had just won the lottery.

Same old DeLancey, thought Maxwell. He had found a new patron.

Watching DeLancey grin and preen made Maxwell think again about his own career. Coming back to the fleet at this late stage—he'd just been promoted to the rank of commander—was definitely not your usual career path. You were supposed to work your way up the hierarchical pyramid. After serving in several different grades at the squadron officer level, *then* you became a department head—operations officer, maintenance officer, administrative officer.

Maxwell had skipped all that. While his contemporaries were serving in seagoing squadrons, he had gone to a cushy flight test pilot job. And then to an even cushier astronaut billet. Now he was back in the fleet as a squadron operations officer, the third senior job in the squadron, and it was no secret that many of his fellow officers thought he hadn't paid his dues. To them he would always be a carpetbagger.

Maxwell and B.J. took their his places with the squadron officers. B.J. slipped into the back row. Maxwell stood with the senior officers, next to Devo Davis. He noticed that Davis looked red-eyed and haggard.

"You okay? You look like you've been on a three-day bender."

"Wish I had. This damned insomnia. Haven't had a decent night's sleep for a week."

On signal from a flag staff officer at the podium, the band swung into "Under the Double Eagle." As they hit the last passage, Whitney Babcock, wearing a fresh set of starched khakis, strutted to the podium. He glanced around, making sure the television crew was in place.

"With a singular act of valor, our own Commander John DeLancey has shown the world what the men and women of the United States Navy are made of. He has proven that Americans will not be daunted by acts of enemy aggression. In the finest traditions of the naval service, this fearless warrior confronted the enemy aircraft . . ."

Maxwell's mind wandered. He found himself thinking about the Iraqi pilot DeLancey had shot. Who was he? Was the guy really hostile, or just inept? Did he have a family? Hopes, dreams, aspirations?

Did he deserve to die?

It occurred to Maxwell that these weren't the thoughts you were supposed to have after combat. Not if you were a warrior. Maybe he wasn't, he thought. At least not like DeLancey.

Babcock droned on for ten minutes. He compared

DeLancey to John Paul Jones, David Farragut, and Butch O'Hare. Finally the moment came. He summoned DeLancey to the podium. "On behalf of the Secretary of the Navy, I confer upon you our nation's third highest award, the Silver Star."

Maxwell heard Davis groaning softly. He glanced over at him. Davis looked white. "You okay, Devo?"

"No. I'm gonna puke." Davis abruptly stepped back and shuffled over to the belowdecks ladder.

Claire Phillips surveyed the scene around her as she positioned her camera crew. A throng of curious sailors had clustered around the brilliantly lit ten-foot-square set. A pair of Super Hornet fighters were parked in the background. Seated in the middle of the set, grinning and flashing a toothy smile, was Commander DeLancey, the subject of her special shipboard interview. The session would be taped and broadcast to millions of television viewers.

Claire was still perplexed about the young woman who had stopped her in the passageway. She was a pilot, judging by the flight suit and leather patch with the wings. The woman was tall, maybe six feet or more. Her name tag read SPAM.

"Ask him how he intends to treat women pilots in his squadron," the young woman said.

The reporter's instinct in Claire came out. "Why? Is there something going on we need to know about?"

The woman's eyes flashed. "Sexism, that's what's going on. Despite all the crap they're telling you, not a damned thing has changed since Tailhook."

Claire nodded. This could turn into something. "Look, Lieutenant, this would make a great interview if you would—"

"No interview. I've still got a career to worry
about." She turned to leave. "Just ask the question.
You might be surprised."

Claire watched the young officer walk away. What
a strange woman, she thought. Marching down the
passageway with those long hammering strides. She
looked less like a pilot than like a gladiator going
to battle.

The camera crew was ready for the shoot. Claire
took her seat on the stool in front of the Navy commander. Looking into the camera, she saw the red-
lighted cue from her set director.

She began the interview with some easy questions
about the action over Iraq. DeLancey surprised her.
Most of her military subjects turned into monosyllabic
lumps when they first peered into that big glass-eyed
television camera. But not this guy. He was coming
back with quick, glib answers, grinning, preening like
a peacock.

Enough, she thought. Time for the hot button stuff.

She looked at him. "What did it feel like," she
asked in a hushed voice, "to kill another man?"

She knew it was a loaded question. But, hell, that
was her job. Claire hadn't earned her reputation for
being a tough reporter by asking pussycat questions.
It was her style to get to the gut issues. That was why
her contract with the network had just been renewed
at twice the old guarantee.

DeLancey seemed to be considering. He turned his
head so that his handsome, lean-faced profile was exposed to the camera. He was wearing his tailored flight
suit with the VFA-36 Roadrunners patch and the
leather name tag showing his gold-embossed wings.

"It was . . . difficult, Claire." DeLancey seemed to

chew on his lip, pained by the memory of what happened. "We were under attack by Iraqi fighters. It came down to a choice—kill or be killed. I had to defend myself and my wingman."

Claire bored in. "But this wasn't your first time, was it? Isn't that how you earned your call sign—Killer?"

Another silence ensued as the camera zoomed in on DeLancey. He nodded his head and gave the camera a thoughtful look. "My job is to defend my country. I've gone up against an armed and deadly enemy four times now. I'm here to report that in each case, I won, they lost." He nodded in the direction of the nearest F/A-18. The camera view switched to the jet, then zoomed in on the name beneath the cockpit: COMMANDER KILLER DELANCEY, CO VFA-36.

Beneath the name were now *four* silhouettes of enemy fighters.

Grudgingly, Claire had to give him credit. The guy was taking control of the interview. Then she noticed that she had another distraction. That civilian from the Pentagon, Whitney Whoever. He was working his way over to DeLancey's side, placing himself in view of the camera.

Time to switch to the *real* hot button topic. "Commander, I understand your squadron has the first two women fighter pilots to deploy on the USS *Ronald Reagan*."

DeLancey nodded, his expression not changing.

"So, tell me, how do you personally feel about women in combat units?"

In the background she heard murmurs, throats clearing, whispered conversation. DeLancey gazed straight into the camera. "I'm glad you asked that question. I happen to think it's the best thing that ever happened to the United States Navy. Women pilots are a terrific asset. In my squadron they will be treated just like any other aviators. No gender bias, no favoritism. No double standard."

From the periphery came more murmurs, more whispers. Claire had to smile. This guy was too much. It was utter bullshit, but he had provided her with a great interview. Every armchair fighter pilot back in the states would be glued to his seat, cheering his new hero.

Time to wrap it up. "Commander John DeLancey, we thank you for your heroism, and I know your fellow Americans thank you." She turned to the second camera. "This is Claire Phillips reporting from the USS *Ronald Reagan* in the Persian Gulf. Back to our studios . . ."

Maxwell rapped on the stateroom door

The latch inside rattled and the door cracked open. Devo Davis was wearing cotton workout shorts and a T-shirt. "That you, Brick? C'mon in."

"What's the matter, Devo? You sick?"

"Something I ate. Couldn't sleep last night."

Maxwell came in and took a look around. Davis looked awful. And he smelled worse.

It was strange, Maxwell thought, how fate kept throwing him and Devo together. During flight training, when Devo had been his instructor in the T-2 Buckeye, the two had become tight friends. Later, when Maxwell reported to his second fleet squadron aboard the USS *George Washington* after the Gulf War, there was Davis again, this time as a squadron department head. When Maxwell went to NAS Patuxent River as a test pilot, Devo was just up the road at the Pentagon. They partied together on weekends, went on double dates on the Chesapeake, served as best man at each other's wedding. Now they were together again. Same ship, same squadron.

On Davis's steel desk stood half a dozen framed photographs. One was of a pretty girl with long blond hair, sitting on a porch swing. She was wearing a white halter, and even in the cropped photo Maxwell could see her terrific figure.

"What do you hear from Eileen?"

Davis went to the safe at his desk and twiddled the dial. "How about a drink?"

Maxwell knew what he had smelled. Davis was a vodka drinker.

"No, thanks." There was no point in lecturing Devo about the long-standing ban on alcohol aboard Navy vessels. Everyone knew a certain amount of clandestine off-duty drinking went on aboard a carrier. Too much temperance, pilots liked to say, took away their edge. Anyway, Devo was the XO.

Davis poured a tumbler full of vodka, and then sloshed a dollop of lime juice into it. He didn't bother with ice. He held the glass up and said, "Skoal, ol' buddy."

Maxwell was still looking at the photograph on the desk. Davis reached over and turned the photo around, facing it backward. "Eileen filed for divorce. Two weeks ago, but she just got around to E-mailing me the news."

Maxwell nodded. So that was it. He had known Devo and Eileen for—how long? Going on fifteen years. It was no surprise, really. He had heard the rumors about Eileen back in Virginia Beach, that she was seeing someone. Maybe more than one.

"I don't have to tell you about how it feels to lose someone," said Davis.

Maxwell didn't reply for a moment. "No," he said in a quiet voice.

"But you're different from me, Brick. You're one of those guys who can deal with it. You think like a machine." Davis's voice cracked. "But, man, I can't handle it . . . I love her so much. I've never loved anyone as much as I love Eileen. I'd do anything to . . ." His words trailed off, and he began to cry.

Maxwell didn't know what to say. Brick and Devo, Debbie and Eileen. The world they had known back there in Patuxent and Washington was history. Debbie was gone, and Maxwell had the gut feeling that Eileen was now lost from Devo's life.

Davis snuffled and turned away while he wiped his eyes with a handkerchief. "Sorry. Fighter pilots don't cry, right?"

"You're human, Devo. You got clobbered from behind."

"No. I saw it coming. But I thought we were gonna get through it."

Davis was weeping shamelessly. Maxwell wanted to leave, but something told him to stay. Davis was a man on the verge of a breakdown.

"You talked to anybody about this?"

Davis looked at him. "C'mon, who would I talk to? The chaplain? You know better than that. DeLancey? I'm supposed to take command of the squadron in four months. You think I'd give him the ammo to ruin my career?"

Maxwell wondered if Davis knew his career was already in trouble. DeLancey had taken to making open jokes about his executive officer and his drinking problem. As far as the chaplain, well, he understood that, too. Fighter pilots didn't confide in shrinks or chaplains. That was an option for the terminally ill and teenage sailors worried about their sexuality.

"How about Knuckles?" Maxwell said. Knuckles Ball was the air wing flight surgeon. "He's a good guy. He can keep a secret."

"I already told him I had a touch of flu. He's got me grounded for a few days."

"Maybe you oughta take some leave. Go back stateside, talk it out with Eileen."

"No way. That would give DeLancey an excuse to shitcan me. I gotta hang in here and cover my six o'clock. Besides, if I leave, there's no one to stand between Killer and you, Brick. He'd love to shitcan you even more than he would me."

At this, Maxwell's eyes narrowed. "Oh?"

Davis poured himself another drink. "It's true. Some kind of bad chemistry between you and De-Lancey. He started running you down even before you checked in. He's never passed up a chance to dump on you."

Maxwell shook his head. "It's a personal thing. He and I were in Desert Storm together."

"Yeah? How come you never told me that?"

"It was no big deal. We just never got along, that's all."

Devo took a drink and shook his head. "It's gotta be more than that. You're one of the best naval officers I've ever known. The best student I had in three years as a flight instructor. The top lieutenant in the squadron when we were in VFA-83, and then you got the test pilot slot to prove it. You could've had any assignment you wanted. Never mind what happened at NASA, the frigging operational Navy is damned lucky to have a guy like you."

Maxwell wanted to change the subject. "All right, tell me something. What's the first thing you're going to do when you take over the squadron?"

"Ask for you as my XO."

"Seriously."

"I am serious. You were born for this job. All I have to do is keep Killer from screwing you out of it. And believe me, he's gonna try."

Maxwell shook his head. "Nah, not even Killer would do that."

"I'd bet my badge on it. He already has his favorite JOs bad-mouthing you, disrespecting you behind your back. By the way, that's the next thing I'm gonna do—straighten some of those little shits out."

Maxwell didn't reply, but he knew Devo was right. He already knew how Killer treated Devo, and it didn't surprise him that Killer was doing the same to him behind his back.

Davis was pouring another drink, this time straight vodka.

"Hey, Devo, what do you say we go to the fo'c'sle and work out."

"Don't patronize me. I'm going to have a couple drinks, then I'm going to write Eileen, tell her . . ." His voice began to crack.

"The booze isn't going to make it better. It's just gonna—"

Davis's face darkened and he turned on Maxwell. "Do not presume to lecture a senior officer. You can either join me in a drink, sir, or kindly get the fuck out of my quarters."

Davis was going to tie one on. Maxwell knew it

wouldn't do any good to warn him that if he was observed by anyone—enlisted man, ship's officer, even some do-gooding teetotaler from another squadron— he would be toast. In the New Navy they made examples of officers who flouted the no-drinking rule.

Maxwell got up. "Have it your way. Just stay in your room and don't answer the phone, okay?"

He took the passageway up to the hangar deck, then made his way toward the ready room. At the far end of the hangar deck, next to a parked Hornet fighter, he saw the cluster of sailors, the bright lights, and the camera crew. He walked over to the periphery of the set.

DeLancey and Whitney Babcock were each shaking hands with a slender, chestnut-haired woman. She was gathering her notepad and attaché case when Maxwell came up.

She looked up. "Sam?"

Maxwell felt an electric charge course through him. No one had called him Sam for years. No one but his father and—

"Sam," she said. "That's you, isn't it?"

She wore her hair short now, in a pixie cut. She had the same willowy build, the graceful swanlike neck. Still stunning, he thought.

"Claire Phillips, cub reporter?"

She laughed. "Sam Maxwell, boy astronaut."

"Former boy astronaut. Now adult fighter pilot."

"So I hear." She ran to him and gave him a hug. "I heard you were aboard, and I was going to find you. They're flying us back to Bahrain in half an hour."

Yes, he thought, holding his arms around her. It was definitely Claire Phillips. She even wore that same perfume he always liked. He remembered the way she felt pressed against him like this.

Maxwell was suddenly deluged with memories.

Back in the Patuxent River days, Claire Phillips was the smartest, sexiest, classiest girl he had ever met. She was on her first real job out of Duke, doing a piece for the *Washington Post* about would-be astronauts. The commandant of the U.S. Naval Test Pilot School at Patuxent River introduced her to Lieutenant Sam Maxwell, who was competing to be in the next class of space shuttle pilots.

The interview lasted three hours, then spilled over into late dinner at the officers' club. They closed down the bar, then went out to the marina pier to talk some more. They were still on the pier when the dawn rose over the Chesapeake.

Brick and Claire became an item. For eight months they spent every weekend together, either at her Georgetown apartment or on the water at Patuxent. She wrote a series about the astronaut selection program that won her an award and a promotion to the international desk.

Claire was offered a post in Reuters's London bureau. Maxwell, in the meantime, learned that he had been selected for a post at NASA. He had orders to Houston to begin astronaut training.

While he was at the Johnson Space Center in Houston, he met another trainee named Debbie Sutter. She had red hair and a pert nose, and until her selection as a shuttle mission specialist she had been a resident cardiologist at Bethesda. Sam and Debbie were married the week after his first shuttle flight.

As if reading his thoughts, Claire said, "I'm sorry about Debbie."

Maxwell looked at her, surprised. But then he realized, of course she would know. Claire was a reporter. It was her job to know.

"You look wonderful, Claire. I'm proud of you."

"You should be. I'm doing what I always wanted. My fantasy job."

"I remember. You were going to blow away Christiane Amanpour."

"I'm doing it. Give me a couple of years."

Maxwell remembered how hurt and angry Claire had been. She had called him one night from Teheran, crying. She still loved him, she said. Within a few months he heard that she married another journalist.

"What happened to—?" Maxwell tried to remember the name. He couldn't.

"Chris Tyrwhitt?" She shook her head. "Didn't work out. Too many women, too much booze. Too much competition between us, probably. We're still officially married, but in the process."

For several seconds, neither spoke. Maxwell remembered again what good company Claire had always been. That quick, dry humor. It occurred to him that he hadn't enjoyed the company of a woman—a civilian woman—for over three months.

He said, "I guess I never got around to explaining about—"

She cut him off. "I'm over it. Believe it or not, there really is life after Sam Maxwell." She gave him a wry smile.

She had half an hour before the COD was to fly her and her crew back to Bahrain. Maxwell took her down to the officers' wardroom.

He brought them a pot of coffee from the server bar. She gave him an appraising look as he sat down.

"Sam, you haven't changed a bit. How do you stay so slim and fit?"

"Same as always. A little weight training, a few miles of running every day or so."

"Running?" She shook her head. "I can't imagine. This ship seems so jammed with people and airplanes."

"It's a big flight deck, about three acres worth. You have to watch out for obstacles, of course."

She laughed and gave him another look of appraisal. For the next twenty minutes they caught up on each other's lives. She talked about her career, how she had graduated from Sunday supplement writer to head of the Middle East desk. He told her about NASA and his shuttle experience. He skimmed over the details of his departure from the space program.

"I've been following your adventures," she said. "How's this for a headline? 'Ace fighter pilot patrols the skies of Iraq.'"

"I like it, except that I'm not an ace. Not even close."

"That would be your commanding officer, Killer DeLancey, right?"

"Close. Four down, one to go. You need five confirmed kills to be an ace."

"But you were there when he shot down the MiG. General Penwell knows your name by heart."

"How did you learn all that?"

"I'm smart and persistent."

"You fluttered your eyelashes and got some guy in JTF staff to run his mouth."

She laughed, and he knew he was right. That was Claire's talent. She could get people to talk.

"What they tell me is all in the public record," she

said. "You just have to know how to piece it together."

A thin man with glasses and a ponytail walked into the wardroom. Maxwell remembered seeing him in Claire's camera crew. "Hey, Claire," the man said. "They want us on deck. Time to blast off."

The clamshell doors of the COD were open, and the crew was loading boxes of gear into the back of the cargo plane. Claire stopped in the doorway to the flight deck and struck a pose. She was wearing a cranial protector and float coat for the flight back to Bahrain.

"Like it?" she asked.

Maxwell had to laugh. "You look like Minnie Mouse."

She made a face. "Where is the *Reagan*'s next port call, Sam? It would be nice if we could . . . you know, meet again. Have a drink and talk. Something like that."

Maxwell caught the reticence in her voice, the sudden shyness. He liked it. It meant that for all her hard-edged toughness as a reporter, she was still vulnerable. In a secret place, she was still Claire Phillips, cub reporter.

"We're overdue for a port call. But after what happened yesterday in the No-Fly-Zone, they probably won't announce the ship's movement until a couple of days before we drop anchor. I'd bet on Dubai, or maybe Bahrain." He looked at her. "Does that mean you'll be there?"

"You know very well what it means, Commander Maxwell. Do the right thing. Ask me for a date."

"A date? Oh." He cleared his throat and said, "Would you, Ms. Phillips, do me the honor of joining me for dinner and drinks at a place yet to be announced?"

"I'll have to think about it." She paused for several seconds. "Oh, what the hell. I'll take a chance." She glanced across the deck at the COD. "Your time's up, sailor. My plane's leaving."

She leaned forward and gave Maxwell a quick, nonlethal kiss. "Be careful, Sam." She trotted across the deck, then stopped at the ramp of the COD. She waved and blew him another kiss.

The two turbine engines cranked up. Minutes later, the blunt-nosed cargo plane hurtled down the track of the *Reagan*'s number one catapult. Maxwell watched until the speck of the COD vanished in the milky sky.

FIVE

Buttwang

The mood in the Buttwang was getting ugly.

"She moved my gear out and took over the goddamn locker!"

"They got better staterooms than lieutenant commanders. Can someone explain why the fuck that is?"

"The tall one with the mouth like a megaphone, calls herself Spam? She went marching into the parachute loft and told the rigger she wanted her call sign stitched on *all* her gear. By tomorrow. And guess what? The maintenance officer told him he'd damn well better do it."

In normal circumstances the Buttwang—the term for the junior officers' bunkroom—served as the sleeping quarters for the eight most junior officers in the squadron. It was a twelve-by-fourteen-foot space that contained four racks of two bunks each. Mounted to the deck was a pair of the ubiquitous Navy gray steel desks. Fixed against one bulkhead were eight storage lockers.

Tonight the Buttwang was the site of an impromptu meeting of the JOPA—Junior Officers' Protective Association. Eleven officers—two junior grade lieutenants and nine lieutenants—were sprawling atop bunks, squatting on the deck, leaning against bulkheads. The only junior officers not present were Lieutenant Bud Spencer, who was the squadron duty officer—and the two new pilots, Parker and Johnson.

The aliens had not been invited.

The litany went on. The women pilots had been in the squadron a total of three days, and already the list of grievances had grown as long as the Congressional Record.

Leroi Jones said, "I checked this Spam out with the replacement squadron training officer back in Oceana. He's a classmate of mine, Ham Hoxe. Hoxe says she shouldn't have made it through the Hornet transition program. Picked up three SODs—signals of difficulty—and would have gotten an evaluation board but she started making threats about a sexual harassment case. They let her through."

At this, the mood in the Buttwang grew uglier. Since the Tailhook scandal in 1991, nothing inflamed the collective anger of male naval aviators as much as the suspicion that women pilots were being judged by a different standard. There had already been several celebrated cases of women pilots who failed fighter transition training, then returned to the cockpit only to fail again. Or worse, to join a fleet squadron, then proceed to scare the living hell out of their COs, their squadron mates, their LSOs, and sometimes even themselves.

"You guys who are section leads had better think about it," said Flash Gordon, a senior lieutenant. Section leads were pilots qualified to lead a formation. "Those two are gonna be your new wingmen."

"We gotta watch our asses," said Hozer Miller. "Especially around the ship, and especially at night. Don't let the aliens get you or your wingman killed."

Undra Cheever spoke from atop a bunk. Cheever was a short, heavyset lieutenant with unruly dark hair that bristled like a cactus. "What about the short one, B.J. Johnson?"

Leroi Jones said, "Ham didn't have anything on her. No SODs, all average grades. Didn't scare anybody when she qualified on the boat."

"Probably sucked up to the LSO."

Undra Cheever cracked up at that. "That's it! How do you think she got a call sign like 'B.J.'?"

The dirty shirt wardroom was busy. Most of the tables were occupied by pilots and crew members. It was the only officers' facility where pilots and crew members could dine informally, wearing their flight suits—dirty shirts—instead of the ship's uniform of the day.

As usual, a cluster was gathered around the stainless-steel ice cream vendor, called the dog machine.

Maxwell spotted B.J. Johnson. She was sitting alone at a table. He sat down across from her. "You mind company?"

"You better not sit there, sir," she said. "You'll catch what I have."

"What do you have?"

"Something awful. So bad that not a single officer in the squadron has dared to initiate a conversation with me since I checked in. Except you."

Brick looked around. "You want some ice cream? I'm going to the dog machine."

She nodded. "Thanks. But here's a stupid nugget question. Why do they call it the 'dog machine'?"

Maxwell grinned and looked over at the machine. "Watch it while it's dispensing ice cream."

She looked over at the great shiny machine. A thick stream of soft chocolate ice cream was oozing from the spigot. She frowned, studying the machine. Suddenly it came to her. "Oh, yuck! That's disgusting. Now that's really a guy thing."

Maxwell shrugged. "You had to ask."

He came back with two cups of ice cream and sat down. He nodded his head in the direction of the junior officers across the room. "Give 'em time to get used to you. It'll get better."

"It's not getting better. It's getting worse."

"How so?"

"Some guy's been calling our room."

Maxwell scooped a bite of ice cream. "Who?"

"No idea. He goes to a lot of trouble to disguise his voice. Last night he said he had some advice for Spam and me."

"What was that?"

" 'Quit while you can.' So I asked him, 'What if we don't quit?' The guy didn't answer for a while, then he said, 'You're going to have one less trap than you have launches.' "

Maxwell listened quietly, not liking what he heard. *One less trap than you have launches.* Somebody wanted to scare them. Maybe scare them enough to make them give it up. "Who do you think it was?"

"Any one of about thirty guys who hate our guts."

"Did you report the phone call?"

She shook her head. "Who to? The skipper?" She forced a laugh. "You know better than that. I already know how the system works. As soon as a female complains about being hassled, she's marked. From then on she's just another troublemaker."

"How did Spam handle it?"

B.J. laughed again. "She's used to it. Spam's a lightning rod. I've been getting the fallout from Spam Parker's battles since we were plebes at the Academy."

Maxwell thought for a moment, trying to imagine who in the squadron would make such calls. Undra Cheever came to mind. Yes, it could be Cheever, who was famous for an obnoxious sense of humor. Or Hozer Miller, almost as bad. Whoever it was, it would be impossible to prove. "I wouldn't make too much of this," he said. "It's probably just some jerk who still thinks women shouldn't vote."

"How many jerks are we gonna have to deal with before we're accepted?"

He looked at her, trying to fathom what she was going through. "Listen, I want you to tell me whenever something like that happens again. I promise I'll look into it. And keep a record of those phone calls."

B.J. nodded glumly and poked at her ice cream. "I thought this would be fun. You know, a great adventure. But it's not. It sucks."

Pearly Gates came in the back door of the ready room, still wearing his LSO outfit. He looked like a panhandler, wearing old fatigue pants, jersey, survival vest, and a black watch cap pulled down to his ears.

Pearly wasn't superstitious, but he made a point of wearing the same tattered old costume when he was waving jets aboard a carrier. The turtleneck jersey and the ratty fatigue pants were the same that he'd had since he qualified as an LSO two cruises ago on the

Roosevelt. Over the jersey he wore the float coat that everyone who worked on a carrier deck was required to wear. The float coat contained a flare pencil and had inflatable bladders in case you were swept off the deck into the ocean.

Pearly's vest had his job title stenciled on the back—VFA-36 LSO. On the front he wore the special embroidered LSO patch—a view of the ramp of a carrier with the motto RECTUM NON BUSTUS.

He took a quick scan of the ready room, then spotted Maxwell. "Hey, Brick, got a sec?" He led Maxwell through the back door, into the locker room.

"What's up?" said Maxwell. "Did I scare you that bad with my last pass?"

"Not you." Pearly glanced around, making sure they were alone. "Brick, you and the XO are pretty tight buds, aren't you? I mean, don't you two go way back?"

"Two or three centuries." Maxwell liked Pearly Gates. He was the kind of officer Maxwell wished the Navy had more of. Though Pearly was only a junior lieutenant, his job out there on the platform entailed enormous responsibility, more than any other squadron assignment. Pearly not only liked the job, he was good at it.

"Devo flew a couple of really ugly passes this afternoon. Boltered once, got a taxi-to-the-one wire next time."

"He's been down awhile with a cold. Maybe he shouldn't be flying yet."

"Maybe he shouldn't." Pearly hesitated, glancing around. "This is between us, okay?"

"Sure." Maxwell was sure he knew what was coming.

"When I debriefed him, I thought I . . . I smelled something."

"Like . . . ?"

"Like booze."

Maxwell kept his expression blank. "Are you sure? Did you ask him?"

Pearly looked uncomfortable. "No. I guess . . . you know, he's the XO, and it's not my place. Most of us think Devo's a good guy, and I didn't want to go to the skipper about it. And, anyway, what if I was wrong? That's why I'm telling you."

"You did the right thing, Pearly. I'll take care of it. You can trust me on it."

"Yes, sir, that's what I thought."

"Bullshit," Davis said.

It was exactly the response Maxwell expected. "Pearly wasn't making it up."

They were standing in the passageway outside the wardroom. Davis waited while a couple of sailors walked past. "He was mistaken. He was probably sniffing the Vicks Nite-All stuff I take to sleep in the afternoon."

"You know you can't self-medicate when you're flying off the boat."

"What are you, my goddamn counselor or something?"

Maxwell knew Devo would react like this. Even if it were true, he wouldn't admit it. And for all he knew, Devo was telling the truth. Maybe he did have sleeping problems.

"No, I'm your friend. You told me you were going to stay grounded for a while. No flying while you got over—"

"DeLancey hit on me. In front of half a dozen JOs.

He wanted to know why the hell I wasn't scheduled to fly in the exercise tomorrow. As much as accused me of being a pussy."

"You should have told him you were sick. Knuckles would back you up."

Davis shook his head. "If I'm gonna take over command of this squadron, I gotta be in the thick of it, like everybody else."

"You scared the hell out of the LSO today. You shouldn't be back flying yet. Look, I'm the ops officer, and I make the schedule. Let me worry about DeLancey."

Davis's eyes looked wet and red. Maxwell worried for a moment that he might break down and cry. Devo was a basket case.

Finally Davis heaved a sigh. "Okay. I'll tell 'em I've got the trots or something. No flying. What's DeLancey gonna do?"

"I don't know. I'll take care of it."

At the moment, he had no idea how he would take care of it. But his first priority was to keep Davis out of an F/A-18 cockpit. Then maybe he could talk him into taking leave, going somewhere to get his head straightened out. Then he would worry about DeLancey.

With his receding hairline and prominent forehead, Spook Morse, the air wing intelligence officer, looked like Ichabod Crane. "That's correct, gentlemen," he said. "The Joint Task Force Commander has ordered all patrolling of the southern No-Fly-Zone to be restricted to the thirty-second parallel instead of the thirty-third."

The pilots in the briefing room were incredulous. "That doesn't make sense," said a Prowler pilot.

"Why the hell would the battle group be pulling back now?"

"That's sixty miles," said Killer DeLancey. "Why are we cutting them that much slack?"

Morse shrugged. "JTF wants to back off and let the tension subside after the . . . uh, shoot-down the other day."

A triumphant look flashed over DeLancey's face. "So they confirmed it?"

"Yes, sir. Your fourth kill. Satellite imagery and *Rivet Joint* both confirm that a MiG-29 was destroyed fifteen miles inside the NFZ."

"Any sign of a response from the Iraqis?"

Morse took his time. Like all intelligence officers, he considered himself God's appointed custodian of need-to-know information. He figured that pilots really only needed to know just enough to complete their narrowly focused little missions. The strategic and vital information—The Big Picture—was the exclusive property of intelligence specialists like himself.

After a sufficient pause he said, "We've obtained some . . . ah, evidence from certain . . . *assets* . . . inside the country that the Iraqis might be gathering a supply of antishipping missiles. Probably from North Korea, transporting them overland through Iran."

"Assets?" asked Craze Manson. "Do we still have inspection teams in Iraq?"

"No." Spook enjoyed feeding the little morsels to the pilots like scraps to a terrier. "Saddam evicted all the United Nations weapons inspectors. But it would be safe to assume, of course, that we still have . . . ah, sources."

"And just what do your sources say happened to the second MiG?" asked DeLancey.

"Possibly destroyed. AWACS lost him before he got back to Al-Taqqadum. They think he might have run out of fuel."

DeLancey pointedly gazed across the room at Maxwell. "Somebody should have shot the sonofabitch before he ran out of fuel."

Maxwell sat with his arms folded, ignoring DeLancey. For an awkward few seconds, no one spoke.

Morse cleared his throat and broke the silence. "Here's the good news. The *Reagan* is scheduled to sail into the southern gulf next week. We'll be conducting a coordinated strike exercise against the Saudi base at Al-Kharj."

"Exercise? What about port call?" asked Lieutenant Bud Spencer.

Spook consulted his fist full of index cards. Now he could really tantalize them. The *Reagan* had been at sea for nearly a month without an in-port liberty period. "Port call? Well, let's see. Oh, yeah, here it is. A week from tomorrow. The *Reagan* will be making a port call in"—he paused, dragging out the suspense as long he could—"Dubai."

The cheering reverberated off the bulkheads. It was so loud it could be heard up and down the passageway, all the way to the O-3 level. Dubai was regarded as the best liberty port in the Persian Gulf.

"Hot damn! Dubai!"

"Hide your daughters, Dubai, here come the Roadrunners."

"BAGs and GAGs! We're on our way, girls."

BAGs was shorthand for British Air Girls. GAGs meant Gulf Air Girls. The hotels and bars and swimming pools of Dubai were renowned for their contingent of lithesome flight attendants.

"We already have a suite booked in the Hilton . . ."

"Party till we puke . . ."

"Met this girl from New Zealand—loved to do it in the Jacuzzi . . ."

Spook Morse sighed and put away his index cards. The intel briefing was effectively ended. He had been around pilots long enough to know that not one of the shallow-minded Neanderthals had the slightest interest in Iraq or the No-Fly-Zone or the geopolitics of Southwest Asia.

It would soon be party time.

"Hi, guys," said the visitor, poking his head into the ready room. "Just introducing myself. I'm Dave Harvey. New shooter, just out of catapult school. Wanted to get to know the pilots in the air wing."

A few Roadrunners looked up from their ready room activities. The visitor was tall and skinny, about six-two, with shiny gold oak leaves on his collar indicating that he was a newly minted lieutenant commander. He had a long neck with an Adam's apple that bobbed like a counterweight.

"What's your call sign?" asked Leroi Jones, looking up from his current task, which happened to be watching Oprah on the ready room television monitor.

"Well, I was a P-3 driver back in my squadron tour. We didn't go in much for call signs."

"Patrol plane puke!" shouted Flash Gordon, causing several more heads to raise. "Man, you must have fucked up big time to get sent to a boat."

The new shooter looked hurt. "Actually, I sort of requested it. You gotta have shipboard duty in your record if you want to get ahead in the Navy, y' know."

More heads raised. This was *really* peculiar—someone who actually *wanted* to be a catapult officer. Volunteering to be on an aircraft carrier like the *Reagan*—without flying.

"Hey, man," said Pearly Gates, "if you're gonna hang around with fighter pilots down here, you're gonna have to get a call sign."

"Aw, I dunno," said Harvey, his Adam's apple bobbing. "Dave has always been my—"

"Not allowed," said Leroi. "No first names, no cutesy nicknames, no patrol plane stuff. You gotta have a real no-shit call sign like the rest of us. Otherwise we won't let you drink with us. You don't want to be an outcast do you, Dave?"

Harvey looked dubious. "I just don't know what my call sign would be . . ."

"You want us to make one up for you?"

"Well, I guess that would be all right. Just so it wasn't something, you know, too . . . raunchy."

"Raunchy?" asked Leroi, his voice dripping with sympathy. "What would that be, Dave?"

"You know, something really gross, like . . ." He had to think for a second, "Oh, something like . . . dog balls."

The instant he said it, he knew it was too late. The ready room swelled with the voices of cheering pilots. "Dog Balls! You got it!"

Harvey heard an alarm signal going off in his mind. "No! No, guys, what I meant was anything *but* that! You know, it's just too—"

"It's perfect. Dog Balls Harvey! It's gonna look great stitched on your vest."

A horrible thought struck Harvey. *These crazy bastards are serious. They're going to label me with the worst name imaginable.*

He began backpedaling toward the door. "Guys, it was really fun kidding with you like this . . ."

"Dog Balls! Dog Balls!"

Bang! He slammed the door behind him and retreated around the corner. Thirty yards down the passageway, the horrible yelling from the Roadrunner ready room was following him. *"Hey, Dog Balls! Come back, Dog Balls!"*

SIX

Al-Kharj

CAG Boyce rapped the pointer—*Whap! Whap!*—on the illuminated chart.

"Al-Karjh air base," he said, whapping the chart once more for effect. "That, ladies and gentlemen, is our target."

The overhead fluorescent light in the ready room reflected off Boyce's shiny pate. He peered out at his audience—thirty flight-suited Hornet and Tomcat crews. "Our force of F/A-18s and F-14s will conduct a simulated strike against the Saudi base at Al-Kharj. The strike package planning was done by Commander Maxwell as part of his strike leader qualification."

A ripple of applause, whistles, and cat calls rose from the room.

"This better be good!"

"Another Hornet fiasco!" said a Tomcat pilot from the F-14 squadron.

Boyce aimed his pointer at the map. "The Navy force—called Blue—will be opposed by the Orange force consisting of U.S. Air Force and Royal Saudi Air Force F-15s. Both the Blue and the Orange forces will be controlled by the same American E-3C

AWACS, using different controllers. Blue will present a dual-axis attack at altitude, until the Orange fighter cover has committed to the respective threats. With the Orange fighters committed, the Blue strikers will turn away and drag the Orange fighters eastward.

"Meanwhile, down on the deck, along a third axis, two divisions of Blue fighters led by Commander De-Lancey will sneak in undetected and engage the Orange fighters from below. If the deception works, the Blue stinger package will kill all the Orange fighters, allowing the Blue strike package to continue to the target."

Boyce lowered his pointer. "Questions?"

A Hornet pilot named Dawg Harrison raised his hand. "What if the deception doesn't work? If the Blue fighters down on the deck get caught by the Orange defenders, looks to me like the strikers are dead meat."

Before Boyce could answer, Killer DeLancey spoke up. "Leave that to me. You suck 'em toward me, I'll kill 'em. I've never lost a fight to an F-15 yet."

That sparked a round of cheering and whistling.

Boyce shoved a cigar into his mouth while he waited for the cheering to settle down. He wanted to tell DeLancey to knock off the goddamn grandstanding. This was a large force exercise, not a solo mission. But Boyce knew he couldn't rebuke DeLancey, at least in front of his adoring fan club.

Settling into his cockpit, Maxwell gazed around the flight deck. The afternoon sun blazed down on the flight deck, making it hot as a griddle. It was always that way in the Persian Gulf, he reflected. Just different gradations of hot, depending on the season.

Maxwell could see all his strike pilots manning their jets. Opposite them, spotted behind catapult one, were the Hornets and the Tomcats of DeLancey's stinger package—the fighters that were assigned to engage the Orange defenders.

He thought again of the four weeks of planning he had put into the exercise, the late nights, the hours spent alone up in the Intel room. CAG Boyce had been impressed with the depth of detail in the strike plan, especially the complex pincers attack that was designed to lure the Orange fighters into the trap.

This was Maxwell's single shot at refuting the prima donna astronaut reputation that he knew DeLancey had been spreading about him. DeLancey wanted everyone to know that Maxwell lacked the fleet experience to carry his weight as a senior squadron officer.

If Maxwell somehow pulled the strike off without any major glitches, he would receive his Air Wing Strike Lead qualification, which was requisite to eventual command of his own squadron. If the mission went to hell and Blue force failed to nail its target, he could kiss it good-bye.

It was exactly what DeLancey was hoping. He would have an excuse to replace Maxwell as his operations officer.

Maxwell finished his pre-start checklist. He closed the canopy, sealing out the wind and din of the carrier flight deck. Inside the cockpit, the digital display screens glowed at him like miniature billboards. On signal from Ruiz, the enlisted plane captain on the flight deck below, he started the right engine, then the left. He swept the control stick through its full range, moving every control surface on the wings and tail. The stabilator—the big horizontal tail slab—he ran to its takeoff trim setting. The flaps were cycled through their full range, then set to half-extended for takeoff.

Five minutes later, he was taxiing forward to the number one catapult, on the carrier's starboard bow. Wisps of steam poured back down the catapult tracks. All four catapults—the two on the angled deck and the two on the bow—were busy now, hurling fighters one after the other into the hazy Gulf sky.

He eased the jet forward, feeling the nose of the Hornet lurch as the nose-tow bar dropped into the shuttle slot. The yellow-shirt standing by the jet's nose gave Maxwell the signal to release brakes. In the center of the flight deck, between the two catapults, the catapult officer was signaling Maxwell to power up.

Maxwell shoved the throttles forward. One last time he "wiped" the cockpit with the stick, making sure the controls were free. He shoved his head back against the headrest and wrapped his left hand around the throttle grip. His right hand came up in a salute to the catapult officer. The ready signal.

Maxwell waited, tensed as always. A half second elapsed . . . waiting . . . another second . . .

KaaaWhoooom! The catapult fired.

The Hornet hurtled down the track, accelerating from zero to 140 miles per hour. Maxwell was rammed back in his seat. He felt his eyeballs flatten in their sockets, felt his guts pressing against his spine. Ahead he could see the edge of the deck, then blue empty sea.

The force of the catapult abruptly stopped. The Hornet's nose lifted. He was flying.

"Ninety-nine Gippers on station," Maxwell said in his mike. "Gipper" was the collective call sign for the *Reagan* air wing strike force.

"Roger, Gipper, your Orange playmates are on station and ready."

Maxwell recognized the voice of Lieutenant Commander Butch Kissick, who would referee the exercise from aboard his orbiting E-3C AWACS.

One by one his strike force jets had launched, then headed for the rendezvous point to join up on the Air Force KC-10 tanker. Two of his jets had gone down on deck for maintenance problems, and the two ready spares were launched in their place.

The big three-engine tanker, a military derivative of the Douglas DC-10 airliner, looked like a giant swan with the swarm of sharp-nosed fighters huddled like baby chicks behind it. When the last jet had completed its aerial refueling, Maxwell took one last look around, then commenced a gentle bank away from the tanker's orbit. He keyed his mike, transmitting the signal that would commence the exercise. "Ninety-nine Gippers, COMEX, COMEX."

The game was on.

On Tracey Barnett's radar screen aboard the AWACS, the strike package looked like a solid cluster of blips. They were aimed on a tangential course toward the Orange home base.

Her boss, Butch Kissick, had assigned her the task of controlling the Blue force raiders from the *Reagan*, as she had requested. It gave her a chance to compete with her counterpart, First Lieutenant Wade Harper. Harper was a freckle-faced computer nerd and, in her opinion, a world-class dork. Already she and Harper had made a wager—dinner and unlimited booze—at the club tonight.

Glancing across the control cabin, she could see

Harper hunched over his own console, talking to the defending Orange force. On her own scope, she was picking up the Orange fighters, three groups of them, taking up their CAP stations.

"Gipper One," she radioed to the Blue leader, "you have three groups heavy, capping north, middle, and south of Al-Kharj."

"Gipper One copies," came the voice of Brick Maxwell.

Seconds later, Tracey saw the cluster of Blue fighters accelerating to nearly supersonic speed. They were still on a course that would take them nose-to-nose with the enemy jets. Only 150 miles separated the two forces.

Tracey began to worry. These Navy jockeys had better have something better in mind than to bore into a head-on fight with the F-15s. They would get hosed like pigeons on a skeet range. Already she could see that nerdly little dork, Harper, gloating over his margaritas back at the bar.

A hundred miles. No way the Orange groups would miss painting that big cluster of ingressing jets. Any second now they would be making their move.

And they were. They were leaving their stations, taking up intercept courses. "North and south groups committing," she warned the Blue leader. "Range one hundred, closing."

Still, the Blue force continued inbound. The two forces were closing at a relative speed of nearly two thousand miles per hour.

Come on, Blue, Tracey implored. *Do something clever or you guys are dog meat.* The Blue strike leader was a guy called Brick. She knew nothing about him except that he had been the second section lead during the MiG shoot last week. He was the only one out there who seemed to understand the rules of engagement. He didn't shoot from the hip.

But what was the guy doing? This would be a great time, she thought, to shoot from the hip.

"Range eighty."

No response. Still merging.

"Range sixty."

Then, from the Blue leader, "Ninety-nine Gippers, stand by . . . Action now!"

Tracey had no idea what the command meant. Action now? What action? But something was definitely happening. The tight cluster of Blue jets had become a milky, indistinct blob on her scope. It meant, probably, that they were dispensing chaff—a cloud of radar-deflecting metal foil. She was picking up the warbling electronic sound of radar jamming, which she knew had to come from the pair of EA-6 Prowlers off the *Reagan,* out there to provide electronic warfare support for the Blue strike force.

Chaff, jamming—something was going on. *What?*

The Blue cluster was no longer a cluster. They were splitting, one group to the left, the other right, diverging at a right angle. And something else . . . Tracey squinted at the scope . . . something else going on . . . concealed in the cloud of chaff and the murkiness of the radar jamming.

Tracey stole a glance over at Harper. He, too, was staring at his scope, wondering what the hell was going on. A smile crept over Tracey's face. She didn't know what the hell was going on either, but she liked it. This was getting to be interesting.

*　　*　　*

Maxwell waited, counting the seconds. This was the crucial part of the plan. Would the split-up of the Stinger package show on the Orange radar screens? Everything depended now on the effectiveness of the chaff cloud and the radar jamming from the Prowlers. DeLancey's Stinger group would now be in their supersonic vertical dive for the deck.

Ten seconds.

Twenty. Maxwell waited, counting.

The fighter section should be leveling off in a few more seconds, ripping along down in the weeds. And, if everything was working right, hidden from the Orange radar.

Thirty seconds. Time for the next surprise.

"Buick and Rambler sections, execute. . . . Now!"

Maxwell rolled his Hornet into a hard ninety-degree turn back to the right. His half of the strike force—Buick section—turned with him. The right half—Rambler section—led by Craze Manson, wheeled into a ninety-degree turn to the left. Behind each section streamed more clouds of chaff.

The strike package was split into two parallel clusters, headed directly for Al-Kharj. The defending fighters would have to split their own forces to intercept the two Blue groups.

Or at least that was the plan.

Come on, guys, Maxwell said to himself. *Take the bait.*

They were taking it.

"Complex tactics," called Harper, the Orange controller in the AWACS. He was trying hard to keep his voice calm. Harper had enough adrenaline in his system now to jump-start a locomotive. "Blue groups diverging now, azimuth split north and south."

"How many groups?" called the Orange fighter lead, an Air Force major. "Two or three? How many, Sea Lord?"

Sweat was trickling down Harper's neck. It was hard to make sense of that mess with all the goddamn chaff and jamming. He squinted into his scope. "Two groups. South group beaming south, north group beaming north."

That was good enough for the Orange lead. He was seeing exactly the same thing on his own radar—two groups separating, obviously setting up to attack on different azimuths. Not very imaginative, really. But what did you expect from people who lived on boats?

"Roger that," replied the Orange lead. "Orange fighters are committing. Exxon flight will take the northern bandits. Mobil flight, target the south."

The Orange lead was also leading the northern, or Exxon flight. The Mobil flight lead, on the southern CAP station, acknowledged the call. Both groups of fighters, north and south, were turning toward the two inbound enemy groups. The middle fighter group, a flight of Saudi F-15s, would remain on station in case things went to hell and the intruders managed to get too close to Al-Kharj.

In the AWACS, Harper studied his scope. It looked like the bandits were turning again. Just as he predicted, the intruders were turning back toward the target. Nose on with the defending fighters.

"Bandits coming nose hot," he called. "Bearing one hundred, range sixty, thirty thousand. Weapons free, Orange lead. Acknowledge."

"Roger, weapons free," replied the Orange lead. It

meant they had the go-ahead to fire simulated missiles as soon as they were in range. He was getting solid radar hits now. Not quite in AIM-120 range, but getting close. This was going to be a turkey shoot.

"Stinger flight is sorted."

It was the message Maxwell had been waiting to hear. DeLancey was reporting that he and his stingers were down on the deck—and they had the enemy fighters located and identified.

Maxwell made one last situational check. His strikers had good separation—ten miles. The Orange fighters were coming at them, probably in afterburner, he figured, judging by the closure speed. Supersonic, and accelerating.

Time for the next move.

"Ninety-nine Strikers, go cold," Maxwell radioed, ordering his flight to turn away from the enemy.

In unison, the two Blue groups executed a hard right turn to the east, which placed them in a trail formation perpendicular to the oncoming Orange fighters.

Rolling out of his turn, Maxwell peered again at his radar—and he saw exactly what he had hoped to see. The Orange fighters were coming after them. Like leopards chasing an antelope, they were in a classic pursuit curve.

Almost in firing range.

Thirty thousand feet below, the Blue fighter package—four F/A-18 Hornets and four F-14 Tomcats—were in a full afterburner vertical climb, streaking upward like rockets from a launcher. Neither group was using radar. They were emitting no electronic warnings to the Orange fighters or to the AWACS.

Directly above them, specks against the milky Arabian sky, were the two groups of F-15s.

The first warning came from Harper, in the AWACS. His voice sounded like he'd been goosed with a cattle prod. "Exxon! Pop-up bandits inside five miles, altitude unknown!"

A second later, more bad news. "Mobil! Threat, snap vector zero-one-zero for ten miles nose hot, climbing!"

The F-15 pilot leading the Exxon group craned his neck, frantically searching. Where the hell were they? Under him? How could they get here without putting out a radar warning . . . ?

Suddenly he knew. Shit! The red radar warning scope light was flashing on his panel like a beacon from hell. Where the fuck did they come from?

He whipped his Eagle into a seven-G turn. "Exxon One, spiked at eight o'clock!" Then he saw it—the distinctive delta shape of an F-14 Tomcat. Coming up at him. Locked on so tight the guy could be shooting spitballs.

A second later he heard the inevitable call. "Splash one F-15, southern group, angels 29, in a hard left turn."

The Eagle pilot was officially "dead." But maybe the rest of his flight would engage the bandits . . .

"Splash two F-15s, southern group."

Two F-15s down. Aw, hell. But they had two more still alive—

"Splash three!"

"Splash four!"

It took less than ten seconds. All four F-15 Eagles

in the southern group were dead. For them, the exercise was over.

The Exxon leader rolled his wings level and glumly acknowledged. He and his entire group were out of the game. It occurred to him that it was probably the shortest air-to-air engagement he'd ever been in. The worst part was that he knew he'd be hearing about this from the swabbies every time they came ashore. Those Navy assholes were merciless.

But he still had the Mobil group. They were in their own furball with another gaggle of Blue fighters. He could hear them chattering like magpies on the radio, calling out targets, yelling that they were spiked.

Maybe the war wasn't over yet.

Killer DeLancey knew even before he flipped on his acquisition radar that he had committed too early. He should have waited another ten seconds, fifteen maybe, before going vertical and popping up. He'd given the F-15s a precious few seconds of reaction time to counter the attack.

His second section, led by Flash Gordon, had managed to get a quick kill on the nearest pair of F-15s. But the second two, with a few more miles of maneuvering room, had turned hard and fast into their attackers—Killer and his wingman, Hozer Miller.

"Take the trailer, Hozer!" Killer barked in his radio. "I've got the leader."

"Copy that," answered Hozer, grunting against the high G load. Hozer would engage the wingman while DeLancey killed the leader.

DeLancey could see it was going to be an old-fashioned turning fight, a classic Lufberry circle with the lead F-15 on one side of the circle, his own Hornet on the other. Nearby, Hozer and the second F-15 were engaged in their own separate turning duel.

This wasn't DeLancey's style of fighting. It was primitive, flying supersonic fighters in a hard G-pulling flat turn like this, trying to get inside the other guy's radius. This was ancient World War One I Richthofen and Rickenbacker stuff. DeLancey preferred to use the spectacular vertical capability of the Super Hornet to swoop and pounce on the enemy like a hawk plucking a mouse.

But it was okay with DeLancey. He had never lost a fight to an F-15 puke, and today wasn't going to be a bit different. It was just more work this way.

Pulling hard, sweat pouring down from inside his helmet, DeLancey kept his eyes on the lead Eagle across the circle. He could see the puffs of vapor spewing from the fighter's wings, a product of the high G load the Air Force pilot was pulling.

But DeLancey could see the angle between them decreasing. In tiny increments, he was gaining the advantage. He knew that in a turning fight, almost no supersonic fighter in the world, including an F-15 Eagle, could beat a Super Hornet. It was just a matter of time, a few more turns of the circle . . . he would have his nose on the Eagle's tailpipes. The F-15 would be dog meat.

In his peripheral vision, DeLancey caught an occasional glimpse of Hozer Miller, flying his own Lufberry circle, closing on the second F-15. Hozer's target was high, pulling hard, trying to evade the missile-firing cone of the pursuing Hornet.

Suddenly the second Eagle stopped trying to evade. Instead, he shallowed his turn, dropped his nose, and pointed his jet across the circle.

At Killer DeLancey's Hornet.

DeLancey had no time to react. "Hozer! Shoot the sonofabitch—"

Too late. "Fox Two! Splash one Hornet," came the voice of the Eagle pilot.

Killer was dead.

A second later—"Splash the F-15." Hozer killed his target—but not before the Eagle pilot had fired his simulated Sidewinder missile at Killer DeLancey.

In his cockpit, DeLancey slammed his fist against the canopy rail. A surge of fury flashed over him like heat from an explosion. He couldn't believe it. That goddamned Air Force prick! It was a cheap shot—totally unexpected and illogical. Stop defending, kill the lead Hornet, sacrifice yourself. A stupid decision in real combat. But this was a war game, and it was perfectly legal.

Ten seconds later, Flash Gordon's section of Hornets dispatched the surviving F-15. "Splash the lead Eagle," reported Gordon.

The fight was over. Four Mobil defenders were shot down. And so was Killer DeLancey.

Maxwell waited until he heard that DeLancey's fighters had engaged the F-15s. Then he called, "Strikers, take heading two-seven-zero."

His strike package was inbound once again to the target. Both groups of strikers—Maxwell's Buick flight and, ten miles abeam, the Rambler flight—accelerated to attack speed.

Thirty miles out, they heard from Tracey Barnett in the AWACS. "Rambler One, bandits on the nose, thirty miles, hot."

Maxwell could see them on his own radar now, the

four remaining Orange defenders. The Royal Saudi F-15s were committing. They were leaving their CAP station, making a head-on attack against the entire strike package. They were Al-Kharj's last defense against the Blue Strike Force.

"Blue Force, go air-to-air," Maxwell transmitted. His Hornets were ready for a face-to-face with the F-15s. The Saudis were good, he knew, but not very imaginative. Four Eagles against eight Hornets, who also happened to be armed with the same AIM-120 radar-guided missiles.

Determined but outgunned, the Saudi pilots came blazing into the fight with the suicidal panache of the Light Brigade. The lead F-15 managed to score an out-of-range shot on Maxwell's dash four, who was flying too wide and stepped down.

It was B.J. Johnson, Maxwell realized. He made a note to himself to debrief her about flying proper combat spread.

It was the last Orange kill of the day. Seconds later, Maxwell reported, "Splash the lead F-15."

"Splash two," called another Hornet pilot.

"Splash three."

"Make that four."

The Orange air defense had been eliminated. Twenty miles ahead, Al-Kharj lay exposed like a ripe garden.

"Ninety-nine Gippers," Maxwell said, again using his group's collective call sign, "push it up."

His Hornets formed a wide combat spread.

"Weapons hot."

Maxwell shoved his throttles into afterburner, rolling into his dive. On either side, he could see his strikers doing the same, each acquiring his respective target on the big sprawling air base.

Streaking downward at supersonic speed, the Hornets ripped over Al-Kharj, dropping their make-believe weapons.

"Buick One off," called Maxwell, flashing past the orange-and-white checkerboard-painted water tower.

"Buick Two."

"Rambler One off."

Each jet reported off, his simulated bomb load delivered on one of the base structures. One by one the fighters screamed over the concrete-and-sand-and-grass patchwork of the air base at nearly nine hundred miles per hour.

Inside Maxwell's oxygen mask, a wide grin spread over his face. He knew the thunder of the sonic booms was reverberating across the air base like the hammers of hell. Glasses were probably shattering, a few windows breaking, someone's china vase cracking. War was hell.

Maxwell knew that when their nerves stopped twanging from the booms, the Air Force blue suits down there would figure out what happened. They had just gotten schwacked by the swabbies.

SEVEN

Sugar Talk

DeLancey was seething. Every vivid detail of the shoot-down—that numb-nuts Eagle driver sacrificing himself so he could take a shot at DeLancey—was still burning like an ember in his gut.

Ahead of him lay the great gray slab of the *Reagan's* flight deck. Behind the carrier trailed a wake of white foam, sparkling in the afternoon sun. DeLancey was stabbing his throttles forward and back, struggling to keep his jet stabilized on the glide path, trying to keep the ball—the amber light that served as the pilot's optical glide path indicator—in the middle of the Fresnel Lens that jutted up like a sign board at the left edge of the landing area.

DeLancey's jet was settling in the groove. "A liii—iiitttle powerrrrrr," the LSO coaxed, using his best sugar talk.

DeLancey responded with a burst of power, shoving the throttles up. Too much.

"Don't go high," said the LSO. But it was too late. Killer's blast of thrust had pushed the jet above the glide path. *"Bolterrrrr!"* Pearly barked into his microphone.

A bolter meant that the jet's tailhook had missed all four wires. Instead of landing, the pilot had to jam the throttles forward and take off again, hurtling off the end of the angled deck and back into the sky. The gray blur of the ship passed beneath and behind him— without stopping. Ahead was the open sky and the sea.

Now Killer was in a rage. Bolters were supposed to happen only to nuggets—pilots who were new aboard the ship—or to pilots who were rattled and had lost their concentration. He was the commanding officer! He had over eight hundred carrier landings in his logbook. He wasn't supposed to lose his concentration.

What galled him most of all was the knowledge that down there in his own squadron's ready room, the other pilots, mostly junior officers who had not flown today's exercise, would be watching the landings on the PLAT—the Pilot Landing Aid Television. He knew what they'd be doing. The insolent little bastards would be cracking up.

He was right.
"Yee-ha!" howled Buster Cherry, a baby-faced lieutenant. "See that? Killer blew through the deck."
"Like soap through a goose," observed Bud Spencer. "Killer the clutcher!"
"Who's he gonna blame that one on?"
"The LSO, of course. For giving the power call."
They loved it. What could be better than watching their own larger-than-life, MiG-slaying commanding officer, Killer DeLancey, having his day in the barrel?
They watched the PLAT monitor as DeLancey made his way around the pattern, setting up for his next pass at the deck.

"Betcha a buck he nails a three wire this time," said Spencer.

"You're on," said Buster. "He'll squat the jet." "Squatting" meant descending below the glide slope, dumping the jet onto the deck and catching the first wire. It was dangerous because it increased your chances of landing short and exploding against the ramp—the edge of the flight deck.

"Killer's cool. He'll get an okay pass."

"I bet on a wave-off," said Leroi Jones, the squadron duty officer. A "wave-off" was a command by the LSO to add full power and go around for another try at the deck.

The ready room fell quiet. The JOs watched the black-and-white image of DeLancey's Hornet appear behind the ship. Superimposed over the jet on the PLAT screen was a set of crosshairs, indicating the jet's position on the glide path.

The jet was below the crosshairs.

"A little low," came the voice of the LSO. "Give me some power."

No one spoke. The audience in the ready room was caught up in the mini-drama of the carrier landing ritual. Carrier landing grades were a matter of pride and heated competition among pilots—and squadrons. To be named "Top Hook"—best carrier pilot—was one of the highest plaudits in naval aviation.

On the VFA-36 "greenie board"—the chart in the ready room on which each pilot's carrier landing grades were recorded—Killer DeLancey's name dwelled somewhere in the middle. At the top of the chart, with stars around it, was the name of the current VFA-36 carrier landing champion—Brick Maxwell. It was a distinction, as everyone in the squadron knew, that irritated the hell out of Killer DeLancey.

DeLancey's jet was still below the crosshairs. "Pow-errrr," called the LSO.

The jet was almost at the ramp. Still slightly low. "Don't go low . . ."

Passing over the ramp, the deck of the *Reagan* safely under him, DeLancey pulled the power off.

He squatted the jet.

Whummppp! The Hornet plopped like a descending dump truck. The jet's tailhook snagged the number one wire—the one nearest the blunt ramp of the deck. The Hornet floundered to a stop on the angled deck.

"Yes!" yelled Bud Spencer in the ready room. He held his hand out, collecting the dollar from Buster Cherry. "That was the ugliest pass since the Marines came out last month."

"I wanna hear the LSO debrief that one," said Leroi Jones. "That's a No-Grade if I ever saw one." A No-Grade was the lowest grade an LSO could assign for a carrier landing. It was equivalent to a black mark on the pilot's landing record.

"That's not the worst part. Did you hear that Killer got morted by an Eagle jockey."

"No shit?"

"He's gonna come storming in here looking for someone to kill."

The laughter ended. The awful realization hit them simultaneously. In a matter of minutes DeLancey would be in the ready room.

Buster Cherry remembered he had paperwork to do. Bud Spencer declared that he had to check on his men in the ordnance department. Leroi Jones glanced at his watch and announced that he was late for a meeting.

"A meeting with who?" demanded Spencer.

"The chaplain. He's gonna take my confession."

"You can't leave. You're the duty officer."

"I thought you might take over for a little while so I can—"

"You're on your own, Jones," said Spencer as he evacuated the ready room.

"First pass—too much power on the start," said Pearly, reading from his handwritten notes. "High in the middle, flat at the ramp and over the wires. Bolter pass."

DeLancey's fist clenched and unclenched the strap on his nav bag as he listened to the LSO. He wanted Pearly to get the goddamn landing debriefing over.

Pearly was carefully not looking at DeLancey. "Second pass . . ." He hesitated, then blurted out the rest: "Not enough power on the start, low in the middle, ease gun at the ramp for a No-Grade, taxi to the one-wire."

DeLancey squeezed the nav bag strap until his knuckles were white. "Are you finished?" he said. "I've heard enough."

He was careful to stop short of actually disputing the landing grade, shit-awful that it was. That was one of the oldest rules in naval aviation—you never argued with the LSO. Even if you were his commanding officer.

But DeLancey was pushing it. "Yes, sir," said Pearly. "Guess you were just, uh, having a bad day."

DeLancey shot him a look that said, *And you're*

gonna have a worse day, mister, if you don't get out of my sight.

Pearly got the message. He and his writer, an LSO-in-training named Nelson, beat a rapid exit out the back door of the ready room.

When they were gone, DeLancey looked around. The place was empty, except for the duty officer, Leroi Jones, who had been unable to escape. Jones was now intently contemplating a spot on the far bulkhead.

In an outpouring of rage, DeLancey wound up and hurled his helmet bag.

Whang! The bag smashed against a metal locker ten feet away. The clatter caused Leroi Jones, still preoccupied with the spot on the bulkhead, to levitate a full six inches out of his chair.

"Jones!" roared DeLancey.

"Sir?" Leroi leaped to his feet. His eyes widened to the size of Frisbees.

"Anybody asks where I am, tell 'em I'm on my way to CVIC. I'm gonna set the record straight about who fucked up this strike exercise."

"Aye aye, sir."

CAG Boyce hung up the phone and turned to the officers assembled in CVIC. "That was Butch Kissick, the airborne commander aboard the AWACS. He sends a 'Well Done.' He's been telling the Air Force pukes over at JTF how the Navy kicked their butts today. When we get into Dubai, he says the drinks are on him."

Boyce had most of his flight leaders in the room. Brick Maxwell, the strike leader, was still wearing his sweat-stained flight suit. Burner Crump, skipper of the F-14 Tomcat squadron, and Rico Flores, commanding officer of the other Hornet squadron, VFA-34, were there.

The only missing player was Killer DeLancey.

"Give credit where it's due, CAG," said Crump. "Strike lead set 'em up."

"Brick pulled it off," said Rico Flores. "He waxed their butts today."

Boyce nodded in agreement. Maxwell was no longer an unknown quantity. DeLancey had almost persuaded him to transfer Maxwell. Too much pointy-headed test pilot, not enough hard ball fighter pilot, DeLancey had tried to tell him, and Boyce had almost agreed.

DeLancey was wrong. The pointy-headed test pilot had pulled off one of the slickest coordinated strikes he'd ever seen.

Just then DeLancey stormed into the briefing room.

"Where you been, Killer?" said Boyce. "Bagging extra traps?"

A titter of laughter rippled through the room. They had all seen Killer's two landing passes on the PLAT.

DeLancey glowered. "The whole exercise was a cluster fuck. We lost two Hornets on the way in. No way that should've happened."

"And you were one of them, right?" said Burner Crump.

More laughter, this time not so suppressed.

Rico Flores said, "Hey, Killer, you're just pissed because the Eagle jockey took you out."

"It wouldn't have happened," DeLancey insisted, "if the strike had been executed right."

Boyce gnawed on his cigar, watching DeLancey fume. It was time to put a stop to this. "Okay, you've made your point, Killer. I don't blame you for being pissed at the F-15 pilot, but you can't blame the strike leader."

"Sir, I still think—"

"Here's the bottom line," said Boyce, his voice more forceful. "We took out all the enemy's air defense assets, losing only two strike aircraft. We destroyed the target—with one minor exception. Intel says one of our Roadrunners—Spam Parker—managed to target the Al-Kharj base hospital instead of the command headquarters building."

This drew howls from the group. Burner Crump said, "She probably thought the big red cross on the building was her aim point."

Boyce grinned and shook his head. "Luckily, the exercise umpire won't know anything about it. The exercise was a huge success, and the credit goes to the strike leader for planning and execution."

Boyce walked over and extended his hand to Maxwell. "Brick, consider yourself a qualified Air Wing Strike Lead."

The flight leaders gave Maxwell a round of applause. Rico Flores clapped him on the shoulder and said, "Shit hot, Brick."

Burner Crump said, "Man, we broke some beer mugs down at Al-Kharj, didn't we?"

The last to shake Maxwell's hand was Killer DeLancey. His face had shed most of its anger. In its place was the famous grin. "I was out of line, Brick. Good job."

From across the room Boyce watched the two men shake hands. The handshake was cordial enough. The words sounded sincere, even conciliatory.

But Boyce knew better. He could tell by their eyes—that cold, hard exchange of looks—that these two despised each other. He didn't know what the root of their conflict was, but he sensed that it went deeper than their disagreement over the MiG shoot last month. Whatever it was, it meant trouble.

Maxwell was sitting alone in the wardroom when CAG Boyce plopped down in the seat opposite him. Boyce helped himself to the coffee. "Okay, open up with me."

Maxwell looked at him in surprise. "Sir?"

Boyce raised an eyebrow. "This pissing contest between you and Killer. I don't need two of my senior officers feuding like a couple of kids in a schoolyard."

"It's old stuff, CAG. No big deal, just a personality conflict."

"Personality conflict, my ass. That's like calling the gunfight at the O.K. Corral a friendly argument. My gut hunch is that there's a story about how this shit started with you and DeLancey."

Maxwell deliberated, drumming his fingers on the table for a moment. CAG's hunch was right. There *was* a story, and it went back over a decade. But it was one he couldn't tell. Not now. Perhaps not ever.

"Sorry, sir. It's personal."

As CAG glowered at him, Maxwell peered across the room at the far bulkhead. He allowed his mind to fly back in time, to a black January night over Iraq.

EIGHT

Night One

USS *SARATOGA*
1930, WEDNESDAY, 16 JANUARY, 1991

He remembered how eerily quiet it had been on the flight deck. No jet engines running, no tugs, vehicles, catapults, arresting engines. The air was still. You could hear a whisper. *Saratoga* had not yet turned into the wind.

"Those guys are counting on us," Lieutenant Commander Gracie Allen was saying as they walked across the deck. "The F-15s, the B-52s, the Stinkbugs—they're gonna get their asses shot off if we don't take out the radars first."

They were walking line abreast—Allen, Maxwell, Rasmussen, and DeLancey. Maxwell could hear the clunk of their flight boots on the steel deck.

"When we get close," Allen said, "take your individual strike lines and assigned altitudes. That's the only way we can de-conflict, because we're gonna be too busy to watch each other."

The briefing had been efficient, without hyperbole. They had devoted the past month to studying their likely targets, planning run-in lines, rehearsing tactics.

Maxwell was a new lieutenant, a nugget only three months in the squadron. His section leader was a slow-talking lieutenant commander named Gracie Allen. The leader of the second section was Lieutenant Commander Raz Rasmussen, a jovial, blond-haired guy with a quick wit. Rasmussen's wingman that night was a cocky, flamboyant lieutenant named John DeLancey.

Even in those days DeLancey and Maxwell hadn't hit it off. Neither could explain the bad chemistry between them, but they both understood that it was an instinctive thing. To DeLancey, the more senior and experienced squadron officer, Maxwell was too cerebral, too introspective to be a fighter pilot. Maxwell, for his part, disdained DeLancey's noisy swaggering and posturing. The two men avoided each other.

Gracie Allen had overall lead of the four-ship flight, with the call sign "Anvil." Their job was to shoot HARMs—anti-radiation missiles intended to snuff out Iraq's air defense radars. The mission was critical because the inbound strike aircraft—other F-18s, F-15s, F-111s, B-52s—all depended on them. The HARM shooters had to take out the deadly barrage of radar-directed antiaircraft guns and SAM batteries or the coalition air forces would be decimated before they reached their targets.

In the stillness of the evening, they manned their jets. Twenty minutes later they launched from the deck of the *Saratoga*. They were headed for Baghdad.

The winter night was clear and smooth. The SEAD—Suppression of Enemy Air Defenses—package amounted to nearly forty jets, F/A-18 Hornets and A-7 Corsairs from *Saratoga*, *America*, and *Kennedy*. They remained in a single cluster until reaching the split-up point, 120 miles from the target.

The lights of Baghdad glimmered on the horizon.
Already they could see flashes, explosions, and tracers
arcing into the sky. It meant that the stealth fighters—
the F-117 "Stinkbugs"—were in the target area.

Maxwell tried to make sense of the hysterical chatter on the tactical frequency. Everyone was transmitting at once, cutting each other off.

As dash two, he was flying on the left flank of the
four-ship. He was nearly overwhelmed trying to keep
track of his leader, check his radar, check his position
and distance to go, and listen to the relentless chatter
on the radio. In the blackness he could no longer see
Gracie Allen out there on his right. At the split point,
each of the Hornets had taken a two-mile separation
and five hundred feet of altitude difference from the
adjoining jet. From now until the missile launch point,
each pilot was on his own.

Then, cutting like a knife through the chatter—
"Bogey! Twelve o'clock, thirty miles!"

Instantly every pilot's head went to his radar.
Where? Whose twelve o'clock? Is it a MiG?

Maxwell tagged him. On his radar he was getting
an EID—Electronic Identification. It was a MiG-25,
code named "Foxbat."

The other three pilots in Anvil Flight picked him
up at the same time. Twenty-five miles, closing fast.

But they couldn't shoot. At least not yet. According
to the rules of engagement read to them at the mission
briefing, an electronic ID was not good enough. There
were too many allied warplanes in the same airspace.
The Hornets were required to obtain a positive identification from the AWACS. Or get a VID—Visual
Identification—which at night was impossible.

Maxwell heard Gracie Allen on the tac frequency. "Request clearance to fire on the bogey."

"Who's that?" said the AWACS controller. "Say your call sign."

Maxwell watched the blip on his radar. Twenty miles. The MiG was coming directly at him. Maxwell selected air-to-air mode on his weapons selector. *Five more miles and I'm gonna shoot.*

Gracie was yelling on the radio. "Anvil Flight has a bogey at twenty miles! We need clearance—"

Bleep.

"—clearance. Do you have PID? State your—"

Bleep.

Each transmission was being overridden by another. Fifteen miles.

Maxwell saw something in his radar, at the far extreme of his gimbals. It looked like—

Shit! Another bogey! A second MiG, two miles abeam the first.

"Trailer!" Maxwell transmitted. "Two miles—"

Bleep. He was cut out. He tried again to send a warning. Then he heard something that chilled his blood—his RWR was howling at high pitch.

A missile was in the air. Coming at him.

Captain Jabbar had no illusions about what would happen. The night sky was filled with enemy fighters. The mother of all battles had been joined.

"Make your peace with Allah," his flight leader, Lieutenant Colonel Al-Rashid, told him before they took off. "We will be joining him tonight."

He and Al-Rashid had barely reached altitude in their MiG-25s when they observed the line of enemy fighters. Jabbar's heart nearly stopped. It looked on his radar like an advancing armada. The line stretched a hundred kilometers. All flying north, toward Baghdad.

Jabbar's *Sirena* was chirping, but it did not yet indicate that they were being targeted. They had the advantage, for the moment.

On the radio, Rashid reported, "I have a lock on the far right fighter. Take the left."

On his own radar, Jabbar slewed his target acquisition box over the blip of another enemy fighter. He prepared to shoot.

A second later, Jabbar saw the white plume of Rashid's Acrid missile rocketing off into the night.

"Anvil Forty-one, spiked and defending!" Maxwell yelled into the radio.

He yanked the Hornet into a max-G break. The RWR was warbling like a crazed parrot.

Hard right and down. Outturn the missile. Pull!

He hit the chaff button, then hit it again, dispensing bundles of the aluminum foil to decoy the Acrid missile's guidance system.

He was turning into the other three Hornets of his flight, but he knew the evasive turn would take him underneath and behind them. In the darkness he couldn't see other fighters. No enemies, no friendlies. It was like knife-fighting in a blacked-out room.

Over his shoulder, he saw the white torch of the missile coming for him. He stabbed the chaff button once again.

It worked. The missile went for the chaff. Then it wobbled, lost guidance, went dumb.

Maxwell kept pulling. Now to get back on the run-in line. Get the nose pointed back at the bogeys.

He found himself under the second section, a couple of thousand feet beneath Rasmussen and DeLancey. He checked his radar, then peered out in the darkness.

Above and to the left—*a plume of fire*! An air-to-air missile leaving its rail. By the distinctive torch of the missile, Maxwell knew that it was an AIM-7 Sparrow missile. The thing looked like a fire-tailed comet.

Raz had taken a shot. But in the heat of battle, he hadn't called a Fox One.

Damn, thought DeLancey, watching the trail of Rasmussen's missile rocketing into the night. He was out of position, a mile too far back. He had been playing catch-up, trying to juggle all the radio calls, checking his position, setting up the armament panel before they got to the HARM-firing point.

Now that goddamn Rasmussen was about to bag a MiG.

DeLancey went to his radar, trying to sort the bogey. *Wait!* Over there, gimbals left, was that another bogey? Were there two?

Which one had Rasmussen taken his shot at?

DeLancey didn't care. Quickly he locked up the lead bogey.

Whoom! His Sparrow missile leaped out ahead of the jet, aiming for the unseen enemy.

"Anvil Forty-two, Fox One," DeLancey called on the radio. "Bandit on the nose."

Jabbar knew that Rashid's missile had missed. It should have impacted by now. The enemy pilot had somehow evaded the Acrid.

Now he and Rashid were too close to get off another shot. In fewer than fifteen seconds they would merge with the enemy fighters. Jabbar's only hope was that they could somehow convert to a stern attack.

Then he heard it. *Chiiiiirrrrrp! Chiirrrrrp!* The *Sirena*. It was howling.

The enemy had awakened to the fact that the MiGs were out here. *Chiiiiirrrp! Chiirrrrrrp!* A radar-guided missile was inbound.

Toward whom? Him or Rashid?

"Break!" he yelled to Rashid. "Break to the—"

Kablooom!

The fireball of Rashid's MiG lit up the sky.

For a moment Jabbar closed his eyes. Then he opened them and saw the flaming debris of the MiG falling toward the black desert. So Rashid was the first to keep his appointment with Allah.

The *Sirena* resumed its slow chirp. Jabbar could not believe his luck. They had targeted Rashid's jet without spotting his wingman. But Jabbar knew it wouldn't last. He had to close the remaining distance between them quickly, before they acquired a missile lock. *Get behind the bastards.*

Jabbar shoved the throttles past the detent. *Baroom!* He felt the two big Tumanksy afterburners jolt him forward like the kick of a mule. He knew he was trailing two great columns of fire, perhaps giving away his position.

So be it. Now he needed speed. Speed was life.

Maxwell saw the bogey explode. He felt like cheering. *Attaboy, Raz!*

Then, seconds later, coming from behind—another missile.

DeLancey, Maxwell realized. It had to be. De-

Lancey was behind Rasmussen, displaced to the right. What was he shooting at?

Fascinated, Maxwell watched the second missile arcing . . . arcing . . . veering downward . . .

Toward the wreckage of the destroyed MiG. With a brilliant flash, the missile exploded in the burning hulk of the Foxbat.

Then Maxwell spotted something else. Off to the right, two bluish streaks of flame. *Afterburners?* Yes, thought Maxwell, peering into the night. The long blue flames were the twin afterburners of a Russian-built fighter.

Another bogey. But where? He scanned his radar, searching.

Nothing. The bogey had vanished. That was bad news.

Jabbar hauled the MiG-25's nose hard left. He completed the 180-degree turn as he came out of afterburner.

Still no warning from the *Sirena*. He was behind the enemy fighters. And they didn't know. The trick now was to lock one of them up and—

There. On his radar. He judged that it was an F/A-18. If the geometry of his turn had been correct, then it was the same fighter that killed Al-Rashid.

It was appropriate, thought Jabbar. An eye for an eye. An F/A-18 for a MiG-25.

He selected ripple fire and squeezed the trigger. *Whoom! Whoom!* The two Acrid missiles streaked out beyond the long, pointed snout of the MiG.

Rashid waited, listening for the shrill warning of his *Sirena*. It was slow-chirping. They still didn't know he was there.

*   *   *

In his peripheral vision, off to the left, DeLancey saw the streaks coming from behind. For an instant he was confused. What the hell? Was someone shooting from behind them? Was that goddamned nugget Maxwell taking a shot?

Or was it . . .

The MiG?

DeLancey felt a sudden stab of fear. How could the MiG have converted them? If he had gotten behind them, he would pick them off like grapes.

DeLancey keyed the mike, about to tell Raz to break hard right when—

Kabloom. An orange ball of fire lit up the night.

Dumbstruck, DeLancey watched Rasmussen's Hornet plunge like a meteor toward the floor of the desert.

"What was that?" he heard Gracie Allen say. "An air-to-air kill?"

DeLancey removed his thumb from the transmit button. There was nothing to say.

Captain Jabbar watched with satisfaction as the fireball plummeted to the earth. Rashid would not die alone tonight.

But now what? He had other Hornets on either side. He wasn't painting them on his radar—and they weren't painting him—because they were nearly abeam. But they certainly knew he was here. They would be searching for him.

In the distance, to his right and to the left, Jabbar could see the flashes of missiles being launched. Air-to-air? Air-to-ground missiles? Anti-radar? They were all rocketing off toward targets in Baghdad.

Jabbar considered his situation. He would love to kill more of the murderous bastards. But he was in the middle of a hornets' nest. If he swung his nose right or left, he would appear on their radars. They would pounce on him like dogs on a rat.

Jabbar decided he would live to fight another day. He eased the throttles of the MiG-25 back to idle and commenced a sweeping descent to the left.

He had avenged the death of his leader, Lieutenant Colonel Al-Rashid. Most surprising of all, he was still alive. For having downed an American fighter, he could expect to receive the highest decoration his country could give him.

That made it a very good night indeed.

From across the CVIC room, Maxwell watched DeLancey. He was describing with his hands how he had shot down an Iraqi MiG-25.

Adrenaline was still flowing. The mood in the debriefing swung from mourning the loss of their squadron mate, Lieutenant Commander Rasmussen, to elation at having conducted the first massive air strike against an enemy since the Vietnam War.

And killing the first MiG.

"I locked the guy up," said DeLancey. "I made sure I had a positive ID, then—Zap—shot him in the face with a Sparrow."

The captain of the *Saratoga* loved it. He clapped DeLancey on the back. "Goddamn, I'm proud of you, son. You're the real thing."

"We got us a MiG killer," chimed in the squadron skipper.

"Hey, now there's a great call sign," said the CAG. "Killer! Killer DeLancey!"

Everyone in the room cheered. It was perfect, they all agreed.

Maxwell watched, saying nothing. He waited until DeLancey was alone, basking in the glow of his new celebrity. DeLancey flashed a cocky grin as Maxwell walked over to him.

"I know who killed the MiG," Maxwell said. "It wasn't you."

The grin evaporated from DeLancey's face. "What are you talking about?"

"Rasmussen shot down the Foxbat."

DeLancey's eyes darted around the room, then riveted on Maxwell. "Rasmussen's dead. How do you know—"

"I was there. I saw it. It was Raz's kill."

DeLancey leaned close to him. "Listen, you fucking nugget. You don't know what you saw. I got that MiG, and no one else. Are you calling me a liar?"

Maxwell hesitated. Yes, he realized, that's exactly what he was doing. But what would it get him? He *was* a nugget. It was his word against that of a senior lieutenant. DeLancey had already been declared a hero by acclamation.

Maxwell had been in the Navy long enough to know what would happen. He would be hung out to dry.

"Okay," he said, turning away from DeLancey. "Keep the MiG."

He felt DeLancey's eyes follow him out of the room. He knew the truth. And DeLancey knew that he knew. He had made a permanent enemy.

NINE

Latifiyah

BAGHDAD
2300, THURSDAY, 15 MAY, THE PRESENT

Tyrwhitt gazed out at the lights of Baghdad. It was warm outside, peaceful now, the lights of the city twinkling in the darkness like a blanket of diamonds. On evenings like this, Tyrwhitt could visualize what it must have been like that night in 1991.

It was the mother of all sound and light shows. Sirens, gunfire, tracers arcing through the blackness . . . Tomahawk missiles cruising like homing pigeons . . . the earth trembling with the impact of bombs . . . sudden eruptions of fire and brick and evil black smoke . . . the veil of darkness cloaking the invisible enemy . . .

From these very windows in the Rasheed Hotel the international press pool had witnessed the dismantling of Baghdad. They had watched the most spectacular display of military pyrotechnics in modern warfare.

When would it happen again?

Soon, Tyrwhitt thought. Sooner than anyone expected.

He turned from the window, feeling the onset of the old familiar loneliness that afflicted him on nights like this. He'd had enough of Baghdad, enough of Iraq and its problems. For too long he had lived in this squalid and oppressed place. He had lived with this same debilitating fear, dreading the day when the Bazrum would knock on his door.

Too long without Claire.

Thank God for the Cyfonika. Since the war the Iraqi telephone system was even more useless than before. International calls to and from Baghdad passed through the Bazrum's eavesdropping operators and were hopelessly delayed or misrouted. At least the Cyfonika satellite communicator permitted him to call anywhere in the world. In order to cloak the device's true purpose from the suspicious Bazrum—transmitting encrypted data to the CIA post in Riyadh—Tyrwhitt made frequent use of the Cyfonika for personal calls. He called his editor in Sydney to discuss new stories. Other times, usually when he'd been drinking, he telephoned old mates scattered around the planet. When he was lonely, as he was tonight, he called Claire.

As expected, she was asleep in her hotel in Bahrain. She was not pleased.

Tyrwhitt explained to her what he wanted to do. They would drive around the countryside of Iraq, viewing the sites the UNSCOM—United Nations Special Commission—inspectors had tried without success to examine. It was a wonderful idea.

"No way," said Claire.

"Not so fast, darling. It would be a great story, showing both sides of the debate. It would be a coup."

"Some coup. It would make me seem as much a suck-up to Iraq as you are."

"What if I arranged an exclusive interview with Saddam?"

"I don't want to interview Saddam. I despise him, and I despise Baghdad."

"Really, Claire, the place has changed. There's a lot to love here."

"Name one thing."

"Me, for one."

"All the more reason not to go."

Tyrwhitt groaned theatrically. "Claire, darling, you're breaking my heart."

"What heart?"

He had to laugh, even though he knew he was getting nowhere. Claire wasn't coming. Okay, he thought, time to to bring out the heavy artillery.

"I suppose," he said, "you know about the incident in the No-Fly-Zone?"

"That shoot-down? Old stuff. As a matter of fact, I interviewed the Navy pilot who shot down the Iraqi."

"Oh? So you're still keeping company with the fly-boys, are you?"

"That's it. I'm hanging up, Chris."

"Sorry. Does your Navy chap happen to know who it was that he shot down?"

There was a pause and he knew he had her attention. "Somebody I should know about?" she asked.

"A fellow named Al-Fariz."

"Wait a minute. I'm getting a pencil. Spell that for me."

Tyrwhitt spelled the name. Then he told her about Captain Hakim Al-Fariz and the young officer's relationship to the President of Iraq. He left out the details about the executions of the officers involved in controlling the mission. The Cyfonika in unencrypted mode was as public as a telephone.

In the long silence that followed, he could hear

Claire Phillips's mind working. "That's pretty interesting," she said finally. "What's going to happen next?"

"I have no idea," he said for the benefit of the
Bazrum eavesdroppers. "Why don't you fly up here
and we'll find out together?"

He heard her groan. "Nice try, Chris. You get the
exclusive on this one. I have other plans."

"What do they call this place?"

"Latifiyah," said Muhammad, his driver.

Tyrwhitt nodded, feigning ignorance. He knew
about Latifiyah. It was forty kilometers south of Baghdad. It had been a weapons depot and a prime target
for coalition bombers during the Gulf War. By the
end of the campaign, the Latifiyah facility looked like
an archaeological dig. During the UNSCOM period,
when frustrated United Nations inspectors tried to
enter Latifiyah, the Iraqis blocked their entry.

Tyrwhitt could see that Latifiyah had been recently
transformed. A complex of new buildings had been
constructed, and by the looks of the walls and the
fortified roofs, the structures were meant to be
bomb-resistant.

"Can we visit the place? You know, just to look
around?"

Muhammad shook his head vigorously. "It is forbidden. We must not approach any closer than we are
now."

They were at least five kilometers from the complex.
Tyrwhitt had ordered Muhammad to stop the Land
Rover at the crest of a hill overlooking the complex.
Down below, he could make out the network of fences
and observation towers. Dust trails rose behind roving
patrol vehicles.

"What do they do there?" Tyrwhitt asked Muhammad.

Muhammad shook his head vigorously. "It is not a matter that concerns us."

Tyrwhitt didn't press him on it. It was a charade they both played. He knew that Muhammad had a very good idea what they did there, and they both understood that it was in neither's best interest to flaunt such knowledge.

Over the past year Tyrwhitt had developed a liking for Muhammad. The Iraqi possessed a sense of humor, and he didn't ask too many questions about these excursions in the desert. Muhammad, who came not from Baghdad but from Samarra in the north, took great pains to keep Tyrwhitt out of trouble, as he was trying to do today.

But this was Iraq. In this troubled country you made no assumptions about loyalty, a commodity more scarce than cow's milk. Tyrwhitt presumed Muhammad was in the employ of the Bazrum. If he was not, he was without doubt subjected to frequent interrogations about his Australian client. Such was the reality of life in Iraq.

Tyrwhitt pulled his Zeiss field glasses from his knapsack. Ignoring Muhammad's distressed look, he stepped out of the Land Rover and focused the glasses on the Latifiyah complex. With the eight-power resolution, he observed something he had not seen earlier—vehicle tracks approaching the buildings. They sloped down a ramp, into a subterranean chamber beneath each building. It meant that whatever the buildings contained was buried deep in the earth, probably encased in layers of concrete.

It was intended to be bombproof.

He noticed something else. At each corner of the perimeter fence was a battery of skyward-pointing large-bore weapons. Fifty-seven-millimeter AA guns, Tyrwhitt guessed. They were on trailers and could be quickly redeployed.

There was more. Over there, at the far end of the facility, was a large-wheeled truck with a sloped track in its bed. And another. Tyrwhitt counted three in all. He was sure there would be more.

Mobile SAM launchers.

Tyrwhitt whistled softly. It all added up. Latifiyah was one of eight new complexes he knew about. This one, more than any other, had the look and feel of a prime weapons assembly facility.

He now had material for two pieces of reportage. The first was for public consumption, describing the heroic struggle of beleaguered Iraq to preserve its sacred sovereignty by barring UNSCOM inspectors from peaceful industrial plants like Latifiyah. For his objective reporting, Tyrwhitt would receive the praise and gratitude of the Minister of Information and, perhaps, even Saddam himself.

The second report, encrypted within the first and transmitted via the Cyfonika, would reach a different audience. It would detail the layout, antiaircraft defenses, and precise coordinates of each structure in the Latifiyah weapons plant. With the information Tyrwhitt supplied, allied warplanes would—

"They're coming!" said Muhammad.

Tyrwhitt swung the glasses to where Muhammad was pointing. Yes, they sure as hell were. A rooster tail of dust rose behind the desert-drab vehicle that was speeding toward them. In the back of the vehicle he could see soldiers holding their weapons at the ready.

Tyrwhitt lowered the glasses. He reached down and touched his ankle holster, making sure the Beretta nine-millimeter was still in place. It was.

"Move over," he ordered. Shoving Muhammad aside, he climbed into the driver's side. He jammed the Land Rover into gear and stomped on the accelerator.

Abdallah Al-Kazeem, the Iraqi Minister of Information, had ghastly breath. Tyrwhitt winced as the minister spoke directly into his face. "You are a friend of Iraq, and a journalist of the very greatest magnitude," said the minister. Then, to Tyrwhitt's disgust, Al-Kazeem kissed him. Not once, but twice.

Al-Kazeem regularly threw these receptions to preserve his relations with the foreign press corps in Baghdad. To Tyrwhitt, the whole thing was a joke. What remained of the Baghdad press corps amounted to no more than a dozen full-time correspondents, down from over a hundred. All the heavyweights—Morrison of Reuters, Hughes from the AP, Amanpour from CNN—had packed up and gone. Baghdad was no longer prime time. Now there were only the second-stringers like Baxter, who toiled for BBC, or Wenger, the super-serious German who wrote dispatches for "Die Welt." And Chris Tyrwhitt, whose employer, World Wide News, was famous for its anti-American bias.

Tyrwhitt knew that he had forfeited most of his own credibility with the overseas press community. They considered him tainted because of his sympathetic atti-

tude toward Iraq. In some circles they had even taken
to calling him "Baghdad Ben."

Screw them was Tyrwhitt's attitude. As far as he
was concerned, the fraternity of foreign correspondents was like a pack of jackals, snapping and stealing
and fighting over their precious little scraps of information. None of their opinions mattered to him.

None except one. Someday, he thought, it would be
nice if Claire knew the truth about her ex-husband.
He doubted if that day would come.

Al-Kazeem finished bestowing compliments and
kisses on Tyrwhitt. While the minister launched into
a speech in Arabic, Tyrwhitt returned to the cluster
of reporters standing in the audience.

"Amazing," whispered Baxter. "Anyone else would
have been tortured and shot after being caught in a
forbidden area."

"They didn't catch me."

"That's because they're incompetent," said Baxter.
"They can figure out who it was they were chasing
out there at Latifiyah. If it were anyone else, he'd be
hanging on a meat hook now. You, they give a medal
and a kiss."

"They respect my reportorial style."

"They respect that servile drivel you write for them.
Like the piece you just did about brave little Iraq
throwing out the oppressive UNSCOM inspectors."

Tyrwhitt shrugged. To hell with Baxter. But the
truth was, it *had* been a close thing—and a foolish
decision—running from the armed security detail back
there at Latifiyah. Thank God for the Land Rover.
He didn't like to think what might have happened if
he had been caught. Some illiterate Republican Guard

sergeant could have performed a summary execution on the spot.

Al-Kazeem was well into his speech, speaking in rapid-fire Arabic. With his rudimentary command of the language, Tyrwhitt understood only about half of what was said. His Arabic was adequate enough to communicate with taxi drivers, order whiskey, and negotiate with the proprietor of the Tammuz whorehouse. That was enough.

"What's he saying?" he asked Baxter.

"Something about Iraq's courageous President defying the American murderers."

"Smart guy. He'll go far."

The minister rambled on, then concluded his speech to unanimous applause. The occasion was not of enough importance to warrant the attendance of Saddam, or even Aziz, the deputy prime minister. The audience was mostly middle-grade government officials and military officers.

The guests were ushered into a hall where tables were laden with fresh fruit and pastry. To Tyrwhitt's great relief, there was a bar. He ordered a scotch, slammed it down, and immediately ordered a refill.

Half a dozen Iraqi bureaucrats came by to shake Tyrwhitt's hand. Several uniformed officers, mostly colonels and brigadiers, their chests laden with dangling medals, introduced themselves and congratulated Tyrwhitt on his reporting.

Standing at the bar, Tyrwhitt became aware of an officer, a hawk-faced man with intense brown eyes, studying him. He returned the officer's gaze. An uneasy feeling crept over him. It was unusual in the Arab world for men to maintain eye contact like this one was doing. The officer was staring at him like a bird of prey.

There was something familiar about the man. Those unblinking dark eyes, the beaklike nose.

Tyrwhitt walked over to him. "My name is Chris Tyrwhitt," he said. "Do I know you?"

"Certainly not," said the man in a voice that sent an alarm through Tyrwhitt. "I am Colonel Tariq Jabbar."

TEN

Liberty Call

DUBAI
1700, FRIDAY, 16 MAY

It sounded like incoming artillery. Heavy metal, drums, electronic strings. The noise was coming from somewhere down the hallway, in the next wing—the same ear-blasting rock music the JOs liked to play non-stop in the Buttwang. Maxwell tried to remember the name of the group. Korn? Pearl Jam? One of those god-awful rock groups favored by the younger pilots. They would be deaf before they hit thirty-five.

It was five o'clock in the afternoon of the *Reagan*'s first day in port. After three weeks on station in the Persian Gulf, the crew of the warship was on liberty.

Maxwell followed the clamor down the hallway of the Dubai Hilton, around a corner to the end of the wing. Inside the half-opened door to a suite, he came to the source. Suite 748 had been established as the official site of VFA-36's Admin Ashore—their private party and recreation headquarters.

Maxwell glanced around the suite. Hozer Miller was stationed behind the bar, mixing drinks from the private stock of booze that had arrived in a gray metal sea locker labeled "VFA-36 Admin Supplies." Flash Gordon, wearing his standard liberty uniform of jeans, polo shirt, and deck shoes, was locked in a conversation with a brunette in a tight sundress. Leroi Jones and Pearly Gates, both in shorts and squadron T-shirts, were in an animated argument about fighter tactics, using their hands as airplanes. Neither could hear the other over the din of music.

Maxwell made a head count. "Where's the skipper?" he yelled to Hozer Miller.

"Patrolling," Hozer yelled back, and gave Maxwell a knowing wink. "He locked up a pair of British Air girls down by the pool."

Maxwell nodded. The Dubai Hilton was renowned as a hunting ground for airline flight attendants. Killer DeLancey was the undisputed king of the hunters. He was famous not only for destroying enemy aircraft, but even more for his relentless pursuit of women when the carrier sailed into port.

On a couch, looking glassy-eyed and disheveled, sat Devo Davis. He clutched a drained cocktail glass in both hands.

Maxwell went over to him. "Hey, Devo, how about a refill?"

Davis stared at him blearily. He held out his glass. His lips moved, but no words came out.

Maxwell took Davis's glass to the bar.

"Lots of water for the XO, light on the scotch," he said to Hozer Miller.

"Roger that," said Hozer. "He was like that when he came in. You ask me, the guy's got a problem." Hozer sloshed a dollop of scotch into a tumbler of water and handed it to Maxwell. "By the way, this came for you a little while ago." He handed Maxwell a pink Post-it. "Some admiral, a three-star named Dunn, wants you to meet him at six o'clock. What's up, Brick? You getting a decoration or a court-martial?"

Maxwell glanced at the note and stuffed it in his pocket. He and Hozer went through the pretense of being friends. Since the MiG shoot-down, the rift between Maxwell and DeLancey had widened. The junior officers had divided themselves into DeLancey supporters and Maxwell backers.

Maxwell knew without a doubt what side Hozer was on. It was well known in the squadron that he was DeLancey's number one snitch.

"Both, maybe. Admiral Dunn is a troubleshooter at OpNav." OpNav was the office of the Chief of Naval Operations.

A perplexed look passed over Hozer's face.

Maxwell could have explained to Hozer that Admiral Josh Dunn was an old shipmate of Maxwell's father. He had known Brick Maxwell since before he could walk. When he was on the road, Dunn never passed up the chance to spend an evening with Harlan Maxwell's kid.

Hozer, Maxwell knew, would report the information to DeLancey. Let him stew over it, he thought.

Another CD was playing now, this one even more metallic and ear-breaking. Flash Gordon was closing the gap between him and the brunette, who had a decidedly British accent, which meant she was either a BAG or a GAG. She was giggling at something he told her. Jones and Gates were still arguing and flying their hands in a simulated dogfight, oblivious to the racket around them.

Maxwell delivered Devo Davis's drink. "How's it going, chum?"

Davis took several seconds to recognize Maxwell's face. Then he said, "He's gonna do it."

"Who's gonna do what?"

"DeLancey."

Davis was having trouble forming the words. "He's gonna get rid of us."

"What do you mean?" said Maxwell, knowing exactly what he meant.

"DeLancey hates our guts. He's gonna get rid of us."

Maxwell glanced around. This wasn't a good place for such a discussion. Davis was shit-faced. "Cool it, Devo. Let's just chill out and have a good time. Okay?"

Davis blinked while his sloshed brain processed the suggestion. He took a slurp from his fresh drink and shrugged. "Yeah, shit, whatever."

Maxwell went over to draw another beer from the keg. He umpired the hand-flying disagreement between Leroi Jones and Pearly Gates, declaring that neither was correct in his analysis of high alpha tactics. Flash Gordon was dancing with the cute brunette, who had been positively identified as a New Zealander and a GAG on a thirty-six-hour layover. For Flash, life was good.

The music was getting to Maxwell. He needed to take a walk. Admiral Dunn's note asked that he meet him at six. It was now five-thirty.

"Listen, guys," he said to Jones and Gates. "Keep an eye on the XO. Make sure he gets to his room okay."

"No problem," said Pearly. "We've got the old guy covered."

Maxwell was almost to the door when he noticed

for the first time the slight figure in the corner lounge chair. B.J. Johnson sat by herself nursing a Coors Light. She was wearing jeans and a T-shirt that bore the likeness of Eric Clapton.

Maxwell went over to her. "Hey, you. Trying to be invisible?"

She gave him a wan smile. "Yeah, I can blend into the wallpaper." She waited until he sat down in the chair facing her. "I wish I had been invisible yesterday, before I got whacked by that Saudi Eagle driver. That was dumb."

Maxwell nodded. "Maybe. Do you know why it happened?"

B.J. chewed on a thumbnail. "Sure. I screwed up."

"That you did. But think about it. What did you do wrong?"

"I guess I was out of position."

Maxwell spread a napkin out on the coffee table. "Look at this," he said, and sketched four winged symbols. "This is a a four-ship combat spread. Look how each section supports the other. If you're dash four, your job is to cover your section leader's right flank." He drew semicircles around the symbols. "Look what happens if you get wider than about five thousand feet from your leader. An oncoming bogey can split your defense quadrants, and you lose mutual support." He drew an arrow between two fighter symbols. "Zap! One of you is dead meat."

B.J. stared glumly at the napkin. "Me, in this case."

"That's what training is all about. Nobody was really morted, and you learned a valuable lesson."

She nodded toward the bar where Undra Cheever and Hozer Miller were huddled. Cheever was cracking up at something Miller said, laughing like a hyena.

"The worst part," B.J. said, "is that those guys get to thump their chests and say they were right about dumb women pilots."

Maxwell looked at the two pilots. Cheever and Miller were the worst of the alien-haters. Each had gone out of his way to make life miserable for the women pilots. One was probably the phantom caller. "Don't worry about them. I happen to know that each of those guys has made dumber mistakes. We all have. It's part of learning to be a fighter pilot."

"I know you're trying to make me feel better. Thank you."

Maxwell folded the napkin and gave it to her. He rose to leave. "You'll get another shot at it. You're gonna do just fine, B.J. Believe it."

B.J. managed a smile. "Okay, Brick. I'll try."

"So you kicked some butt over at Al-Kharj yesterday."

"Yes, sir," said Maxwell. "And we took out all their fighter assets."

A broad grin split the face of Admiral Joshua Lawrence Dunn. He refilled both their wineglasses. "I love it," he said. "The way they're telling it at JTF, it was a damn turkey shoot. Both the ACE and the Fifth Fleet Commander were over there rubbing the Air Force's noses in it. They say you suckered in those F-15s like ducks to a blind." Dunn cracked up thinking about it.

Josh Dunn was a gangling, six-foot-four former attack pilot who had flown 140 missions over North Vietnam. Having survived to command a squadron, an air wing, a carrier division, and, ultimately, the U.S.

Navy's Sixth Fleet, Dunn was in the twilight of his forty-year career.

"I can't wait to tell your old man about this," he said. "Harlan Maxwell's boy—leading the whole goddamn large force exercise, and kicking their asses from here to Riyadh. He's gonna swell up like a toad."

"Probably not. Dad's still mad because I left NASA to come back to the fleet."

Dunn nodded. "Well, that's the way fathers are. He was so proud that his kid was an astronaut. When you walked away from the space shuttle program, it nearly broke his heart."

Maxwell remembered. It was almost a year ago now, but the phone call was still vivid in his mind. His father, a retired rear admiral, had been incredulous. "Sam, for Christ's sake, think it over. Everything you've worked and studied for. I know you've suffered a loss, but trust me, son, you'll get over it and . . ."

Suffered a loss. Yes, recalled Maxwell, that he had. But his father had been wrong about one thing. He wouldn't get over it. Some things you didn't get over. What happened on the cape was burned into his memory. What he had lost was irreplaceable.

He never wanted to fly into space again.

Josh Dunn took a sip from his wineglass. "So tell me. How's it going in your new squadron?"

"Oh, pretty good," Maxwell said carefully.

"Getting along with the famous Killer DeLancey?"

Maxwell couldn't tell if Dunn was fishing, or just making conversation. He took the cautious route. "More or less." You didn't spill your guts to a three-star admiral, even if he was like your uncle.

"Not what I hear. Back at OpNav the rumor is the

MiG shoot last week put you and DeLancey in a major pissing contest."

"We had a disagreement about rules of engagement."

Dunn tilted back in his chair and looked around the room. A pair of crystal chandeliers bathed the room in a soft yellow light. The only other guests in the Dubai Hilton dining room were a party of a half-dozen Europeans having a quiet dinner and a couple of Arab businessmen huddled over coffee.

"DeLancey served under me during the Kosovo operation," said Dunn. "I was running CarGru Eight. I wanted to court-martial the sonofabitch for violating the ROE, but I got overruled. He had patrons high up in the Navy Department. Goddamn civilians who thought he wore a mask and a cape. So he got decorated and promoted instead."

Maxwell nodded. Some things never changed, he thought. "Sounds like Killer."

"All I'm saying is you better watch your six o'clock. A commanding officer like that will ruin your career. Don't trust the sonofabitch."

Maxwell had to smile at that one. *Don't trust Killer DeLancey?* The one thing you could trust about DeLancey was that you couldn't trust him. "I'm watching my six o'clock."

The admiral regarded him for a moment, then he leaned across the table and lowered his voice. "Listen, Sam, I'll deny I ever said this. But I can arrange for you to get orders to another squadron. It would solve everyone's problem. DeLancey will give you an unsatisfactory fitness report and ruin your chances of getting your own command someday."

"No, sir," said Maxwell so quickly he surprised him-

self. "I appreciate what you want to do. I have to deal
with Killer my way."

"What way is that?"

Good question, thought Maxwell. He had no idea.
But he couldn't allow a high-ranking friend of his father's to bail him out. "I'm going to do my job the
best I can. I'll let the system take care of the rest."

"Killer *is* the system. He'll derail your career."

Maxwell shook his head. "Thanks for the offer,
Admiral."

Dunn sighed and leaned back in his chair. "I knew
you'd say that." For several seconds he stared into
his wineglass. "You know something? You're just as
pigheaded as your old man."

Claire Phillips waited at a cabana table, sipping a
vodka tonic. She glanced at her watch again. How long
had she been sitting here? Twenty minutes? Damn,
she thought, a cigarette would taste wonderful. Never
mind that she had given up smoking three months
ago. Why was she nervous? *Come on, girl, get a grip.*

It was past eight o'clock. She wondered if he had
gotten the note she left with the concierge, who promised to deliver it to Commander Maxwell's room.

11 A.M., 16 May
  Dear Boy Astronaut,
  *We have a date, remember? I'm in town to cover
a press conference at the ambassador's residence
at seven. Then I'm free (for dinner, I mean). Let's
meet in the Hilton Cabana bar at eight.*
  Love,
  Cub Reporter

The press conference, just as she expected, was a god-awful waste of time. The ambassador was a wealthy California automobile dealer and a political crony of the President. He was famous for convening these events for no other purpose than to have himself videotaped in the presence of visiting dignitaries. The dignitaries in this case amounted to a couple of admirals and their staffs, and that self-promoting twit, Whitney Babcock.

That was okay. As Claire well knew, out here in the Gulf journalism and politics were intertwined. Someday she would be asking for the ambassador's help with a breaking story, and she would have credit. She would see to it that the ambassador's pointless news conference got coverage. She showed up at six-thirty with her producer and two cameramen. The conference amounted to a pronouncement by the ambassador about how the U.S. Navy intended to protect oil tankers, regardless of their flag, as they transited the Persian Gulf.

Mercifully, the pronouncement had been brief. Claire interviewed the ambassador, making sure to mention the dignitaries, then capturing all their beaming faces on videotape. She thanked everyone and got the hell out.

In the cabana bar, the white-jacketed waiter came by her table. She ordered another vodka tonic. The cabana was swathed in light from the array of Japanese lanterns strung in the palms. Half a dozen guests—three men and three women—were sitting at the long, curved bar. A lone musician in a safari shirt was producing warbling electronic music with his keyboard.

The drinks were beginning to settle her now. She'd

finish this one, and if he didn't show up, she'd pack it in. That was a bizarre turn, she reflected. Her journalistic beat—the Middle East, Europe, Southeast Asia—was filled with men, many of whom were powerful and well known, who would kill to meet her, take her out, just be seen with her.

Right, she thought. *So why are you sitting here by yourself waiting for—*

He stepped into the cabana. She saw him pause for a moment, standing in the light of the lanterns, peering around. Claire's heartbeat quickened.

Watching him, she wondered again, What was it about him? He wasn't especially handsome, at least not in a conventional way. He had that craggy face, with high cheekbones and those riveting blue eyes. His lanky, narrow-waisted build made him look more like some kind of athlete—ski bum or a tennis pro—than a career naval officer.

He spotted her. In long strides he came to her table. "Claire, I'm really sorry. I couldn't make it any sooner."

"That's okay," she heard herself saying. "I just got here myself."

He flagged down the waiter, and they ordered more drinks. The moon, Maxwell pointed out, was just coming up over the eastern wall of the hotel courtyard. Why didn't they stay right there for dinner? Through a bottle of Pinot Grigio and a dinner of calamari and grilled swordfish, they talked about the old days—Washington, D.C., Patuxent River, the little bar they loved in Georgetown, the quaint way the fishermen spoke out on Tangier Island. And old friends they both knew.

"Where's Devo?" Claire asked. "I heard you two were in the same squadron again."

"Devo? Yes, he's here. He—he said to say hello, but he'd had a long day. He probably hit the sack."

She noticed the hesitation. "Eileen? Are they still—"

"Splitting up. Devo's not handling it well."

She nodded. She gathered by his voice that he didn't want to pursue the subject. Eileen Davis, she remembered, was a girl who demanded a lot of attention. It wasn't surprising that she would be discontented with a husband who spent half his life at sea. Claire wondered again how it might have been if she and Sam had stayed together.

She tried getting him to talk about the situation in Iraq. Maxwell artfully dodged the specifics of what the *Reagan* and its battle group might do. She kept trying.

"Okay, Sam, just tell me one thing."

"Maybe. What?"

"You were there that day your skipper shot down the MiG in the No Fly Zone?"

"Yes. And?"

"Why didn't you shoot the other MiG?"

Bogey!

Possible target, not yet identified. DeLancey was the only one who saw it.

The Roadrunner BAG and GAG patrol was making an early return to base. The three—DeLancey, Miller, Cheever—had decided to cut their losses and head for the admin on the seventh floor. At least the booze was cheap, even if the women were nil. But DeLancey was still scanning for targets of opportunity.

Crossing the Hilton lobby, DeLancey saw something

interesting in the corner of the bar, like a distant target against the horizon. He said nothing, and kept it to himself.

"Listen, guys," he said. "Go up and put some music on. I gotta make a phone call, then I'll be along."

He waited until the elevator door closed on Miller and Cheever. Then he retraced his route across the lobby, to the bar on the mezzanine. He saw a long, shiny blond mane and a short skirt. He couldn't see her face—her back was to him—but she was showing a considerable length of tan legs.

He pressed on in. As he closed the distance, DeLancey began to notice she looked very much like . . . but it couldn't be . . .

It was.

Spam Parker was perched on one of the high stools at the bar, talking to some guy whom DeLancey vaguely recognized. He was a lieutenant commander from CAG staff, an NFO—Naval Flight Officer—who sometimes back-seated with the EA-6B squadron.

DeLancey stood there for a few seconds sizing up the situation. It was trouble, he thought. He should just walk away, go back to the elevators, and up to the admin. A voice inside him reminded him that nothing good could come from this.

But what the hell. It wouldn't hurt to look.

She turned and saw him. "Skipper! I was wondering where you were."

She was wearing a short black leather skirt—one of the tight minis that women were not allowed to exhibit in public in Arab countries, even in a liberal Muslim state like Dubai. She had on a thin white halter that showed she had no interest in a bra, which would have gotten her into even more trouble on the street.

Christ, thought DeLancey. Who would have thought she looked like *that* outside of her baggy flight suit? The woman had the body of an amazon. And she was showing it off for the benefit of this google-eyed back-seat puke. The guy was swilling his beer and looking at her like a kid having his first wet dream.

She'd had a lot to drink, he could tell. Her tone had that breezy familiarity. Too breezy, too sexy for a junior officer to be using with her CO. But that was Parker's style. Like the miniskirt and the halter.

"Tom Batchelder," said the NFO, extending his hand. He was a friendly young man, tall and slender with a brown crew cut, wearing an Izod sport shirt over Dockers khakis. "CAG staff."

DeLancey eyeballed him. He ignored the proffered handshake. "I'm Killer DeLancey," he said. "Her commanding officer." Intimidate, then liquidate, he always figured. Get the skirmishing over with.

The NFO blinked, suddenly worried. His eyes darted up and down the bar. He was sensing clear and present danger, and it was time for a quick reassessment.

"Uh-oh, look at the time." He made an exaggerated study of his enormous wrist chronometer. "I've got to cut and run. I'm late to meet someone upstairs." He slammed down the rest of his beer. "See ya, Spam. And, uh, it was really nice meeting you, Commander."

Spam waited until the NFO had made his retreat. "Wow! Do you always intimidate people that way?"

"Just protecting you."

She giggled and took a sip of her drink. "Is that what a skipper is supposed to do? Protect his women pilots from horny CAG staff officers?"

"A good skipper looks after his own."

She gave him a knowing look, then leaned forward a little. "You know something, Killer—it's okay if I call you Killer, isn't it? I have an enormous respect for you. And you're such a clever and persuasive man. I'm so glad I'm in your squadron."

There it was again. She had just ratcheted the familiarity level up another notch. He knew she was stroking his ego, but he didn't mind. She was just being female.

Spam stirred her drink with her finger, then inserted the finger into her mouth. With her eyes locked on his, she withdrew her finger, leaving it against her pursed lips. She curled her fingers into a ball and rested her chin on it.

DeLancey was getting a signal from his internal radar. There was distinct danger here. He should just get the hell out of here. But he was feeling a surge in his groin.

"I don't suppose it occurred to you," he said, "that that's a very sexy outfit you're wearing."

"Really?" She batted her eyelashes again and looked down at the leather skirt. "This old thing?" She laughed and recrossed her legs. "Do you think it's too . . . flashy?"

"The locals might get upset. But that's their problem."

"Does that mean you approve?"

He didn't answer right away. He made a show of examining her legs. They were bare and surprisingly tan. He eyeballed her tiny skirt, her thin cotton halter.

"Yeah," he said finally. "You pass the DeLancey test."

"That's good." She leaned forward again, giving

him a view down the front of the halter. "Because I really want you to like me, Killer. And not just as an officer. You know what I mean?"

DeLancey knew what she meant. And it definitely exceeded the rules of engagement. But there were times, he told himself, when you had to break the rules. No guts, no glory.

DeLancey waved the bartender over and signed the tab. He and Spam exchanged looks. No words were needed. Her eyes, gray, half-closed, said it all.

She nodded, and they rose together. Keeping a discreet distance between them, they made their way across the lobby, to the elevator. She waited primly while he pushed 6.

The doors closed.

They lunged at each other. For twenty-five seconds, while the elevator ascended to the sixth floor, they pulled at each other's bodies. They kissed, groped, rubbed, fondled, stroked, until—

Ding. The door opened on the sixth floor and the outside world reappeared. A middle-aged European couple stood there, regarding them curiously. Resuming their three-foot separation, DeLancey and Spam made a wobbly but dignified exit from the elevator. They walked down the hallway in a stately promenade.

To Room 612. DeLancey made a quick check in each direction. All clear.

He unlocked the door and let them in.

Thunk! She kicked the door closed and pressed her body into him. "I know I shouldn't be here," she said in a throaty voice. "I don't care. I want you. I've wanted you since that day I first saw you . . ."

*   *   *

Brick and Claire sat in the sand at the water's edge.

Over a distant loudspeaker they heard a muezzin wailing the morning call to prayer. The eastern sky was glowing orange, gold, and pink. Overhead, Venus was a brilliant dot, offset by the sliver of a crescent moon—the symbol of Islam.

In the harbor, an ancient dhow was getting under way, drawing a V-shaped wake through the glassy water. Barely visible in the distance was the gray shape of the USS *Ronald Reagan*. Maxwell knew that the crew of the warship—those who were not ashore in Dubai—would be getting about the business of the day.

She broke the silence. "You miss it when you're not there, don't you?"

Maxwell nodded. She was reading his mind again.

It was like the time five years before, when they first met. They had talked until the sun came up. With Claire, it was easy, he remembered. It was natural.

They talked about the good times, her passage through the labyrinthine world of international reporting. He told her more about his time at NASA. They hung on each other's stories, filling in the gaps of the past five years. By silent agreement they steered around the bad parts. There would be time for that later.

Claire was different in one way, he noticed. She seemed to possess an inner confidence that she lacked before. During the journey from cub reporter to becoming one of the top print broadcast journalists in the business, she had acquired self-assurance. She was not particularly happy, Maxwell guessed. He didn't know why; maybe it was just a look in her eyes. Perhaps, he thought, she would tell him.

Claire leaned forward and scooped a handful of
sand across her bare feet. Maxwell watched her, noticing the smooth curve of her legs from her ankles, past
her knees to her thighs, up to the hem of her dress.

Looking at her bare legs, he remembered something. It was a vision that had remained in his memory
for the past five years like a secret treasure.

"Do you still have the scarf?" he asked.

She looked surprised. She shook her head and said,
"No. Not after we broke up."

He remembered now. They were at her apartment
in Georgetown. It was her birthday, and he was taking
her to dinner. He surprised her with a gift.

He still saw the excitement in her eyes when she
unwrapped the package. The scarf was silk, with gold
brocade and a floral pattern. She held it up to the
light. Tears sprang to her eyes, and she said, "Oh,
Sam, that is . . . absolutely . . . the loveliest gift I have
ever received."

She kissed him. Then, impulsively, she declared that
she would wear it that very evening. But first she
wanted to run upstairs and change.

Maxwell waited for her to come back. He waited
for what seemed a long time, but was, in fact only five
minutes. Finally, she appeared at the top of the stairs.

Maxwell had to catch his breath.

"Well," she said. "Do you like it?"

Claire was wearing the new silk scarf around her
neck. And nothing else.

"I like it," he said as he ascended the stairs.

They never made it to dinner.

"You're staring, Sam."

Her voice returned him to the present. "Sorry. You
caught me."

She brushed the sand off her feet and tugged the dress over her knees.

"Do you still think I'm pretty?"

Maxwell looked at her face. She was peering at him the way she used to back in the old days, with that quizzical, teasing expression. He remembered how much he had loved that look. He hadn't expected ever to see it again.

He was feeling an unmistakable stirring inside him. It was good to be next to her, sitting with her like this. He wondered if she felt the same way.

"Yes," he said. "I think you're prettier than ever."

Claire moved closer to him and laid her head on his shoulder. "I like that," she said.

They fell silent again.

The red-orange ball burst above the rim of the sea. At the same time, a breeze rippled from the water, wisping Claire's closely cropped chestnut hair. The morning air was turning warm and balmy, a prelude to the day's desert heat.

Claire said, "So you're not going to tell me what happened?"

That was the other thing about Claire he remembered. The relentless curiosity. "Happened? When?"

"Don't tease. You were in the No-Fly-Zone the day of the MiG shoot-down."

"You already know. One MiG-29 down. The other bugged out. End of story."

Claire eyed him skeptically. "So Sam Maxwell, astronaut-turned-fighter-pilot, didn't shoot down the MiG?"

"Did you stay up all night with me because you wanted to be with me, or because you needed a story?"

"Both." She squeezed his hand. "But I'll settle for just being with you."

He looked in her eyes for any trace of insincerity. Claire was a good reporter—and a hell of an interrogator. Maybe she was just pumping him for a story. But he was sure they had more between them than just a news story. He could feel an electricity.

"Let's make a deal. I'll ask the Command Intelligence Officer what I can and cannot say. Then I'll get official clearance from the Public Affairs Officer to talk to you."

She nodded excitedly. "Terrific. What's my half of the deal?"

"It might be expensive."

"Anything you want."

He liked that answer. He gave her a grin, and she grinned back.

"Dinner first," she said.

"No more interrogation?"

"No more interrogation." Then she reconsidered. "Well, maybe a little. No more than necessary."

He gave it a second, pretending to deliberate. "Sounds like a deal."

They stood up and brushed the sand off.

"Well, since you've kept me up all night, why don't you take me to breakfast? I'd kiss you for a coffee and a croissant."

"Another deal."

They kissed, then held it several moments longer than necessary. Claire stepped back and peered at him. "Whew," she said. "You haven't forgotten anything, have you?"

*　　　*　　　*

DeLancey needed a break.

Actually, he decided, what he needed was a transfusion. Never in his career had he encountered a female with such prodigious sexual energy. She had used him like a stud animal. Then she wanted more. More to drink, more attention, more sex. She was insatiable.

He needed to get the hell away.

Getting her out of his room was difficult enough. She was ready for a matinee session, and he just didn't have it in him. Anyway, he was sober enough to start worrying. What if his wife called? These phones didn't have caller ID. Who might stop by his room? That was all he needed, CAG or some flag staff puke or, worse, some journalist to catch him shacked up with one of his female officers.

So he suddenly remembered he had a ten o'clock meeting with CAG. He ushered Spam and her black miniskirt out into the hall.

"Will I see you tonight?" she wanted to know.

"Sure. I'll give you a call this afternoon."

"You know my room? 842?"

"Yeah. Let's meet in the admin. About four or so, okay?"

He closed the door and leaned against it.

His skull ached from all the scotch. They'd gone through a fifth and a half. It was crazy, he thought. Dangerous, reckless, irresponsible. Suicidal even.

Why did he do it?

Simple. Because it was the most mind-blowing erotic encounter he'd ever had. Parker represented his wildest sex fantasies bundled into one steaming, pulsating package.

It occurred to him that he was probably the latest

in a series of career-advancing studs she had used like this. *What if she talks?*

He didn't want to think about it. He needed a beer. That was the best way to clear your head after an all-nighter. Get some air, slam down a beer or two, you'd be ready again.

DeLancey dressed, went to the elevator, and rode it to the lobby. He hadn't bothered to shave. He was wearing wrinkled chinos and a polo shirt. It didn't matter. It was early, and no one would be in the bar yet.

Passing the coffee shop, he caught the scent of strong Arabian java. That was what he needed—coffee and a Danish to get his heart started.

Then he stopped. Sitting inside the shop was Maxwell, talking to some babe.

Curious, DeLancey stepped inside. He recognized her—that Phillips woman who interviewed him on the ship after the MiG kill. She was wearing some kind of sexy sundress that showed off nice cleavage. She was engrossed in conversation with his least favorite squadron officer, Maxwell.

Okay, time for some command presence. He put on the Hollywood smile and moved in.

Maxwell said, "Claire, you remember my commanding officer, John DeLancey?"

"Just call me Killer." DeLancey shook her hand, holding it longer than necessary.

Claire regarded him with interest. "Of course I remember you, Killer. You were a good subject."

DeLancey slid his bar stool in closer, inserting himself between Claire and Brick. "Anytime I can help you, just let me know. If you'd like, I'll arrange another shipboard news conference." He took an appreciative glance at her crossed legs. "As long as Saddam keeps sending me MiGs, I'll keep shooting them down."

"It shouldn't be too difficult if they're all like the last one."

DeLancey looked at her quizzically. "The last one? The Iraqi pilot entered the No-Fly-Zone with hostile intent."

"Not what I hear. I understand he was a student fighter pilot on his first operational mission."

The smile stayed frozen on DeLancey's face. "What are you talking about?"

"Hakim Al-Fariz. He was probably lost and strayed over the boundary when you shot him down."

"How would you know that?"

"I'm a journalist. It's my business to know such things."

"Look, Miss Phillips—"

"Just call me Claire." She smiled and recrossed her legs."

"I don't know who's been telling you that crap." He looked pointedly at Maxwell. "But I can guess."

Maxwell caught the accusation. "Claire has sources all over the place."

DeLancey looked at each of them. "What the hell is this? *60 Minutes* or something?" He glowered at Maxwell. "It looks to me like you've been passing classified information to the media."

"Not at all," Claire said. "Commander Maxwell hasn't told me anything." She reached over and squeezed Maxwell's hand. "Despite my best efforts."

DeLancey stood up. The Hollywood smile was gone. "I wish I could say it was nice seeing you again,

Miss Phillips. By the way, the offer for another interview is canceled. Commander Maxwell, you and I will
talk later."

They watched DeLancey march out into the lobby
and disappear.

"So that's the real Killer DeLancey," said Claire."

"The one and only."

"He's rather handsome actually. Shorter than he
seemed when I interviewed him. Probably has a Napo-
leon complex. A shame that he's such a pompous ass."

Maxwell had to grin at that. "Didn't take you long
to figure him out."

"And he's your commanding officer. Too bad." She
looked at him. "I hope you realize that the man hates
your guts."

"I sometimes get that impression."

"Are you going to tell me why?"

For a moment Maxwell considered telling her what
happened that first night of the Gulf War. It would
be a relief to share the truth with someone. Someone
he cared about.

"No," he said finally.

DeLancey raged as he rode the elevator back to the
sixth floor. *The snotty bitch!* The kind that would cut
your throat while she's giving you that phony smile.

In his room, he went directly to the phone. He rang
up Bouncer Oswald, a Navy commander who ran the
intelligence staff for the Joint Task Force.

"Claire Phillips?" said Oswald. "She's married to a
guy named Tyrwhitt. We call him 'Baghdad Ben,' because he writes bullshit about how we're killing all the
poor malnourished children of Iraq. Every time we hit
one of their SAM sites, he says we're bombing some

school or orphanage. And she's the one who somehow picked up the story about the pissing contest between the Air Force and the Navy over the MiG shoot last month."

"Besides her husband, where does she get her material?"

"She's a woman, isn't she? I hear she's not bad-looking."

DeLancey smiled. "What would you say if one of our air wing officers turned out to be sleeping with her?"

Oswald didn't answer right away. "You trying to tell me something, Killer?"

"Maybe."

"I'd say we got ourselves an informer."

ELEVEN

Recall

Dusk was settling over the delta.

From the cockpit of his F-16 Viper, Captain Catfish Bass could see only a continuous blanket of cloud. Beneath the cloud deck lay the wide marshy valley of the Tigris River. To the east stretched the border of Iran. To the west, Iraq and the disputed No-Fly-Zone.

For two hours the four U. S. Air Force F-16s and their escort, a Marine EA-6B Prowler, had been on station. Twice now they had plugged into a KC-10 refueling tanker.

They were skimming the eastern rim of the No-Fly-Zone, near Basra, on a routine patrol. Ironclaw, the Grumman EA-6B, was busy probing and cataloguing the emissions coming from Iran. Nothing had come up except an occasional hit from Iran's IADS—Integrated Air Defense System.

Situation normal. Nothing from the known sites in Iraq.

That was smart of them, thought Bass. Each of the F-16s was carrying a HARM missile—a radar-seeking weapon—which they were authorized to fire if they received a warning that an air defense site had locked them up.

Bass and his flight leader, Major Scrapes Williams, had just left the tanker. The second pair of Vipers was taking their place, plugging into the refueling boom. That was the preferred way to conduct the NFZ patrols—two on, two off. If someone got into a fight, he had a fresh pair of F-16s ready to cover him.

Bass peered down at the cloud layer directly beneath. He hoped Scrapes had a good handle on their position. Somewhere in the vicinity of Basra was an SA-3 ring. SA-3s were an old variety of Russian-built surface-to-air missiles. Primitive, but still lethal if you gave them an easy shot.

He didn't like flying low and slow over a cloud deck, especially one that overlay enemy SAM sites. Bass knew the F-16's RWR would pick up an inbound SAM, and he was fairly sure the EA-6B, with its array of electronic warfare equipment, could jam the enemy's control radar. Still, it was better when you could see the damned things coming at you.

Bass glanced at his nav display—then looked again. Shit! A shot of adrenaline surged through him.

"Scrapes," he radioed, "check our position. I show us five south of Basra."

"Negative. We're now twenty—uh-oh. Stand by."

Bass was getting a bad feeling. He saw Williams's Viper begin a hard left turn.

"Coming back to the south," called Williams. "I, uh, plugged the wrong waypoint in the inertial."

Bass stayed with him, flying a combat spread formation. Fucking beautiful, he thought. Scrapes was taking them *right over* the goddamn SA-3 ring. That wouldn't be so bad if they were hauling ass at five hundred plus knots. But they were poking along at a leisurely two-sixty to conserve fuel. And the Ironclaw was probably not watching that close because . . .

Eeeooowweeowww!

His RWR. It was warbling.

"Burner Three Hot!" came the warning from the Ironclaw.

An SA-3 was in the air.

Bass heard the warble change in his headset. *Two SA-3s!*

Scrapes heard it too. Bass saw the lead F-16 roll out of the turn, begin to crank the other way, then reverse. Scrapes was confused.

Then Bass saw it—the SA-3—popping out of the cloud deck. It looked like a telephone pole trailing a long plume of fire.

The missile was drawing a bead on Scrapes Williams.

"Hard left, Jugs Lead!" the Electronic Warfare Officer in the Ironclaw called, using their flight call sign. "Hard left now!"

Williams got the message. It was definitely time to get out of Dodge. The afterburner of Williams's jet ignited. The F-16 honked into a maximum-G turn. Bass stayed with him, selecting his own afterburner and opening the chaff dispenser.

Then he saw that Williams had forgotten to put out his own chaff—confetti-like metal foil that obscured targets on radar. "Chaff, Scrapes!" he yelled on the radio.

A second later, a cloud of chaff appeared in the wake of Williams's hard-turning Viper.

It was working. The SA-3 stopped flying a pursuit curve, and was veered onto a path perpendicular to

Williams's fighter. The missile wobbled, then tilted over in a ballistic arc.

Bass took a deep breath. Jesus, that was close . . .

Another warning: *Eeeeoowww!*

The second missile erupted from the clouds like a fiery comet. It was flying a perfect pursuit curve. But this SA-3 was not aimed at the lead F-16.

It was locked on to Catfish Bass.

Bass dropped the nose of his jet and pulled harder. Eight and a half Gs. Nine.

Even in full afterburner, the F-16 was losing airspeed in the hard turn. *Turn! Turn inside the missile!*

He pulled until the jet shuddered. It wasn't enough. The SA-3 now had an energy advantage. Bass tried to tighten the turn. The missile was nearly within detonation range.

BLAM! The concussion came from behind.

Bass could feel pieces departing his jet. The SA-3 warhead had detonated close to the tail, he guessed.

Bass saw the fire warning light come on. The F-16 skidded, then went into a sickening roll. The control stick went dead.

"Mayday! Mayday!" Bass yelled in the radio. He reached for the ejection handle.

Maxwell awoke in the early afternoon, possessed by an idea. He had a mission to perform. He would have to hurry before the market closed. He dressed in a hurry and left the hotel.

The souk in old Dubai was just as he remembered it. All the wares of the Middle East were for sale in the vendors' stalls—carpets, gold, leather goods, T-shirts, sandals, live poultry.

Maxwell wandered through the rows of stalls, perusing the merchandise, until he found the kiosk he was looking for. He examined each of the scarves, holding them up to the light. Finally he found a scarf that was very close to the one he remembered. It was black, with gold stitching and the image of a bird in flight.

"How much?" he asked the leather-faced vendor.

"For you, three hundred dirhams."

It was a bargain, but the vendor would be insulted if he did not at least negotiate. Maxwell countered with an offer of one hundred dirhams. The vendor came back with two-fifty. Finally a deal was struck at two hundred Emirian dirhams, which amounted to about seventy-five dollars. For an extra ten dirhams, the vendor agreed to gift-wrap the scarf.

When Maxwell returned to the hotel, a message was waiting for him. He was to call the Air Wing Duty Officer.

He couldn't believe it. "Damn!" Maxwell grumbled into the phone. "Why?"

"Can't say," said Frisby, the duty officer. "But it's no drill. Everyone's due back by six o'clock."

Something had happened. No one knew anything, only that the party was over. The *Reagan* was sailing.

Maxwell could imagine the groaning going on throughout Dubai at that moment. After nearly a month of continuous flight operations, working twelve- and fourteen-hour days, the crew of the USS *Reagan* had been in port exactly three days. It was supposed to be a time for relaxation, partying, chilling out, forgetting about the requirements of the United States Navy and the USS *Ronald Reagan* and the politics of the Persian Gulf.

Instead, an emergency sortie. The *Reagan* was headed to sea.

Maxwell knew the drill. All hands ashore were being ordered back to their stations. In a mass migration toward the fleet landing, two thousand sailors and officers would come walking, riding, staggering, and in some instances being hauled comatose to the utility boats that would shuttle them out to the carrier. As always, a few enterprising sailors would get wind of the recall and lie low. *No, sir, I swear. Never knew a thing about it till I saw the ship headin' out . . .*

Maxwell called Claire's number. She didn't answer. He left a message with the concierge, letting her know their date was on hold. He promised he would E-mail her from the ship.

He took his place in the line of disgruntled officers waiting to check out of the Hilton. No one was happy.

"Another fucking exercise," said a pilot from the Tomcat squadron.

"It's punishment," said a young lieutenant. "We were having too much fun."

"It's our commander in chief," said a lieutenant commander from the S-3 squadron. "He got caught with his pants down again. This means war."

Maxwell's taxi pulled up to the landing. More than two hundred sailors and several dozen officers were already clustered on the concrete pier waiting for the next boat. In the evening twilight, the temperature had cooled.

Waiting on the landing when he stepped from the cab was Claire Phillips. She wore a Levi's jacket over a polka-dot dress.

"You heard the news," he said.

"I deliver the news, remember? I couldn't let you go without saying good-bye."

"Sorry about our date tonight."

"I had you for one whole evening. That's a beginning."

She gave him an impulsive kiss. Then he noticed Killer DeLancey and Hozer Miller at the edge of the landing. They were watching him curiously.

Another gray 120-man utility boat came gliding up to the pier. A boatswain's mate snubbed the bowline to the dock. Sailors lined up to step onto the loading ladder.

"You're the reporter," Brick said. "What's going on? Did something happen?"

"Yes. Something happened. And I can guess what's going to happen next."

Then she leaned forward and told him, very quietly, what happened that afternoon to cause the USS *Reagan* to haul anchor and put to sea.

Brick listened, nodding. When she finished telling him the news, he glanced over at the crowd. Most of the clustered sailors and officers had boarded the utility boat.

Except DeLancey. He was still there, staring at them.

Suddenly Maxwell remembered the package. He pulled it from his carryall bag. "I, uh, was going to give you this at dinner tonight. I know it's not your birthday."

She felt the package, recognizing its contents. "It will be. Come back to me in one piece, Sam."

TWELVE

Jabbar

(SYNDICATED WIRE SERVICE,
17 MAY, BAGHDAD
BY CHRISTOPHER TYRWHITT)

BAGHDAD, Iraq—Iraqi military officials reported the downing of an American Air Force F-16 Viper Friday morning during a predawn incursion of Iraq's airspace near the southern No-Fly-Zone. An Iraqi official declared that the American jet was destroyed by an anti-aircraft missile battery, which returned fire when attacked by the American jets. The only reported damage, the official said, was to a clearly-marked school building.

A U.S. State Department spokesperson has confirmed the loss of the jet, adding that the pilot safely ejected and was rescued soon after the incident.

Tensions have heightened along the United Nations-imposed No-Fly-Zone since the downing last month of an Iraqi MiG-29 interceptor jet by U.S. Navy jets flown from the aircraft carrier USS Ronald Reagan. The fate of the Iraqi pilot has not been disclosed.

Since the imposition of the No-Fly-Zones after the end of the Gulf War in 1991, American and British warplanes have frequently targeted Iraqi air defense sites. Today's action was apparently a continuation of the stepped-up pressure on the Iraqi air defense system.

President Saddam Hussein has sworn retaliation for such hostile acts by United States forces, and the downing of the American fighter was hailed in Iraq's press as a confirmation of his resolve.

It was incredible, thought Colonel Jabbar. He was alive.

Not only was he alive, he was flying.

Had Jabbar been a true believer, which he was not, he might have attributed this miracle to the Divine Being. This would seem to be an undeniable instance of intervention by Allah. That Colonel Jabbar's life had been spared at the very moment of his execution by firing squad was simply too miraculous for any other explanation.

Except, of course, for one. The sudden reversal of his fate as he stood facing the loaded carbines of the Republican Guard was exactly the sort of capricious melodrama that Saddam loved to orchestrate. Immediate death sentences, instant reprieves—all were rendered and reversed in the presidential court of Saddam Hussein like alternating weather reports.

But here he was, alive. And flying again.

Jabbar nudged the MiG's throttles forward a notch. Beneath him swept the monotonous brown desert of western Iraq. To his right, stepped up a thousand feet, was his wingman, Captain Suluman Faisal.

They were flying low and fast, skimming the floor of the desert at a speed of over eight hundred kilometers per hour. Faisal was his safety pilot, peering out ahead for danger while Jabbar concentrated on low-level navigation. Faisal was a competent airman, unlike the hapless Captain Al-Fariz, deceased nephew of Saddam.

Faisal, of course, was not happy about today's training mission. He had been told nothing about the purpose of the mission, nor what sort of munitions delivery they were simulating. Like most fighter pilots, Faisal preferred to be up in the stratosphere where they were supposed to engage enemy fighters. Instead, they were hurtling across dunes and dwarf trees like lowly air-to-ground attack pilots.

"Be alert, Red Lead," came Faisal's voice on the tactical frequency. "Vehicles ahead, twelve o'clock, three kilometers."

"Red Lead is looking."

Jabbar peered through his windscreen. *What are they? Military trucks? One of the Shiite caravans on the move . . .*

He spotted a column of dust. Half a dozen rickety trucks with homemade containers strapped to the beds were bumping down the unpaved road. Smugglers, probably, hauling contraband on their return trip from the Kurdish-held territory near the Turkish border.

Jabbar dipped the MiG's right wing, altering course just enough that he would go blasting directly over the column. The trucks were moving eastward. They wouldn't see the fighters bearing down on them from behind.

Jabbar dropped the MiG down until he was no more than fifty feet over the tops of the trucks.

Closer . . . closer . . . Jabbar saw a passenger in the back of the truck look up, suddenly spot the fighters. His mouth opened . . .

Wharrrrooom! The MiG-29 roared over the truck column at nearly supersonic speed.

Jabbar pulled up and rolled the MiG into a vertical bank so he could look back over his shoulder. The lead truck had careened into a gully beside the road. The other trucks in the column were stopped. Their occupants were sprinting into the desert like ants from a mound.

Jabbar had to laugh. That would give them some excitement, he thought. Smuggling had become a routine business in Iraq since the sanctions. Now the terrified buggers would think that Saddam had sent attack jets out to seek and destroy their miserable vehicles. They wouldn't stop running until they'd put several kilometers between them and the convoy.

Jabbar returned his thoughts to the training mission. Back to low-altitude navigation, flying over the floor of the desert. Back to training for the real mission. Jabbar eased the MiG down again to a hundred feet above the sand.

Too bad, he thought, focusing his gaze on the landscape blurring past him. Too bad that the real mission wouldn't be as easy as sneaking up on smugglers. The real enemy would not be so easy to surprise. And most certainly the real enemy would not run for the desert like a frightened rabbit.

The thought filled Colonel Jabbar with a cold dread. It was why he had been spared from the firing squad. He had been given an assignment that was as deadly as standing before a squad of Republican Guard riflemen.

Jabbar still didn't know what weapon—or weapons—would be mounted on his MiG-29. But already he had managed to piece together parts of the puzzle, like an elaborate mosaic. He could deduce that it was almost certainly an air-launched missile. He was sure that it was a weapon that could be deployed from very low altitude at a distance of at least 350 kilometers from the target.

Now he was certain of another fact: The weapon possessed massive destructive power. Enough to obliterate a hundred-thousand-ton warship.

Walking toward the ready room, Maxwell could feel the movement of the ship under him.

The recall of the *Reagan*'s crew had been very successful. Fewer than a hundred sailors were unaccounted for, a statistic that amazed old hands who could remember when a recalled aircraft carrier would head to sea leaving a quarter of its complement behind in local brothels and bars.

One more way in which the New Navy was different, thought Maxwell.

When he entered the Roadrunner ready room, Undra Cheever, the squadron duty officer, was chewing on a doughnut. His face lit up when he saw Maxwell come into the ready room. "The skipper wants to see you in his office ASAP."

Maxwell nodded. It meant that DeLancey was back in attack mode.

After a quick coffee, he checked his mail, then headed up the passageway to DeLancey's office.

As usual, DeLancey didn't invite him to sit. He got right to the point. "You're a security risk, Maxwell. I'm going to have you relieved."

Maxwell had no idea what he was talking about. This was DeLancey's style, to lead with an outrageous statement. Throw you off balance before getting to the point.

"May I ask how you've determined that I'm a security risk?"

A knowing smile spread over DeLancey's face. "The Phillips woman. You've been screwing someone known to be antimilitary, then spilling classified information to her."

Maxwell's eyes rolled skyward. It explained the peculiar look DeLancey gave him while they were waiting back at the fleet landing for the boat. It was absurd.

"I presume you can prove this?"

"I don't have to. She's getting information from someone. It's you she's been with. That makes you a security risk. You can save yourself and the Navy a lot of trouble by simply resigning."

Maxwell was getting the picture. DeLancey wanted him to cave in and quit. He considered for a moment, then he reached for the telephone on DeLancey's desk. "Do you want to call the Judge Advocate General's office now?"

"JAG? Why?"

"You're going to be a defendant in a defamation case. If Miss Phillips doesn't do it, I promise you I will."

"This is the United States Navy. You can't sue your commanding officer."

"And you can't have an officer relieved because of your own perverted suspicions. I'll remind you, Killer, slander is a violation of the military code of justice." He picked up the phone and held it out to DeLancey. "Want me to make the call? Might as well get started."

The smile was gone from DeLancey's face. "Don't pull that lawyer shit with me. We both know that you're banging that reporter. And we both know that one way or another, I'm gonna get you busted out of here."

"Thanks for the warning, Skipper. Will that be all?"

DeLancey glowered at him in silence.

Maxwell turned on his heel and left.

"When?" Tyrwhitt asked.

"Soon. Two weeks. Perhaps a month."

"That's pretty indefinite."

"What do you expect?" the man snapped. "A printed timetable? This is Iraq."

"Of course. I'm sorry."

Tyrwhitt reminded himself to be careful. *Don't push too hard.* The man was obviously sensing danger. He might get spooked and run.

As arranged, they met in the old souk, the one in the north part of the city near the B'aath building. This time the man was already in the stall, examining carpets. He had purchased one cheap Persian and was fiddling with another.

He seemed more nervous edgy this time. Tyrwhitt gave him a moment to calm down. "Do you know the source?"

"North Korea. Probably by way of Afghanistan."

The usual suspects, thought Tyrwhitt. The fraternal brotherhood of terrorist countries.

"How are they delivered?" asked Tyrwhitt.

"Overland, by truck at night. You know about Iraq's oil business?"

"I thought Iraq was forbidden to export oil."

"It's quite clever, really," said the man. "They use these trucks with tanks welded to the long flat beds. Every night they transport the refined oil across the

desert. They deliver it to the Kurds in the north, Shiites in the south, to the Iranians in the northeast."

"Iraq's sworn enemies?"

The man shrugged. "Capitalism thrives in strange
circumstances." Tyrwhitt thought he glimpsed a wry
smile beneath the man's cloaked face. In the shad-
owed stall, he couldn't see the man's face clearly, but
that voice—yes, it could be. The colonel he met at the
minister's reception.

"They sell it at one-quarter the world price," the
man went on. "The oil is forwarded to depots in Turkey and Jordan and Iran and resold at twice the
amount. Everyone makes money. For the return trip,
the tanker trucks are flushed and converted to dry
cargo carriers. The trucks haul goods over the desert
back to Baghdad."

"What goods?"

"Items that the sanctions have denied Iraq. Everything from canned food to drugs to ammunition."

Tyrwhitt was beginning to get the picture. "And
missiles?"

"Of course."

It was so obvious—and workable. High-tech weaponry was being smuggled along the same ancient
routes used by nomadic traders for the past thousand years.

"Do you know what type?" Tyrwhitt asked.

"Kraits. The new long-range versions, manufactured
in China. They now have at least ten with mobile
surface launchers. I know of two more that have been
prepared for air launch."

Tyrwhitt tried to fix the numbers in his mind. The
information was too vital for him to get it wrong.
"What about warheads? Do they have any?"

The man didn't answer right away. "Everything the coalition suspected that Saddam had, he has."

"You mean—"

"Anthrax. Sarin gas. Botulinum toxin. Aflatoxin. Weaponized and ready for munitions delivery."

Tyrwhitt nodded. It was worse than he expected. Everyone knew that Saddam had biological weapons, despite the efforts of the United Nations inspection teams. But no one seriously believed that he had the means to deploy them. How could this be going on without the coalition's intelligence services picking it up? Or had they?

Great Christ Almighty, thought Tyrwhitt. Biological weapons, deployed aboard missiles. That meant urban and industrial targets. The populated centers of Iraq's enemies—Tel Aviv, Kuwait City, the military and commercial complexes of Saudi Arabia—all within range of the Krait missiles.

To use such weapons against civilians would be the most heinous crime in history. Surely Saddam knew that retribution would come from—

Tyrwhitt caught himself. There had to be more. Of course there was. Biological weapons would not be effective against well-prepared military sites, especially armored and movable sites like aircraft carriers.

There *was* more.

Tyrwhitt had to force himself to ask the next question. "You said 'everything the coalition suspected.' Does that mean Iraq possesses—"

"Nuclear warheads?" For the first time, the man looked directly at Tyrwhitt's face. He had brown, somber eyes. The intense brown eyes seemed to peer right into Tyrwhitt's thoughts. "Certainly. And he will use them." The man sniffed and turned his face away. "Tyrwhitt, must you always stink of whiskey?"

Don't let the bastards see you cry.

B.J. Johnson had to keep telling herself that. She was near the breaking point. She knew she should have expected something when she came into the ready room. She should have known by the way Undra Cheever and Hozer Miller were lurking in the front of the room, watching her like a couple of vultures.

The dirty tricks were getting dirtier. One day last week when she suited up for flying, she discovered that her torso harness—a nylon outer garment with fittings that attached the pilot to the Hornet's ejection seat—had a lacey push-up bra neatly sewn inside. She had forced a laugh and let it go. Frat boy stuff.

Then a few days later she found her flight suit bristling with white objects. They were tampons, protruding like white pennants from the sleeve pockets. Again she ignored it. She knew that if she threw a tantrum about such things, the bastards would never let up.

The anonymous phone calls—*one less trap than you have launches*—had stopped, but now she was getting these notes. They were the same stuff, nasty and anonymous. She hadn't shown them to Maxwell as he had requested. It would just make it worse, she thought, having a senior officer spring to her defense like a white knight. She would be branded as another wimpy female who couldn't take the heat.

As usual, she had entered through the back door of the ready room and gone directly to her chair. The chairs were airline-style recliners with the name patch of a squadron pilot Velcroed on the headrest. Beneath each chair was a drawer in which the pilot kept briefing sheets, kneeboards, personal gear. It was also a message drop.

The ready room was filled this morning. Killer De-Lancey was in the front of the room, on the phone with someone. Brick Maxwell was standing at a briefing table talking with Pearly Gates.

B.J. had opened the drawer beneath her chair. Inside the drawer lay an unfamiliar object—a cloth bag with a note attached. Without thinking, she immediately opened the bag. She took out the objects inside.

It was a pair of shiny steel balls.

She could feel Cheever's and Miller's eyes riveted on her as she read the attached note.

To the Alien,
   This is what you have been missing. The Navy forgot to issue them to you when they gave you wings. Wear these proudly.

A deathly silence had fallen over the ready room. She could feel every pilot's eyes on her. DeLancey was staring, a look of intense interest on his face. Maxwell had stopped what he was doing and was looking at her. B.J. wanted to hide. Cram the insulting note and the bag back inside the drawer. Slam it shut and get out of this hateful place.

It was too late. Everyone had seen her open the bag and read the note. Cheever and Miller were cracking up, chortling like a pair of baboons. The other pilots were gawking like rubberneckers at a car wreck. They were waiting, she realized, for her to break down. They expected her to scream, sob, go on a world-class crying jag. It would prove everything they held true about women pilots.

The truth was, that was exactly what she felt like doing at this moment. Her lower lip trembled. She couldn't deal with any more of this shit. *Wear these proudly.* All she wanted to do now was sit down and bury her face in her hands.

But she couldn't. Not here. *Don't let the bastards see you cry.* That was her mantra these days.

She looked around the room. Cheever and Miller were still cackling. Not much doubt about who the ball-donors were. Maxwell had figured it out too. His face was a dark mask, glowering at the two. If she didn't do something, the white knight was going to come out.

She did something. She held up the steel balls, letting everyone see them. Clacking them together in her right hand, she walked over to where Cheever and Miller were parked at the squadron duty desk. "Did you guys do this?"

They stared back at her. Neither answered. Even Maxwell was peering at her with curiosity.

She clacked the balls together again. Actually, she thought, she rather liked that hard metallic feel of the spheres in her hand. Clacking them together like that seemed to embolden her. What the hell, it worked for Captain Queeg, didn't it?

As she turned to exit the ready room, she looked again at Cheever and Miller. They weren't laughing. "Thanks, guys," she said. "Now I have the balls, and you don't."

*　　*　　*

No doubt about it, thought Whitney Babcock, studying his reflection in the mirror. He had that look about him, the look of a man destined to command.

He was wearing his favorite shipboard outfit—the starched military khakis with a web belt and a black name tag that bore a simple gold-embossed inscription:

Whit Babcock,
Undersecretary of the Navy.

He reminded himself to arrange some publicity photos in this outfit.

He turned from the mirror and faced Killer De-Lancey. "Maxwell? The ex-astronaut in your squadron?"

"That's him," said DeLancey. "He busted out of NASA, then his father got him orders to my squadron. CAG overrode my request to get rid of him, and now he's my operations officer."

"He's a security problem? How long has this been going on?"

"Quite a while, we think. We know he's been seeing the Phillips woman since Dubai, but probably long before that."

"You think she's pumping him for classified information?"

"I'm almost certain," said DeLancey. "But I don't want to jump to conclusions. He's still one of my officers. Rather than destroy his career with a scandal, I thought it would be best just to have him reassigned."

Babcock nodded. "Well, it's commendable, Killer, being concerned about your people. But if we've got a security leak, we have to take measures."

"I thought, sir, that—"

Babcock waved his hand. "Just call me Whit."

"Okay, Whit. I thought that a call from you might cut through all the red tape. We could get a quick security check on this reporter to find out what damage might have been done. And maybe Maxwell could just be quietly transferred."

"I have a conference call with the Secretary of the Navy and the White House this afternoon. When I'm finished, I'll tell someone in the department to put a detailer on the Maxwell matter."

"I appreciate your help, Whit."

The two shook hands. Babcock waited until De-Lancey left the office, then he resumed studying his image in the mirror.

THIRTEEN

Basra

USS *RONALD REAGAN*
0545, MONDAY, 19 MAY

Wearing his starched khakis, Babcock strode to the podium and adjusted the microphone. He delivered a steely-eyed gaze at the flight-suited aviators filling the room.

"I just got off the line with the President," he said, letting the weight of the title settle over his audience. "He has given the go-ahead for a retaliatory strike against the Iraqi emplacements that downed our fighter yesterday."

Babcock paused and struck a pose that, everyone guessed, was intended to summon an image of Douglas MacArthur. Or Theodore Roosevelt. Or, some supposed, Michael Douglas.

"This is a historic moment, ladies and gentlemen. Today it will be your privilege to strike a blow on behalf of civilized nations around the globe. The world will be watching. The President has faith in you, and so do I."

Babcock stood there for a moment, waiting for a reaction from his audience. No one applauded. The pilots stared back at Whitney Babcock in total silence.

After a few seconds, Babcock rallied and said in

a booming voice, "Good hunting!" He gave them a Hollywood salute and left the ready room.

An awkward silence fell over the group. CAG Boyce rose and walked to the podium. He glanced at the door, making sure Babcock was gone.

"Okay, none of what I'm gonna say is to be repeated outside this room." Boyce paused a second and looked over at Admiral Mellon, sitting in the front row. Mellon gave him a barely perceptible nod.

Boyce went on. "Despite what you just heard, this ain't Desert Storm. It's not even a concerted military strike. It's a simple, one-shot, pissant punitive raid. A little message that our President wants to send to their President. Saddam is being told he better mind his manners, or we'll take out what's left of his crummy infrastructure.

"But I want everybody to get this. These are *not* high-priority targets. I don't intend to lose jets or pilots taking out one of those worthless bridges or chicken coops at Basra. I want you to keep it high, stay away from the hot spots, come home in one piece. I'd better see every one of your ugly faces back in here this afternoon for the debrief."

Boyce shoved a half-gnawed cigar into his mouth and returned to his seat.

Spook Morse, the intelligence officer, then came forward to give the latest target data. He talked about tankers, weather over the target area, transponder squawks, collateral damage avoidance, and all the nuances of a coordinated raid.

As Boyce listened to Morse go on about SAM site updates, target area weather, he looked at his strike pilots. Some looked better than others. They had been yanked out of a full-scale liberty session in Dubai. He knew for a fact that some of them had world-class hangovers. He also knew it wouldn't do any good to tell the most afflicted to take themselves off the flight schedule. He sure as hell wouldn't, and neither would they. This was combat, and no self-respecting fighter pilot was going to stay behind if he could help it.

Thank God, he thought, for resilient bodies and young reflexes.

Devo Davis, perhaps the most hungover, sat in his usual place in the second row. He had only the vaguest recollection of how he left the hotel. Someone—Leroi Jones or Undra Cheever or some other JO—must have rolled him out of his room and shepherded him onto the liberty boat.

Devo was on his third cup of gut-burning black coffee. He could tell by the ache in his skull that life was returning to his body. All he wanted was to get through this goddamned mission.

Davis remained in his seat until the ready room had emptied. He was about to leave when Maxwell came up.

"You okay, Devo?"

"Superb. Haven't felt so fucking terrific since I had scarlet fever. I want to thank you for sticking me on a HARM station."

"Wasn't me. The skipper made the assignments."

"With Spam Parker of all people. A nugget on her first combat sortie. What am I, the designated spear catcher?"

"Want me to try and change it?'

Davis shook his head. "Can't do that. If I'm gonna take over this squadron some day, I gotta be willing to fly with anybody." He glanced around to make sure they were alone. "Even aliens."

"We'll rendezvous overhead at seventeen thousand," said Devo in the briefing booth.

"Why?" demanded Spam Parker. "Why don't we just join up on a tacan radial away from the ship?"

Devo took a deep breath. "Because," he said patiently, "that's what the air wing tactical procedures require—an overhead rendezvous. Now, after the rendezvous, we switch—"

"I still think it would be better if we joined on a tacan radial."

Devo felt his headache worsening. He told himself to stay cool.

"Fine, Spam. Nice that you have an opinion. But today we're gonna do it my way."

"Why? I mean, it just sounds so . . . pedantic."

Devo couldn't believe this shit.

"Here's the reason," he said, his voice rising an octave. "I'm the flight leader, you're the wingman. Here's another: I'm a commander, you're a lieutenant. Or try this one: I'm a three-tour strike fighter pilot, you're a nugget. We're gonna do it my way. Understand?"

Spam started to protest again, but she caught the look on Devo's face. She crossed her arms and sat tapping her boot on the deck.

Devo went on with his briefing. After their rendezvous, they would proceed to their battle station, where they would orbit, ready to fire their radar-seeking

HARM missiles at any enemy SAM site that was tracking the strike group.

Devo knew their chances of seeing action were almost nil. And he knew too that someone—De-Lancey probably—was violating protocol by assigning the executive officer such a minor role in the strike.

But Devo wasn't arguing about it. Not this time. He still wasn't back to a hundred percent of his old self, and he had a huge freaking headache.

Devo had no illusions about his ability. He was an average aviator who, on a good day, could turn in an above average performance. But lately the good days had been far between.

Devo knew that he had lost something. Even though he was the squadron executive officer, the second in command, he no longer had credibility with the other officers. They neither feared nor respected him, as junior officers were supposed to do. He could sense it in the way they talked to him—that condescending, too-familiar manner. Devo Davis was no longer a force to be reckoned with.

Well, he'd fix that problem. Today all he wanted was to get through this strike. Fly the mission, shoot the HARMs if necessary, get back aboard the ship.

Plus, keep this mouthy nugget from killing them both.

Devo finished the briefing. "Maintain a combat spread. Stay in position, out where I can see you."

Spam seemed bored. He couldn't tell whether she was listening or not. "Any questions?" Devo asked. She shook her head. "See you on deck," said Devo.

*   *   *

Christ, it's hot. Devo thought he would melt in the cockpit of his F/A-18. The Hornet's air conditioner was good, but not effective in the hundred-degree heat of the flight deck.

He emptied the water bottle that he had planned to drink en route to his battle station. He was desperate to get off the ovenlike flight deck and into the cooler sky.

What he needed was a shot of vodka. His head was pounding like a drum. In fact, he thought, he'd trade his gonads for a Bloody Mary right now. *Why the hell aren't they getting this launch off?*

The carrier's nose swung slowly into the wind. The jet blast deflector rose in front of Devo's jet, and he saw the Hornet on catapult one go into tension. The thunder of its engines shook Devo's jet. Devo grimaced inside his oxygen mask.

The catapult fired with a bang, flinging the combatloaded jet into the hazy sky over the Persian Gulf. Devo winced as a searing pain coursed through his head. Even the flow of pure oxygen through his mask wasn't helping.

The deflector came down. It was Devo's turn.

Following the yellow-shirt's directions, he taxied up to the cat track, then lowered the launch bar fixed to the nose gear. Slowly, carefully, he eased forward, felt the "clunk" as the launch bar engaged the catapult shuttle. Obeying the cat officer's signals, he released the brakes and throttled up to full power. He wiped out the flight controls, scanned the engine instruments, then looked at the cat officer.

It was Dog Balls, the new shooter the pilots liked to pick on. *Be gentle, brother.* Dog Balls was peering back at him, waiting for Devo's salute.

Devo saluted. He tensed for the cat shot.

WHAM! The catapult fired.

The Hornet hurtled down the track. Devo felt himself slammed back against the seat. The pain of his hangover became a white-hot spear somewhere behind his eyes.

The heavy fighter cleared the deck and began to climb. The pain in Devo's skull receded to a dull throb.

He could see the bomb bursts as the strikers hit their targets in the Basra delta complex. They were in their assigned orbit at twenty-eight thousand feet, thirty miles southeast of the target area. The strike seemed to be going as briefed.

Devo scanned his HARM display. He had seen no sign of electronic activity from inside Iraq. No SAM sites, no gun-tracking radar. The Iraqis were lying low. They had been through this before. All they had to do was stay hunkered down until the bombs quit falling. Within a couple of months they'd have their sites back up and running. It was part of the game.

Devo was feeling better now. The pure oxygen helped, but he still had that dull throb in his skull. He was thirsty as hell. It also helped that things were quiet on the electronic warfare front.

He turned onto the inbound leg, pointing back toward Basra. He saw columns of smoke rising from the three main target areas. There were no new bomb bursts. The last striker called off target.

Devo looked over at his wingman. Spam was out of position. Anyone else he would order to dress it up, and it would be done. With Spam, it would be a goddamn airborne debate. She'd insist she wasn't really out of position.

It wasn't worth it. His head ached too much for an argument and—

He saw a missile.

One of Spam's HARMs was streaking from beneath her wing toward Basra. Devo watched in disbelief as the antiradiation missile arced away in a smooth flight path.

"Magnum, magnum," came Spam's voice over the strike common frequency. "Nail Forty-two, magnum— Burner Three, Basra."

She was announcing that she had launched a radar-seeking missile against a SAM threat.

For a moment the strike frequency was silent. Then bedlam. Everyone wanted to know what the hell was going on.

"Say type and direction of threat!"

"Who's being targeted?"

"Burner Three where? Anyone got a visual?"

Devo was checking his own HARM display. It was blank. No indication of an enemy radar. He reset the RF gains and looked again. Nothing. He was getting a bad feeling.

On the back radio he said, "Spam, tell me what kind of threat you saw."

"I had an SA-3 on the HARM display," she answered. "The box was there and it showed active tracking. So I took the shot. They were probably tracking the last of the strike group."

"What do you mean, a box? An SA-3 displays as a *triangle*. What the hell did you shoot at?"

Her voice became more insistent. "I just told you,

an SA-3 site near Basra. Box, triangle, who cares? I know very well what I shot at."

Devo's headache came back. He had seen the way the HARM left Spam's Hornet. It was flying in a smooth arc, not the jerky, snakelike path a HARM took when it was locked on to a radar-emitting target. It wasn't tracking.

Fucking beautiful, he thought. When they returned to the carrier, it would be his job to explain why he let his knuckleheaded wingman pickle off a half-million-dollar missile. At nothing.

It had been a milk run. They were en route back to the *Reagan*. Except for Spam's HARM, they had expended no weapons.

Then, 150 miles out, they received a call from Surface Watch aboard the *Reagan*: "Nail Forty-one, this is Alpha Sierra. We need you to check out a surface contact that is approaching the battle group."

Alpha Sierra gave Devo the range and bearing of the unknown vessel.

Devo groaned to himself. "Nail Forty-one copies," he said. "Descending to have a look."

Devo reduced power and lowered the Hornet's nose. Spam was late following. She floated high, then had to use full speed brakes to keep from shooting out in front.

Devo leveled off at a thousand feet above the water, flying at a comfortable three hundred knots. "Fly abeam, slightly high. Keep at least a mile separation and watch for small boats and gunfire."

"Roger."

Devo's radar was painting the surface contact straight ahead. "Alpha Sierra, Nail Forty-one flight has the contact on the nose twenty miles, stand by for ID."

Half a minute later, he could see the profile of the ship on the horizon. "Tally ho on the nose," he called to Spam. "I'll take it up the vessel's starboard side and arc around to the left. Stay a mile abeam my right wing and hold your altitude."

"Roger that."

She still was out of position—too high, and closer than a mile abeam. But she wasn't in a position to hurt anything. It was the best he could expect for now.

"Nail Forty-one descending out of a thousand," called Devo. "Keep me in sight at all times."

"Roger."

He eased down to one hundred feet. He could see white caps and the varied colorations of the sea below him. Salt spray was peppering the windscreen. At this altitude, there was no room for error. With only a second's inattention, he would be fish food.

As he streaked over the stern of the ship, Devo saw that it was a merchant vessel. He could see the ensign of the Islamic Republic of Iran, but he couldn't pick out the vessel's name painted on the stern.

He would have to come back for another pass.

Devo started to pull up and turn back. It was then he saw a blur over his right shoulder.

Spam's Hornet! The belly of the jet was coming at him.

Shit! She had lost sight of him.

Devo jabbed the stick forward, punching the jet's nose down. Instinctively he hunched down in his seat. He saw—and felt—the roaring mass of Spam's Hornet slide over his canopy.

Somehow they missed.

Devo's heart resumed beating. It was close, too damned close. He'd missed a collision by inches and—

"Altitude! Altitude!" It was the synthesized voice of "Bitchin' Betty," the Hornet's aural warning system.

Devo yanked back on the stick. He glimpsed the digital altitude indicator counting to zero.

FOURTEEN

Inquest

Where the hell is Devo?

Spam eased the nose up and started her climb back to ten thousand feet. She glanced around, left, then right. No Devo.

"Devo, you up?" she said on the number two radio. No answer.

That was just like him, she thought. Take off and leave his wingman. Particularly if the wingman was a woman.

Leveling at ten thousand feet, she tried calling Devo again. Still no answer. She was getting a bad feeling about this. Something weird had happened back there over the freighter. Like a good wingman, she had stayed with him as they passed over the ship. She remembered looking down at the ship, and then when she looked back up—Devo's jet wasn't there.

He should have been more explicit in the briefing about what he wanted her to do. Instead, he had wasted time with all that picayune shit about where they would rendezvous. As though she needed lecturing from a . . . drunk.

He had probably hauled ass back to the *Reagan* and

left her out here. That would be the typical move of your classic male chauvinist fighter pilot who thinks women ought to be darning their socks. She'd get his ass roasted on a spit when they got back to the ship. She'd tell Killer what a jerk his executive officer really was.

Now she had to get back to the ship by herself, and she wasn't sure what the hell she was supposed to do. One more thing he didn't cover in the briefing.

She could hear the other returning jets calling on the CATCC—Carrier Air Traffic Control Center—frequency. Spam checked in using her call sign: Nail 42.

"Roger, Nail Forty-two," said the controller. "You got Nail Forty-one with you?"

"Negative."

Several seconds ticked past, then a different voice came over the frequency. "Nail Forty-two, this is the captain. Look, we're not painting Nail Forty-one's transponder squawk, and we think he might be a nordo." A "nordo" was an aircraft with lost radios. "Take a look around and see if your flight lead is with you, maybe on your wing."

Spam took a quick glance to either side of her jet. Empty sky. No radioless jet flying on her wing. "Negative. He's not here."

Spam wondered what the hell was going on. The *captain of the ship*? They were worried about Devo. It didn't occur to them that he had abandoned his wingman. She was getting a feeling that something had gone wrong, and she had learned by now how the male-biased Navy operated: The bastards were going to blame it on her.

Spam stopped thinking about Devo. It was time to *land* on the thing.

Her first pass was unstable, causing the LSO to give her a frantic wave-off close to the ramp. Overcorrecting on the second pass, she missed all four arresting wires and boltered, back into the pattern.

Her third pass was within limits, but ugly. High in the groove, settling at the ramp, with an urgent power call from Pearly, ending with a number one wire—the closest to the blunt unforgiving ramp of the deck.

Taxiing forward to where the director was signaling her to her parking spot, she began preparing herself for the debriefing. Already she could hear the accusations, and she would be ready with the answers. The LSO tried to make her look bad by yelling these hysterical commands on the radio.

And Devo. The man was a blatant sexist. He shouldn't have been flying. His briefing was unprofessional and erratic. Whatever happened to Devo was his own fault.

CAG Boyce sighed and hung up the phone. He closed his eyes and massaged them with the tips of his fingers. This was the part of his job he hated most. In twenty-three years as a naval aviator, he had seen his share of mishaps. It never got any easier.

He swung around in his chair and faced the officers seated at his conference table. "They found debris," he said. "Five miles from the Iranian freighter."

"Did the freighter fire on him?" asked Killer DeLancey.

"No, there wasn't any indication of hostile action."

"Any clue that he ejected?" asked Maxwell. "Locator beacon or . . . ?"

Boyce shook his head. That would be wishful thinking, and they all knew it. No beacon, no raft, no floating survivor. When you hit the water at three hundred knots, there wasn't much left.

Losing a guy like Devo Davis was tough. Boyce and Devo went all the way back to the A-7 days together on the *Kitty Hawk*. Devo, for all his faults, was someone Boyce could count on to tell him how things really were.

Now he couldn't shake this feeling that he had helped kill Devo.

He had heard the rumors about the drinking. As Air Wing Commander, he was also aware that Devo was having problems in the cockpit. But they had already had a private talk about all that, and Devo convinced him it was a passing thing. He was having trouble getting over the split with Eileen. Nothing serious. He was coming out of it.

Then, while the *Reagan* was in port in Dubai, Killer DeLancey had come to his office. He wanted Devo replaced and sent home. Killer thought that Devo was a drunk and a poor role model for the junior officers.

Boyce turned him down. Devo, he told DeLancey, would come out of it. Devo was a good executive officer, he would make a good commanding officer. Just cut him a little slack, and Devo would get a handle on his problems.

That, of course, was a lie. His real reason for keeping Devo Davis was more critical. He needed someone he could trust to watch Killer DeLancey.

The recovery team completed its sweep of the surface around the crash site. To no one's surprise, they found only a few baskets of floating debris—nothing that would yield a reason for the crash of Devo's Hornet.

The Aircraft Mishap Board convened the next morning in the air wing conference room. Boyce named Commander Spike Mannheim, of the VFA-34 Blue Tails, senior member of the board. Maxwell, as the Roadrunners operations officer, was assigned to the board, and so were Craze Manson, the maintenance officer; Bat Masters, the safety officer; and the air wing flight surgeon, Knuckles Ball.

Spam Parker was the first witness called. She sat at the end of the table facing the five board members. She wore her dress khakis, her blond hair tied back in a bun.

Mannheim asked the first question. "Lieutenant Parker, please describe Commander Davis's demeanor during the brief."

"What do you mean?"

"Was he . . . alert? Upbeat? Perceptive?"

"He seemed irritable. He was probably hungover."

"We're not asking you to make judgments. Just tell us how he conducted the brief."

"Very unprofessional, in my opinion."

"Explain, please."

"Devo kept making a big deal about this overhead rendezvous, like it was some sort of religious thing with him."

Mannheim frowned. "You disagreed with your flight leader about the rendezvous?"

"It just made more sense to rendezvous on a tacan radial."

Mannheim scribbled a note on his yellow pad. "Even though the air wing tactical procedures specifically call for an overhead rendezvous?"

Spam didn't like the questioner's tone. "You asked me to tell you about the briefing. I just told you."

Mannheim studied her for a second. "Okay, let's talk about the mission. Tell us what happened."

Spam described the HARM patrol.

When she finished, Maxwell spoke up. "I'm curious, Spam. How did you happen to fire a HARM? Why didn't Commander Davis take the shot?"

"I guess he wasn't watching his display. He didn't see the Burner-Three indication."

At this, Mannheim picked up a manila file folder. "We have reports here from both AWACS and *Rivet Joint*. They saw no Burner-Three activity at all. It looks like the HARM you fired went inert, without tracking."

Spam looked at each of them. She was receiving clear danger signals now. They were on a fishing trip. "I just told you. I had an SA-3 site locked up on my HARM display. There was a definite SAM threat to the strike force, and I fired a missile."

"Did Commander Davis say anything to you about your missile shot?"

"I don't remember."

Mannheim looked at his notes again. "Here is a transcription of your HUD tape. After you fired the HARM, you and Devo had a radio exchange. He said, 'What do you mean, a box? An SA-3 displays as a *triangle*. What the hell did you shoot at?' " Mannheim looked at her. "Well, Lieutenant?"

Spam was sure of it now. They were trying to set her up. "Excuse me, but what has this got to do with Devo's crash? Am I on trial here?"

"We're trying to reconstruct the entire sortie," said Mannheim.

"It seems to me you're trying to blame me for something that has nothing to do with the accident."

Mannheim glanced at his colleagues, then made a note on his pad. "Very well. We'll come back to that later. Tell us about the Iranian freighter you and Devo overflew."

Spam related how they received the call from Alpha Sierra to check out the unidentified ship.

"Did you observe any hostile activity?" Maxwell inquired. "Any sign of firing from the ship?"

"No. Nothing at all."

"What were Devo's instructions to you about tactical formation?"

Spam considered for a moment. They had the transcript from her HUD tape. They were trying to trip her up. "As I recall, he said to fly a mile abeam and higher."

"And is that, in fact, what you did?"

"Of course."

Maxwell thought for a second, then said, "So you saw Commander Davis's jet hit the water?"

"Not exactly. I was . . . trying to get the name of the ship."

"I don't understand," interjected Mannheim. "If he was overflying the ship, and you were a mile abeam, how could you also be getting the name of the ship?"

Spam's anger was rising now. The bastards were definitely trying to trap her. "That was our job, identify the ship. That's what I was trying to do."

Mannheim again consulted his file. "Alpha Sierra has told us that your two radar contacts were converging as you approached the freighter. At the time they lost Devo's radar signature, the two of you were superimposed on the radar display." Mannheim put down the file and looked at her. "As Commander Davis's wingman, you were supposed to be a mile abeam. Can you explain why you did not have him in sight when he impacted the water?"

Spam knew for sure now where this was going. It was just as she expected. "What is this? An inquisition?" She shoved her chair back and stood up. "I don't have to sit here and submit to this. Not without a lawyer."

"Sit down, Lieutenant," said Mannheim. "This is a hearing, not a court of law. The purpose of all these questions is to learn the circumstances of the mishap flight."

"No. Your real purpose is harassment of a female officer."

Mannheim looked like he had been slapped. "Did you say—"

"Harassment. You know what that means, Commander."

He exhaled a long breath and glanced at the other officers. "I know exactly what it means. Okay, Lieutenant Parker, we're going to take a break. You're excused for now."

Spam executed a smart about-face and exited the conference room.

Closing the door behind her, she allowed herself a smile. She was right. They *were* trying to pin this whole thing on her. Blame the new female pilot so they could get rid of her. Well, she had put a stop to that—at least for now.

The H word. In the New Navy, it was the ultimate weapon.

* * *

DeLancey glanced each way down the empty passageway, then said, "You told them *what*?"

"It was just a warning," Spam said. "To make them back off a little."

"Harassment is a serious charge these days," he said. "Whenever someone uses that word, it means the commanding officer is supposed to initiate a JAG investigation. Is that what you want?"

"They were hassling me about Devo. Trying to make everything my fault."

"For example, what did they say was your fault?"

"The HARM I shot, for one. And then they're saying that I wasn't watching Devo's jet when he flew into the water."

DeLancey froze for a second and looked at her. "You *were* watching your leader's jet, weren't you?"

"Don't you start. You sound just like them."

"I need to know," said DeLancey. He took another look down the passageway. "Were you in combat spread when Davis hit the water?"

"I don't like these questions. You're trying to intimidate me."

"Answer the goddamn question."

"This isn't like you, Killer. If you're going to act this way, I won't talk to you."

DeLancey was nearing his limit. He slammed the edge of his fist against the steel bulkhead. "Listen, damn it. They're going to roast you in the mishap report if you go on letting them think you fucked up that overflight of the freighter. They'll hang the accident on you."

"No, they won't."

"Really?" DeLancey said. "And why not?"

"Because you won't let them."

DeLancey blinked, not comprehending. "What do you mean?"

"You know what I mean. You're the commanding officer. You'll have to do something."

DeLancey peered at her as if seeing her for the first time. Her gray eyes looked right back at him, unblinking.

Red Boyce finished reading the official Mishap Investigation Report. He slammed it down on his desk. "I don't fucking believe this."

"I knew you'd say that," said Mannheim.

Boyce just shook his head. "That sonofabitch."

Mannheim had personally delivered the 102-page report to Boyce's office. In the report Mannheim and his fellow board members concluded that the MP—Mishap Pilot, in the report—lost situational awareness while overflying the Iranian merchant ship and permitted his aircraft to impact the surface.

In other words, Devo Davis accidentally flew into the water.

It was the board's further conclusion that a contributing factor to the MP's loss of situational awareness was his wingman's failure to maintain a deconflicting flight path during the overflight of the freighter.

In other words, Spam Parker probably caused Devo to hit the water.

But then, as an attachment to the report, was the endorsement of the MP's commanding officer, Commander DeLancey. While agreeing with the conclusion that Devo Davis had killed himself by flying into the water, DeLancey emphatically rejected the second conclusion.

"The conjecture that Lieutenant Parker did not take

appropriate separation during the overflight of the
freighter is not supported by fact or testimony. Lieutenant Parker was fully cognizant of her duties as
Commander Davis's wingman, and the evidence cor-
roborates her statement that she executed her mission
precisely as briefed. Nothing in this report should be
construed as a reflection on Lieutenant Parker's aero-
nautical or military ability."

Boyce picked up the report and waved it at Mannheim. "What is this bullshit, Spike? Killer just neutral-
ized your report. Goddammit, he knows just as well
as we do what happened. What's going on with him?
Has he turned into some kind of closet feminist?"

Mannheim just shrugged. They both knew it was a
rhetorical question. CAG didn't expect him to dispar-
age a fellow senior officer. Even a grandstanding ego-
maniac like DeLancey.

Hozer Miller had a smirk on his face. He handed
the message board to Maxwell in the ready room and
said, "Bye-bye time, Brick."

Maxwell saw that Miller had been thoughtful
enough to highlight the message with Maxwell's name
on it.

> *From: O-5 Assignments Officer, Bureau of Per-
> sonnel, Department of the Navy.*
> *To: Commander Samuel Joseph Maxwell, USN*
> *Subj: Permanent change of station.*
>
> *Within one week upon receipt of these orders,
> you are detached from your duties at Strike Fighter
> Squadron Thirty-six, deployed aboard USS Ron-
> ald Reagan. Not later than 15 June, you will report*

*to the commanding officer, Training Squadron
Twenty, at Naval Air Station Kingsville, Texas, for
duty involving operational and training flying.*

Pearly Gates looked over Maxwell's shoulder. "Training squadron? Man, that's the end of the earth."

Maxwell nodded. "No, it's purgatory." For a fighter pilot with the rank of commander, assignment to the training command was the terminus of a career. He could forget about ever flying fighters off a carrier deck again.

Maxwell copied a set of the orders on the ready room Xerox, then returned the message board to Hozer.

On his way to the wardroom, he tried to make sense of what had happened. Killer had done it, he was certain. But why did CAG Boyce go along with it? It didn't compute. Boyce was a crotchety guy, famous for outbursts of temper, but he was a straight shooter.

The wardroom was busy, each of the long tables half-filled with officers having coffee or consuming ice cream dispensed by the big stainless-steel machine in one corner. Maxwell poured a coffee, then sat by himself. He was going through the morning's stack of mail and squadron read-and-initial messages when he sensed that he was being watched.

He was. They were standing at the other end of the wardroom, near the lunch buffet line. Whitney Babcock, trying to look like Chester Nimitz in his starched khakis, standard-issue web belt, and Navy flight jacket, was studying him. His head was nodding in agreement as DeLancey said something in his ear.

Maxwell gave them a wave of recognition. They

averted their eyes and continued their conversation with their backs turned.

Looking at the two men, Maxwell suddenly understood. It had to be Killer and his new patron. DeLancey had persuaded Babcock to intervene directly with the assignments office and get him shipped out.

Maxwell considered his options. He could approach Babcock directly to explain his case. Then he quickly rejected that idea. Babcock had become such an admirer of DeLancey, he would disbelieve anything Maxwell said about DeLancey. He could go to CAG. But then CAG must have signed off with an endorsement. So much for Boyce being a straight shooter.

He felt a pang of regret, thinking back to the dinner in Dubai with Admiral Dunn. *I can get you transferred to another squadron.*

Dunn had warned him about DeLancey. He had been too proud. Now it was too late.

"Sit down, Killer," said CAG Boyce. "Coffee black, no sugar, right?"

"Yes, sir." DeLancey took a seat at the long, empty conference table. It was midmorning, and both men were wearing the standard-issue G-1 fur-collared flight jackets over their khakis.

Boyce poured the coffee. Then he tilted back and sipped from the big porcelain mug with the air group insignia on one side and the title CAG emblazoned on the other.

As usual he clutched an unlit cigar, which he liked to gnaw on when he was doing business. He wished he could light the thing up like he used to in the old days. In the health-freakish New Navy, the environment Nazis turned you in to the EPA.

"We need an executive officer for your squadron, Killer."

DeLancey nodded. "I figured we'd get one of the prospective COs just finishing requal training. I was thinking of Jake Kovacs. He could be out here in a couple of weeks—"

"I've already got someone in mind."

A wary look passed over DeLancey's face. "Who would that be?"

"Brick Maxwell."

DeLancey's coffee cup stopped halfway to his mouth. His mouth twitched. "You gotta be joking."

"Brick's nearly the right seniority. He's already proved he's a damn good strike leader. And most important, he's up to speed on the situation out here. If we wind up going to war and something happened to you, I wouldn't want an inexperienced XO taking over the squadron."

DeLancey was shaking his head adamantly. "No, it can't be Maxwell."

"What's your problem with Maxwell? You know something I don't?"

"Well, for one thing, he's got orders. He's on his way outta here."

Boyce stared at him. "How can that be? He just got here three months ago. He's not due for rotation."

DeLancey's mouth twitched again. "He's been reassigned to the training command at Kingsville."

Boyce picked up the unlit cigar and stared at it for a second. How did this get by him? Something was going on—

Ping! It came to him.

"Killer," he said slowly, "did you by any chance go over my head to get Maxwell transferred?"

"I was gonna tell you, Red. I was talking to Whit— Mr. Babcock—and he—"

"Babcock? That little peckerhead civilian who thinks he's Lord Nelson? Don't tell me you went to him with this."

DeLancey swallowed hard and said, "I mentioned that I thought Maxwell might be leaking information to a female reporter. The Undersecretary said he'd take care of it. I was just as surprised as you when the orders came in."

Boyce felt a tantrum coming on. "Goddammit! I oughta have *you* relieved and shipped outta here. Did anybody ever explain to you what chain of command means in the Navy?"

"Yes, sir. It was on my agenda to tell you about it."

Boyce exploded. He stood and aimed the cigar like a weapon. "You listen to me, mister. You don't *tell* me about capers like that. You come to me first! You understand that? You got a problem with your squadron, you talk to the Air Wing Commander, not some dipshit civilian who you think will advance your illustrious career. One more stunt like that and I promise you won't have a career. *Do You Read Me?*"

Killer nodded. "Yes, sir. But it's already done."

"The hell it is. Those orders are canceled as of this minute."

"Sir, with all due respect, I don't think you ought to do that."

"Why? Are you going to Babcock about *me* now?"

"Of course not. I just don't think keeping Maxwell as XO is gonna work out."

"It's too late for this discussion. You had a chance to tell me what you thought, and you blew it. Now I'm telling you. You got a new XO, and it's Maxwell."

DeLancey nodded, showing no expression. "You're the boss."

Boyce and Maxwell leaned against the rail of the open deck and watched the crews below respotting aircraft for the next launch.

"He's a goddamn hero," said Boyce. "Everybody in the Navy Department, including that little prick Babcock, thinks he shits gold bricks. If I fired him, they'd hang me in effigy from the Pentagon flagpole."

Maxwell wondered where Boyce was going with this. They both knew it was highly unusual—even improper—for an Air Wing Commander to be so candid with a subordinate officer.

"DeLancey's got four months to go as the Roadrunner skipper," said Boyce. "Then he'll be rotated stateside and become somebody else's problem." Boyce paused, and looked directly at Maxwell. "In the meantime, I want you to take over the executive officer's job."

Maxwell wasn't sure he heard right. It was too unbelievable. "Sir? Executive officer? You know that I've only been in the squadron—"

"I know exactly how long you've been there, and I know where you came from. And I happen to be a pretty good judge of people. We may have a war coming up. I need someone I can trust to keep DeLancey from going off the deep end."

"I'm flattered that you think I'm up to it, CAG. But there's a problem. Killer wants me gone, out of his squadron."

CAG just shrugged. "That's his problem, not yours. He'll have to accommodate. Anyway, there ain't any law that says a skipper and his XO have to go steady. Well, will you take the job?"

For several seconds, Maxwell didn't answer. He reflected on how life kept changing. From the fleet to outer space, back to the fleet. His career was in the tank, or so he thought. For all he knew, it still might be.

"Yes, sir, I'd be honored to take the job."

"I'll make the announcement today." Boyce paused and looked at Maxwell. "By the way, are you going to tell me now why DeLancey hates your guts?"

For a moment Maxwell didn't answer. What happened during the Gulf War—when Killer DeLancey had taken credit for another pilot's downed MiG—was a story he had kept to himself all these years.

He still would. "You'll have to ask Killer that question, CAG."

"Do you think he'd tell me?"

"No," said Maxwell. "I don't think he'd tell anyone."

FIFTEEN

Requiem

The rifles of the Marine honor guard crackled once, twice, three times. With each volley the crowd on the hangar deck jerked.

It was appropriate, Maxwell thought, that the service for Devo Davis would take place on such a day. The Gulf had turned choppy, and a ragged deck of clouds scudded low over the *Reagan* battle group. A warm breeze wafted through the space where most of the air wing officers were now huddled.

The chaplain, a Lutheran minister with the rank of lieutenant commander, had delivered a brief eulogy capsulizing the forty-one years of Commander Steve "Devo" Davis. He recounted the details of Devo's life—his Midwest origins, his graduation in the upper quarter of his Naval Academy class, his rise through the echelons of naval aviation. "God gives, and God takes away," the chaplain said. Devo Davis, he assured them, was a man who loved God, his country, and the U.S. Navy.

On a linen-covered table lay a collage of objects—Devo's gold aviator's wings, a ceremonial naval officer's sword, photographs of Devo as a midshipman, as a young nugget aviator, as a senior squadron officer. In one photo, a radiant Devo and his new bride passed under the crossed swords of his fellow officers as they emerged from a chapel.

On a little dais lay a triangularly folded American flag, which was supposed to be delivered to the next of kin. Seeing the flag, Maxwell wondered about Devo's next of kin. He tried to imagine how Eileen had reacted when she learned that she was a widow. Saddened, probably. He guessed that she also felt relieved. Her inconvenient status as a naval officer's wife was officially ended, without the messiness of a divorce.

The melancholy sound of taps reverberated across the hangar deck. Each mournful note of the bugle seemed to swell in the air, then vanish in the cold steel bulkheads.

The soul of Devo Davis was committed to the Almighty.

Maxwell stopped outside DeLancey's stateroom door. He rapped twice, then heard DeLancey's voice. "Come in, it's open."

It was their first meeting since CAG had tapped him to be the squadron executive officer. Maxwell wished he could have seen DeLancey's reaction.

DeLancey sat at his desk shuffling through a pad of notes. He didn't bother looking up. "Sit down."

Maxwell sat on the steel chair and glanced around. It was a typical senior air wing officer's quarters— single bunk on one bulkhead, a steel bureau with pull-out drawers, a couple of padded chairs. An oriental throw rug lay on the deck. On one bulkhead hung a framed portrait of DeLancey standing beside his Hornet with the kill symbols beneath the cockpit. Next to it was a framed collage of DeLancey's awards and decorations, including the new silver star.

Maxwell glimpsed his own name at the top of one of DeLancey's note pages.

Finally DeLancey said, "Contrary to my expressed wishes as commanding officer, you are going to be the XO of my squadron."

Maxwell said nothing.

"How did you pull that off? Was it your old man, the admiral?"

Maxwell ignored the question. "I'd like to say I look forward to working with you, John. Sounds like you don't feel the same way."

"Let's get something straight. You may address me as 'Skipper,' or by my call sign. You and I will never be on a first-name basis."

By tradition, squadron commanding officers and executive officers dropped military protocol and began a bonding process. So much for tradition, thought Maxwell. "Okay, if that's the way you want it."

"As far as I'm concerned, you're a temp. You may be the CAG's golden boy, but you are by no means a permanent replacement as my XO."

DeLancey picked up the sheaf of papers. "These are documented deficiencies in your performance. As a squadron department head you were a flop. As an aviator, I consider you average at best, and in my opinion your act of cowardice in combat is worthy of a court-martial. Besides all that, you were never a team player in this command. I'm going to write you a fitness report as operations officer that will end your career. Those orders to the training command were the only route you had to a graceful retirement."

Maxwell did not respond. It was nonsense. Since he

had arrived, the squadron's scores were at an all-time high. With the exceptions of the late executive officer, and the recent problem with Spam Parker, all the pilots were trained and combat ready.

DeLancey went on. "I don't care what CAG said about your strike lead into Al-Kharj. As far as I'm concerned, it was a disaster. Right now he's the only man standing between you and the brig. I have good reason to suspect your loyalty to your country. I'd like to pull your security clearance, given that you've been shacking up with that reporter—"

Maxwell felt a wave of anger pass over him.

"—but you can read all about it in your next fitness report," DeLancey said.

Maxwell knew there was nothing he could do about his fitness report. Commanding officers could say anything they wanted.

DeLancey tilted back in his chair. "Here's the bottom line. VFA-36 is my squadron. You will carry out my orders immediately and without question. You take no action without my approval. Understood?"

"Yes, sir."

"Much as I hate to afford you the privilege, you'll need to occupy the XO's stateroom. You'll conduct squadron business in there, and I don't want it to look like there's a rift between us."

DeLancey regarded Maxwell for a moment. "Don't get too comfortable. As far as I'm concerned, your real job is in Kingsville, and my advice is that you should take it and run. CAG might think you're here for the duration, but he doesn't necessarily have the last word, either."

Maxwell didn't reply. The meeting with DeLancey had gone as he expected.

DeLancey kept his gaze on him. "First whiff I get you're trying to stir something up with the CAG or the admiral, I'll have you in front of a court-martial. Do you copy?"

Maxwell didn't answer right away. For a moment he was tempted to dredge up the past—the real reason DeLancey despised him. Maybe this was a good time for them to bury it. *The MiG you claimed in Desert Storm? You can have it. It's over.*

He saw DeLancey's narrowed, hate-filled eyes, and he realized the truth. It would never be over.

"I copy, Skipper."

"Good. Get the hell out of my office."

Maxwell emptied the drawers in Devo's locker, neatly folding and placing all the clothing in a wooden shipping container. On a yellow legal pad he listed each article that went into the container. Then he gathered the items from Devo's desk—photographs of his wife, videocassettes that he guessed were tapes he exchanged with Eileen, and a stack of letters. He and Eileen were childless, which had been a frustration for Devo. Maxwell remembered that sometimes, when Devo was drinking and feeling contemplative, he would mention that Eileen had never wanted children.

In a desk drawer he found another stack of photos. In one of the shots, he was startled to see the four of them—Devo and Eileen, Brick and Claire. It was taken on the Maryland seashore, while Maxwell was still waiting for his assignment to NASA. The four faces smiled at him from the photograph. Maxwell felt an overwhelming sadness come over him. He sank into the desk chair. The face of Claire Phillips smiled at him from the photo.

He remembered that day, the breeze blowing in from the gulf, the seagulls and the sand crabs. Devo had been full of himself, cocky and proud. He had his orders to a strike fighter squadron as a department head. Someday in the not-too-distant future he would be an executive officer and prospective commanding officer. The only thing better than being an astronaut, he gloated, was getting command of your own fighter squadron. To a fighter pilot like Devo Davis, that was the ultimate success—your own command. It didn't get any better.

It didn't happen. That was before Killer DeLancey, before Eileen announced that she was splitting. Before the *Reagan* and a bad day over the Persian Gulf.

Before Spam Parker.

Maxwell sighed and laid the photograph back on the stack. He wished again that he had stood firm and insisted that Devo's name be removed from the flight schedule that night. Of course, it would have given DeLancey the final ammunition he needed to relieve Devo of his duties as executive officer. Devo would be disgraced, but alive.

Then it would be Devo cleaning out this room, Maxwell thought. He would gather his effects and quietly disappear from the *Reagan*, transferred to some meaningless billet back in the states. Devo would hate it, and after a few weeks he would put in for retirement. He would then drink himself into an early grave.

The thought made Maxwell even gloomier. One way or the other, Devo Davis had been a doomed man.

He returned to the task of packing Devo's effects. He filled the wooden container with clothes from the drawers. He placed all Devo's personal papers in a manila envelope and sealed it. Then he removed the contents of Devo's safe—five bottles of vodka, one a quarter full, and a half-empty flask of brandy. Devo's nightcap stock.

He poured the liquor into the sink, rinsed the insides of the bottles, then slipped the empties into a plastic bag. After nightfall, the bottles would join their owner in the dark waters of the Persian Gulf.

Maxwell picked up the photo again. Claire was wearing the scarf he had given her. She looked happy, as if she were was in love.

Maxwell decided that he would keep the photo. Devo would approve.

In his room, Maxwell put on the new Berlioz CD he bought in Dubai. He placed the photo from Devo's room on his desk, next to the one of Debbie. He sat at the desk, letting the music wash over him, and he thought about the shambles that had become his life. A numbing sadness settled over him like a shroud.

Everything he loved had turned to dust. He had lost Debbie. His once-brilliant career was probably at a dead end. His father, whom he admired above all men, had walked out of his life after his resignation from NASA. His best friend lay at the bottom of the Persian Gulf.

He had nothing of value left. Nothing that mattered.

Debbie smiled at him from the photograph on the desk, and he felt the hole in his heart opening wider. Maxwell closed his eyes, fighting back the tears.

For the thousandth time he remembered that day on the Cape.

*   *   *

It was one of those dazzling Florida afternoons. From the gantry tower Maxwell could see eastward far beyond the beach, all the way to the rim of the Gulf Stream. The air was crisp, the horizon as sharp as a pencil line.

She waved at him as she boarded the orbital vehicle. Like the other six crew members, Debbie was wearing the orange pressure suit with the mission patch and wings on the left breast, the American flag emblazoned on the shoulder.

It was a dress rehearsal for the actual launch in two days. They would take their stations and run through the checklists, do a power-up and test of the command and control consoles, and then simulate a countdown to ignition. It was a routine procedure they did before every launch.

Debbie Sutter loved being an astronaut. Though she wasn't a pilot, she intended to be someday. Eight years of college and med school, then four years of internship—there'd been no time for flight training. She'd been a cardiologist when she made the cut for astronaut training. She was assigned as a human factors specialist, and for the ten-day mission of the space shuttle *Intrepid,* her job was to study and quantify the effects of prolonged weightlessness on cognition, memory, and sleep patterns.

They had been in the vehicle for nearly an hour. The boarding hatch of the shuttle was closed and sealed so the vehicle could be pressurized, just as it would be for the real launch.

Maxwell watched from the gantry observation room. On the monitor he could see views of the command cabin, where the shuttle commander and the pilot sat. In the cabin he could see the mission specialist stations. Debbie was in her reclining launch seat, facing a console with instruments and a panel of labeled switches.

All the astronauts were wearing the sealed pressure helmets. Their suits were plugged into the onboard oxygen system, and they communicated via the ship's closed-circuit interphone.

As the pilot read off the checklist, another astronaut would perform the required action, then acknowledge.

"Crew compartment hatch 212 closed," called out Jeff Beamish, the pilot.

"Hatch 212 closed," confirmed Anton Vevrey, a payload specialist.

"ER loop automatic control."

"ER loop automatic," replied another astronaut.

"Perform cabin leak check."

"Cabin leak check in progress."

They went through the litany of prelaunch items, checking cabin pressurization, communications systems, flight controls, thrust-management parameters.

"Main engine controller bite check."

"Main engine controller bite check okay."

"Terminate liquid oxygen replenish."

Maxwell heard Debbie's voice give the response. "Liquid oxygen replenish is terminated."

"Okay. Open the liquid oxygen drain valve."

"Liquid oxygen drain—*Aahhhhh!*" Debbie's voice stopped abruptly.

The hair on Sam Maxwell's neck stood up. Every face in the observation room whirled to the monitor that watched the aft crew compartment. Thick black smoke was filling the compartment.

"Oh, shit!" Maxwell heard a controller say. "Fire in the crew compartment!"

A shrill, clanging alarm went off. On the wall over the door, a red light started flashing.

New voices came over the channel, all issuing desperate commands. "Depressurize! Close the liquid oxygen valve! Get the goddamn hatch open!"

Maxwell watched helplessly while they rushed to open the hatch. A cloud of bilious smoke gushed from the crew compartment. Paramedics rushed across the cantilevered gantry platform and boarded the vehicle. Within a minute they were dragging out orange-suited astronauts, yanking off helmets, slapping on oxygen masks.

The two pilots, Cutler and Beamish, were wobbly but okay. Nancy Rehman, an astrophysicist, came out on her own power, though she was shaking uncontrollably. The Japanese payload specialist, Nomuru, had breathed in smoke and was coughing badly. So was the Swiss mission specialist, Vevrey, but both revived when they were given oxygen.

The last to come out were the two astronauts in the aft crew compartment, Bud Feldman and Debbie Sutter. The paramedics hauled them out on gurneys.

Both were dead.

Two veteran astronauts who had been there in the gantry held Sam Maxwell's arms, restraining him. "Go down below, Sam. Don't stay here."

Maxwell wouldn't leave. He stood there transfixed while they removed her helmet.

She had not died from smoke inhalation, but from fire. The flames had entered her suit, torched her face and hair and her lungs. Her final seconds of life had been spent in excruciating pain.

They would have been married a year the next month. After Debbie's rookie space flight, they were going to take a trip somewhere, maybe to the Bahamas. They would celebrate, rejoice, think about starting the family they planned to have someday. They had already become famous as the shuttle couple, the husband-and-wife astronauts, the high fliers. *Newsweek* did a piece on them. They appeared on *CNN Live*, *Good Morning, America,* and *Oprah.*

They wanted to interview Sam Maxwell again. They wanted him to explain for their viewers the depth of his grief. Give the public a look at his Tom Selleck features while he maybe shed a tear or two on camera.

Maxwell refused. He hung up when they called. He ignored them when they approached. When a Houston reporter pursued him across a parking lot, Maxwell seized him by the collar, shoved him over the hood of a Lexus, and promised him if he saw him again, he would stuff his digital Nikon up his ass.

The inquiry into the tragedy went on for a month. In the final analysis, they declared it a freak accident. It had been a one-in-a-million combination of circumstances—a tiny fracture in the liquid oxygen drain valve, a leak in the crew ventilation system, and a simultaneous spark from the faulty console switch activated by Debbie as she complied with the prelaunch checklist. There was nothing inherently wrong with the space shuttle, even though *Challenger* and *Intrepid* had now killed a total of eight astronauts.

An enraged Sam Maxwell refused to accept the findings. The director of NASA ordered him to take a thirty-day leave, clear his head, then report back for duty at the space center in Houston. Instead, Maxwell went home and drafted a letter of resignation.

*   *   *

He opened his eyes and let them focus on the two photographs standing side by side on the desk. Debbie and Claire.

After a while Maxwell powered up the Compaq notebook computer on his desk. He logged onto the net and, a minute later, saw the flashing notice that he had mail waiting.

From: Claire.Phillips@MBS.com
To: SMaxwell.VFA36@USSRonaldReagan.
    Navy.mil
Subject: Port Visit

Dear Sam,
    You sure know how to get a girl worked up, don't you? I should be exhausted after staying up all night. But I wasn't the least bit tired the next day. To borrow from Shakespeare, perhaps the sweeter rest was ours.
    Of course I'll be happy to meet you at your next port visit. Do you really think it might be Bahrain?
    I don't want you to think I'm worrying out of turn, but please be careful out there. With the political situation this tense, God only knows what could happen. For what it's worth, I have a bad sense about your CO as well. I just don't want anything to happen to my favorite fighter pilot.
    I am proud of you, Sam Maxwell. You know you've always been my hero.
    Love,
    Claire

Through a blur of tears Maxwell read the note. A swarm of mixed feelings spilled over him. He gazed again at the photograph, at the smiling, happy girl with the new scarf.

He felt something tugging at him, dragging him out of his black mood. *Admit it, Maxwell. You want to see her.*

He went back to the computer and began typing a reply.

SIXTEEN

The Trailblazer

(COMMONWEALTH NEWS SERVICE,
19 MAY, BAGHDAD
BY CHRISTOPHER TYRWHITT)

BAGHDAD, Iraq—Eleven schoolchildren were reported killed during an early morning attack by United States warplanes against civilian targets in the southern Iraqi city of Basra. According to reliable sources, U.S. Navy F/A-18s from the aircraft carrier USS Ronald Reagan fired radar-guided missiles at the clearly marked Al-Humbhra school complex, destroying one building and killing or injuring more than a hundred Iraqi children.

Though officials of the United States State Department quickly issued a denial, claiming that the objective of the attack was an anti-aircraft missile site, photographic evidence from the site strongly suggests that the Al-Humbhra school was, in fact, the focus of the raid.

In a terse statement to his assembled cabinet, an angry Iraqi President Saddam Hussein declared that the cowardly American murderers of Iraqi children would be punished.

Jabbar awoke bathed in sweat. He sat upright in his bed. His pulse was still racing from the vividness of the dream.

He could still see the rippled surface of the sea skimming beneath his jet, the high cloudless sky over the Gulf. And in the distance, that great gray death slab on the horizon.

It looked so benign.

The MiG was flying at only a hundred feet above the sea at nearly twice the speed of sound. Somehow he had come this far without being killed by American jets. He didn't know why. Surely their airborne sentry ship—the AWACS—would have detected him. At any second he expected to hear the shrill chirp of his *Sirena* radar warning receiver announcing the threat of an air-to-air missile.

Jabbar had no illusions about his own survival. He knew his death had been preordained when he locked gazes with the riflemen of the firing squad. But he would die like a warrior. Also mounted to his MiG was a cluster of air-to-air missiles. His final act as a fighter pilot would be to engage as many of his enemies as possible before he was blown out of the sky.

As the angular silhouette of the great ship swelled on the horizon, Jabbar's finger went to the launch button on the control stick. Mounted beneath the right wing of the MiG was the Krait. Jabbar knew that even today the American Navy had nothing that could intercept a low-flying, supersonic missile.

He knew what would happen when he pressed the button. The Krait would leap from its station beneath the MiG's wing and streak toward the demon ship out there on the horizon. The missile would pierce the double-layered steel hull, not detonating until it had penetrated the vital organs of the warship. When the warhead exploded, the USS *Reagan* would erupt in a hellish mushroom of fire and molten steel. America's most powerful warship—and its five-thousand-person crew—would be vaporized.

Jabbar knew he should feel a hatred for the *Reagan*. From its deck had come the Hornet fighters that killed Captain Al-Fariz—the incident that ignited this new war. But Jabbar could also admit the truth. The goat-brained Al-Fariz had been ripe for killing anyway, blundering as he did into the forbidden territory.

Jabbar had often wondered why he too had not been shot down in the same engagement. Still burned into his memory like an indelible scar was that moment of terror, hearing the shriek of his *Sirena,* waiting for the Hornet pilot to kill him with another missile.

But the missile hadn't come, and Jabbar did not know why. Did the American lose his nerve? Did he decide that shooting Al-Fariz was a mistake? Did he feel merciful?

Jabbar was sure that he would never know the facts, only that an American fighter pilot had spared his life. And now Jabbar had been ordered by Saddam Hussein to launch a nuclear-tipped missile against the American aircraft carrier.

It was insane, thought Jabbar. Saddam was a maniac. But like many maniacs, this one possessed a demented genius for retribution. Jabbar knew that other missiles—launched simultaneously from surface vehicles—would be en route to targets in Israel, Kuwait, Bahrain, and Saudi Arabia. The cities were even more defenseless against the Krait than the American fleet. The much vaunted Patriot missile had been a great joke during the Gulf War, doing more damage to the territory it was defending than to the incoming

Scud. Even its successor, the Revere, was ineffective against the lethal Krait.

It would be a slaughter. A very ugly slaughter, because for most of the intended targets the Krait warheads transported Anthrax toxin and Sarin gas. Saddam did not wish his enemies a merciful death.

The Middle East would become a biological and nuclear wasteland.

Jabbar sat upright in his darkened room, wet with perspiration. Outside, the dawn had not yet come to Baghdad. Saddam's war was still only a bad dream.

He still had time. He had to do something.

"Listen carefully," the man said.

Tyrwhitt listened. They sat at adjoining tables in the sprawling al-Amarz coffee house. Swarms of passersby jostled each other, shuffling past the tables and the harried waiters.

The man's features were now familiar to him—the hawklike nose, the intense brown eyes that drilled into him like lasers. No question, he was the colonel from the reception at the Ministry of Information. Tyrwhitt wondered again about him. What motivated the man? What did he do in the Iraqi military? Why was he taking such a terrible risk?

"Latifiyah," said the informant in a low voice. "It is the assembly plant as well as the Krait missile propellant factory. Each building is fortified with a minimum of a meter of concrete. The complex has not only antiaircraft and SAM defenses, it is within the protective umbrella of the Al-Taqqadum fighter interceptor base. Now pay very close attention. I will give you the current air defense order of battle." He stopped and peered at Tyrwhitt with his piercing brown eyes. "Are you sure you can remember this?"

Tyrwhitt sighed and gave him a withering look. "As I told you before, I remember everything."

He caught the Iraqi's humorless smile. Obviously he didn't believe it. But it happened to be true. Even after half a dozen scotches, Tyrwhitt still possessed his computerlike ability to retain reams of arcane data. It was the single attribute that made him an effective journalist. And spy.

The Iraqi went on in his rapid, accented English. He related details about the state of Iraq's air defense radar, the disposition of its surface-to-air missile batteries, the timetable for the launch of the Kraits.

Tyrwhitt nodded, absorbing the information. He noticed that as the Iraqi spoke, his eyes were in constant motion, scanning the crowded shop.

Abruptly he stopped. He drew the folds of his kaffiyeh around his face. Tyrwhitt could see only the intense dark eyes. "We are in danger here. You must leave immediately."

He nodded toward the far end of the coffee house. Two brown-suited men were walking through the open-walled entrance. They had the unmistakable look of the Bazrum.

Tyrwhitt rose, turning his back to the entrance. "Will we meet again?"

"I don't know. It is very dangerous for us now. Go quickly."

Tyrwhitt inserted himself into the throng of passing people. Assuming the standard hunch-shouldered posture of the Iraqi male, he shuffled toward the far end of the coffee house. He didn't look back.

*   *   *

Tyrwhitt pulled the old Halliburton suitcase down from the shelf in the closet. He tossed in three clean shirts and enough underwear and socks for three days.

He stopped and peered out the window. It was still only three-thirty in the afternoon. He was in good shape to catch the six o'clock Middle East Airlines flight to Bahrain. It was one of only three daily commercial flights leaving the country. Even though the U.N. sanctions had been eased in the past year, air travel from Iraq was still a bitch.

It had been a close thing back in the coffee house, he reflected. The Bazrum agents had spotted him, which he now realized was what the informant intended. In their eagerness to trail Tyrwhitt they had failed to notice the Iraqi colonel, still huddled at his table with his face cloaked in his kaffiyeh.

Tyrwhitt led them on a hide-and-seek chase through the B'aath district. Walking briskly through the crowded plaza, he took a sharp turn into a vendors' lane, then darted between a row of crumbling low buildings. When he doubled back to the opposite end of the plaza, he spotted a rusting Trabant taxi idling in the outer lane. He jumped into the taxi and told him to drive swiftly to the Rasheed.

The two puffing Bazrum agents came trotting out a side street in time to see the Trabant pulling away. Tyrwhitt gave them a cheery wave.

By the time he arrived back at the Rasheed, he had reached a decision. This new information was too explosive, too detailed to send by encryption. He would have to fly to Bahrain.

It had taken a couple of calls on the Cyfonika. As it turned out, he had no problem getting a seat on the

MEA flight, which was a 727 with over a hundred seats open. Iraq was so poor, few of its citizens could travel by air.

His editor in Sydney was agreeable to Tyrwhitt taking some rehab time. Everyone knew that Baghdad was a hardship assignment and, anyway, Tyrwhitt could justify getting out for a few days by cranking out a feature article. In Bahrain he could write something about the skirmishes between the emirate government and the Shiites who were raising hell in the streets. Old stuff, but it would cloak his real reason for being in Bahrain.

Latifiyah. If the Iraqi informant was to be believed—and Tyrwhitt was convinced of the man's veracity—time was against them. It was urgent that he have one of his rare one-on-one debriefings with his CIA handler. The secrets of Latifiyah were ticking in his head like a time bomb.

Tyrwhitt threw his toilet kit into the suitcase. After a moment's hesitation he removed the ankle holster and the Beretta nine-millimeter and stuffed it in the dresser drawer. For the past five years, since he'd been through the CIA school in Langley, Virginia, he had regarded the concealed pistol as life insurance. Without it he felt defenseless. He had no choice now—no way could he get through Baghdad's airport security with a firearm.

He glanced at his watch. Almost an hour remained before he had to leave for the airport. Tyrwhitt settled into the deep desk chair and tried to put everything into perspective. His meeting with Ormsby, his CIA handler, would take no longer than half a day. Bahrain would be a holiday. Short, but still a holiday from the grimness of Baghdad. It would feel peculiar not to be startled by each unusual sound, every soft footstep in a hallway, not to lie awake wondering when the Bazrum would smash through his door and haul him away.

Bahrain was an enlightened Muslim country with a plenitude of good restaurants. Bars. Nightclubs . . .

Wait. In the frenzy to gather the information about Latifiyah, he had nearly forgotten. When he last spoke with Claire, wasn't she on assignment? Yes, of course she was. She had been infuriated that he woke her up, suggesting she join him in Baghdad.

Claire was in Bahrain.

He picked up the Cyfonika satchel and walked to the window. He extended the antenna of the satellite device and began punching in the numbers.

Chuff. Chuff. Chuff.

Maxwell rounded the corner at the fantail, then started back up the starboard side. Jogging on the hangar deck involved a certain risk. You had to be wary of aircraft tie-down chains that could snag an ankle and make you a cripple. You had to dodge the tow vehicles that shuttled back and forth, darting in front of you, dragging jets around the deck.

He was on his second lap when he heard someone coming up from behind.

"Mind if I tag along, XO?" B.J. Johnson appeared beside him, matching his easy stride. She was wearing nylon warm-ups and a white headband. Maxwell noted her level, relaxed pace. B.J. was not a jogger. The kid was a serious runner.

"I'd probably just hold you up."

"You're doing a good eight-minute-mile pace," she said. "Suits me."

"Looks like you've done this before."

"Once or twice," she said, breathing easily. "A whole slew of ten-kay runs, and the Marine Corps marathon last fall. Three hours twenty-five minutes. Not bad for a girl, huh?"

"Not bad at all. You beat me by five minutes."

She smiled at that. "So?"

They made a half-dozen circuits of the hangar deck, maintaining the eight-minute pace. "How many laps to a mile?" she asked.

"I don't know. Twenty laps takes me forty-five minutes. What's that? Six miles?"

"Close. How far you gonna go?"

"Six. Then I'm wiped out." He looked at her again and said, "What's on your mind, B.J.? You didn't come up here to run laps with an old guy."

She kept her eyes straight ahead. "I need somebody to talk to. Spam is no use. She's on another frequency. To the other guys in the squadron, I'm still an alien. I thought maybe I could run something by you."

"Sounds heavy. What's the subject?"

"Me. I'm going to quit."

Maxwell slowed to a halt. "If we're gonna talk about this, I have to be able to breathe. C'mon with me."

"Where are we going?"

"You'll see. A special place."

A twenty-knot wind swept over the catwalk, tousling B.J. Johnson's hair and ruffling the collar of her flight suit. Eighty feet below they could see the bow of the *Reagan* slicing like a cleaver through the Gulf.

B.J. stared down at the water and said, "Back when

I got my orders to flight training, I thought it was such
a bright shining opportunity. Then to get Hornets—
absolutely my wildest dream come true. It was supposed to be a great adventure.''

Maxwell knew what she meant. He could remember
his own flight training days—the exhilaration of going
off to Pensacola, beginning a career in naval aviation.
It never left you.

"So you changed your mind?"

"About the adventure part, no. I still love flying.
But the opportunity part, that stuff about the wings of
gold and the camaraderie of naval aviators—it didn't
happen, Brick. It's not happening. Not for me, not for
any women aviators. It's a lie."

He had never heard B.J. speak so bitterly before.
It gushed out in an angry burst. "Nobody said it was
going to be easy," he said.

Her eyes were filling with tears. "Damn it, don't say
that! I never wanted it to be easy. If it was easy, it
wouldn't be worth doing. It's just that . . ." Her voice
trailed off.

"You don't think it's worth doing anymore?"

"I don't think I *can* do it anymore." She began to
lose her composure. "I don't want to be a trailblazer.
I don't want to set a damned example. I just want to
go someplace where I'm accepted for what I can do."

She dabbed at her eyes with the sleeve of her T-shirt.
"Sorry. Fighter pilots aren't supposed to cry, are they?
They're supposed to be like John Wayne."

"John Wayne wasn't a fighter pilot. He was an
actor. You, on the other hand, are a real-life fighter
pilot. Feel free to cry."

Maxwell knew what she meant. B.J.'s troubles were

the same every minority faced when they broke into a fraternity like naval aviation. Just because you made it through the door didn't mean they invited you to the table.

"It's no secret," she said. "They really want us to fail."

"Who's 'they'?"

"Those who feel threatened by us. The Undra Cheevers and Hozer Millers who cheer whenever one of us bites the dust. It's like . . . we have no friends. No support group."

For a while Maxwell said nothing. He knew what she said was true. Women in military aviation were isolated, without the traditional bonds that male warriors took for granted. He thought about his own nugget years. Yes, he'd had a built-in support group. Not only did he have fellow male aviators with whom he lived and trained, he had mentors. He had his father, salty and opinionated. He had Josh Dunn, his father's best friend. He had a sequence of mentors— flight instructors, department heads, commanding officers.

For men, mentors were natural and necessary. For women fighter pilots like B.J. Johnson, they were nonexistent.

"Okay, let's start one," said Maxwell.

"Start what?"

"A support group. Consider me the founder and president of the official B.J. Johnson support group."

B.J. looked skeptical. "You're making fun of me."

"Not at all. The group has just been founded. There's only one thing you're not allowed to do."

"Uh-oh. What's that?"

"Quit."

B.J. turned and gazed out to sea. Off on the eastern horizon lay the low, mottled coastline of Iran. To the north was Iraq. Enemies everywhere.

"What would it prove? They're still gonna hate me."

"That's their problem. It's your life, not theirs."

B.J. didn't respond. She peered around, taking in the panoramic view. "I see why you like it up here."

"Out here at night, especially in a storm, you feel infinitesimally small. It puts your problems in perspective."

"Is that how you felt in outer space? Infinitesimally small?"

"Yeah, if you can call a two-hundred-fifty-mile-high orbit 'outer space.' "

She looked dreamily off into the distance. "I once thought I wanted to do that."

"You still can. You could be an astronaut, B.J."

She shook her head. "This is hard enough, just proving that I can fly the Hornet. Then I would have to somehow get into test pilot school, go through the same bullshit again. Proving myself. Then NASA. I can't be a trailblazer anymore."

Maxwell felt a shock run through him. He stared at her. "What did you say?"

She looked at him peculiarly. "Trailblazer?"

Maxwell turned his face out to the open sea. His mind was racing back in time. "That's what she called herself," he mumbled into the wind.

"She? You mean . . ."

"Deb." Maxwell gripped the rail with both hands. "She always called herself a trailblazer."

"Deb was your wife, wasn't she?" B.J. said gently. "I heard what happened. I'm sorry."

"Don't be. I'm over that."

"She was an astronaut too, wasn't she?"

"Almost. She was training for her first shuttle flight."

B.J. waited a moment. "Is that why you quit?"

Maxwell didn't answer right away. He had locked those memories in a dark compartment of his psyche, not to be shared. "It was more complicated than that."

"But you did quit. You resigned from the astronaut program."

"Yeah, I resigned."

She folded her arms over her chest and faced him. "No disrespect, sir, but doesn't it seem a little . . . contradictory, you giving me a pep talk about not quitting?"

The ship was heeling to port. As the *Reagan*'s course altered to the south, the glare of the afternoon sun spilled over them. Maxwell pulled his sunglasses from the sleeve pocket of his flight suit and put them on. "You're not me, and this isn't the space shuttle we're talking about. You're already a fighter pilot, and you have to have a better reason for throwing away your career than because the guys don't like you."

She sighed and looked out over the rail again. The sun was low over the Saudi coastline. "What was she like? Your wife, I mean."

"Smart. Good-looking. Gutsy."

"What would she say about what I'm doing now?

He looked at her questioningly. "What *are* you doing?"

"Being a trailblazer. Like her."

He nodded. "She'd say don't quit."

*   *   *

Outside her room, the late afternoon sun had settled below the rim of the high rise buildings across from the hotel. As she listened to the man's voice on the other end of the line, she felt a rush of emotion. She was surprised that Chris Tyrwhitt still had the power to rouse her.

"How did you know I was in Bahrain?" said Claire.

"Lucky guess."

"Are you still trying to get me to Baghdad? Forget it. I'm not coming."

"You don't have to. I'm coming to you."

A silence followed while Claire digested the news. She could hear him breathing on the phone. It sounded eerie, as if his voice were being channeled through outer space.

"I'm very busy," she said finally. "The divorce is still in process and we shouldn't—"

"We have to talk, Claire. Really. I need to see you."

"It won't change anything. Too much has happened."

"I don't care what's happened. I'll make it up to you. You don't have to believe me, just give me a chance. Can't we at least have a drink, maybe dinner together?"

She hesitated. She wished he didn't have this effect on her. Damn him, he was a masterful charmer, which was why she had fallen for him the first time around. She had learned her lesson. Once with Chris Tyrwhitt was enough, thank you.

But what the hell, he could be good company. He made her laugh, made her feel wanted, made her feel sexy. Which, of course, was the dangerous thing about Chris Tyrwhitt.

Don't see him, she told herself. *You're finished with Chris Tyrwhitt.*

"Okay," she heard herself saying. "We can meet for a drink."

SEVENTEEN

Bahrain

MANAMA, BAHRAIN
0930, FRIDAY, 23 MAY

A mini-tornado of dust swirled beneath the CH-53E Super Stallion helicopter as it alighted on the embassy landing pad. The khaki-clad naval officers trotted away from the helo in single file, clutching bags and hanging on to their caps. Each was running in the hunched-over position that fixed-wing pilots always took when they were forced to walk beneath the whop-whopping blades of a rotary-wing aircraft.

Of all the Gulf emirates, Maxwell liked Bahrain the most. The prosperous little archipelago was separated by a single causeway from the great Saudi peninsula. Though the same family—the Al-Khalifas—had ruled it for over two centuries, the emirate had received a heavy dose of westernization during a century of British occupation.

Maxwell dropped his bag at the edge of the concrete helo pad and gazed around. Bahrain looked just as he remembered. He could still see vestiges of the British colonial past in the architecture, in the way shops and stores were set back from the street. Bahrain was the most liberal and westernized of the Gulf states, and that was reason enough to be glad they were here.

All fifteen designated strike leaders, as well as every squadron commanding officer from the *Reagan*'s air wing, had been summoned to the briefing. For the strike leaders, it didn't matter what the reason was. It was a weekend off the ship.

Because the U.S. military's Bachelor Officers Quarters in Bahrain was too small to accommodate the attendees to the strike conference, the *Reagan* contingent would stay at the Holiday Inn. A bus was waiting at the edge of the helo pad to transport them to the hotel.

As the bus lurched out of the embassy compound, CAG Boyce yelled to the back of the bus. "Check into your rooms, then show up for beer call at seventeen hundred." He jammed a cigar in his mouth. "I mean everyone. No excuses."

The bus wound through the narrow side street, then onto the main thoroughfare of downtown Manama, the capital of Bahrain. The Navy pilots stared at the clean, well-kept buildings, the recently paved streets, the neatness of the city. They passed Sheikh's Beach, which was one of the few places in the Middle East where you could see women in bikinis.

They drove past a residential complex where, in one block, stood four identical houses. One of the Tomcat pilots knew the story. "Some rich local guy has four wives. According to the Koran, a man can have multiple wives, but he has to treat them equally. So the poor schmuck had to build a house for each one."

The Holiday Inn was a sprawling two-story building. It had a richly carpeted lobby, ornamented with brass and marble, and it was staffed by a brigade of what they called TCNs—Third Country Nationals—mostly Pakistanis and Filipinos, who were in perpetual motion delivering messages, fetching cocktails, emptying ashtrays.

The pilots stood in the lobby and gazed around. After the steel-encased dreariness of a Navy warship, the hotel looked like an imperial palace. It also possessed the most vital of accoutrements—a long, brass-railed bar extending just off the lobby. Through a glass-paneled door they could see the other essential component—a swimming pool and poolside bar where, if fortune should smile on them, they would encounter flight attendants in transit or a cluster of female tourists.

Directly across the street stood another palace, the Gulf Hotel, where it had been confirmed that a contingent of GAGs were staying. Bahrain was an even happier hunting ground than Dubai.

Maxwell was the last to check in. The desk clerk handed him the room key and said, "Message for you, Commander Maxwell. It came an hour ago."

On his way up the elevator he read the pink note sheet.

Dearest Sam,
   Miss you terribly. Please keep dinner open. I'm across the street in the Gulf Hotel, room 238. Call ASAP.
   Kisses, hugs, everything else,
   Claire

Maxwell's room was spacious, with sliding doors that opened on a sunny verandah with a table and patio chairs. He went to the phone, and punched up the number for the Gulf Hotel.

"Room 238, please."

No answer.

After he'd unpacked his duffel bag and hung up his uniform, he put on his swimming trunks and went down to the pool. Most of the *Reagan* strike leaders were already there. He saw DeLancey and Manson were at the poolside bar making moves on a couple of bikini-clad European women.

Maxwell swam half a dozen laps, then flopped in a lounge chair and let the sun dry him off. After several minutes, he went to the bar and picked up the phone. He tried the Gulf Hotel again. While the phone rang, he waved at DeLancey, who was eyeing him from across the bar.

Still no answer.

Maxwell ordered a beer, then chatted with a young British Airways first officer who was on a crew layover. At ten minutes after four, Maxwell went back to his room to get dressed for CAG's beer call.

He tried Claire again. Still no answer.

"Do you want to leave a message?" asked the hotel operator.

Annoyed, he hesitated, then said, "No."

CAG Boyce took a test puff on the Cohiba, then exhaled a long stream of smoke. He smiled in approval to the bartender. That was one of the blessings of deploying overseas. You could obtain real Cubans, not the knockoffs they sold back in the States for which they charged you twenty bucks.

From his stool at the end of the bar, Boyce watched his pilots. They were slamming down beers, telling flying stories, maneuvering their hands in the way fighter pilots always did at bars. Most were wearing chinos, polo shirts, loafers. By the short haircuts and the way they moved their hands, there was no mistaking them

for anything but U.S. military jocks. Each held the
rank of either lieutenant commander or commander
and was either a squadron commanding officer or a
strike leader.

Hanging out like this with his pilots was a treat for
Boyce. Being the Air Wing Commander was a lonely
job. He wasn't directly in command of a squadron,
just the overall boss of the flying units aboard the
Reagan. What he sorely missed was the daily hands-
on business of running his own fighter squadron.

He couldn't help thinking about the real reason they
were here. Behind the joking and hand-flying was a
serious purpose. Boyce remembered how it had been
during the Gulf War, and again during the punitive
raids they had delivered on Iraq throughout the last
decade. The procedure was simple. Take out the SAM
sites first, the AA positions, drop a few bridges, put
some smart bombs on their command and control
facilities. Inflict a little pain.

This time, he had a feeling, would be different. The
targets were not benign. If they didn't succeed in erad-
icating the threat, the threat could eradicate them.
Somebody else would be inflicting the pain.

At the end of the bar, DeLancey was telling a story.
Craze Manson was glued to his side, paying rapt attention and chortling in the right places with his goofy
laugh. Boyce noticed that Brick Maxwell stood apart
from DeLancey's group, drinking a beer by himself.

Boyce waited until DeLancey had finished his tale,
then he ambled down to the end of the bar.

DeLancey was on a roll. He saw CAG coming and
said, "Smoking those things will make your hair fall
out, CAG."

"It's worth it." Boyce took another puff on the

cigar. "Update me on the female pilot problem. The mouthy one, Parker. Is she getting her act together?"

A look of alarm flashed over DeLancey's face, then quickly vanished. "Spam? Oh, sure, she's gonna be all right."

"Doesn't look all right to me. She's been scaring the hell out of the LSO. The air boss and the captain both called me about it."

"She's showing a lot of improvement, CAG. I think she's gonna work out fine."

Boyce knocked the ash off his cigar. Something just didn't compute, DeLancey sticking up for a woman pilot. He had been one of the loudest female-bashers in the strike fighter community. Now he sounded like a women's-libber. Why?

There was one frighteningly obvious possibility.

Boyce placed his cigar in the big marble ashtray. He looked around, then said in a low voice, "Killer, would you by any chance be screwing Lieutenant Parker?"

DeLancey broke out in a laugh. "C'mon, CAG, give me a break. I'm her commanding officer, for Christ's sake. You know I wouldn't—"

"You'd screw a pile of rocks if you thought there was a snake in it."

DeLancey kept smiling, but his eyes darted around, making sure no one else was listening. "Not if it had 'U.S. Navy' stamped on it. I know better than that. I just think the kid deserves a break. Hell, she's a good pilot. In fact, she's already approached me about being a section lead."

"Section lead?" Boyce nearly choked. "Tell her she'd better learn how to get aboard the ship first.

Next cruise, maybe we'll talk about section lead." *If she's still around,* he thought.

DeLancey nodded. "I'll tell her."

Boyce puffed his cigar back to life. He hoped Killer wasn't bullshitting him. When a female pilot was having flying problems, it was a no-win situation. If you saved her life by kicking her out, you faced a sexism charge. If you kept her in the cockpit and she hurt herself, you were to blame. Either way, everybody lost.

At exactly six o'clock Boyce finished the stub of his cigar. "Drink up!" he bellowed. "CAG's hungry."

He knew a restaurant called Cico's which, he informed them, had the most superb Italian food in the Middle East. Maybe in the whole damned world. Boyce knew this because his mother was Italian. No one argued. The pilots understood the realities of military life. CAG was boss; they were on their way to a joint called Cico's.

Maxwell thought once again about the Gulf Hotel and Claire. Why hadn't she answered his calls? Damn it, she knew he was here. She had left the note.

On the way through the lobby, he tried phoning again. Still no response. This time he left a message with the concierge that he would call after dinner.

The food at Cico's, just as Boyce had promised, was excellent. He presided at the head of a long table with a red-and-white-checkered cloth. Bottles of red wine were passed up and down the table. Boyce told a story about when he'd been on exchange duty with the Royal Air Force in Oman and they'd gotten drunk and stolen a camel. Everyone laughed, though most of the senior pilots had heard the story a dozen times.

The pilots liked CAG Boyce. He was a traditional fighter jock, not one of the politically astute fast-burners on his way to higher command. Boyce was an old warhorse who, everyone figured, had gone as far as he would in the Navy's pyramidal rank structure.

The conversation around the table dwelled on the usual subjects: airplanes and women. The only subject not being talked about was the one most on their minds—why they were in Bahrain. If asked, the pilots had been warned to say only that they were here on weekend liberty. Sea duty was a bitch, you know. This was the New Navy, and they had to give you time on the beach to blow off some steam.

Leaving the restaurant, the group dispersed. Boyce and a contingent of his strike leaders piled into taxis and headed for a jazz place. DeLancey and his followers announced they were laying siege to a gin mill called Henry's. They had gotten reliable intelligence reports that a flock of GAGs had been sighted on the premises.

Maxwell watched them depart, then took a taxi back to the hotel.

"Come on, Claire, be a sport. Let's drink up and go to my room." Chris Tyrwhitt gave her a bleary smile. "For old times' sake."

Claire Phillips swirled the ice in her vodka tonic and regarded him over the rim of her glass. He hadn't changed. Still ruddy-faced, probably from all the drinking. He was wearing the same old clothes—wrinkled khaki shorts, long stockings, safari shirt. His mop of reddish hair had begun to show flecks of gray. "You haven't forgotten how to make a girl feel wanted, have you?" she said. "Is that still all you ever think about?"

"When I'm with you, yes."

"You haven't been with me for—what? A year and a half?"

"Nineteen months, sixteen days, and"—he made a show of looking at his watch—"nearly seven hours. Your choice, not mine."

"I remember. After you'd spent the night with that Danish woman, the consul's wife. Or was it the other one, the German floozy who—"

"She wasn't a floozy. She was a cabaret singer with a voice like Piaf."

"And a disposition like Himmler. Wasn't she the one who threatened you with castration?"

"No, that was the Ukrainian girl who worked over at the Reuters bureau. And I'm pleased to report that she didn't succeed. Since you believe nothing I say, however, you may wish to verify that fact for yourself."

She ignored the suggestion while she fumbled in her purse for a half-empty Marlboro pack. She had nearly kicked the habit. These days she smoked only when she was stressed out. She pulled a cigarette from the pack, then changed her mind and left it unlit in the ashtray.

"Baghdad must be pretty boring now," she said. "Most of the embassies shut down, no major news services except your own. What do you do for amusement?"

"The usual thing. I've developed a relationship with a certain female named Martha."

"Martha? Is she Iraqi . . . ?"

"Hard to tell. She's a camel, but I'm not sure of her nationality."

Claire had to laugh. It was that wacky outback humor that had drawn her to him in the first place. She reminded herself to be careful. This was a guy who could flaunt every code of moral conduct—especially the seventh commandment—and have you laughing about it.

"Do the Iraqis censor your dispatches?"

"Sure," he said. "But they like what I write, so it's no problem."

She crossed her legs and tugged the hem of her skirt closer to her knees. "Is that why you write such ingratiating bullshit? Like that piece about the school-children in Basra? Are you on their payroll?"

He didn't seem to be insulted. "I wouldn't exactly put it that way." He gave her a wink.

"You know what the U.S. military calls you out here? Baghdad Ben. They think you're the Iraqis' mouthpiece."

"How do you know what the U.S. military thinks? Still hanging out with the Yank flyboys?"

"I'm still a reporter."

"Anything for a story." He tipped his glass up and drained it. "Basically, we're all whores."

"That's pretty tasteless, Chris."

"We do what we have to do."

She bristled but let it go. After all, that was Chris Tyrwhitt's style. Three years ago, back in Washington, she had thought he was terrifically funny, that disarming Crocodile Dundee manner. She had known him only a couple of months before they were married. He was witty, good-looking, and when he felt like working at it, could be a competent journalist. What she learned later was that Chris Tyrwhitt seldom worked at anything except drinking and philandering.

Tyrwhitt put his hand on her knee. "I really have missed you, you know."

"You missed me so much you went to Baghdad."

"You threw me out, remember?"

She was about to make a sarcastic reply when she noticed he wasn't looking at her. Tyrwhitt was gazing at something over her shoulder. She turned to see what he was looking at.

Sam Maxwell stood in the entrance to the bar. His eyes were locked on the two of them.

"Do you know that chap?" Tyrwhitt asked. "He's been standing there staring at us."

For a second, their gazes met. Maxwell's face was a frozen mask. Claire was suddenly aware that Tyrwhitt's hand was still on her knee.

Maxwell turned and walked away.

"Oh, damn!" she said, and yanked Tyrwhitt's hand off her knee. She ran over to the entrance of the bar. "Sam?" she called, looking around.

He was nowhere in sight.

The bus that took them to the strike conference was the same one that had delivered them to the hotel yesterday, but instead of the smiling young Bahraini at the wheel, their driver was a Marine gunnery sergeant. He wore a sidearm and a UHF radio headset. Two more Marines in full combat gear, each carrying an M-16 and wearing their own headsets, occupied the front and the rear rows of the bus.

The bus wound through a labyrinth of back streets, while the guards maintained a watchful lookout. Not until they stopped did the pilots realize they were back at the old American embassy, an under-used facility that contained the only SCIF—Special Compartmentalized Intelligence Facility—this side of Riyadh. The SCIF had a blast door and another squad of armed guards. The exterior shell of the facility was shielded against monitoring or electronic intrusions.

Maxwell took a seat with the other pilots in the large, windowless briefing room. A half-dozen tiers of seats faced a narrow dais with a lectern and a row of folding chairs. Behind the lectern sat a khaki-clad admiral with two stars on his collar, and two civilians. By their ubiquitous button-down shirts and wing tips Maxwell knew they had to be spooks—either CIA or Defense Intelligence.

Next to the admiral, wearing his own khaki outfit, sat another civilian—the Undersecretary of the Navy. Whitney Babcock smiled and came over to shake hands with Boyce and DeLancey.

Rear Admiral Dinelli, whose title was a convoluted military acronym, COMUSNAVCENT—Commander U.S. Naval Forces Central Europe—took the lectern and opened the conference. "As you know, gentlemen, the Iraqis have been scaling up their threat posture steadily since last month. It began, as you might also suspect, precisely on the afternoon of 18 April."

Several pilots nodded. "When Killer flamed the MiG," someone volunteered.

"Correct. But not just any MiG. It happened to be a jet flown by a pilot named Al-Fariz, who, we have determined, was the nephew of the President of Iraq."

Someone in the room whistled. Several cast sideways glances at Killer DeLancey. DeLancey, for a change, was not grandstanding. He maintained a stoic expression.

"Since that day," the admiral went on, "things have heated up. They've been lighting up their air defense radars. On 17 May, they managed to bring down the F-16 at Al-Basra. We have reason to believe they may have more ambitious plans than ever before."

The admiral turned to the wall behind him. "Chart, please," he said, and an eight-foot-square illuminated map of Iraq lowered from the overhead. The admiral aimed a laser pointer at the map, positioning the beam directly over a spot to the south of Baghdad.

"Latifiyah," he said, making a tiny circle around the spot. "Iraq insists the facility is a pharmaceutical plant. They have, of course, denied United Nations inspectors access to the facility." The admiral aimed the laser again. "Here, at Al Fallujah, and another one five kilometers south of Baqubah." He pointed to a spot in the fertile valley northeast of Baghdad.

"Excuse me, sir," said a lieutenant commander from the Blue Tail squadron. "I remember Latifiyah from the Gulf War. I know for a fact we nailed that place."

The admiral nodded. "You did. It was gutted. Now they've rebuilt and gone deep underground. We have evidence that Latifiyah is the most heavily bunkered facility in the country with the exception of Saddam's own headquarters in Baghdad. Baqubah and Al Fallujah were also bombed and have been totally reconstructed with fortified storage containers."

"Storage for what, sir?" asked CAG Boyce.

The admiral seemed to consider the question, then he nodded to the seated civilians. "I'll let Mr. Ormsby of the Central Intelligence Agency take that one."

Ormsby took the lectern. His plump face was punctuated with round oyster-shell framed glasses beneath a receding hairline. "For the past six years, after the first U.N. inspection team was thrown out, Latifiyah was developed as a chemical and biological weapons plant. We have new evidence that it is being used as a rocket propellant facility and probably a missile assembly shop."

"What kind of missile?" asked Burner Crump, the F-14 squadron commander. "The new Scud?"

The spook shook his head. "Not a Scud, and not even a Silkworm, though the Iraqis would have no trouble obtaining them. Something not seen before in the Middle East." Ormsby turned to the screen behind him. The map of Iraq vanished and was replaced by a projected color image of a long, tapered missile cradled in a mobile launcher. The missile had sharply swept-back guide vanes and a concave indentation in its body.

"The Krait," he said. "Developed in China, brokered and sold by North Korea. Uses cheap and efficient global positioning satellite guidance—courtesy of our own Defense Department. The surface-launched version of the Krait has a range of three hundred miles and a speed in excess of Mach three."

Murmurs came from the assembled pilots. Each was doing the same quick calculation.

"That's right," said Ormsby. "Operating in the extreme northern Gulf, the *Reagan* battle group could be within range of the surface-launched version."

"You said 'surface-launched version,'" said Gordon. "Does that mean—"

"It does. Our sources report that they are reconfiguring several Fulcrums at Al-Taqqadum as strike fighters. We've observed what appears to be extensive low-altitude pilot training being conducted in the north, in the Mosul area. If they use the Fulcrum as a launch vehicle for the Krait, then every target in the Middle East will be vulnerable. Including the *Reagan*."

Tyrwhitt emerged from the windowless gloom of the SCIF. He stood for a moment on the curbside, blinking in the sudden brilliant sunlight. Even with the dark glasses it was painful.

The blue Toyota was waiting. "Hilton Hotel," Tyrwhitt said as he climbed in the back. He recognized the driver—a young Bahraini in the employ of the American consul.

As the Toyota headed down the road that paralleled the access to the SCIF, Tyrwhitt looked back at the front entrance. He saw the bus that had just delivered the American Navy pilots. They were getting their own briefing, most of it based on the information he had just delivered to his handler.

The pipeline of secrets, he thought. It flowed through the Middle East like crude oil.

His handler, Ormsby, was a pompous twit. He had conducted the debriefing as if it were a therapy session, delivering all this professional wisdom to the amateur spy. He even saw fit to admonish Tyrwhitt about drinking and exercising discretion with local women. The slightest lapse in discipline, you know, could jeopardize the balance of power.

For nearly three hours Ormsby had grilled him about the reports from the Iraqi military informer. What did the informer want? He didn't know. What was his job? No idea. Why was he willing to inform? He didn't say. Did he want to defect? Apparently not. Could he be trusted? Of course not. Could anybody?

The trouble with Ormsby, Tyrwhitt finally concluded, was that he was a prude. But so were most of

the Americans he had encountered in the espionage
business. Tyrwhitt was sure that Ormsby had never
gotten drunk or laid in a shithole like Baghdad.
Ormsby had probably never been in a whorehouse, at
least in the Middle East. The pink-cheeked twit knew
nothing about real life.

Now they were in the end game. Though Ormsby
hadn't said as much, they both understood that Tyrwhitt's return trip to Baghdad was probably his last.
The danger level had ratcheted off the scale. It would
soon be time to effect the egress plan.

The Toyota turned onto Al-Faisal Avenue. It was
barely ten o'clock, three hours before his flight departed. He had time for a few beers at the hotel. He
might even try seeing Claire again. Once more for old
times' sake.

Maxwell tried to focus on the briefing, but the image
kept reappearing in his mind—Claire and the guy with
his hand on her knee.

Again Maxwell pushed the picture from his
thoughts. A Navy captain from the NAVCENT intelligence unit was talking about fleet defense and target
critical nodes. He had a voice as monotonous as a
twenty-eight-volt motor.

". . . if the launch vehicles—the Fulcrums—were to
penetrate the battle group's two-hundred-mile defense
perimeter, not even our shipboard Phalanx batteries
would be guaranteed to stop an incoming Krait . . ."

*The two of them at the bar, the guy's hand on her
knee . . . It looked natural . . . She was used to it.*

He should have known better. After five years, she
had a life that did not include him. It was better this

way. He had enough problems without becoming involved with a female reporter.

"The Latifiyah propellant facility"—the captain was
aiming a pointer at the chart on the screen—"is identified by this fortified bunker with these ventilation
stacks." He indicated a series of concrete funnels protruding from what looked like a low, one-story
building.

The captain droned on through the high-value target list, identifying critical nodes for each, topographic
details, then discussed the current state of Iraq's air
defense system. When he finished, he looked at his
boss. "Anything else, Admiral?"

Before he could respond, Whitney Babcock rose
from his chair. "I have a few comments."

The admiral looked dubious, but he had no choice.
"Gentlemen, I think you all know Mr. Babcock, the
Undersecretary."

Instead of his Navy khakis, Babcock was wearing a
bush jacket with the belt tied behind. He looked like
the great white hunter. "Fellows, I want to tell you
that I've just spoken with the President about this situation. He wants you to know he is behind you one
hundred percent."

Several pilots exchanged bemused glances. Someone guffawed.

Babcock ignored this and continued. "I think you
all know me to be a straight shooter, right? Well, trust
me when I tell you this, the President is determined
to get tough with the Iraqis. Once and for all, he's
going to put a finish to the Iraqi threat. You can take
my word for it, gentlemen, your commander in chief
is one hell of a warrior."

At this, a titter rippled through the room.

The admiral looked pained. Standing behind Babcock, he glowered at the group and shook his head vigorously. CAG Boyce peered around at his pilots and let them read his lips: *Shut the fuck up.*

Silence fell over the group.

Babcock came to the end of his pep talk. "So, from one fighting man to another, let me tell you I have the utmost confidence in you." He paused for effect, then pulled off his glasses and said in a booming voice, "Good hunting, chaps."

Several seconds passed. Someone tried clapping, but it quickly sputtered out. An anonymous voice said, *"Chaps?"*

It was afternoon, nearly two o'clock, when the bus returned them to the Holiday Inn. A cloud formation was scudding in from the Saudi peninsula, carrying with it cooler temperatures and a hint of approaching rain. The briefing had taken them through the lunch hour, so most of the pilots headed directly for the poolside bar to order food. At four-thirty, the bus would return them to the helo pad, and they would be on their way back to the *Reagan*.

Maxwell went to his room to pack. The message light was blinking and a written note had been slipped under the door.

> *Where have you been, Sam? It's noon, and I will not leave this room until you call! Please, please call. Better yet, come by. In case you forgot, it's room 238.*
>
> *Love and kisses, C.*
> *P.S. It's still my birthday.*

As he stuffed his clothes and dop kit back into the duffel bag, he debated with himself. Call her and tell her what you think. Ask her what that scene in the bar was all about.

No, drop it.

He went to the phone and picked it up. Then he changed his mind. Drop it.

After several minutes he picked up the phone again, punched room service, and ordered a club sandwich. He finished packing, then watched CNN until the waiter delivered the sandwich.

He was leaving the room when the phone rang. He paused, listening to it ring. He closed the door and walked on down the hallway.

At the checkout desk, he scanned the lobby. He saw a half dozen of his fellow pilots from the *Reagan* and several Bahraini businessmen sipping coffee at tables. He paid his bill, which included the beers yesterday afternoon and all the unanswered phone calls to the Gulf Hotel and came to nine dinars—nearly thirty dollars.

She wasn't anywhere in sight. That was probably good. He didn't want a scene, and anyway, he knew he was not in control of his feelings. Still fixed in his mind was that hand on her knee. *Who the hell was that guy?* Someone familiar enough to fondle her in public.

Why the hell did it matter? he asked himself. It didn't. Let it die.

He was nearly to the coffee shop when he heard her voice. "Sam?"

He froze.

"Sam, I've been looking for you." She was wearing the same outfit, a sleeveless, knee-length silk dress, he had seen her in last night.

He thought she looked stunning.

The other pilots saw her at the same time. De-Lancey was walking from the elevator. He stopped in midstride and stared. So did Craze Manson. And CAG Boyce.

She ran to him and gave him a warm hug. Maxwell felt awkward, angry, foolish.

"Why didn't you call?" she said. "Why didn't you answer your phone?" She looked at his face. "Are you angry, Sam?"

He didn't answer. He felt everyone in the lobby watching him. He wanted to say, damn it, he *had* tried to call her. She hadn't answered because she was out with that dissipated-looking asshole who had his hands all over her.

Instead, he said, "I was tied up this morning."

"Why didn't you stop when you saw me in the bar last night? I was waiting for you, Sam."

He was aware of DeLancey and the whole crowd watching them. "Let's talk outside," he said.

She followed him to the sidewalk. The afternoon heat still lay over Bahrain like a blanket. The bus was already there, waiting on the semicircular drive to transport the pilots back to the helo pad. Most of the pilots were clustered around the door of the bus.

She stopped and looked at him. "I know why you're upset. Please listen to me. What you saw last night isn't what you think."

"Go ahead. I'm listening."

"I didn't expect that Chris would be here. I haven't seen him in months. We've been separated for over a year. The divorce papers are in New York waiting for signature."

Maxwell felt foolish. "Your . . . husband? The guy who writes the anti-American stuff from Baghdad."

She nodded. "Chris Tyrwhitt."

"Saddam's mouthpiece. Are you feeding him information, or vice versa?"

She looked like she had been slapped. "Neither. I was having a drink with him while I waited for you to show up."

The pilots were coming through the revolving door, carrying their bags. Maxwell saw CAG Boyce standing by the bus, watching them.

"You don't believe me, do you?" Claire's voice was breaking.

"Why are you here?" he demanded. "To pry another story out of me?"

"I'm here because I wanted to see you. I don't understand you. Why are you so cold?"

Maxwell didn't know. He didn't know anything. He wanted to take her in his arms, but he couldn't. He was paralyzed. He remembered DeLancey's accusation about her being a security risk. Now he didn't know.

Claire's eyes were brimming with tears. "Damn you, Sam Maxwell!" She said it loudly enough that all the aviators boarding the bus stopped and gawked at them. "You idiot! I love you. Don't you know that?"

Maxwell stared at her, totally confused.

"I've always loved you." She whirled away from him. She disappeared from his view around the corner of the hotel.

The bus driver beeped the horn. Maxwell turned and saw that the other pilots were all aboard, watching him through the windows.

CAG Boyce appeared in the door of the bus. "Get in the bus, Brick. We need to talk."

He took the seat next to Boyce in the last row.

As the bus rumbled out of the parking lot, Boyce said, "You may be a hell of a pilot, Maxwell, but you got a lot to learn about women."

"Sir?"

"That girl back there on the sidewalk. You stood there like a lump of cow crap and let her run away."

"We, ah, were having a disagreement, CAG."

"I know all about your disagreement with Claire Phillips."

Maxwell looked at Boyce in surprise. "Excuse me? You know—"

"She called my room last night, and I went down to meet her in the lobby. She kept me up well past midnight, while she told me all about herself. And you."

Maxwell had to shake his head in wonder. There was no end to the ways Claire surprised him. Nor Boyce.

Boyce went on. "She was worried that I—or the Navy—would think she was a security threat, being close to you. And the truth is, I thought she might be. But I realize now that the woman understands more about Middle East problems than you or I and probably our intel staff."

"Did she tell you about last night in the bar?"

"Yeah. While she was talking to her ex-husband, you stormed off like a kid who got stood up on his first date." Boyce shook his head in disgust. "That was pretty damn dumb."

Maxwell nodded, remembering the rage he had felt. Okay, that *was* dumb. He hadn't given her a chance.

Boyce gnawed on his cigar for a while, watching the bleached scenery of Manama roll past. The bus arrived at the embassy gate. The Marine sentry saluted, and the bus continued to the pad where the CH-53 Sea Stallion waited.

Boyce waited until the other pilots had exited the bus. "Assuming it's not too late—and it might be, after your sterling display of ineptitude—you might consider getting on your knee and begging forgiveness. For some reason that defies my understanding, that girl is in love with you."

EIGHTEEN

The XO

Killer DeLancey made love, Spam Parker reflected, like he flew fighters. Fast, furious, without preliminaries. He was pumping away in quick, relentless strokes, like a man in a hell of a hurry.

They were in DeLancey's stateroom, in his down-quilted bunk. It was two-thirty in the afternoon. Most of the squadron officers were either flying or working in their respective offices.

Of course, this *was* DeLancey's office. Here the commanding officer conducted squadron business, and here he met with his subordinate officers. And here this afternoon, while the *Reagan* cruised the Persian Gulf, he was fucking Lieutenant Spam Parker.

She had recognized the look in his eye when they were down in the ready room after the all-officers meeting. She and DeLancey were going over her monthly matériel division report. Like the other pilots on the day's flight schedule, she was wearing her green-gray flight suit, but not the standard baggy suit that looked like a potato sack. Spam's flight suit had been tailored, taken in at the waist and tightened around the legs, so that it accented her longish, narrow-waisted figure. The front zipper was far enough down so that when she leaned over to retrieve a document from her file case, DeLancey got a glimpse of cleavage.

His eyes fastened on her like heat-seeking sensors. She glanced down, as if she'd just noticed the gaping flight suit. She tugged the zipper up a couple of inches. She gave him a knowing smile.

It was enough. DeLancey glanced around, cleared his throat, and said, "Uh, I need to go over that report once more before we submit it to the air wing. How about dropping it by my office at, say"—he glanced at his watch—"fourteen hundred?"

Her eyes met his. The meaning was unmistakable. "Yes, sir. I'll be there."

It had been so easy.

DeLancey's breathing was becoming faster, more urgent. She began to moan softly. Not too loudly, just enough to give him encouragement. He liked that, she had learned. It was good for his ego.

She felt him tense, and she arched her back, emitting a low, throaty groan. DeLancey finished in a flurry of pounding and pumping.

It was over too soon, she felt like telling him. The guy did it like a jackrabbit. But she knew he wouldn't like that. She would let him think he was terrific.

They lay together in the bunk, the perspiration dripping from them onto the sheet. "Did you really want to see my matériel report?" she asked.

"What matériel report?"

She giggled. He was actually a pretty cool guy when he wasn't being the World's Greatest Fighter Pilot.

They dressed in silence. As she laced her boots, she said, "I flew with Craze Manson this morning."

"Yeah? How'd that go?"

"Very good. He said I was an excellent wingman." It wasn't exactly what he said, she remembered, but it was close enough.

DeLancey just nodded.

"So don't you think it's time I moved up to section lead?"

DeLancey shook his head. "I ran it by CAG, and he said not yet."

"CAG? Why do you have to have his permission? Isn't this your squadron?"

"It's his air wing. And he's taken a special interest in the . . . women pilots."

"Aliens, you mean."

"You know what I mean. You and B.J. are the only two women in his air wing. You're high profile, and CAG wants to be careful."

She noted the way DeLancey was watching her. He had a worried look on his face, like a man who had just seen an armed intruder.

Good, she thought. He was beginning to get the picture.

Maxwell peered around the corner of the passageway. The officers' berthing area was deserted. It was midmorning, with flight operations in progress, and all the inhabitants of the staterooms were in their respective offices or ready rooms.

All but one.

He glanced at his watch. He'd been there fifteen minutes now. No one had left or entered the area since he'd been standing there.

After five more minutes, he heard the lock turn in a stateroom door. The door cracked open. The head of Hozer Miller popped out and glanced quickly in each direction. Seeing nothing, Miller ducked back inside his room. "All clear," he said in a low voice.

The pudgy shape of Yeoman Third Class Diane Grotsky emerged from the room. Her chambray shirt flapped loosely over her blue dungarees. Grotsky's disheveled hair looked like a bird's nest.

Stopping in the passageway, she peered to the left, then the right—and a look of absolute terror flooded her round face. She was gazing directly into the face of her squadron executive officer.

Maxwell nodded to the terrified woman but said nothing. He swept past her to the closing stateroom door.

Clunk! The door wouldn't shut. Maxwell's right foot was inserted in the threshold.

Inside the room, Hozer Miller was seized by a sudden desperation. *Clunk! Clunk! Clunk!* He kept trying to slam the door.

"Open up, Hozer," said Maxwell. "It's come-to-Jesus time."

Hozer stopped trying. Maxwell heard a long sigh of resignation. The door slowly opened.

Hozer Miller stood in the doorway, barefoot and shirtless. He was wearing his boxer shorts. Miller looked at Maxwell and his shoulders slumped. Life as he knew it was over.

Maxwell glanced back in time to see the back end of Yeoman Grotsky, moving at an unusually brisk pace, disappearing around the corner of the passageway.

He walked past Miller and entered the room. He glanced around at the strewn clothes and rumpled bedding. The place looked like a grenade had gone off. Hozer was your basic slob, Maxwell observed.

"I should have known you'd find a way to get me," said Hozer bitterly.

Maxwell looked at him. "Why do you think I'd try to get you?"

"Because of the ration of shit I've been giving you. You know I'm one of Killer's guys. And Killer wants you gone."

Maxwell nodded. At least they could agree on something. "I suppose you know the consequences of fraternizing with an enlisted woman."

"I have a pretty good idea."

"It's a court-martial offense, Hozer. This is the New Navy, and there's no tolerance. You stand to lose your commission, your wings, everything."

The life oozed out of Hozer Miller. He slumped into the desk chair. "This is all I ever wanted to be since I was a kid—a fighter pilot on a carrier. Now . . ." Hozer had to fight back the tears. "Now I've blown it."

Maxwell was seeing a different Hozer Miller. Gone was the old smirk, the mock-respectful manner, the barely concealed insolence. Hozer looked like a beaten animal.

"How long's it been going on?" Maxwell asked.

"Since Dubai. It's not her fault. She's just a kid. She thinks I'm some kind of white knight because I'm an officer."

Maxwell thought about the plain-faced, plump enlisted woman, whose facial expression never seemed to change. He guessed that Diane Grotsky hadn't had many boy friends, at least of the sort who were likely to enhance her self-esteem. She had probably joined the Navy right out of high school, hoping to change her life. A romantic involvement with an officer and a pilot, even a tawdry shipboard affair, must have seemed like a fairy tale.

Maxwell asked, "Who else knows about it?"

"No one."

"Are you sure?"

Hozer looked up at him. "I may be stupid, XO, but I'm not suicidal. I wouldn't let anyone know that I was having an affair with an enlisted woman."

"So you're willing to tell a court-martial that you accept full responsibility for the affair? That the woman was not at fault?"

Hozer put his face in his hands and said, "Yes, sir."

"Even though it will be the end of your career? At the very least, you'll lose your commission and get a dishonorable discharge. Maybe worse."

Hozer shuddered and said, "I'll take whatever I've got coming."

Maxwell regarded him carefully. For all his flaws, Hozer Miller was actually showing minuscule traces of being a decent human being.

"You made a stupid choice, Hozer. After Tailhook, the press loves this stuff. This will get the Navy back on *60 Minutes*."

Hozer slumped farther into his chair, saying nothing.

"You put the careers of yourself and another person and the reputation of a whole squadron at risk."

Hozer nodded miserably. "Where will they hold the court-martial?"

Maxwell didn't answer right away. He looked around the room some more, seeing the photo of Miller's wife and two children on the desk. On the wall was the photo of Hozer receiving his naval aviator's wings.

Finally, Maxwell said, "This squadron needs fighter

pilots. We have a war to fight, and a court-martial at this time will take up valuable resources." He leveled his eyes at Hozer. "I want your word as an officer that the Grotsky affair is over."

A look of pure astonishment passed over Hozer Miller. "You mean . . . I won't lose my career?"

"I didn't say that. Give me your word."

"Yes, sir, you have my word it's over. I promise you."

Maxwell continued staring at him. Hozer Miller wore the look of an inmate who had gotten his first view of death row. "Good. I suggest you clean up this mess and get back to work."

Outside, in the long starboard passageway, Maxwell stopped and considered what had just happened. He knew it was his responsibility, as a senior officer, to file charges against Miller. The affair would serve as a warning to anyone who considered violating the military's sacred fraternization rule.

But, he reminded himself, he was the executive officer. It was his call, and in his judgment he had just achieved the best possible result. He had put an end to an illegal and potentially explosive situation. And he had scared the crap out of Hozer Miller.

"Pow-werrrrr!"

Pearly Gates was using his sweetest LSO sugar talk. But it wasn't working tonight. The Hornet in the groove was settling below the glide path, sinking toward the blunt killer ramp of the landing deck.

"Same damn thing," he muttered to Chesney, the assistant LSO. "She's outta here." He hit the button on his pickle switch, causing the red lights on the Fresnel Lens to flash. "Wave off, wave off!" Pearly barked into his radio.

Twin tails of fire shot from the tailpipes of the Hornet as the engines went to full power and the afterburners ignited. The fighter's nose pointed upward, back into the night sky.

"I hate this shit," said Pearly, watching the lights of the jet pass overhead. It was the pilot's third unsuccessful pass at the deck. Pearly knew he shouldn't blame himself, but damn! It pissed him off when he couldn't get one of his pilots aboard.

The sound-powered telephone rang. Pearly knew before he picked it up who it would be.

"Goddammit!" came the voice of CAG Boyce. "What's the problem out there?"

Holding the handset away from his ear, Pearly gazed up at the red-lighted, glass-paned space in the carrier's superstructure. He knew Boyce was up there gnawing on his cigar, glowering back at him. "Same as last night, CAG. She's overcontrolling, not giving me power when I call for it."

"Can you get her aboard, or do we bingo her?" Diverting the fighter to a shore-based airfield instead of landing back aboard the carrier was sometimes safer than letting an unnerved pilot try again for the deck.

"Let me work her one more pass," said Pearly. "I think I can get her down."

CAG didn't answer right away. Pearly knew that Boyce was peering at the Hornet out there in the pattern, thinking of all the consequences. "All right. One more pass. Make sure you take good notes, because if she doesn't get her shit together, I'm gonna convene a FNAEB on her."

Like everyone else, Boyce pronounced it "Fee-nab." A FNAEB—Fleet Naval Aviator Evaluation Board—was appointed whenever a pilot's flying was erratic or dangerous. The board's task would be to determine whether the pilot should lose his—or in this case her—wings.

The Hornet was back in the groove. "Hornet ball, Parker, nine-point-two."

"Roger ball."

Spam Parker's Hornet started down the glide path. She had a decent pass going, observed Pearly. This time she was steady in the groove, flying a center ball. So far so good.

Then the Hornet started settling.

"A lii-itle pow-werrrr," said Pearly, using his best sugar talk. "Just fine-tune it for me, Spam."

Pearly saw the Hornet climb back up to the glide path. "Hold what you got."

The lights of the Hornet drew nearer the ship. Pearly could make out the sleek silhouette of the approaching jet. It was settling again.

"Power! Fly the ball!"

He heard the engines power up. The Hornet rose back to the glide path.

"Don't go high. Fly the ball."

The Hornet leveled off, then plummeted toward the ramp.

Whump! The jet plunked down on the deck like a dropped bowling ball. With a shuddering roar, the Hornet lurched to a stop.

"One wire," called out Chesney. Spam had again landed short of all four arresting cables. Pearly Gates shook his head in disgust. He realized his hand was soaking wet from perspiration. He turned away from the scene on the deck and gazed out to the blackened sea. Sometimes he hated this goddamn job.

"A FNAEB?" Spam stared at him in disbelief. It was the worst thing that could happen to a pilot. "What's the problem?"

"The problem," said DeLancey in a level voice, "is your landing grade average."

"No, it's not." Spam's eyes flashed. "The problem is Pearly. He's giving me lousy grades because I'm a woman. He wants me to look bad."

"You make yourself look bad when you catch six one wires in a row. You got two wave-offs and a bolter on top of that."

"You sound just like Pearly," she snapped. "I thought you were on my side."

DeLancey looked exasperated. "I'm quoting the record. That's why we keep a record, you know—to spot a trend. The LSOs think your trend is dangerous."

"Are you going to support me or not?"

"I'm the commanding officer. I have to do what's best for the squadron."

Spam drew herself up to her full height so that she was peering down at DeLancey. Her voice rose to a crescendo. "You will put a stop to this. Do you understand? You cannot convene a FNAEB on me."

"What are you talking about? I'm the commanding—"

"You know exactly what I'm talking about. You won't be the commanding officer of a garbage scow if I tell them about us."

DeLancey's eyes widened as if he'd just seen an apparition. "Did you say what I thought you said?"

"If you allow this FNAEB, I'll tell the world that

the highly decorated Killer DeLancey is having sex with one of his female pilots. How do you think that will play on *Nightline*?"

DeLancey was too stunned to answer. He stepped back and stared as if he were seeing her for the first time.

Maxwell sat by himself at the end of the conference table while DeLancey convened the squadron department heads meeting. The safety officer, Lieutenant Commander Bat Masters, sat across from him. Lieutenant Commander Craze Manson, the maintenance officer, and Lieutenant Spoon Withers, the administrative officer, were ensconced along the far side of the big table.

Everyone knew DeLancey hated such meetings. His routine was to make a few brief announcements, then turn over the business of soliciting department head reports to the executive officer.

Today DeLancey seemed distracted. "As you know, CAG insisted that we get a new executive officer right away," he told them. "For that reason Commander Maxwell has been named the new acting executive officer of the Roadrunners."

Maxwell noted the "acting." Really magnanimous of Killer to be so congratulatory. He nodded to the assembled officers while they gave him a smattering of applause.

DeLancey glanced at his watch. "I've got an air wing staff meeting, so I'll turn the meeting over to the XO. I know you guys are going to give Commander Maxwell the same kind of cooperation you gave Devo Davis."

Maxwell noticed the smirks around the table. It was

no secret that the other officers had generally ignored
Devo. Now they planned to do the same with Maxwell. Okay, it was time for a change.

He waited until DeLancey was gone. "First item of
business," he said, "is a new operations officer. That's
going to be Bat Masters."

They all looked surprised. Manson blurted, "What's
going on? I'm senior to Bat. I should get the ops job."

"Bat already has experience in the ops department," said Maxwell. "I need you in maintenance."

Manson shook his head. "What's the skipper say
about that?"

"He said I'm the XO. He told me to make the call."

"We'll see about that," Manson muttered. He tilted
back in his chair and went into a sulk.

Maxwell ignored him and said, "Starting this afternoon, I'm going to visit each of your offices and go
over your records and schedules."

More surprised looks. Manson tilted forward in his
chair and said, "What for?"

"To get a quick snapshot of the squadron. I want to
know what's going on in each of your departments."

"Devo never did that."

Maxwell ignored him again. "Admin is my first stop.
I'll be there at thirteen hundred."

"Yes, sir," said Spoon Withers, jotting the time in
his notepad.

"Maintenance department at fifteen hundred,"
Maxwell went on. "That a good time for you, Craze?"

"No," said Manson. "I've got a suggestion. Why
don't you just chill out, Brick? Our departments ran
fine without Devo getting involved. They'll do fine
without you poking around." Manson looked around
the group. "Isn't that right, guys?"

No one answered. The other officers glanced at each other, unsure whose side to take. Bat Masters busied himself scribbling on his pad. Spoon Withers was studying the far bulkhead.

Manson stood up and made a show of consulting his pocket calendar. "Looks like I've got another appointment now. So long, everyone."

"It'll have to wait," said Maxwell. "We're having a meeting."

"Sorry. I'm busy."

Manson left the room, letting the door slam with a clunk behind him.

Several seconds passed while no one spoke. Maxwell felt the other officers watching, waiting to see what he would do. He rose and said, "Nobody move. I'll be right back."

Manson was still in the passageway. "Craze, wait a minute," Maxwell said. "I want to talk to you."

"Yeah?"

Maxwell glanced around. The passageway was empty. Craze Manson was about his height, but pudgy and thicker at the waist.

He seized Manson by the collar and—*Wham!*—rammed him against the steel bulkhead.

Tightening his grip on Manson's collar, he yanked his head forward. Craze Manson's eyes bulged.

"What the hell? Are you crazy or—"

Wham! Maxwell slammed him back into the bulkhead. "Listen to me, Craze. If you ever utter a disrespectful word to a senior officer in this squadron, I will personally kick your ass up between your shoulder blades."

Manson's face was filled with disbelief. "Hey! I'm a

lieutenant commander in the Navy. I don't have to take this shit from—"

Wham! Manson's head ricocheted off the steel bulkhead. His eyes were watering.

Maxwell tightened his grip even more, clamping down on Manson's windpipe. "Do you understand what I'm telling you, Craze?"

Manson stared back at him.

He gave Manson a violent shake. "Do you understand me, Craze?"

"Yes," Manson croaked. "Yes, *sir*."

Maxwell released him. "That's good. You know, as the new XO I really appreciate your cooperation, Craze. Now, don't you agree that we ought to continue the department head meeting?"

Manson hesitated. Maxwell gave him a nudge forward. Manson straightened the collar of his uniform, then trudged back toward the conference room.

The squadron department head meeting continued without any further rancor. Maxwell made notes while he listened to each of the weekly reports. He assigned the upcoming duty watch periods, then thanked the officers for their support.

The meeting was ended. As Maxwell excused himself and left the room, he noticed that each of the officers rose and stood at attention. Even Craze Manson.

Maxwell came into his room and went directly to the laptop on his desk. He clicked the Power button, then while he waited for the computer to labor through its boot-up, he slid a Berliner Philharmonic CD—Mussorgsky's "Pictures at an Exhibition"—into the disc player.

When he finally got on-line, he checked his mailbox. It was empty.

No surprise, he thought.

He listened to the swelling symphonic music while he tried to compose an E-mail message. He could still see her face, the tears, the anger and disappointment. *Damn you, Sam Maxwell. I love you . . .*

After he had pecked out the message on the notebook keyboard, he reread the note, then deleted it. He wrote another. And deleted it.

After the third try, he tilted back in the steel chair and stared at the screen.

Dear Claire,

You used to ask why my call sign was "Brick." Now you know. Describes how my brain works. I let you run away from me without telling you what I most of all needed to say: I WAS WRONG.

It was an unforgivable, brick-headed mistake, and I'm sorry. It is too much to expect that I would get a second chance. I had that already. But if you should choose to see me again when the Reagan *comes to port, I promise I will do better.*

I love you.

Sam

He pushed the Send button and logged off.

NINETEEN

The Ramp

The blackness.

Spam hated it. She hated night flying in general, and in particular she hated launching and recovering on an aircraft carrier at night. Most of all she despised the inky, vile blackness that clung like a shroud over the Persian Gulf.

It was stupid. Why were they droning around in the dark up here on the CAP station? They called it Combat Air Patrol, but she knew that no one in the region, least of all the Iraqi Air Force, was crazy enough to venture out in this evil blackness.

Only the U.S. Navy. So typically stupid.

"Runner Forty-five," came the voice of Killer De-Lancey, her flight lead. "Check your position. You're too far abeam."

"I'm just where I want to be," she answered. "What's the problem?"

"Your station is supposed to be a mile abeam. Move it in."

She felt like telling him to shove it. He could pull that world's-greatest-fighter-pilot crap with everyone

else, but not with her. She didn't have to put up
with it.

She knew why Killer was her flight lead on tonight's
sortie. He was checking on her. He wanted to see how
she performed as a wingman. She was being evaluated.

On every sortie for the past week, Spam had found
herself assigned to fly with a senior officer. And they
never gave her anything meaningful to do. Nothing
but these goddamn boring CAP assignments.

Yesterday she'd flown with Craze Manson, who
was a jerk. And the day before with Maxwell, the
ex-astronaut that DeLancey hated so much. To her
surprise, Maxwell seemed like an okay guy, which
made her wonder why DeLancey was always bad-
mouthing him. Spam reminded herself to check that
story out. You never knew when such a thing could
be useful.

At least she'd heard no recent talk about a FNAEB.
Killer had gotten the message loud and clear. The
cocky little bastard had figured out that if he wanted
to keep his job, he had best look out for the interests
of Lieutenant Spam Parker.

Sleeping with the boss. It always worked. The best
career insurance you could have.

"Runner Forty-five, we're leaving CAP for the
marshal."

"Roger that," she replied.

It was too early. She had expected that they would
remain on the CAP station another ten minutes. The
marshal was a stack of holding patterns thirty miles
behind the ship where the inbound aircraft positioned
themselves for recovery aboard the carrier. Each pilot
was supposed to time his turn in the marshal pattern

so that he "pushed"—departed the stack—at a precise time that would keep him in sequence with the other jets.

She knew why they were going early. Killer was worried she would have trouble getting set up in the marshal pattern and screw up the approach sequence.

Like last night. She had gotten out of sequence during the push. But it wasn't her fault, she remembered. It was those dumb shits in CATCC—Carrier Air Traffic Control Center—who kept issuing totally incomprehensible instructions to her. They had deliberately caused her to arrive late at the marshal pattern, which in turn caused her to push at the wrong time, which had forced a couple of other Hornets to wave off their approaches to the ship. Then they tried to blame it on her—

"You're ten miles from marshal," she heard De-Lancey say. "Make a left-hand entry and start your timing. Don't screw this one up."

Spam felt a burst of anger. How dare he talk like that when everyone could hear? Then she realized that she was hearing him on the back radio, the secondary frequency used for plane-to-plane private communications.

"I know what I'm doing," she snapped back. "Save the lecture for those idiot CATCC controllers."

That should shut him up.

In the briefing room before the launch, DeLancey had tried to intimidate her with that male senior-fighter-pilot act. Admonishing her about flying a good pass at the ship, staying in position, getting set up in marshal.

She had shut him up him by mentioning her upcoming interview with the senator from California.

DeLancey had nearly choked. "With who?"

"You know, the woman senator who's investigating the reports about the Navy mistreating women pilots."

After that he sulked. He was strangely quiet as they rode the escalator to the flight deck. On the radio he was surly and curt, giving her this unnecessary advice.

The two Hornets passed over the marshal holding fix at twenty-two thousand feet. Killer flashed his lights, signaling that Spam was detached from the two-ship formation.

She entered the holding pattern—and became confused. Was the holding radial two-thirty or three-twenty? What was her push time? How the hell was she supposed to get back to the fix when—

"Runner Forty-five, this is Marshal. Where are you going? Your push time is now."

"I was getting established in this stupid pattern. What's the hurry?"

"Roger, Forty-five, turn to a heading of zero-five-zero. Start your descent now."

Spam was rattled and angry. On the back radio, she said, "Damn it, this is your fault. You dropped me off too close to the stack. You're gonna hear about this!"

I hate that bitch. The thought kept playing like a refrain in DeLancey's head.

He was descending through eight thousand feet. On the marshal frequency, he could hear the controllers issuing instructions to Spam. She had missed her push time and was out of sequence. And, of course, she was arguing.

She was hopeless, thought Delancey. Spam Parker

couldn't navigate her way out of a parking lot. Yet she had everyone—from the captain of the ship to the air traffic controllers—treating her with kid gloves. No one wanted a war with such a belligerent female.

Including Killer DeLancey.

Why did I do it? he wondered again. It was insane, getting involved with her. It was the worst mistake you could make in this business, thinking with the wrong part of your anatomy. Getting laid had taken priority over keeping his job.

He had to find a way out.

Twenty miles from the ship, passing five thousand feet, he called, "Runner Forty-one, platform."

"Roger, switch to final controller."

On the final control frequency he could no longer hear Spam and her ongoing dispute with the marshal controller. She was still ten miles behind him. That was fine with him. He'd heard enough of her bitching.

A half mile from the carrier, he picked up the glimmer of the deck lighting and the amber meatball. De-Lancey flew a steady pass to the deck, snagging the three wire.

Following the lighted wands of the taxi director, De-Lancey parked his jet forward of the carrier's island superstructure. He shut down the engines, but left the battery switch on while he listened to the UHF radio.

Just then, he saw the dark silhouette of a Hornet flash past the port side of the ship. A second later, he heard the roar of twin afterburners—*Whooom!* A jet was being waved off from its pass at the deck.

Spam, he realized. Getting another wave-off by the LSO. This was going to be interesting.

On his UHF radio display he selected the channel on which the LSO was working Spam's jet. Then he heard rapping on his Plexiglas canopy. Ruiz, the plane captain who maintained DeLancey's jet, was standing on the boarding ladder.

DeLancey raised the canopy. "There's something wrong with the radio," he yelled over the din of deck noise. "It dumped the loaded frequencies. I have to reprogram it."

"Never mind, sir," Ruiz yelled back. "I'll do that."

DeLancey shook his head. "No, I remember the frequencies. I can do it." He closed the canopy and busied himself punching numbers into the UHF display. Ruiz shrugged and stepped back down the boarding ladder.

On the radio DeLancey could hear Pearly Gates using his sweetest sugar talk: "—not enough power, then you came on with too much. Go easy with it next time, Spam."

"You go easy!" Spam snapped back. "I was doing okay until you started giving me all those power calls."

Listening to the radio exchange, DeLancey began to have an idea. There was a way. Maybe, just maybe, he had found a way out of his predicament.

"You tell me," Boyce barked. "Why the hell is that pilot still wearing wings?"

Maxwell didn't reply. They both knew it was a rhetorical question. And they both knew why Boyce was asking the question in a loud voice. The skipper of the *Reagan*, Captain Stickney, had just stormed into CATCC.

The room was flooded in an eerie, red-lighted glow. Flickering consoles were arrayed along each bulkhead.

Controllers sat hunched over their displays, directing the *Reagan*'s jets through the night sky.

Stickney was wearing his old battered Navy flight jacket. "We're running out of sea room on this heading," he said. "We're bearing down on Kharj Island and a cluster of Iranian oil platforms. You've got five more minutes to get her down or she bingoes."

Boyce nodded. "Yes, sir. We've got the tanker hawking her on the downwind."

Stickney didn't look happy. He turned to leave, then said over his shoulder, "Why *is* that pilot still wearing wings?"

Spam tried to concentrate. Down there in the ready room, she knew all the other pilots—*the men*—were glued to the PLAT, cackling and making bets and having a good old time watching the alien trying to get aboard. Bolter, bingo, or barbecue?

She was on final approach, a quarter mile from the ship. Close enough to see the ball clearly. It was a little low, and that was fine with her. It made for a better pass, she believed, if you kept it on the low side all the way in. It gave you a better shot at the wires.

"Don't go low," she heard Pearly say. "A lii—tttle powerrrrr. . . ."

She responded with a jab of the throttles.

The ball was coming up, almost in the middle . . .

"Eeeeasssy with it." The LSO's voice sounded different, she thought.

Then, the same voice, "Don't go high!"

It didn't sound like Pearly. CAG must have assigned another LSO to take over.

She snatched the throttles back again.

She heard a garbled transmission. The new voice again: "Don't go high. Right for line up."

Obeying, she dipped the right wing, swinging the jet's nose slightly to the right.

And dropping lower.

Much lower. The ball was descending to the bottom of the lens.

More garbled transmissions. She didn't understand. *What was he saying?*

The red wave-off lights were flashing.

The ball was flashing red at the bottom of the lens. She saw the gray mass of carrier looming out of the darkness ahead.

She saw the ramp.

Spam jammed the throttles forward. Seeing the blunt end of the deck swell in front of her, her mind froze.

"Power! Wave off! Wave off! Burner!" Pearly Gates was yelling—screaming—into his radio.

It was as if she didn't hear him. The jet was descending like a rock toward the blunt ramp of the carrier. Suddenly Pearly knew what would happen next.

His only escape was the survival net that hung out over the water beneath the platform. He took one last glance at the approaching jet, then dropped his handset. With a running leap, he hurled himself over the side of the platform. Astonished, the two other LSOs dropped their notebooks and leaped behind him.

In the next instant, the F/A-18 struck the ramp.

KABLOOOM! The jet broke in half, and the internal fuel tanks exploded.

A torrent of flaming jet fuel swept over the aft flight deck, engulfing the LSO platform.

The aft portion of the fighter, tailhook still attached, slid up the deck and snagged the number one arresting wire. The tail of the jet lurched to an abrupt stop, burning fiercely.

The forward half of the Hornet was wrapped in flame. As if in slow motion, it tumbled end over end down the angled deck. At the end of the angled deck, it pitched into empty space and disappeared in the blackness of the Gulf.

A sheet of flame covered the ramp of the landing area. Trapped in the arresting wires, the aft fuselage was a bright orange fireball. The LSO platform and its electronic console were ablaze.

Klaxon horns blared. The air boss's voice boomed over the loudspeakers: *"Fire! Fire! Fire on the flight deck aft and amidships. Away all support teams. This is not a drill!"*

It was a scene of horrific beauty. Whipped by the thirty-knot wind over the deck, the flames cascaded into the sky, lighting up the flight deck. Behind the ship, the surface of the sea shimmered in an orange glow.

Firefighters in asbestos suits moved like mechanical toys over the illuminated deck. Hoses gushed streams of white foam onto the blaze.

DeLancey watched from the cockpit of his parked Hornet. He was alone. All the deck crewmen had run to join the fire-fighting team. DeLancey allowed himself a smile of satisfaction.

TWENTY

The Cave Dwellers

USS *RONALD REAGAN*
0900, TUESDAY, 27 MAY

Pearly Gates was a mess. Both eyebrows were singed away, and his left arm was bandaged. His ankle was sprained from having the other LSOs land on top of him in the net.

He was taking Spam Parker's death hard. The worst thing that could happen to an LSO was to lose a pilot he was controlling. He kept shaking his head. "I tried to help her. She wouldn't respond. She wouldn't answer my calls."

"Nobody's blaming you," said Maxwell. "You did your best."

To his surprise, Maxwell's name had appeared on the letter appointing the investigation board. As squadron executive officer, he wouldn't normally sit on an investigation. But then he realized the board's composition had been decided several weeks before the accident, when he was still the squadron operations officer.

The senior member was Commander Duke Zybrowski, executive officer of VFA-34. Also appointed to the board were Craze Manson and the flight surgeon, Knuckles Ball.

"Big Mac got it the worst," Pearly told the assembled board. "He was the last into the net and he was on top. He got second-degree burns on his back."

"You guys were lucky," said Zybrowski. "The LSO platform was roasted. The Fresnel Lens was trashed. It was amazing that no one was killed." Then he corrected himself. "Except Parker, of course."

Pearly was still shaking his head. "It was so weird. Like . . . she was getting other instructions."

"Other instructions?" asked Maxwell, puzzled. "What do you mean, other instructions?"

"I don't know exactly. It was like she was doing the *opposite* of what I was telling her."

"Did you hear anything else on the frequency?"

"No, sir. But I had this feeling that . . . I wasn't getting through."

Maxwell's brain was still processing this information. It didn't compute. *Other instructions?*

"Could she have been listening on another frequency?" he asked. "Her back radio?"

"I had good comm with her when she called the ball," said Pearly. "But when I tried calling her that she was going low, it sounded like the frequency was jammed."

Maxwell stared at the bulkhead for a moment, trying to reconstruct the scene. Something was nagging at him—a tiny, vague image lurking in the back of his brain.

The board called Killer DeLancey.

He flashed the trademark grin and said, "Okay, guys, fire away. What do you want to know?"

"We're having a problem establishing Spam's radio

setup the night of the crash," said Zybrowski. "You were her flight lead. We have the tape record of all transmissions on the number one radio between you and the ship's controllers. But we can't find a record of any dialogue between you and Spam on the number two radio."

"Probably because there wasn't any," said DeLancey. "The mission went as briefed. Nothing needed to be discussed on the second radio."

Maxwell found that peculiar. "You mean Spam didn't argue or discuss anything while you were airborne? Wasn't that a characteristic of hers, always making spurious radio calls?"

DeLancey shook his head. "Not anymore. I straightened her out on that. Her attitude had really turned around."

Maxwell was dubious. From everything he knew, Spam Parker's attitude, if anything, had gotten even more argumentative. "How about your number two radio? What were you using for a tactical frequency?"

DeLancey gave him a withering look. "What do you think? Squadron common, 295.7 megahertz, just like we're supposed to."

Maxwell held up a rectangular card. "This is your kneeboard card from the flight. You didn't fill in the box with assigned frequency. But there's a symbol jotted down here—'X-W.' What does that mean?"

DeLancey peered at the card. " 'X-W'? No idea. Something I jotted down while we were briefing. Maybe it meant 'crosswind.' Spam was having trouble figuring out wind and drift in the marshal pattern, and I was helping her with it."

The board members asked more questions about

Spam Parker's flying discipline—or lack of. DeLancey handled all the queries with an easy nonchalance.

The board had no more questions for DeLancey.

"It's a damn shame," he said as he rose from his chair. "Parker was turning into a good fighter pilot."

The board members looked at each other. No one offered a comment.

After DeLancey left the room, Zybrowski asked the others, "Do you think he really believes that shit?"

Lieutenant Commander Big Mac MacFarquhar had a walrus mustache and a booming voice. "Yeah, that was me who flattened Pearly. I was the last one in the net."

Maxwell winced. Big Mac weighed in at an easy two-fifty. Having an object the size of MacFarquhar land on you from twenty feet above could be lethal.

MacFarquhar peeled back his flight suit and showed Maxwell the bandages on his back. "The fire was already on us when I jumped. One more second and I would've been a flame-broiled Big Mac."

They were in the air wing office, where MacFarquhar had his own cubicle with his name on it. Big Mac was the senior LSO aboard the *Reagan*, and it was his job to supervise all the other squadron LSOs.

Maxwell looked at the yellow pad on which he had jotted notes during the interview with Pearly Gates. "Pearly said it seemed to him as if Spam were getting 'other instructions.' What's your take on that?"

"At first I thought so too. It was like one of the other LSOs had cut in and told her, 'Easy with it,' or something like that. But I checked the tapes. Nobody said squat."

"Then what made her dump the jet onto the ramp?"

MacFarquhar shook his head. "Pilot error. Arrogance. Parker flew into the spud locker. Period."

"Then why was she even allowed to be out there?"

"You guys tell me. She was your problem, not mine. I told Killer we oughta send her packing."

"What did Killer say?"

"He said to keep her in the loop, don't worry because she was getting better."

"But she wasn't getting better."

"Yeah, and now she's dead. And pardon me if I don't get all remorseful about it. That dumb broad nearly killed me and all my LSOs." MacFarquhar glanced around, then lowered his voice. "Good riddance, I say. Too bad it had to cost us a Hornet. I'll tell you this much, I've got no stomach for any more fucking social experiments like Spam Parker."

Maxwell let MacFarquhar rant for a while. Big Mac was a good LSO, but Maxwell knew he was not an objective witness. He was still reliving the horror of the fireball on the flight deck.

Finally Maxwell thanked him and left the office. Walking down the passageway, he pondered again what little he had learned. Why did DeLancey, a fervent antifeminist, not act when the LSOs told him they wanted Spam taken off flying status?

Why did Spam Parker, who wasn't known to be crazy or suicidal, ignore the radio calls that would save her life?

It didn't add up.

*   *   *

Petty Officer Third Class Jose Ruiz was still wearing his flight deck float coat. His cranial protector lay on the padded seat next to him. He scratched his head and said, "Well, sir, it was dark, and I wasn't paying that much attention."

They were sitting in the back of the ready room. Maxwell prompted him. "But you definitely saw Commander DeLancey remain in his cockpit after he landed and you had secured the tie-downs?"

"Yes, sir. When he raised the canopy, he told me he was going to reprogram the radio."

Maxwell tried to visualize DeLancey reprogramming his radio. Something wasn't making sense. "Why would he do that?"

Ruiz chuckled. "He said he screwed up and forgot to use the 'crypto hold' function that saves the frequencies."

"Isn't it your job to reprogram the radio when that happens?"

"Sure, but the skipper said he needed the practice. He's a cool guy, Commander DeLancey. Most of the pilots just walk away and leave that stuff to us."

Maxwell thought for a second, mentally reconstructing the scene on the flight deck the night Spam Parker crashed. "So Commander DeLancey was sitting in his cockpit when Lieutenant Parker's jet hit the ramp?"

"Yes, sir, I believe so."

"Weren't you there?"

"As soon as the fire broke out, I ran over to man a hose." Ruiz looked worried. "Did somebody do something they weren't supposed to, Commander?"

Maxwell wondered briefly how perceptive the nineteen-year-old enlisted man was. Had he read anything into the questions? "No, not at all. This is what we do when we investigate an accident."

The young plane captain shook his head. "Do you know what happened to Lieutenant Parker? Do you know why she flew into the back of the ship?"

"Not yet, but I'm going to find out, Ruiz." With that thought, Maxwell looked up, over Ruiz's shoulder. In the front of the ready room, DeLancey was watching them intently.

Half an hour later, DeLancey stopped him in the passageway outside the Roadrunner ready room.

"You're off the Mishap Investigation Board. As of now."

Maxwell tried to read DeLancey's expression. Nothing the man did surprised him anymore. "It's not a good time, Skipper. The board is in the middle of making its report, and I'm—"

DeLancey cut him off. "You heard me. Butt out. You shouldn't have been on the board in the first place. As executive officer, you've got real work to do. Right now you're supposed to be up in strike planning putting together the coordinated ops plan."

There was no use arguing. "Yes, sir. Who's taking my place on the investigation board?"

"Lieutenant Cheever. Hand over all your notes and material to him. He'll finish the report."

Maxwell watched DeLancey walk away. DeLancey now had his acolytes, Craze Manson and Undra Cheever, on the board. It meant that he controlled the investigation.

The phone in Maxwell's stateroom rang.

"It's B.J. Johnson, XO. Can we talk?"

Maxwell glanced at his watch. "I've got an intel briefing in about an hour. How about the wardroom in ten minutes?"

"Someplace more private would be better."

He thought for a second. "Okay, the hangar deck, by the number two elevator."

"See you there."

In another few minutes, they were walking along the perimeter of the hangar deck. Maxwell said nothing, letting her talk.

"Spam never actually *told* me something was going on," said B.J. "But she was my roommate, you know. You get a sense of these things."

She paused to watch a tug hauling an F/A-18 across the deck to a maintenance bay. The *Reagan* was between flight operations cycles. Blue shirts were respotting jets, shuffling aircraft from the flight deck to the hangar deck, getting ready for the next aircraft recovery.

"What things? For example?"

"For example, I'd come in, and she'd be talking on the phone with someone—she wouldn't use a name. But I could tell by her voice that it was someone . . ." B.J.'s voice trailed off.

"Someone she was intimate with?"

B.J. nodded. "That was Spam. It didn't surprise me. She called it 'stud du jour.' It was just her style. Wherever she was, she had a boyfriend."

"She never told you who it was?"

"No."

"But you have a pretty good idea, right?"

B.J. nodded again. "It must have been after Dubai. It was like, her attitude changed. She suddenly stopped badmouthing everyone, going on about how we were being screwed over by the establishment, like she used to. She talked about how she was going to get moved up to section lead. She was really upbeat." B.J. paused, and said, "For a while."

"Just for a while?"

"She was having trouble coming aboard, as you know. She was blaming it on Pearly. But then she started worrying about a FNAEB. She was afraid they would take her wings. I heard her say one time, if he let them FNAEB her . . ." B.J. didn't finish the thought.

Maxwell gave it a moment. "Who was 'he'?"

"She never actually said. But I could guess. So can you."

He could. "The skipper?"

"It's just a hunch. Call it intuition if you like."

More than a hunch, Maxwell knew. They both knew she was right. He was shocked, but not surprised. It wasn't unheard of in the Navy that a senior officer, even a squadron commander, might become involved with a female subordinate. It would explain De-Lancey's coddling of a weak pilot.

B.J. was looking at him. "What do you think? Could it have had anything to do with her getting killed?"

"I don't think so," he said, trying to sound sure of himself.

He could see by her expression that she didn't believe him.

"When?" CAG Boyce said, repeating the question. "That's up to the President. Could be as soon as tomorrow. Or the day after."

On the bulkhead behind him was an illuminated map of Iraq. All his strike leaders were assembled in the intelligence briefing space.

Boyce went on. "It seems that our intelligence assets in Baghdad have been compromised. But they sent an alert that Iraq has completed its weapons assembly project and is ready to push the button. The United Nations is now going through all the usual posturing. They've issued a forty-eight-hour ultimatum to Saddam to open up all his weapons facilities and submit to inspection."

A Hornet pilot piped up, "Hey, great. Saddam's gonna invite the inspectors over to his palace for tea and then give them all his new toys. We can all go home."

A ripple of laughter ran through the room. Boyce said, "Yeah, right. What it means is he gets two free days to hit us before we hit him. And we can forget the element of surprise. He's gonna know we're coming."

Boyce walked over to the map. "Strike leaders, I want each of you to finalize your strike plans. Replot all your run-in lines according to the latest threat assessments. These will be updated hourly based on satellite and recon data."

"What about the air-to-air threat?" asked a Tomcat pilot.

"Al-Taji and Al-Taqqadum still have small units of flyable MiGs, but they shouldn't have any ground-controlled intercept capability left. Anyway, the Brit Tornadoes are tasked with eliminating the interceptor threat on the ground before we get there."

*   *   *

It was a place only bats could love.

The Carrier Air Traffic Control Center was as dark as the inside of a cave. What little light there was in CATCC came from the greenish glow of the radar scopes and the large Lucite grease board that covered the opposite wall.

Chief Petty Officer Mark Williams, the senior enlisted controller, greeted Maxwell. "Good morning, Commander, how can I help you?"

"I'm looking for tapes from the ship's air traffic control communications on the night of the Hornet crash, Chief."

"We've already made copies of all that for the Aircraft Mishap Board, sir."

"I know, but we don't have anything with the mishap aircraft's tactical communications. You know, transmissions made on the squadron discrete frequencies."

Chief Williams scratched his chin. "I'm sure we made copies of your squadron's tac freqs—both of them—for the board. You say there was nothing on them from the mishap aircraft?"

"Hardly anything. Maybe they were using another freq." Maxwell was fishing now.

"If they were, we wouldn't be taping it down here. Maybe she was just using good radio discipline that night."

Maxwell had to smile at that one. One thing Spam Parker had never been known for was radio discipline. "Yeah, maybe so. Well, thanks for your help anyway."

A dead end, he decided. He walked back toward the lighted passageway.

Williams called after him. "Just a minute, sir."

"Yeah, Chief?"

"Sometimes the spooks down in Surface Plot monitor the battle group's transmissions to make sure we aren't breaking EMCON or broadcasting any classified information. They're the guys who monitor the spectrum and report EMCON violations. Maybe they could help."

"Good call, Chief. Thanks a lot."

Maxwell's mind went into high gear. Why hadn't he thought of it before? The spooks were equal opportunity spies, he thought. They didn't just eavesdrop on the enemy—they did it to everyone.

Surface Plot was almost as bad as the CATCC cave—dark and lit mostly from the glow of the various wall-sized electronic boards. Maxwell asked a dungaree-clad petty officer where to find the Surface Watch Officer.

"Through that hatch, sir, and buzz in at the entry portal. He's back in the SCIF." SCIF stood for Special Compartmentalized Information Facility. It meant beyond Top Secret classification. Eyes only, need-to-know.

Maxwell was out of his element. He was far below-decks, down in the spaces of the carrier's Surface Plot, called Alpha Sierra. They called this black shoe country, and it was occupied by surface Navy officers, who wore black shoes with their khaki uniforms. The black shoes looked in disdain at the brown-shoed aviators who, they were convinced, were incapable of rowing a canoe.

Maxwell stood in front of the remote camera and pressed the buzzer.

A voice from an invisible speaker said, "May I help you?"

"Commander Maxwell, VFA-36. I'd like to see the Surface Watch Officer."

"Present your ID card."

Irritated, Maxwell removed his ID. He wondered if the spooks knew the carrier had been under way now for three weeks and that not a single spy had been seen swimming out from the shore.

"Place the card in the drawer."

Maxwell placed his card in the drawer next to the buzzer switch. After several seconds, the voice said, "You may enter, Commander."

The door buzzed and popped open as the electronic latches released.

It was chilly inside the darkened space, and Maxwell rubbed his arms for warmth. A bespectacled, khaki-clad commander strode up and extended his hand. "Chris Foley, Surface Watch Officer," he said. "What brings an airedale down into the bowels of the *Reagan*? Too hot on the flight deck?"

"We ran out of ice cubes and heard this was the coldest place on the ship."

"You heard right." He smiled and waved his arm. "This stuff is extremely temperature-sensitive. What can we do for you?"

"We're investigating the F/A-18 mishap the other night. I heard that you sometimes monitor the battle group radio frequency emissions, for content and such."

"We monitor a lot of frequencies—and not just our battle group."

"Do you keep track of airborne transmissions from our aircraft?"

"Sure. Especially when the BG is under emissions

control. The admiral wants to know if we're keeping strict radio silence, and if anyone breaks it, he wants to know who. The command ship *Blue Ridge* does most of it, though. We're sort of the auxiliary.''

"Were you guys keeping track of the upper UHF spectrum the night of the Hornet crash?"

"As a matter of fact, yes. You're the second air wing officer to ask that question today."

Maxwell stared at the watch officer. "Someone else was down here?"

"Your skipper, I think. You know, the one who shot down that MiG—"

Maxwell felt sick to his stomach. "DeLancey?"

"Yes, that's the one."

"What did he want?"

"Same thing you're looking for."

"Did you give it to him?"

"The tape? Oh, sure. We were about to throw it out anyway."

Maxwell tried to sound calm. "You mean you didn't keep a copy?"

"No, we don't keep that stuff unless there's some level of intelligence interest."

Maxwell felt a pall of gloom descend over him. He knew he had been on the right trail, but he was too late. The trail had gone cold. Now he was out of ideas.

He thanked the watch officer and left.

Outside the frigid Surface Plot area, the air seemed hot and stagnant. As Maxwell turned down the long passageway he saw DeLancey, standing four or five hatches away. DeLancey nodded, and gave him a smile.

*   *   *

Maxwell returned to his room. He put on a Vivaldi CD, then turned on the computer and checked his E-mail.

Nothing. No surprise, he thought. It was over.

He tried again to make sense of the Spam Parker accident. He remembered again what he had learned about accident investigations when he was in test pilot school. They liked to compare an investigation to an archaeological dig. You worked with an event that was frozen in time, and you tried to re-create what actually happened. It was like looking at the remains of a fossilized dinosaur and guessing how it died. You could invent theories about why this or that happened, but in the final analysis, that's all you really had—theories.

But this wasn't archaeology, he reminded himself. They weren't dealing with ancient history. This was a recent event, and they damned sure ought to be able to come up with credible evidence. The trouble was, you could gather as much good evidence as you wanted—and still come up with the wrong answer. Especially if someone was hiding the critical piece of evidence. Or planting a red herring.

For a while Maxwell ruminated, listening to the bright, warbling sound of the baroque music. Then, abruptly, something else came to him. It was an old adage—one they used to teach back in test pilot school about accident investigations. *Remember your first impression—it's almost always the right one.*

Well, he remembered his first impression about this accident, unthinkable as it was. He had nothing else to go with it, just an impression—a hunch, really. It was too bizarre, too inconceivable to even discuss it with the other members of the board.

No evidence, no clues. Just an impression.

His mind was clicking forward again. Maxwell turned off the CD player and picked up the phone.

TWENTY-ONE

The Noose Tightens

BAGHDAD
2130, WEDNESDAY, 28 MAY

Tyrwhitt was afraid.

He had been afraid before, but this time was different. In every situation before, he had possessed a sort of cockiness. He knew he could outwit them. It was all a game, and he was a superior gamesman.

But now the game had changed. Before, it had been easy to lose the mush-witted agents assigned to tail him. They were amateurs, always attired in the same drab safari suits, too slow to anticipate his sudden detours through the teeming market places and whorehouses. Sometimes he would let them stay on his trail, just to lull them into thinking he was unaware.

No more.

The agents who were trailing him this afternoon from the Rasheed Hotel weren't wearing the same old brown safari suits. And they hadn't been fooled by the sharp turn at the whorehouse. These were trained operatives. They were watching every move he made.

Why?

Darkness had settled over Baghdad. The streets were bathed in a dirty yellow light. Tyrwhitt hailed a passing taxi, a beaten-up Toyota. He jumped in and urged the driver to move out, leaving the two Bazrum trailers gawking from the sidewalk. Seconds later, he saw a black Fiat swing out of the alley across the street and fall behind.

Tyrwhitt directed the taxi driver across town, all the way to the northern souk, then southward again toward downtown and the B'aath building. The lights of the Fiat remained behind them, several hundred meters in trail. They passed over an ancient arched bridge that spanned the Tigris River. The bridge was narrow, with barely enough room for two opposite-direction vehicles. Looking back, Tyrwhitt saw the Fiat slow to allow a rickety panel truck to pass.

At the end of the bridge, the road made a hard right turn. For the moment the taxi was hidden from the Fiat's view. Tyrwhitt crammed a fistful of dinars into the driver's shirt pocket. "Go!" he yelled at the driver. "Keep driving. Go fast!"

He opened the door and jumped out.

Ducking into a darkened portico, Tyrwhitt watched the taxi pick up speed and clatter away. A few seconds later, the Fiat rounded the corner. Tyrwhitt could see three men hunched inside the black car. They were all peering ahead, watching the taxi.

Still in the darkness, Tyrwhitt pulled on a black, loose-fitting cotton jacket, then put on the kaffiyeh. He removed the Beretta from his ankle holster. He chambered a round, then slipped the pistol into his right jacket pocket. From his trouser pocket he removed a Buck switchblade and inserted it in a strap around his right wrist.

The black Fiat did not return, but he knew it would be back when they realized he had abandoned the taxi.

He was a good three kilometers from the dead drop—the prearranged location where his contact was supposed to leave the packet of information. They had agreed that it was too dangerous to conduct any more meetings in the souk. The contact—the anonymous Iraqi officer—suspected that he was being tailed. Tyrwhitt had already noticed the stepped-up surveillance of his own activities, the replacement of the gum shoed safari suits with grim-faced men in black. The game was nearly over.

Tyrwhitt stayed to the darkened side streets. It took fifteen minutes, zigzagging at right angles along the narrow streets, before he came to the Mirjan Mosque. It was an ancient building, erected in the fourteenth century, and now in a state of preserved decrepitude.

He looked out over an empty plaza at the front door of the mosque. It was surrounded by a high wall with a wooden gate in front. Minarets rose from each of the four corners. A pair of yellow streetlamps illuminated the large wooden front door.

Tyrwhitt remembered what the officer had told him. "Look for the southern wall of the courtyard. In it is a niche, indicating the direction of Mecca. Directly beneath the niche is a stone box, half a meter high. It contains a stone that supposedly came from the Kaaba, the central Muslim shrine in Mecca. There you will find the packet containing the information you have requested."

"What if the packet is not there?" Tyrwhitt asked.

"It means we have been compromised," the officer said, "and you are in deadly danger. You must execute your egress plan." At this, the officer looked directly at him. "You do have an egress plan, don't you?"

Tyrwhitt was surprised by the question. He tried to sound positive. "Of course."

From across the plaza, Tyrwhitt studied the gate of the mosque. A couple of motor scooters and a half-dozen bicycles leaned against the outer wall. No one was entering or leaving.

Tyrwhitt started across the plaza. When he was still thirty feet from the front gate, he heard it, then looked over his shoulder and saw it turning the corner.

The black Fiat. Its lights were extinguished. It was coming toward him.

Tyrwhitt tried to affect a creaky shuffle, like that of a man twice his age. He continued shuffling toward the gate.

It seemed to work. The men in the Fiat appeared not to recognize him in the kaffiyeh and black jacket.

He reached the front gate as the Fiat slowly crossed the plaza. He opened it and entered. The courtyard of the mosque was deserted. He peeked through the door to the prayer hall and saw half a dozen worshipers inside.

Even in the half-light, he had no trouble finding the niche in the southern wall, with the symbol indicating the direction to Mecca. At the base of the wall, just as the informant had said, was the ancient box.

He raised the solid slab cover. Inside, at the bottom of the box, lay the blackened stone, the relic from the Kaaba.

And nothing else.

He ran his hand around the inside of the box. It was empty except for the stone. He looked behind the box, around and beneath. There was no packet.

Tyrwhitt backed away from the box and tried to think. He was almost precisely on time. The informant had been specific. *Eight o'clock.* No earlier, no later. Something was wrong.

Tyrwhitt's heart began to race. Outside waited the black Fiat and the Bazrum agents. What did it mean? Had the informant been dragged in and interrogated? Had he told them about the dead drop? Did they know?

Of course they knew, he thought. Why the hell else would the Fiat have homed in like the fucking angel of death to this decrepit old mosque? The bastards were expecting him.

But they hadn't recognized him as he entered the mosque. The disguise—the kaffiyeh and black jacket and old man's shuffle—had worked. Or had it?

Tyrwhitt again opened the door to the prayer room. The worshipers did not look up at him. At the back of the room he saw another door. He shuffled through the room and tried the door. It opened to a darkened alleyway.

He closed the door behind him, blinking in the darkness. Something—a cat or a large rat—scurried beneath him, making a hissing noise.

He had walked ten meters when he nearly ran into him. The man wore black trousers and a jacket. He wasn't moving, just standing there watching. One of the Bazrum agents from the black Fiat.

Waiting for him.

Bluff, thought Tyrwhitt. Shuffle on past the agent. There was nothing else he could do. Maybe the disguise would still work.

The agent threw up an arm, blocking his way. In one abrupt motion he snatched the kaffiyeh from Tyrwhitt's head, exposing his shock of red hair. "Haaa!" the agent said in a triumphant voice.

Tyrwhitt saw the agent's hand—the same one he threw up to stop him—sliding into his jacket, going for his weapon.

Tyrwhitt didn't wait. With all his weight he stiff-armed the man under the chin, shoving him straight back into the wall of the mosque. The agent bounced back in a crouch. His hand came out of his jacket clutching an automatic pistol.

And then his eyes widened. He stared at Tyrwhitt in disbelief.

He tried to raise the pistol, but it slipped from his hand. He gazed down at his shirt. The grip of Tyr-whitt's six-inch switchblade was protruding from his chest. Blood was spurting through his shirt from his pierced heart.

The man's eyes bulged and went white. He slid down the wall, sprawling into the alleyway. His sight-less eyes stared upward into the night.

Tyrwhitt retrieved his knife. He could see that the agent was a short, muscular man, perhaps thirty-five or forty, with a heavy black mustache. He cleaned his knife blade on the dead man's jacket, then removed his kaffiyeh, which was still clutched in the man's hand. *Tough luck, mate. Better you than me.*

He peered in the darkness up and down the alley-way. There had been three agents in the Fiat, and surely they had a radio. He had only minutes left. Seconds, perhaps.

He turned and began to run.

The faded blue Volkswagen was still in the shed where he had stashed it. The top was covered with droppings from the birds that nested in the rafters. On either side, wheelbarrows loaded with plaster filled up every square inch of space. The Beetle's upholstery had long since faded and split from the effects of the harsh Middle East sun. The fenders looked like they had endured a demolition derby. That suited Tyrwhitt. The car looked no different from the thousands of other rattletrap cars that clattered around Baghdad, with one single exception. Its engine and running gear were in perfect condition. The Beetle could get him out of Iraq.

Outside, he could hear the city stirring to life. It had taken him nearly all night to get here. By this time they would be scouring Baghdad looking for the reporter who had killed the Bazrum agent. He had made his way slowly, slipping into darkened doorways and alleys whenever he heard a vehicle approaching.

Now all he had to do was drive away. But to where? He was in the center of Iraq—375 miles from Zakho, on the Turkish border, which required driving through a no-man's-land where he would be prey not only to Iraqis but Kurdish rebels and bandits. The border of Jordan was the same distance but nearly unreachable by a normal wheeled vehicle. Syria was as close as Turkey, but there he would surely be detained at the border and handed back to the Iraqis. And he could forget Kuwait, at least by the direct route. The border was still heavily patrolled by the Republican Guard.

His safest choice was Saudi Arabia. He could drive southward through the desert, remaining west of Kuwait, then enter Kuwait from the south. He might be picked up by Saudi border patrols, but that was okay because they would deliver him to the Americans in Riyadh.

The problem was, the roads amounted to nothing more than camel trails. You needed a jeep or a

Humvee to navigate the ancient routes. If the Beetle broke down, he would be stranded in the vastness of the desert. He and the faded Volkswagen would join the carcasses of the thousand scorched tanks, armored cars, and smugglers' trucks.

Of course, he could summon help.

The Cyfonika.

You idiot! Tyrwhitt thought, as he stood in the darkened shed. The goddamned satellite phone. He had left it back in his room at the Rasheed.

Tyrwhitt cursed himself. Why had he left the damned thing? It was cumbersome, nearly ten pounds with the battery pack, and anyway, he had expected to return to the Rasheed.

Not that he felt any sense of duty to protect the secret technology built into the Cyfonika. But he could at least transmit the news that there would be no further news—the game was up. Saddam's holy war, for all he knew, would commence after morning prayers.

With the Cyfonika he could tell the agency that he was skipping the country. He could even tell them exactly where he was if the situation got nasty.

And then he nearly laughed. Why would they come? Why would the haughty CIA consider sending an armed unit into a hostile country to rescue one of their "assets"? He was as expendable as toilet paper. If trapped, he was supposed to do the expedient thing—destroy his data and equipment, mainly the Cyfonika, and then, of course, himself. Leave no prize for the enemy.

But if they thought he was alive—and about to fall into Iraqi hands . . . ? Wouldn't his life suddenly have immense value?

He needed the damned phone.

Tyrwhitt could see the gray dawn light seeping through the cracks of the door. It was still early. Perhaps they hadn't yet connected him to the killing of the Bazrum agent.

He had to retrieve the Cyfonika.

In the predawn coolness, he could see wisps of vapor trailing off the helicopter's rotor blades. Like all fighter pilots, Maxwell distrusted the whirling, gyrating, impossibly complicated machinery of a helicopter. Too many moving parts, too much to go wrong.

It was a short ride, he reminded himself. In the gray light he could already make out the irregular silhouette of the command ship, USS *Blue Ridge*. They were skimming the surface of the Gulf at fifty feet.

Maxwell felt the helo slow, then begin its descent to the pad on the cruiser's aft deck. Half a minute later he stepped out, clinging to his uniform cap in the downwash of the still whirling rotor blades.

Waiting for him was a first-class petty officer, who led him belowdecks, directly to the SCIF.

The facility was a cavelike chamber much like the one aboard the *Reagan*. But here aboard the *Blue Ridge,* which was a command ship, the level of security was cranked up even higher. This, Maxwell observed, was really spook country.

"We're ready for you, Commander," said a bespectacled young lieutenant, wearing khakis. "I've already pulled the tapes from that three-hour slice you requested."

He led Maxwell to a console that mounted an array of three-foot tape reels. "We've got the whole RF spectrum covered, but I narrowed the search down to the ultra-high-frequency band you flying types use.

There's your headset. When you're ready, I'll show you what we found."

Maxwell slipped on the earphones, then gave the lieutenant a thumbs-up. The reels began to wind.

He listened for nearly twenty minutes. Then he heard it. Urgently, he signaled the lieutenant to stop the tape. "Right there. Run it again, please, the last three minutes."

Maxwell pressed the earphones to his head, straining to hear every nuance. As the tape played, Maxwell's head began to nod in understanding. It was all coming clear. Finally he had more than just a hunch. *Your first impression is almost always the right one . . .*

TWENTY-TWO

Trapped

Baksheesh. An immensely civilized tradition, thought Tyrwhitt. The custom of paying gratuities, tips, bribes, in order to accomplish your purpose. It had greased the wheels of commerce in the Middle East for centuries.

He hoped the custom would continue as he slid the five green bills bearing the portrait of Andrew Jackson into the palm of Ibrahim Ibrahim, the night porter at the Rasheed. Ibrahim was a skinny man with a sharp, hawklike profile and several missing teeth. He had a wary look about him, with the narrow, cynical eyes of a man who trusted no one, believed in nothing. Nothing but baksheesh.

Tyrwhitt was also counting on the fact that Ibrahim disliked the safari-suited Bazrum thugs as much as he despised the administration of Iraq's President. He had lost a son in the Gulf War, and another had returned from captivity permanently deaf, the result of a fuel-air bomb detonated directly over his bunker.

They stood in the pantry, just inside the back service entrance. Ibrahim counted the bills, then slid them into his vest pocket. It was more money than he earned in a year at the hotel.

"Two hours ago," said Ibrahim. "They were here. They entered your room, then they left."

"Did they take anything?"

"Like what?"

"A leather bag." Tyrwhitt gestured, indicating the shape of the Cyfonika satchel.

"No. I think they were looking for you, not a bag."

Tyrwhitt nodded. It was possible, he thought. The Bazrum agents were vicious, but stupid. They might not think to retrieve the articles in his room until they realized he was gone.

He gave Ibrahim instructions on where to search for the satchel, in the trunk against the foot of the bed.

"I will find it," said the porter. "Stay here, out of sight. It will take five minutes."

Tyrwhitt waited in the pantry. It was broad daylight outside now, and he could hear the din of honking horns and unmuffled motors on the busy street. The streets would be clogged with the unruly traffic of downtown Baghdad.

He peeped through the drawn curtains and checked the narrow street that arced around the back of the hotel. He saw no agents. No black Fiats. So far, so good.

He settled onto Ibrahim's wooden stool. He felt suddenly fatigued, deprived of sleep. He knew he would go many more hours, a day perhaps, before he could sleep again.

He slid his right hand into his jacket pocket and wrapped it around the Beretta. It was odd that he felt no remorse about killing the Bazrum man. Maybe that would come later. He'd never killed before, but he'd always wondered how it would make him feel. Idly, he wondered what Claire would think—

Ibrahim came back. The pantry door swung closed behind him. In his hand was the Cyfonika satchel. "Come with me," he said.

Tyrwhitt rose from the stool, about to follow. Then he stopped. Something, a nagging sensation, warned him.

Ibrahim's eyes. Gone were the narrow, cynical eyes. Ibrahim's eyes were wide open, darting about like those of a frightened animal.

"Where are we going?" Tyrwhitt asked.

"To safety. You will see." The eyes avoided making contact.

Tyrwhitt withdrew the Beretta. Ibrahim's eyes widened even farther. "Who is out there?" Tyrwhitt demanded. "How many?"

Ibrahim's eyes looked toward the pantry door just as it flew open.

A Bazrum agent, dressed in a dark safari suit, burst inside. His pistol was already raised. A split second elapsed while he fastened his eyes on Tyrwhitt.

It was too long. *Kaploom!* The first round from Tyrwhitt's Beretta struck him in the chest. The shot sounded like a cannon firing in the closed room.

The man staggered backward, trying to aim his weapon.

Tyrwhitt fired again—*Kaploom!*—opening a purple hole in the man's forehead.

As the man dropped, Tyrwhitt saw the second agent, directly behind him. The man was retreating through the door.

Tyrwhitt fired once, missing him. The agent turned and bolted through the door. *Kaploom!* Tyrwhitt fired again, hitting him in the temple. The man went down, caroming into the opposite wall.

The spring-loaded pantry door slammed shut.

Tyrwhitt dropped to a crouch and scuttled away from the door. Ibrahim was flattened against the wall, trying his best to be invisible. His eyes had expanded to the size of saucers.

Tyrwhitt listened for noises outside the door. He could hear only the raspy sound of Ibrahim's breathing. He aimed the pistol at the porter. "How many, goddammit?"

"Only those two."

You lying asshole, thought Tyrwhitt. *Then why are you trying to become part of the wallpaper?*

"Where was the satchel?"

Ibrahim nodded toward the door. "They had it."

Tyrwhitt tried to think. They had been expecting him. And they would not be in a hurry to storm the room again. First they had to close off the escape routes. And probably get reinforcements.

The Volkswagen was parked a hundred yards from the back entrance. Or at least he hoped the damned thing was still there.

He had to run for it.

He looked again at the sprawled body of the Baz-rum agent. Blood was oozing from the hole in his forehead. On the other side of the door lay the second agent. That raised the score to three.

Then he looked at Ibrahim, and anger swept over him. *I can make it four.*

Still crouched, he shuffled over to where Ibrahim was pressed against the wall. Ibrahim's eyes filled with terror. Tyrwhitt jammed the muzzle hard against his temple. Ibrahim began to tremble.

Tyrwhitt shoved his hand inside the porter's vest. He felt around, then came up with the five twenty-dollar bills. Ibrahim's eyes followed the departing currency like a dog watching a piece of meat.

"No baksheesh today," said Tyrwhitt, stuffing the money into his trousers. *"Manyouk."* It was his favorite Arabic expression. It meant "fuck you."

He gathered up the Cyfonika satchel. Opening the back door, he peeked around, then darted outside.

At 0545, the phone rang in Boyce's stateroom aboard the *Reagan.* "It's a go," said the watch officer. "The strike is on."

"It is now T-minus ninety-eight minutes," said Spook Morse, the wing intelligence officer, peering out at his audience of flight-suited pilots. "The *Reagan* is presently two hundred miles southeast of Basra, heading north. By launch time we'll be one hundred eighty miles, and be in the same position for recovery."

Morse aimed his laser pointer at the map. "Tanking for the strike force will be from KC-10s on these four stations." Two of the stations were over Saudi airspace, and two over the Persian Gulf. "Because of the tankers' vulnerability, they will not be permitted to go closer than fifty miles from Iraqi airspace. If you come out of Indian country needing fuel, you're gonna have to make it to the tanker station.

"Our current weather is some high cirrus over the target area, with scattered cumulus between five and ten thousand en route. Right now we have some ground fog along the Tigris River and over the lake region in the northwest, but that's expected to burn off by your target time. Visibility is forecast to be unrestricted. Looks like excellent bombing weather."

"More like excellent anti-aircraft weather," added an anonymous voice.

Morse ignored him and continued. "Combat Search and Rescue will be provided by a force of Marine helos holding offshore"—he pointed to a spot below the Iraqi shoreline—"here. They will be escorted by Marine F-model Hornets coming out of Bahrain."

Morse's briefing covered the rest of the mission details: transponder squawks, bingo fuel requirements, bull's-eye navigation reference points, code words, weapon loads, maintenance problems, avoidance of collateral damage.

When Morse was finished, CAG Boyce walked up to the podium. "I know that for most of you, this is your first shooting war. Put your trust in your strike leaders, stick with the plan. Remember, this is not just another punitive exercise. This is for real, and the placement of your bombs will determine whether the enemy will be able to strike back at us and our allies."

In his seat in the third row, Maxwell listened to Boyce's briefing. As he jotted notes on his kneeboard, he thought about the strike. He would be leading a four-ship division of Hornets armed with laser-guided GBU-24 bombs. His second section, on whom he would depend to protect his flank, was led by Craze Manson, with Hozer Miller flying as his wingman. Maxwell's own wingman was B.J. Johnson.

Some lineup, he thought. Two guys who hated his guts and a nugget wingman who had never seen combat.

He glanced across the row of seats. B.J. Johnson

looked nervous, he thought. She was clutching something in her right fist, squeezing it, unsqueezing. Well, he thought, that was normal. Anybody who wasn't nervous before they launched on a combat mission ought to have their brain examined.

B.J. saw him looking her way. She opened her right hand and showed him what she had been squeezing—two shiny steel balls. Her gift from Cheever and Miller.

Maxwell almost laughed out loud. He nodded and flashed her a thumbs-up.

At the podium Boyce finished his briefing. He pulled a fresh cigar from his flight suit vest pocket. "Okay, folks, that's it. Let's go rip 'em a new one."

But the briefing wasn't over. Before anyone could leave, Whitney Babcock stepped to the front of the room.

"Ladies and gentlemen," he said, taking the microphone, "the forty-eight-hour grace period the United Nations issued has now expired, and Iraq has been officially notified that its weapons facilities are subject to immediate destruction."

"Why don't we just send 'em our battle plan?" said someone.

Barely subdued laughs rippled through the room. CAG's face darkened and he shot a fierce warning look at the offenders.

Babcock appeared not to notice. He rambled on for several more minutes. Finally, he said, "The President is confident that your efforts today will show the world that America will not tolerate the rogue ambitions of a country like Iraq. Good hunting, ladies and gentlemen."

No one applauded.

CAG said in a loud voice, "Strike leaders, brief your people. Everyone draw their sidearms in your ready rooms." Then he added, as an afterthought, "Try not to hurt yourselves with them."

A tall African-American Marine sergeant arrived in the VFA-36 ready room to issue the automatic pistols. One by one the pilots checked out their weapons. Though they had all qualified with small arms early in their training, most had long ago forgotten what they knew about the nine-millimeter pistols.

The sergeant was not happy. As he watched the pilots fumble with the weapons, a pained expression came over his face. He couldn't help noticing that Leroi Jones was trying to stuff the ammunition magazine into the pistol backward. Horrified, he saw Flash Gordon peering down the barrel of his own pistol.

Carefully, the sergeant reached over and directed the muzzle away from Gordon's eyeball. He said to the group, "Gentlemen, take my advice and just keep those things in the holsters, okay?"

"Yeah, good idea, Sarge."

Maxwell's own sidearm, a pearl-handled Colt .45, was the one handed down to him by his father. He was loading the magazine of the automatic pistol when DeLancey walked up to him.

"Where'd you go this morning?" DeLancey demanded. "You were late to the brief."

"I had a job to do."

"You went someplace in the ship's helo. I want to know where."

"To check something out over on the *Blue Ridge*."

DeLancey was eyeing him warily. "I gave you a

direct order to butt out of the investigation. You were to stop snooping."

Maxwell holstered the Colt. "I found out what happened to Spam Parker."

The nervous chatter in the room abruptly ceased. A heavy silence descended on the assembled pilots. They stared at Maxwell and DeLancey. DeLancey looked like he'd received an electrical charge.

Maxwell picked up his helmet and nav bag and walked out of the ready room.

He rode the escalator to the gallery deck, then stepped up onto the flight deck. Red-shirted ordnance crews were going from jet to jet loading and arming weapons. Every strike fighter carried a full load of weapons.

Maxwell looked around for his jet. It was spotted on the number two elevator, just forward of the ship's island.

As he arrived at the parked Hornet, he saw DeLancey come marching up behind him. The fury showed in his face. "What the hell do you mean, you found out what happened to Parker?"

It occurred to Maxwell that he could almost enjoy this. Never before had he seen DeLancey look scared. "You almost got away with it," he said. "The 'X-W' on your kneeboard card. It meant 'Check Winchester,' right? Funny, I'd almost forgotten the old Winchester frequency—303.0. That's what you use when you don't want anyone else to hear you."

"Prove it. There's no record of it."

"None on the *Reagan* because you destroyed the only tape. But I found out about the *Blue Ridge,* the command ship. They still had it in their RF spectrum scan." Maxwell reached into his shoulder pocket and pulled out a tape cassette. "I've got it right here."

DeLancey's brows lowered like hoods over his eyes. "That doesn't mean shit. It could be anyone's voice on that tape."

"The legal officer tells me that voice printing is easy to identify, and it's very admissible evidence. The tape happens to be date-and time-stamped, by the way, at exactly the time Spam crashed."

DeLancey's jaw muscles were clenching. "Give me that tape, mister. That's an order."

Maxwell stuffed the cassette back into his shoulder pocket and zipped it closed. "You'll get a chance to hear it," he said. "At your trial."

DeLancey reached for him, shoving Maxwell against a rack of two-thousand-pound bombs. "I gave you an order. I want that goddamn—"

A hand grasped DeLancey's shoulder and pulled him back. "Hey," said CAG Boyce, "if you guys want to fight, then get in your cockpits. We've got MiGs to kill."

He almost made it.

In fact, thought Tyrwhitt, he would have made it from the Rasheed without being spotted if it hadn't been for the damned Cyfonika. He was on Tammuz Street, only three blocks from the hotel, trying to get the antenna extended on the thing. It had to protrude through the window of the Beetle to get a clean signal to its satellite. He had to stop the car in order to keep the antenna at the correct azimuth to the satellite.

He transmitted his message in the open. No more encrypted intelligence reports embedded inside official news releases. The game was up. It no longer mattered that the Bazrum could intercept his transmissions.

He transmitted the news that the Baghdad operation was compromised. He knew that they would infer that Iraq's missile attack was imminent. He then reported, without being specific, that he was making his egress from Baghdad. He would call again when he was clear of the city.

Just as he concluded the transmission, he saw him— one of the safari suits, standing in the street, holding a walkie-talkie and staring at him like he had just seen an extraterrestrial.

How ironic, Tyrwhitt thought. He had put his life at risk to retrieve the satellite phone because he thought it would get him out of trouble.

Now he was in real trouble.

In his rear view mirror, he could see the Fiat pursuing him. There were at least three in the car. Tyrwhitt could tell that the driver was handling the automobile well. That was more bad news. Now his only chance of escape was to lose this guy quick before the Bazrum scrambled every black Fiat in Iraq.

He sped eastward, across the Tigris and into the dense Al-Karrada district. The streets narrowed, lined with street vendors and produce stalls. Pedestrians and bicyclists peeled away as he blew his horn.

Tyrwhitt was alternately flooring the accelerator, then stomping on the brakes, screeching around corners in a four-wheel slide. The four-cylinder VW engine was screaming like a tortured buzz saw. It would have been great fun, he thought, if the nasty little buggers back there weren't trying to kill him.

Ahead lumbered an ancient lorry stacked with baskets of vegetables. Tyrwhitt jammed his fist on the horn. The lorry driver's left arm extended, flashing an upraised finger.

Shit! thought Tyrwhitt, slowing behind the lorry. In the mirror he saw the Fiat closing on him.

Tyrwhitt swerved to the left, looking for an opening. There wasn't enough space to pass between the lorry and the row of vendors' stalls.

The Fiat was close enough for Tyrwhitt to see the faces of the men inside.

He stomped on the accelerator and roared alongside the lorry. The angry driver yelled and shook his fist.

And then, too late, Tyrwhitt saw them.

Chickens. Crates of them, stacked atop each other ten feet high, extending halfway into the street. The owner of the chickens was gesturing wildly as he ran for his life.

Whap! The Volkswagen plowed into the crates.

Tyrwhitt lost sight of the road ahead. The Beetle's windshield filled with feathers, flapping chickens, shattered crates, bird droppings.

Whang! He felt the VW sideswipe something—the lorry? Then he emerged from the cloud of feathers.

The way ahead was clear. The windshield was a mess, festooned with chicken droppings and feathers. He looked in the mirror. Behind him the lorry lay on its side, blocking the street. Baskets of vegetables were spilled in the street. A white flurry of chickens flapped and squawked and ran loose.

The black Fiat was not in sight.

Tyrwhitt whipped the VW around the next corner. He was coming into the Babil district in the southeast section of the city. He had to stay off the main avenues, keep working his way southward, then intercept the road to Al-Mussayyib.

After that, the desert.

He again crossed the Tigris River, driving southward over the old Al-Jami'aa bridge. The streets were
filled with bicycles and mopeds and battered automo-
biles. He came to a roundabout in the Al-Jazair sub-
urb. The circle was clogged, and traffic had slowed to
a crawl.

Tyrwhitt was beginning to relax. It was good, he
decided, that it was morning rush hour. The shabby
Volkswagen, shabbier than ever with its coating of
dung and feathers, was inconspicuous in the chaos of
Baghdad traffic. All he had to do now was blend in.
Keep driving south—

Fucking hell! A wave of fear swept over him like
an arctic chill.

Two of them, waiting at the far periphery of the
circle.

One was a marked police car, the other a black Fiat.

Tyrwhitt's heart raced. He saw the Bazrum agent
standing beside the Fiat, scanning the traffic. The
agent suddenly spotted the Volkswagen halfway across
the circle.

He stopped scanning, and for an instant he and Tyrwhitt locked gazes.

The agent yelled to the policemen. Then he reached
inside the Fiat and snatched something that looked
like a transceiver. Still looking at Tyrwhitt, he began
talking into the transceiver.

Tyrwhitt peered around him. He was locked in the
glut of traffic. Vehicles surrounded him on either side,
in front and behind.

He was about to jump from the car and run. Then
he saw an opening. There, to the right, a hundred
yards before the waiting Bazrum agents. It was a nar-

row street, threaded between two rows of ancient stuccoed buildings.

He veered the Beetle into the stream of traffic. *Clang!* He banged fenders with an old Trabant in the next lane. The outraged driver leaned out his window, yelling obscenities.

Tyrwhitt gave the man a wave. *Sorry, mate. Send the bill to Saddam.* He pulled in front of the Trabant— *Scrunch!*—tearing off the East German car's front bumper.

He cut across the outer lane, knocking over an old man on a bicycle. A rusty taxi, honking its horn, careened onto the walkway and whanged into a stuccoed wall.

Tyrwhitt jammed down on the accelerator. Gathering speed, the Volkswagen barged into the side street.

And then his heart sank.

The street extended only about three hundred meters. Laundry flapped from overhanging ledges. Plastic crates of garbage lined both sides.

No matter, thought Tyrwhitt. *You're committed. Go for it and hope for the best.*

He gunned the car on down the street, knocking over crates of garbage. Dogs and old women and children scurried out of the way.

He reached the end of the street and—*Thank God!*—another narrow lane diverged to the left. Tyrwhitt swung the VW hard to the left. He saw that the narrow lane extended for many blocks.

He saw something else, coming out of an intersection.

A desert-colored Army truck, carrying a squad of soldiers. Republican Guard, Tyrwhitt could tell. The truck pulled into the street, blocking his way.

Tyrwhitt slammed on the brakes and threw the VW into reverse. As he did, looking over his shoulder, he saw the familiar shape of a black Fiat. The Fiat entered the street and stopped, blocking his exit.

He was trapped.

Tyrwhitt brought the VW to a stop and sat there for a moment regarding the Fiat. Three Bazrum agents, wearing their brown safari suits, climbed out and began walking toward him. He looked back in the opposite direction. The Republican Guardsmen were piling out of the truck. A dozen of them, carrying their weapons, were advancing toward him.

Tyrwhitt waited. He was no longer in a hurry. He had sometimes wondered how it would feel when it came down to this. Every game had an end. Over the past six months, usually after several scotches, Tyrwhitt had reviewed in his mind all the possible endings. This was one he had rehearsed.

One thing had changed. His heart was no longer racing. He was calm.

He wrapped his right hand around the Beretta in his jacket pocket. Then he opened the door and stepped out. He turned to face the Bazrum men.

The morning was still cool. A dampness glistened on the cobbled street. On a balcony above the street, a woman was hanging out laundry. The woman stopped and stared at the scene below.

One of the Bazrum agents yelled an order to the soldiers behind him. Tyrwhitt understood the order— *Don't shoot.*

They wanted him alive. Tyrwhitt knew why.

Tyrwhitt gave the Bazrum agents a big grin. Let them know he was surrendering. It was a good chase, right? Great sport, actually. He waved and began walking toward them. The agents waved back.

When he was fifteen feet away, Tyrwhitt pulled out the Beretta. *"Manyouk!"* he said, speaking in Arabic. *Fuck you.* He shot the nearest agent in the chest. Firing quickly, he dropped the second agent with a bullet in the belly. He fired at the third man. The round missed, blasting a patch of stucco from the wall behind.

The panicked agent was running, his head ducked. He yelled back at the Guardsmen.

Tyrwhitt followed him with the Beretta. He squeezed off the shot just as the fusillade of bullets tore into him.

TWENTY-THREE

Bandits

At her console in the AWACS, Tracey Barnett uttered a silent prayer. *Please, God, don't let me screw up.*

On her tac display she could see the Air Force F-15s, flying high-fighter sweep, preceding the low-flying F-15Es to their target at Al-Taji. To the southeast, she saw the cluster of blips that represented the strikers from the *Reagan*. They were commencing their ingress to their target at Latifiyah. Almost to their targets were the Brits, streaking low over the desert in their Tornado strike fighters.

"Sea Lord, this is Gipper Zero-one," called the leader of the *Reagan* strike group. "Any activity on the Purple Net?"

Tracey recognized the voice of Red Boyce, the strike leader. Air wing commanders didn't usually lead strike groups, but she knew Boyce. He was the kind of commander who led from the front.

"Negative, Gipper. Picture clear."

Purple Net was the AWACS data link with all the other information-gathering sources. Boyce was wondering the same thing they were. *Where were the MiGs?*

On her tactical display in the great lumbering AWACS, Tracey could see the Iraqi radar sites lighting up like tiny penlights. Iraq had awakened to the fact that they were under attack.

"Burner Two, Burner Three active," she called. "East Reno, ten miles." Burner Two and Three were SA-2 and SA-3 surface-to-air missiles.

Butch Kissick, the ACE, appeared behind her. "Where the hell are the HARM shooters?"

"There." She pointed to the phalanx of blips—F/A-18s—sprawled across her screen. "They're thirty seconds out."

"Too damn close," said Kissick. "The F-15s and the Tornadoes are almost in the Target Area."

Tracey nodded. It *was* close. If the HARMs didn't snuff out the air defense radars, the SAMs would make dog meat of the strike jets. She repeated the silent prayer.

Thirty seconds later, she heard the report. "Magnum! Magnum!"

The radar-killing HARMs were in the air. One after the other came the reports, "Magnum! Magnum!"

Fascinated, Tracey watched the attack unfold on her display. She saw several of the Iraqi radars shutting down. They had picked up on the bad news that they were targeted, and they were hoping to elude the incoming barrage of HARMs.

Too late, bubbas, thought Tracey. The HARM had a memory like a killer elephant. Once it found a radiating source, it locked the target's position into its guidance system.

The Brits were the first on target. She saw the blips of the Tornado strike jets streaking across the Shayka Mazhar air base, southeast of Baghdad. They were dropping antipersonnel and armor munitions— APAM—intended to crater the runway and make it unusable for the squadrons of MiG-29s and MiG-25s based there. Tracey always shuddered when she thought about how the APAM worked. The stuff would shred every object on the field—man or MiG— that stood taller than waist-high.

Tracey heard the Tornado lead. "Sledgehammer is off target, one hundred over one hundred."

"Hammer copies," answered Butch Kissick. "You are green south, green south."

Kissick glanced over at Tracey and winked. It was good news. The Tornado leader was reporting that they'd put a hundred percent of their munitions on target—with no losses.

So far, so good, thought Tracey. No MiGs would be taking off from Shayka Mazhar today. But they still had Al-Asad and, most of all, Al-Taqqadum to worry about. *Where are the MiGs?*

Jabbar had to laugh.

From the cockpit of his MiG-29, sitting parked under its camouflage netting, he could see the Krait missile. Saddam's priceless death weapon looked like a section of drainage pipe, resting on its loading cradle out in the middle of the tarmac. It was exposed to attack from the air.

That was precisely what Jabbar expected to happen.

When he received the report that Shayka Mazhar air base was under attack, he knew they had only minutes left. Al-Taqqadum would not be spared.

Standing beside his fighter, he had summoned the commander of the ordnance crew. "Remove the Krait missile from my aircraft."

The commander, a round-faced captain, stared disbelievingly. "Sir, I do not have that authority."

"You do now. I just gave it to you."

"But, Colonel, what will I do with the weapon?"

"I suggest you shove it up Saddam's ass."

"But, Colonel—"

"Move, you idiot!" For emphasis, Jabbar produced his Makarov semi-automatic pistol. He pointed it in the officer's face. "Unload the missile."

Possessed with a new understanding, the ordnance officer leaped to his task. Within five minutes, he and his loading crew had detached the Krait missile from the fighter.

Jabbar ordered his seven best pilots to man the remaining MiG-29s. He himself would fly the specially prepared MiG that, until minutes ago, had been designated to conduct the doomsday mission against the American aircraft carrier.

Fuck doomsday missions, thought Jabbar. And fuck the maniac who dreamed up an attack that would ensure the total destruction of Iraq. In a single act Jabbar had spared his country an unspeakable horror.

Sitting in his cockpit, Colonel Jabbar felt a sense of calm satisfaction. His old red helmet—the same one he had worn for ten years—rested on his cockpit rail, ready to don. He was prepared do what he did best— fight the enemy in the sky.

It was futile, of course. This fine May day would surely be the last for him and his gallant young pilots. But if they kept their composure and pounced when the enemy was least ready—

Jabbar saw a car driving across the ramp. It was a black Fiat.

The Fiat was followed by a truck with two dozen Republican Guard in the back. In the car Jabbar could see at least four Bazrum agents.

They stopped to inspect the unloaded Krait missile. Jabbar saw the agents looking around. One of them pointed at his MiG parked under the camouflage net.

Jabbar knew it was time. He called down to his crew chief. "Hurry, Suliman! Remove the camouflage net! We're starting engines."

Puffy black mushrooms were erupting two thousand feet below them. Fifty-seven millimeter, Maxwell guessed. Or maybe eighty-eight. The AA was coming from somewhere near the Latifiyah complex. None of the bursts was yet above twenty thousand.

Maxwell wished for a moment that he could roll in on the gun positions. It would be nice to treat the inhabitants to a shower of high explosive. But not this trip. Today they had more important business.

No SAMs were in the air, at least not yet, and that suited Maxwell just fine. If the HARMs had done their job, the SAM sites were now a smoldering ruin.

Both Chevy flights—DeLancey's division of four Hornets, and Maxwell's own flight of four—were approaching the initial points. Strangely, the chatter had subsided on the tactical frequency. Maxwell could see that the lead division was in a shallow dive now, and though he couldn't see the actual weapons, he knew that the laser-guided GBU-24 bombs would be dropping from the fighters and soaring toward their destinations.

That was the beauty of smart bombs, he thought.

Not just that you could thread them through an opening no larger than a ventilator shaft. You did it while remaining outside the killing range of the antiaircraft guns. For a strike fighter pilot, it was life insurance.

On his FLIR display Maxwell picked up his assigned target—a row of low buildings on the inner periphery of the Latifiyah complex. They housed a missile assembly line—for another minute or two, anyway.

In the adjoining row of structures, he saw a building erupt in a geyser of debris, and he could imagine hearing the explosion—*Kaploom*.

A second later—*Kaploom*—the adjoining building.

One after the other—*Kaploom Kaploom Kaploom*—Chevy One flight's bombs were exploding on their targets. One building after the other was vanishing in a dirty brown puff.

As Chevy One's bombs rained down on their targets, Chevy Five flight, Maxwell's next flight of four Hornets, approached the initial point.

Maxwell shoved the nose of his Hornet over in a shallow dive. He took a glance to either side. They were out there in combat spread—B.J. on the left, Craze and Hozer on the right. Each was busy acquiring his own target with the jet's laser designator.

For an instant Maxwell worried about his wingman. If a nugget's nerve was to fail, this was the moment. He pushed the mike switch for the back radio, the frequency shared only by his flight. "Are we having fun yet, Chevy Six?"

A sassy voice answered, "No sweat, boss. Just a walk in the park."

Maxwell smiled inside his oxygen mask. So much for his wingman's nerve. B.J. Johnson was cool.

In his HUD, Maxwell slewed the laser designator over the target . . . fine-tuned it . . . sweetening the designation just a little left . . . up just a smidgen . . . *there* . . . right over the transom of the front door . . . *Release*!

Now the hard part. Waiting, letting the laser designator illuminate the target while the GBU-24 plunged like a hawk to its quarry.

Twenty-five seconds to impact.

Ten seconds.

Maxwell knew that if he did his job right, the brown, nondescript building in his HUD—he'd been told it was a missile propellant lab—would be converted to a smoking crater.

Five seconds.

Zero seconds. The GBU should be—

Kaploom.

Maxwell felt like cheering. Not quite a bull's-eye, he calculated. More like three or four feet. Close enough for government work. No more propellant lab. No more building.

He saw the other Hornets' bombs arriving. *Kaploom. Kaploom. Kaploom.* The geysers erupted in rapid succession. More brown puffs, more vanished buildings.

"Chevy Five off target," Maxwell called.

"Chevy Six off."

"Chevy Seven off."

"Chevy Eight."

Maxwell pulled up hard, rolling the Hornet into a right bank. All his jets were off target, weapons delivered. Grunting against the Gs, he peered down at the target area. Smoke was billowing from the ruined complex. The Latifiyah assembly plant had just been transformed to a complex of landfills.

It was the best possible result, Maxwell thought. They'd nailed the target and, best of all, they came through unscathed. All they had to do was rejoin and egress. It was time to get out of town.

On the tactical frequency, he heard DeLancey calling AWACS. "Sea Lord, Chevy One. Picture?" He wanted to know if they had intruders.

"Picture clear," came the voice of Tracey Barnett. "No, wait! Pop-up target—East Boston—five miles."

Maxwell instinctively swung his head to peer over each shoulder, scanning the horizon. Pop up target! It had to be the MiGs. The bastards hadn't bothered trying to deflect the bombing attack. Instead, they stayed low and waited until the Hornets were coming off the target.

When they were most vulnerable.

The tactical frequency filled with excited chatter.

"Chevy One, bandits two o'clock low!"

"Snap Vector, Chevy One, tactical, one-five-zero, ten miles."

"Chevy Three, hound dog at three o'clock, engaging."

"One copies, Three, cleared to strip."

"Bandits, bandits! Eight o'clock, three miles!"

Maxwell peered in each direction, trying to pick up the bandits. *Where the hell are they?* DeLancey's flight was engaged. Had to be Fulcrums, Maxwell figured, probably up from the Al-Taqqadum air base, less than fifty miles away.

It was classic, Maxwell thought. Just when you started thinking your enemy was on the ropes, he surprised you with a shot to the groin.

The MiGs were all around them.

B.J.'s voice crackled over the radio. "Brick, break right! Bandit, your four o'clock low."

Maxwell jammed the stick to the right and pulled. Straining against the sudden G load, he peered over his right shoulder. *Where is*—

He saw it. A Fulcrum, low and fast. It looked like a double-finned shark, coming after him.

But the guy was too eager, Maxwell noted. His convergence angle was too acute. Maxwell pulled hard into the attacker and kept turning. He could see that the MiG was going to overshoot, go wide behind him. He would set up the kill for B.J.

"Stay in your turn, Brick," called B.J. "I'll have a shot in ten seconds."

Maxwell pulled harder. *You'd better have a shot,* he thought. They were both going to be toast in about fifteen seconds. The MiG jockey had buddies out there.

Maxwell was losing sight of the MiG as the Russian-built fighter overshot the turn and disappeared behind him. This was the hard part. His instincts told him to reverse the turn, pull up in a vertical, execute a pirouette, and come back down on the MiG. But this wasn't a one vee one. He had a wingman.

It was B.J.'s job to cover his tail. *Stay in your turn. I'll have a shot in ten seconds.* Could she do it? He would soon find out.

Maxwell stayed in the turn.

Bandits high at nine o'clock. DeLancey had both MiGs in sight, but he didn't call them out. If he called a break turn now, Undra would turn into them and then both would get away.

DeLancey started a turn to the left, keeping his nose down. The lead Fulcrum looked like he was blowing through. The guy was fast, probably trying to get the hell out of town before he got whacked. But the second Fulcrum was out of position, high and wide. He didn't yet see the Hornets below him.

The second Fulcrum was a sitting duck.

DeLancey selected an AIM-120 radar-guided missile and turned his Hornet hard into the second MiG. As he pulled his nose around for a firing solution, he thought for a second about his own useless wingman. Undra was still back there somewhere. It occurred to DeLancey that Undra could be in trouble. What if the lead MiG didn't just blow through, and decided instead to take a shot at Undra?

DeLancey considered for a second. Perhaps he should delay his turn while he talked Undra back down to the formation. The two Hornets would again have mutual support.

But that would take precious seconds. Time was critical. If he waited for Undra to rejoin, he would lose the MiG.

His fifth kill.

Screw it, thought Killer DeLancey. Undra Cheever was on his own.

Speed is life.

It was the fighter pilot's mantra, and it was flashing through the mind of Colonel Tariq Jabbar as he led his MiG-29s in a supersonic charge at the enemy Hornets.

He had almost been too late. He was still starting the second engine when the Bazrum staff car came skidding up to the revetment. Jabbar had shoved the number one throttle all the way to the stop and came blasting out of the revetment in a storm of sand and thunder.

Too late, the driver of the oncoming black Fiat saw the big fighter coming at him. He swerved, rocking up on two wheels, just as the MiG slammed into the car.

Jabbar felt a lurch. The left wing rose up, then came back down. Jabbar guessed that the main landing gear had run over the Fiat. Looking back over his shoulder, he saw that the automobile was flattened as if it had gone through a crusher.

It occurred to him that he had probably done some damage to his aircraft. He wondered briefly whether the jet was still flyable. It didn't matter, he decided. He would take off anyway.

Russian airplanes were tough. Tougher than Italian cars.

In pairs his fighters roared down the runway at Al-Taqqadum—just in time to nearly collide with the wave of incoming British Tornado jets. As the MiGs lifted from the runway, the Tornadoes sizzled across the field, spewing their loads of antipersonnel bombs.

The last pair of MiGs didn't make it. Caught on their takeoff roll by the deadly shredder bombs, both MiGs burst into flame and fireballed off the end of the runway.

Now they were six.

They stayed low, gathering speed as they hurtled toward Latifiyah. Jabbar's plan was simple. Keep up the speed and rip through the flight of enemy Hornets, picking off as many as they could. Attack from one side, blow through and exit on the other side. *Speed is life.*

Soon he saw them, dead ahead, just coming off their

bombing targets at Latifiyah. Two Hornets, one low, the other pulling up. Beyond them, two more. And beyond them, still more. Jabbar had plenty of targets from which to choose.

Jabbar selected the high one in the lead section. He was obviously a wingman, but with his nose pointed up, he was blind to his leader, who was accelerating out ahead.

Convenient, thought Jabbar. He banked hard to the right, opening up a lag between him and the Hornet. Then he cranked back hard to the left and pulled up nearly vertical.

There!—an easy low-deflection shot at the Hornet's tailpipes.

Jabbar waited, gaining a positive lock with the Archer missile's heat-seeking warhead. He had a good tone, well within range, less than a thousand meters.

He squeezed the trigger.

Whoom! The Archer leaped off its rail. Behind the missile Jabbar could see the thin gray trail of smoke. He watched the Archer quickly overtake the climbing Hornet.

Undra Cheever looked wildly around him. He had to fight hard to suppress the panic that was swelling up in him.

He couldn't see anyone. Not the skipper, whom he was supposed to be following, and not the goddamn MiGs that were all over them like a cheap suit. *Where are the MiGs everyone is jabbering about?*

His overriding thought after pulling off the target was simple. *Get out of Dodge.* Get the nose up, get away from those motherless anti-aircraft gunners

down there who might get lucky and whack you with
an eighty-eight millimeter.

He had lost sight of his leader. *Where is Killer?*

"Chevy One," Undra called, "Chevy Two is blind
on you."

"Your twelve o'clock low, engaged," DeLancey answered. "Get your nose down."

Engaged? Shit, that meant Killer was already in a
furball with a MiG, trying to score another kill. Killer
didn't give a fat rat's ass about his own wingman.

Undra pushed over, rolling up on his side to scan
the terrain ahead. He picked up DeLancey's Killer's
Hornet low, in a left turn.

Then he glimpsed something over his left shoulder.
What is that? He saw a glint of sunlight, a trail of
gray smoke.

Suddenly he knew what he was seeing. *Oh, shit, here
comes a . . .*

In the next instant, he sensed the flash of the missile's warhead. Then the explosion. It was the last
thing Undra Cheever felt.

"Fox Two!" called B.J.

About time, thought Maxwell, still in a hard left
turn. The MiG was still behind him somewhere. The
radio call from his wingman meant that she had just
taken a Sidewinder shot.

Maxwell kept turning. Any second he ought to be
hearing—

"Splash One!" B.J.'s voice had a throaty, triumphant ring.

Then Maxwell saw it over his right shoulder. The
MiG-29 was falling like a shotgunned dove. B.J.'s Hor-

net was still locked on to his tail, prepared to launch another Sidewinder.

Seconds later, the MiG's canopy separated. Maxwell saw a flash, and the tiny insectlike pilot's ejection seat popped up and behind the stricken jet. The parachute canopy blossomed and floated toward the desert.

Maxwell couldn't help thinking about the Iraqi pilot. He wondered how the guy would feel when he found out he had made history. He was the first jet fighter pilot to be shot down by a woman.

He and B.J were nearly abeam now, the same altitude. Maxwell realized the fight wasn't over.

He saw two specks. *MiGs*. They were coming at them from three o'clock.

"Chevy Six, break right, bandits three o'clock level!"

The fight was on again.

Maxwell barely had time to roll into the oncoming MiGs. Too late for a head-on shot. They merged.

Whoom! They passed nose-to-nose with over a thousand miles per hour closure speed. The lead MiG swept past so close Maxwell could see the MiG pilot's head in the cockpit.

He was wearing a red helmet.

Coming off the target at Latifiyah, Flash Gordon could see his wingman, Leroi Jones, a quarter mile abeam. Gordon and Jones were the second pair of Hornets in Killer DeLancey's four-plane division.

Through all the garble on the tac frequency, he was getting the picture. *Pop-up targets!* But how many?

He glanced at his situational display, then peered outside at the hazy desert sky. Killer and Undra were out there somewhere, already engaged. It was the job of the second section—Flash and Leroi—to cover them.

Then he heard Leroi's voice on the tac radio. "Bandits eight o'clock converging. I don't think they see us."

He looked. He saw only empty sky. "No joy, visual, press!" *I don't see them but I have you in sight. You have the lead.*

"Roger, Leroi has the lead. Hard left, Flash! Bandits low, nine o'clock. I'm pulling nose on to them."

Damn! Flash still couldn't see them. He followed Leroi's left turn and pulled hard.

"Keep your turn in," Leroi said. "We're gonna have a shot."

A shot at what? Flash still saw nothing but sand and sky.

There. Low and nearly invisible in their desert-colored paint schemes. He had a good visual ID. They were definitely Fulcrums moving fast on a nearly parallel track.

"Tally two, visual," Flash said.

"I got the leader," answered Leroi.

"Okay, Flash has the trailer."

He was getting a lock now with the APG-73 radar, which confirmed that the target was a MiG-29. At this speed the range was at the extreme end for a Sidewinder shot. An AIM-7 Sparrow would be a good choice, Flash thought. An AIM-120 AMRAAM active radar-guided missile would be even better.

Flash's thumb selected AMRAAM on the side of the Hornet's stick grip. He pushed the castle switch forward, commanding the radar to bore-sight search. Instantly it locked on to the MiG. Peering through the

HUD, he confirmed that he had the trailer MiG boxed inside the in-range circle. At the top of the acquisition box in the display, he was getting a flashing cue: SHOOT.

Flash squeezed the trigger.

Whoom! The AMRAAM roared away from the Hornet like a mad dog in a meat locker, trailing fire and gray smoke.

"Chevy Three, Fox Three," he called, signaling an AMRAAM shot.

Three seconds later, he heard Leroi Jones. "Chevy Four, Fox Three." In his peripheral vision, Flash saw Leroi's missile arcing through the sky toward the lead MiG.

Both MiGs abruptly broke to the right. Flash turned with his target, keeping his MiG locked up and in sight. He knew that the Fulcrum pilots were getting an urgent radar warning signal. By now they knew missiles were in the air.

From the trailer MiG spewed a trail of silver radar-defeating chaff.

Too late. The missile slammed into the Fulcrum just aft of the canopy. Still in its hard right evasive turn, the MiG broke apart. An instant later, the jet's center fuel tank erupted in a billowing orange fireball.

"Splash One!" called Flash Gordon, watching the burning hulk of the MiG fall like a comet.

The lead MiG's turn was nearly abrupt enough to elude Leroi's missile. But as the missile overshot the tail of the fighter, the proximity fuse detonated the warhead. Pieces of the jet's big vertical fins broke away, followed by sections from its destroyed tail surfaces.

The MiG went into a sickening skid, then began a roll to the left. Flash saw the canopy separate from the jet. The rocket-propelled ejection hurtled the pilot clear of the destroyed fighter.

"Splash One!" called Leroi Jones.

Over his shoulder, Flash kept the tiny figure of the MiG pilot in view as he fell toward the desert. After what seemed like minutes—it was actually less than five seconds—he saw a round beige-colored parachute canopy pop open like a parasol.

Flash raised his hand in a salute.

Things were going badly, Jabbar thought. At least four of his MiGs were down. They'd killed only one Hornet—the one he had taken on his first pass through the attacking force.

Now this. He was in a turning fight.

He couldn't believe his own stupidity. Or arrogance. He had violated the tactical doctrine he tried to impress on his young pilots: *Fly through the enemy. Shoot and exit.*

You didn't engage an F/A-18 in a classic dogfight. The big MiG-29 was a powerful, brutish fighter, but its greatest assets were its speed and its vertical capability. In an old-fashioned turning, gyrating dogfight, it was outclassed by the more agile F/A-18.

When he passed the lead Hornet, he knew he should have continued straight ahead. His great speed advantage would have taken him out of range before the Hornets could reverse and target him.

But as the two fighters merged, something happened. During the second when they passed canopy to canopy, he and the Hornet pilot had locked gazes.

It was as though a silent challenge had been issued.

Some primal voice inside Jabbar had commanded him. *Stay and fight.*

Jabbar pulled the MiG-29's nose up in a vertical climb. He rolled the jet ninety degrees on its axis to look for his enemy. If the Hornet was still in a tight turn down below, he would swoop down and—

Jabbar saw the Hornet. He wasn't down below. He was three hundred meters away, in his own vertical climb. Jabbar could see the pilot in the cockpit staring at him.

The red helmet. Maxwell wondered what it meant. Some kind of personal statement? Iraqi fighter pilots weren't reputed to be flashy or demonstrative. Nor were they known to be aggressive. The Iraqis liked to hit and run. They never took on a coalition fighter in a one-vee-one.

Until today, thought Maxwell. *Who is this guy?* Maybe he was a Russian, or some ex-Eastern Bloc fighter pilot. He was flying the Fulcrum like he had seen lots of combat.

"You with me, Chevy Six?"

"Chevy Six tally one, visual, free," answered B.J. "You defensive?"

"Engaged, neutral. Watch for spitters."

It was B.J.'s job to prevent another MiG from sneaking into the fight and taking a shot at him.

"You're covered, Chevy Five." Brick's Hornet and the MiG were too close to allow B.J. a safe shot. She arced around outside the fight looking for a shot, and for other MiGs.

Maxwell knew that his vertical climb would top out before the Fulcrum. The Fulcrum had more initial energy. It could keep going up like a rocket, waiting for the Hornet to start back down, then take a shot.

Maxwell's airspeed was decreasing rapidly. He eased the Hornet's nose over, delicately working the rudders, watching the angle of attack. If he lost control here, let the jet depart and go into a spin or a falling leaf, he was dead meat. The MiG would have an easy shot.

He already had an AIM-9 Sidewinder selected. In his earphones he was getting the low growl from the missile's seeker unit. The MiG was within forty-five degrees of the Hornet's boresight centerline, well within the AIM-9 seeker cone. But the range was close, perhaps too close.

It might be his only shot.

He squeezed the trigger.

Whoom! The Sidewinder leaped off the left pylon and streaked toward the climbing MiG.

Watching the missile fly to its target, Maxwell felt the Hornet trying to drop from under him. He was nearly out of airspeed, hanging in the air on the thrust of the Hornet's engines.

He saw the missile pass several hundred feet behind the tail of the MiG. And keep going.

A clean miss.

The range was too close. The Sidewinder needed three seconds to arm. There hadn't been enough time or space.

But the MiG pilot had seen the shot. His nose was coming down. Maxwell knew he would not get another easy shot.

Both fighters plunged downward, each gaining precious maneuvering energy. Bottoming out, they passed nose-to-nose again.

Maxwell pulled hard on the stick, hauling the nose of the Hornet back upward. He grunted against the seven Gs, looking over his shoulder to keep sight of the MiG. He remembered the old dictum: *Lose sight, lose the fight.*

He saw the MiG's nose crank around in a rolling scissors. This guy was no amateur, Maxwell realized. He was flying the hell out of the Fulcrum. In another turn, he would have his nose on Maxwell's Hornet.

Maxwell countered. He turned into the MiG, matching the scissors. Again they passed, spiraling upward. Maxwell glimpsed again the red helmet. Once more he wondered, *Who is this guy?*

Approaching the apogee of the vertical scissors, Maxwell balanced the Hornet on the thrust of its engines. He was indicating barely more than a hundred knots—a speed at which most other fighters would tumble out of the sky.

Carefully working the rudder pedals, Maxwell slewed the Hornet around its axis. Out the side of his canopy he could see the MiG.

The MiG was slow, almost out of flying speed. His nose was coming down.

It was the moment Maxwell was waiting for.

Jabbar understood what was happening. Grudgingly, he could almost admire the skill of the Hornet pilot. He was using his fighter to its maximum advantage. The American knew how to make the Hornet stand on its tail, pirouette, and change direction. Jabbar knew that the F/A-18, from such a perch, could strike like a cobra.

As it was doing now.

The long tapered nose of the Hornet was coming

down, toward him. Jabbar countered, rolling into the Hornet.

He knew he was too late. The Hornet had managed to open a space between them. Now the F/A-18's nose was pointing behind Jabbar's MiG.

But the range was close. Too close, Jabbar hoped, just as it had been before. The Hornet's first missile had flown past him without detonating.

Jabbar turned hard, peering over his shoulder. He could see the Hornet behind him. Very close. Jabbar was sure there would not be a missile at this range—

He saw a flash in the nose of the Hornet. For an instant, he was confused. *What can that be . . . ?*

Then he saw the tracers arcing over his right wing. He felt a stab of fear.

Guns. The world's oldest and most primitive air-to-air weapon. He remembered that the F/A-18 possessed a rapid-fire twenty-millimeter cannon.

Over his shoulder he could see the Hornet. In the nose of the fighter, the muzzle of the air-to-air cannon was blinking like a strobe light.

He felt the impact—*Ratatatatatat*—like hammer blows resonating through the airframe of his MiG. The big Russian fighter was tough. It could take hits. But not like this.

He saw a line of cannon holes stitched across his right wing. *Ratatatatatat.* It felt as if a buzz saw were cutting through the MiG.

The right wing separated. The MiG-29 snapped to the right, rolling over and over. Its nose dropped and the big fighter plunged toward the earth.

Jabbar felt himself flung against the side of the cockpit. His head smashed into the canopy.

Nearly senseless, he tried to reach the ejection lanyard. He couldn't move his hand. His arms were pinned by the jet's whirling force.

Jabbar struggled to reach the lanyard. His hand wouldn't move. Through the canopy he saw the brown Iraqi desert whirling toward him.

TWENTY-FOUR

Blue on Blue

AL-HILLAH, IRAQ
0845, FRIDAY, 30 MAY

Maxwell was deep inside Iraq, heading north.

He checked his fuel state. *Six point one.* Six thousand one hundred pounds of JP-5. The furball with the MiG had consumed all his reserves. He would be fuel critical by the time he got to the KC-10 tanker. Running out of gas over a country you had just bombed was a lousy idea.

But first he had to collect his wingman. "Chevy Six, say your posit and state."

"Your twelve o'clock, fifteen miles, Chevy Five," answered B.J. Johnson. "I'm eight-point-zero. You want me to anchor here and join on you?"

Maxwell studied his situational display. He saw the blip of B.J.'s Hornet to the south of his position, with the rest of the strike group. She had more gas than he did, but she wasn't fat either. "We won't waste fuel joining up. Egress south, B.J. See you at the tanker."

"Roger that. By the way, I confirm your MiG kill. Congratulations."

"You too. YoYo for now."

"YoYo" was tactical brevity for "You're on your own."

Maxwell had to grin as he remembered how he had worried about his wingman. A nugget—a *female* nugget—on her first combat sortie. From this day on, B.J. Johnson would be considered the equal of any pilot in the squadron.

Maxwell was still more than twenty miles northwest of Latifiyah. He could see columns of black smoke billowing skyward from the ruined complex. One of the buildings was still blazing fiercely. Probably one of the propellant storage facilities, Maxwell guessed.

He gave the complex a wide berth.

In his situational display, he saw that all the *Reagan* group strikers were now southward bound. No targets on his radar, no data-linked targets from the AWACS.

It meant that he was the last Hornet out of the target area.

But then he looked again. *Wait a second.* There was something else. Another blip was showing up on the display. He wasn't alone out here.

DeLancey made one last sweep along the northern arc of the target area. If any MiGs were still alive and flying out here, he wanted them.

He'd already had a sweet day. The big number five! A number six would be even sweeter.

Too bad about Undra, he reflected. It was his own fault. If the dumb shit had stayed in position, maybe he wouldn't have gotten whacked by the MiG.

With his radar DeLancey was sorting out the Hornets as they egressed the target area. His own second section, Craze and Hozer, had been the first out of the target area. They were almost to the tanker at the southern Iraq border. Not far behind were Flash and

Leroi, who had each collected a MiG before making their egress.

By listening to the tactical frequency, DeLancey knew that Maxwell and his female wingman had also gotten MiGs. Now she was on her way south, on her own.

Maxwell was the last one in the target area.

DeLancey had the symbol of Maxwell's Hornet in his situational display. He was almost straight ahead, ten miles. He was slow, probably to conserve fuel.

DeLancey switched off his radar transponder—the device that identified him on the AWACS radar screen. He steered the nose of his Hornet toward the symbol for Maxwell's fighter. He had a thirty-knot speed advantage.

Peering through his HUD, DeLancey picked up the grayish profile of Maxwell's Hornet.

"Chevy One, this is Sea Lord," came the voice of the woman AWACS controller. "Do you read Sea Lord?"

DeLancey did not answer.

"Chevy One, we're not getting a transponder squawk. If you read, squawk mode two."

DeLancey ignored the call. He left his transponder switched off.

He saw Maxwell's Hornet make a thirty-degree turn to the right. Maxwell knew he was back there, and he was getting a visual ID.

"Chevy One, is that you at my five o'clock?" he heard Maxwell call.

DeLancey kept his silence. On his stores display, he selected SIDEWINDER. He heard the low growl of the seeker unit as it acquired its target.

*　　*　　*

Maxwell was getting an uneasy feeling.

The guy behind him was definitely a Hornet. But why wasn't he talking or squawking a code? Perhaps he had combat damage and had lost his radios. If so, he would need help getting home.

Maxwell slowed his jet down and started a right turn. The radioless Hornet could join up, and Maxwell would escort him back to the ship on his wing.

But the Hornet wasn't making any attempt to join up. Instead he was bore-sighting Maxwell with the nose of his fighter.

As if he were tracking him.

A warning signal went off in Maxwell's brain. He looked again at the Hornet behind him. The range was close for a missile shot, but within limits. With his left hand he reached over and touched the hard rectangular lump of the audio cassette in his breast pocket.

Like the last pieces of a puzzle, it was coming together. The pilot in the Hornet behind him was the same one who killed Spam Parker by talking her into the ramp. The same one who claimed a MiG in Desert Storm that someone else shot down.

He knows that you know.

Maxwell slammed his jet into a hard turn.

A second later he saw it. A flash on the Hornet's right wing tip. The missile was off the rail. Behind it trailed a telltale wisp of gray smoke. It looked like a stubby pencil, flying a pursuit curve toward him.

Turning hard inside the curving path of the missile, Maxwell hit the flare dispenser. Flares were decoys. They were supposed to fool the Sidewinder missile's heat-seeking head.

The missile wasn't fooled. It was boring straight toward Maxwell's jet.

Maxwell felt the sweat pouring down from his helmet into his eyes. His only hope was to outturn the missile at the last second.

He forced himself to wait. It was his only chance. *Wait. Wait until the missile is almost—*

Now. He hauled back hard on the stick and shoved the throttles into full afterburner, using the extra thrust of the afterburners to tighten the Hornet's turn.

He winced as the Sidewinder passed behind the Hornet's tail.

There was no explosion.

The hard turn in afterburner had been too much for its finned control system. The missile hadn't come close enough to Maxwell's Hornet to detonate the proximity fuse.

DeLancey's Hornet was in a steep bank, going for Maxwell's tail. With his speed advantage, DeLancey was almost in gun range.

Maxwell knew he had to keep DeLancey outside his turn radius. Keep him from drawing a lead with his twenty-millimeter Vulcan Gatling cannon.

He knew the odds were against him. Killer DeLancey was the toughest air-to-air opponent in the fleet. And the most successful.

He saw DeLancey's jet slide to the outside of the sharp turn and pitch up into a high yo-yo. He was conserving his airspeed, trying to set up for a shot with the cannon.

Maxwell reversed his turn. He rolled back into DeLancey's jet.

The distance between them had narrowed. Because of DeLancey's greater speed, and because Maxwell's turn had been tighter, the two Hornets were nearly parallel.

They turned into each other, passing nearly nose-to-nose.

As Maxwell turned hard again back toward De-Lancey, he heard the robotic voice of Bitchin' Betty, the F/A-18's aural warning system: "Bingo. Bingo."

He was almost out of fuel.

But he couldn't exit the fight. The two jets were in a classic scissors duel. Neither could quit without exposing his tail to a shot from the other. It was a fight to the finish.

By the third reversal, neither had gained any advantage. Each pilot was flying his Hornet to its maximum. Maxwell knew that DeLancey would stay in the fight until they ran out of fuel. Or until one of them was dead.

Another reversal, another head-on pass.

Maxwell realized it couldn't last much longer. De-Lancey would know that he was low on fuel. All he had to do was wait for Maxwell to flame out.

Okay, Maxwell said to himself. *Let it happen.*

He pulled both throttles back. As if the engines had flamed out, the Hornet lost airspeed rapidly.

Maxwell rolled out of his steep turn and rocked his wings. It was a signal of surrender. DeLancey could either fire on him now or wait and strafe him in his parachute.

He saw DeLancey's Hornet roll in for the kill.

The Hornet was closing rapidly. He hoped De-Lancey was eager. So eager he would wait for an extremely close range before he opened up with the twenty-millimeter. The Hornet carried only four hundred rounds of ammunition. At the Vulcan cannon's high rate of fire, the ammo would be gone in a few seconds.

He saw the shape of the Hornet swell behind him. A thousand yards back, closing.

Eight hundred yards. *Any second the Vulcan would fire—*

Now. Maxwell rolled the Hornet inverted and jammed the throttles forward to full thrust. He pulled hard on the stick, yanking the nose of the Hornet toward the earth below.

He saw tracers arcing past his wing. The surprise move had gained him a split second's advantage. But no more. DeLancey was dangerously close behind him.

Maxwell was betting everything on DeLancey's ego. DeLancey had been so sure of a kill, he might make a mistake. He would follow him down.

And he did.

Maxwell abruptly reversed his own turn and hauled the nose of his jet back up. Up towards a vertical line.

DeLancey's nose was already deep below the horizon, and he was too fast. He was committed. By the time he reversed, pointing his Hornet upward again, it was too late. He had veered outside Maxwell's tight climbing turn.

Maxwell had a precious altitude advantage. Keeping the nose of his Hornet pointed high, he reversed direction again. Beneath his nose he saw DeLancey going into a high-G roll, trying to initiate another scissors duel.

Maxwell didn't join the scissors. He kept his jet perched on its tail as he executed a rudder pirouette, changing directions, pulling his nose back below the horizon.

DeLancey's F/A-18 was directly in front of him.

Maxwell rolled upright and eased the nose of his fighter back up, fanning his speed brake to keep from overshooting. He was pointed at DeLancey's jet, so close he could read the numbers on the tail. He pulled the throttles back to keep from overrunning.

DeLancey's jet was inverted, at the apogee of its scissors roll. The sleek gray shape of the Hornet filled Maxwell's windscreen.

Maxwell's radar gun director was locked on. He tracked DeLancey's jet with the gunsight pipper in his HUD. The range indicated only five hundred feet.

Peering through the gunsight, he flew the pipper onto the forward half of DeLancey's jet.

He had a clear view of DeLancey's helmet in the cockpit. He slid the pipper directly over the helmet. His finger wrapped around the trigger.

He hesitated.

You can't do this. For an instant he argued with himself. *You can't kill a friendly.*

But DeLancey was trying to kill him.

Maxwell squeezed the trigger. And held it.

Brrrrrraaaaaaaaaaaap! The airframe of the fighter vibrated as the Vulcan spewed out bullets at six-thousand-rounds-per-minute.

He was shocked by the ferocity of the cannon. The cockpit where DeLancey's helmet had been exploded in a blur of fragments.

Brrrrrraaaaaaaaaaaap! The stream of bullets worked aft, opening the fuselage like it was a tin can. The F/A-18 in his gunsight disintegrated. The fuselage fuel tank ignited. DeLancey's Hornet erupted in a pulsing orange blob of fire.

A cloud of debris appeared in front of his nose. Instinctively, Maxwell ducked.

Whap! Thunk!

He emerged from the cloud into clear sky. No more debris. No more hostile fighters. No one trying to kill him, at least for the moment.

But his troubles weren't over. He glanced at his fuel quantity display. He was down to less than one thousand pounds of fuel.

He wouldn't make it out of Iraq.

He heard something else. "Engine left, engine left," said Bitchin' Betty, the robotic aural warning.

His left engine was no longer running.

Butch Kissick ran his hand through his close-cropped hair. "Would someone tell me what the fuck is going on?"

"I had two targets," Tracey Barnett said. "Chevy Five and someone else."

"Whaddya mean someone else? Someone *who* else?"

"I don't know. Maybe another Hornet. Chevy One went EMCON, no squawk, no reply. It could have been him. But now he's gone."

"You mean—"

"Like he was morted, Butch. It looked like they were in a furball. Then something happened. Someone—or something—took him out."

Kissick stared at her. "You mean Chevy Five? No. It doesn't make sense."

"I know. But I didn't see anything—"

"Sea Lord," came a voice over the tac frequency. "This is Chevy Five."

Kissick and Tracey looked at each other. Kissick

grabbed his microphone. "Sea Lord copies, Chevy Five. What's going on out there?"

"I'm low state. I'll flame out in five minutes. I need the tanker."

"Texaco tanker is on East Chicago station. Can you make it that far?"

"Negative. My left engine is shut down. I don't have the fuel to make it out of country."

Kissick lowered the microphone and stared at the console. Jesus, this entire strike was turning into a world-class cluster fuck. One Hornet confirmed lost, another probably down under *very* strange circumstances. Now Chevy Five was about to punch out over a country full of extremely pissed-off Iraqis.

He needed a miracle.

"Hang in there, cowboy," Kissick said. "I'm working on it."

"Texaco Tanker, this is Sea Lord. Got a hot vector for you. You ready?"

The voice of the KC-10 tanker pilot crackled back over Butch Kissick's headset. "Say the bearing and distance, Sea Lord."

"He's heading south, Boston one-four-five degrees, two-two-five miles."

"Sorry, Sea Lord. Unable."

Kissick blinked as if he'd been slapped. "Guess I didn't copy right, Texaco. Sounded like you said 'unable.' "

"Affirm, Sea Lord. Rules of engagement. We can't go in country."

Kissick couldn't believe this shit. He knew that big lumbering tankers like the KC-10—a militarized version of the DC-10 commercial jetliner—were considered too vulnerable to send into combat areas. Instead, they orbited at the periphery of hostile territory, like airborne gas stations.

But damn it, this was war. You did what you had to do. You took risks.

"What are you talking about, rules of engagement? We got an egressing shooter about to flame out in Indian country."

"Rules are rules, Sea Lord. Wish I could help."

Kissick's eyeballs bulged to the size of golf balls. *Rules are rules?* Kissick wanted to wrap his hands around the tanker pilot's windpipe. He knew the guy from back in Riyadh. He was an Air Force captain named Dexter who could quote chapter and verse from the operations manuals. Dexter was going to make a great airline pilot someday.

"Listen, jerk face, I don't give a flying fuck about your rules. This is Hammer, your Airborne Command Element, and I'm in charge here, understand? I'm giving you a direct order. Steer three-five-zero degrees and descend to twenty-two thousand feet." Kissick's voice was rising in a crescendo of wrath. *"Now! Do you copy?"*

Kissick knew that he had overplayed his hand. He glanced over at Tracey Barnett. Her lips were moving in a silent supplication.

For several seconds the frequency was quiet.

They heard the tanker pilot's voice. "Texaco copies. We're steering three-five-zero and descending. We'll try to pick up your shooter."

Kissick sighed and put down his microphone. Before this day was over, he knew he'd be on the carpet in the general's office. Dexter was right about rules being rules. But what the hell. He'd had a good career. Maybe it was time to go fishing.

Forty miles.

They were closing rapidly, but not rapidly enough. Still 120 miles inside Iraq.

As much as he hated doing so, Maxwell forced himself to glance again at the fuel quantity indicator. Three hundred pounds. It was no longer a precise number. At such a low quantity the Hornet's fuel quantity indication system could have a plus-minus error of several hundred pounds.

Thirty miles. He saw the distant speck appear in his windscreen.

On his situational display, he could see that the tanker was in a turn. By the time the big ship had completed the 180-degree turn, Maxwell would be in position behind him.

If he didn't flame out. He glanced down again.

Two hundred pounds.

"Chevy Five, this is Texaco. You got us in sight?"

"Gotcha, Texaco."

"That's good. You gonna last long enough to plug in?"

"If I don't, you'll be the first to know."

Almost close enough to glide out of country. But not quite. He was down to twenty thousand feet. From this altitude, he still wouldn't make it clear of Iraq. Maxwell checked the service Colt .45 still holstered beneath his torso harness. He reached down and reassured himself he could find the ejection handle. Just in case.

The speck in the windscreen was growing in size. The big three-engined ship was still in its turn. Maxwell could see the basketlike refueling drogue trailing behind the tanker.

He reached down inside his cockpit and actuated the switch that extended the Hornet's refueling probe.

One hundred pounds.

It was a joke among fighter pilots that air-to-air refueling was easy—except when you really needed it. You had to fly the probe that was affixed to the side of your jet into a three-foot basket dangling at the end of the tanker's long refueling hose. If the air were turbulent or, worse, you were so filled with adrenaline that you missed the basket, then you had to back off and try again. That was providing you hadn't broken your canopy with the flailing basket. And providing you had enough fuel for another try.

Fifty feet behind the drogue. He slid the jet down, flying beneath the great mass of the KC-10. He had no time to waste making his approach to the drogue. He had fuel for one shot.

Maxwell lined up the Hornet with the drogue, then eased forward.

Ten feet. He knew the fuel quantity was indicating zero.

Five feet. *Hurry. Keep it moving.*

Two feet.

Klunk. The probe poked into the center of the drogue. A bow briefly rippled down the length of the hose as the probe shoved the basket forward.

"Here comes your gas, Chevy Five," came the voice of the tanker pilot. "Now can we get the hell out of this place?"

TWENTY-FIVE

Deliverance

Through the window on the admiral's bridge, Maxwell could see the flat brown shoreline of Bahrain. A jagged row of modern hotels and office buildings rose above the ancient dwellings along the seafront. The *Reagan* had dropped anchor off Bahrain exactly twenty-five minutes ago.

Admiral Mellon, CAG Boyce, and the *Reagan*'s captain, Roger Stickney, sat across from Maxwell. They were listening to the tape player in the middle of the table. They heard the voice of Killer DeLancey.

"Eeeeasssy with it."

A couple of seconds later, "Don't go high, don't go high!"

It was easy to imagine Spam Parker's jet descending through the darkened sky toward the deck.

"Easy with it," they heard DeLancey say again. "Right for lineup."

"That was a bogus lineup call," said Maxwell, "just to get her to drop the nose and go lower on the glide slope."

A steady aural tone sounded on the tape.

"What's that?" asked Stickney.

"He's holding the Transmit button down," Maxwell said. "It's blocking out the LSO's calls on the other radio. Right now the LSO is yelling for her to add power, to wave off, but it sounds garbled to her because she's hearing both radios transmit at once."

Click. The tape abruptly ended. "The tape is time-stamped," said Maxwell. "That's exactly when Parker hit the ramp."

For a while no one spoke.

Finally, Admiral Mellon said, "I don't know what to say. This is just too hard to believe. Her own commanding officer killed her."

"And then tried to kill his executive officer," said Boyce. "You all saw Brick's HUD tape. Killer fired a Sidewinder at him, and Brick took him out with the gun." Boyce banged his fist on the table. "I wish I'd had the chance to shoot the sonofabitch myself."

Stickney was shaking his head. "Killing a woman pilot, then a deliberate blue-on-blue engagement in a war zone. All based aboard America's newest and most expensive aircraft carrier. This is going to look great on the evening news. It's gonna make Tailhook look like a taffy pull."

"What about Congress?" said Boyce. "Wait till that woman senator finds out how the Navy treated one of her precious female pilots."

No one wanted to touch that one.

Admiral Mellon seemed not to be listening. He rose from the table and stood gazing toward the Bahrain shoreline, his hands clasped behind his back.

He said in a low voice, "Thirty-four years." He continued looking out the window. "I've seen it all—Vietnam, the Gulf, Tailhook, the Balkans, downsizing, rebuilding, downsizing again."

None of the officers spoke. Maxwell thought that the admiral looked old and tired. His shoulders seemed hunched, his thinning hair whiter than before.

"Enough is enough," Mellon said, speaking to no one in particular. "I'm not going to give them another sword to use against us."

He turned to the officers at the table. "Okay, gentlemen, get this straight. Here's the way it's going down. Commander John DeLancey will get a memorial service with full honors and a posthumous Navy Cross."

The three men at the table stared at him. Boyce could not restrain himself. "But, Admiral, the sonofabitch—"

"Listen carefully, all of you. During yesterday's strike, DeLancey shot down another enemy aircraft, becoming the first active-duty ace since the Vietnam war. He is a national hero. Regardless of what else he did, we won't take that away from him."

Boyce shook his head. "Admiral, that still doesn't account for what he did to Spam Parker. And it doesn't explain how he happened to get killed."

"DeLancey was killed in action. We don't know how. He was the last jet out of the target area. Whether it was a SAM or a MiG or a lucky AA hit, we'll never know."

"What about the AWACS controllers? Don't they have an idea what happened?"

"I'll call Joe Penwell, the Joint Task Force Commander. He doesn't want this to explode in our faces any more than we do."

"What about the tapes?" said Stickney. "Brick's HUD tape and that audio tape we just heard prove that DeLancey was a murderer."

Mellon didn't reply. He walked over to the VCR and extracted the HUD cassette. Then he picked up the audio tape player and ejected the tape. Ignoring the curious stares of the three men at the table, Mellon pulled a metal gun case from his desk drawer. He slipped the two cassettes into the case.

He shoved open the door to the outside catwalk. Using a sidearm swing, he hurled the case in a high arcing path, over the rail and out to sea. He watched the gun case disappear in the murky water.

Admiral Mellon strode back into the flag bridge. "What tapes?"

No one answered.

He dusted his hands off and said, "That, gentlemen, was probably the last significant act of my naval career."

"Sir?" said Stickney. "You don't mean you're—"

The admiral picked up a sheet of paper from his desk. "My orders came in on the fax this morning. I've been relieved."

The three officers stared at him, surprised.

"In two weeks I turn over command of the *Reagan* battle group. I'm taking mandatory retirement, by directive of the Undersecretary of the Navy."

Stickney was aghast. "That doesn't make sense, Admiral," said Stickney. "Is it because of the alpha strike? Did anybody look at the intel photos? Don't they realize the attack on Latifiyah was a total success?"

Boyce spoke up. "Admiral, if I may say so, sir, you and your staff ran the most effective coordinated strike I've ever participated in."

"No," said Mellon. "It's Mr. Whitney Babcock who gets the credit for the strike. And he did it despite the interference of me and my bungling staff. At least that's the way it's being reported in Washington. Babcock's at the White House this very minute accepting congratulations from the President. The word is that he's going to be promoted to the National Security Council."

Boyce jumped to his feet. "That's bullshit!" he exploded. "Damn it, sir. Somebody in this Navy has to stand up to that little prick. We'll set the record straight."

Mellon shook his head. "It's the system, Red. Civilians oversee the military, not us old squareheads. It's the way the founding fathers set it up. It may be a flawed system, but it's the one we have taken oaths to support."

The admiral paused and gazed out the window again. "It's time for me to exit. I've had a great career, with damn few regrets." He looked pointedly at the empty tape player on the table. "And that includes what I just did here today."

An awkward silence settled over the room.

"There's just one other item," said Mellon, "and that concerns you, Commander Maxwell."

"Sir?" Maxwell rose from his chair, not sure what was going on.

"Your new orders."

Here it comes, thought Maxwell. *I'm the next to retire.* "Orders to where, Admiral?"

"CAG needs a new skipper for VFA-36." Mellon shuffled through another set of papers from a tray on his desk. "For once Red and I agreed on something."

Mellon found the papers. "Let me be the first to congratulate you, Brick. You're the new commanding officer of Strike Fighter Squadron Thirty-six. You'll be a great skipper."

Maxwell shook Mellon's hand, then accepted handshakes and backslaps from Boyce and Stickney.

He felt as if he were dreaming. So much had happened in the past two days, most of it bad. He had been attacked by both enemy and friendly fighters. He had shot down one of each. He had almost flamed out over a hostile country.

Strangest of all, he had killed his own commanding officer. In the United States Navy, that was not considered a great career move. But here he was, back aboard the *Reagan*. Instead of court-martialing him, they were giving him the best job in the world.

There was only one explanation, Maxwell figured. Someone was looking out for him.

General Joe Penwell had worked himself into a red-faced fury. "You two are under house arrest," he roared.

First Lieutenant Tracey Barnett, United States Air Force, and Lieutenant Commander Butch Kissick, United States Navy, exchanged glances and kept their silence. They were still wearing their flight gear from the AWACS mission.

Penwell was pacing behind his desk, slamming a fist into his palm. Across the room, standing next to the wall-sized Middle East chart, was Commodore Ashby, bespectacled and dour-looking.

"How dare you usurp the theater commander's authority? That's my authority, mister!" Penwell demanded. "Ordering that tanker in country was a clear violation of the rules of engagement."

"We saved a Hornet pilot's ass," offered Kissick.

Penwell ignored him. "You're going to get a court-martial out of this, Kissick. And I promise you, you're not going to get special protection from any candy-ass Navy lawyers. This is Air Force country, and your butts are roadkill out here."

"Sir," interjected Tracey, "you have to understand something. We saw an occurrence out there—"

Penwell turned on her. "No, *you* understand something. I am a lieutenant general in the United States Air Force and you are a goddamned one-bar woman officer. Do not presume to lecture me."

At this, Tracey Barnett's eyes flashed. She locked gazes with the general. Then she glanced at Kissick. He gave her a nod. "Okay, General, we understand about the tanker. Can we knock off the bullshit and talk about what really happened?"

Penwell stared at her. "What did you say? Knock off *what*?"

Tracey gulped. What the hell? They were going to get court-martialed anyway. "With all due respect, General, Butch Kissick is the best ACE in theater. The best I've ever seen. I stand by his decision to send the tanker in and save that fighter. But there's more, sir. It's clear to us that you're deliberately avoiding the real issue here."

"Lieutenant, I hope you have a good lawyer, because you're going to need one."

"You didn't haul us in here to talk about why we diverted the tanker, did you?"

Penwell placed his hands on his desk and thrust his head forward. "Why else would I bring you here? To pin a damn medal on you?"

"Because you know what we saw on our display during Chevy flight's egress. We saw a blue-on-blue engagement in country, and now we want an explanation for what we saw."

"I don't know what the hell you're talking about."

"We saw Chevy One in a furball with Chevy Five. We had clear indications of an engagement, and then—"

Hrrrrruumph. From across the room, Ashby was making a great show of clearing his throat. "If I may," he said in his monotone voice. He walked over to Penwell's desk and whispered in the JTF Commander's ear. He turned back to the AWACS crew. "Perhaps it should be explained to Lieutenant Barnett and Lieutenant Commander Kissick that what they think they saw may not have been what they, in fact, saw."

Tracey looked at each of them. Ashby wasn't making a bit of sense. Neither of them was. "Excuse me?"

"What the commodore means," said Penwell, "is that in the confusion of the strike egress, you may have seen something in your display that didn't happen. Or you missed something that did happen."

Tracey nodded. She was beginning to see where this was going. "What we saw was pretty plain, General. There weren't any bandits anywhere near Chevy One and Five—"

"Of course there were bandits. They weren't all shot down."

Tracey had to think for a second. That much was true. They had painted five Fulcrums in the air at Latifiyah. Only four were reported shot down. The survivor, presumably, had experienced some kind of near-death epiphany and bugged out for the north country.

Penwell continued. His voice was less strident now. "Let's say the bandit stayed low, did a visual vertical attack on Chevy One, emitting no radar signal, then went back for the deck. With all that was going on, isn't it possible that you might not have spotted it?"

Now Tracey knew for sure where it was going. She looked again at Butch. He just shrugged. "Well, sir, I guess it would be possible. We definitely lost the last Fulcrum. It might have been him."

Penwell clasped his hands together. "Without question, it was the Fulcrum. The Fulcrum took out Chevy One. A damned shame, too, but in the thick of battle, unavoidable things happen." Penwell paused, then looked at both of them. "Is that not the way you saw it, Captain Barnett? And you, Commander Kissick?"

"Captain? I'm a first lieutenant—"

"Let me be the first to congratulate you," said Penwell. "You've both just received field promotions."

Tracey was too surprised to answer. She looked over at Butch. He was grinning and nodding with the new understanding of what they had seen. It meant, Tracey guessed, that they were no longer under arrest.

The coxswain barked an order. The boatswain's mate heaved the bowline to the sailor on the landing. The big gray utility boat bumped gently against the piling, and the crew snubbed the lines fast.

Maxwell stepped ashore.

The air was dry and warm, with a light breeze from the sea. He was wearing civvies—khaki trousers, a knit polo shirt, deck shoes. In one hand he carried his blue overnight duffel bag.

He stood there on the fleet landing for a moment. He set the bag down while he looked around. He didn't see anyone except the shore patrol detail and a row of taxis waiting for the flood of sailors that would soon arrive from the *Reagan*.

She didn't come.

Why should she? he asked himself. Not after the time in Bahrain. Not after he let himself get swept up in all that paranoia about reporters pumping Navy officers for information. Claire was a journalist, not a spy, which he had known all along. But he had let his brain go dead when he spotted her with the guy in the bar that night. He had insulted her, then compounded his stupidity by not owning up to it and apologizing.

After all these years, Maxwell realized, he still hadn't learned zip about women. Nada. Probably never would. But he knew when he'd blown it.

Still, he had hoped she might be there. He picked up the duffel bag and headed toward the row of taxis. *She didn't come.* Okay, another place, another life—

He saw her.

She was standing in the shade beneath a towering palm. She was wearing a sleeveless summer dress, the same kind she used to wear when they went out on the Chesapeake. She had the scarf around her neck . . . the one he had given her in Dubai.

She stood there watching him. For a moment Maxwell had the thought that she was there to meet someone else, and he just happened to show up.

Stupid thought, he told himself. No more stupid thoughts.

For what seemed to Maxwell like an hour, but in fact was only five seconds, they regarded each other. Neither spoke. Claire's face was expressionless, her somber blue eyes fixed on him. Maxwell tried to read her thoughts. He couldn't.

Finally, she smiled.

He went to her and put his arms around her.

"Sam," she said.

"Claire."

He didn't know what to say after that, so he kissed her.

They stood that way for a while, their arms around each other, neither speaking. It was a beginning, thought Maxwell. After all the false starts, it was another beginning. This time, he promised himself, he would get it right.

In the gathering dusk, the temperature was dropping rapidly. The sun lay low over the high western ridge. At this elevation, nearly two thousand meters above sea level, the vegetation was reduced to scrub brush and a few patches of scrawny weeds.

The convoy clattered over the last rise, then began the long descent to the border. Each of the six trucks hauled a load of crude oil in the tank welded to its frame. Over each tank flapped a ragged tarpaulin.

All in all, it had been a routine journey. The convoy had begun with nine vehicles. Two had broken down with engine problems, and one was stolen at gunpoint by Kurdish tribesmen. It was the cost of doing business.

"Look," said the driver of the lead truck. He nudged his passenger who had dozed off again. "Ahead. You see? They are waiting for us."

The passenger blinked and looked through the dirt-encrusted windshield. Ahead lay a checkpoint. He saw jeeps and soldiers in red berets.

"The border," said the driver. "We have arrived."

The passenger was awake now, even though he had

not truly slept for two days. A stubble of beard covered his face, and his arm was aching again. With his good hand, he adjusted the sling that kept the broken wrist bound to his side. Soon he would receive medical attention and the broken limb could be set.

An officer came to the passenger's window. He was very polite. He asked their identities.

The passenger didn't reply at first. He peered up at the sign that covered the border entrance. It read WELCOME TO TURKEY.

"I am Colonel Tariq Jabbar," he said. "Formerly of the Iraqi Air Force." A broad smile spread over his face. *Hayat jaeeda,* he thought. *Life is good.*